T0279394

The LIES of ALMA BLACKWELL

ALSO BY AMANDA GLAZE

The Second Death of Edie & Violet Bond

The LIES of ALMA BLACKWELL

AMANDA GLAZE

UNION
SQUARE
& CO.

NEW YORK

UNION
SQUARE
& CO.

NEW YORK

UNION SQUARE & CO. and the distinctive Union Square & Co. logo are trademarks of Sterling Publishing Co., Inc.

Union Square & Co., LLC, is a subsidiary of Sterling Publishing Co., Inc.

ISBN 978-1-4549-5192-6 (hardcover)
ISBN 978-1-4549-5193-3 (e-book)
ISBN 978-1-4549-5194-0 (paperback)

Library of Congress Cataloging-in-Publication Data

Names: Glaze, Amanda, author.
Title: The lies of Alma Blackwell / by Amanda Glaze.
Description: New York : Union Square & Co., 2024. | Audience: Ages 14–18. | Summary: "Seventeen-year-old witch Nev Blackwell reckons with a terrible inheritance when a stranger arrives at her ancestral California mansion with a dark warning"—Provided by publisher.
Identifiers: LCCN 2024003568 (print) | LCCN 2024003569 (ebook) | ISBN 9781454951926 (hardcover) | ISBN 9781454951940 (trade paperback) | ISBN 9781454951933 (epub)
Subjects: CYAC: Witches—Fiction. | Supernatural—Fiction. | Haunted houses—Fiction. | Grandmothers—Fiction. | Mystery and detective stories. | BISAC: YOUNG ADULT FICTION / Paranormal, Occult & Supernatural | YOUNG ADULT FICTION / Family / Multigenerational | LCGFT: Paranormal fiction. | Detective and mystery fiction. | Novels.
Classification: LCC PZ7.1.G5882 Li 2024 (print) | LCC PZ7.1.G5882 (ebook)
    DDC [Fic]—dc23
LC record available at https://lccn.loc.gov/2024003568
LC ebook record available at https://lccn.loc.gov/2024003569

For information about custom editions, special sales, and premium purchases, please contact specialsales@unionsquareandco.com.

Printed in the United States of America

2 4 6 8 10 9 7 5 3 1

unionsquareandco.com

Cover and interior design by Marcie Lawrence
Cover art by Elena Masci

For Blake, always

The LIES
of ALMA
BLACKWELL

Chapter One

The whispers follow me as I walk down Ocean Avenue, a low hiss that rises above the gentle breeze sliding in from the sea. A veil of damp, somber morning fog blurs the picturesque Victorian store-fronts, but it's not heavy enough to hide the eyes that narrow as I pass. Not thick enough to obscure the lips that flatten into grim lines at my approach.

There's been another drowning.

A foghorn sounds beyond the rocky shores of the Pacific Ocean, and I think about the red whistle the janitor found floating next to Mr. Harrison in the shallow end of the high school pool. No one in Hollow Cliff needs a reminder that Tom Harrison was an excellent swimmer, that he coached our championship-winning water polo team for the past fifteen years, or that he won the open-ocean swim race every summer. They don't need a reminder that his drowning couldn't possibly have been an accident, but that's exactly what that whistle was.

The spirits always claim their kills.

The churning fury of their rage is what woke me up in a cold sweat an hour before dawn this morning, the unnatural chill of their touch scraping clawlike against the barrier of my mind. They're never satisfied with the single life they take. Each drowning only makes them more ravenous. More desperate to break through the binds that rein them in. More savagely determined to complete the vengeance they began more than a century ago.

When I pass by the central square, it's not only Mr. Harrison's name swirling in the misty summer air. His death is a stark reminder to the people of this town that in a week, I'll become the youngest Blackwell ever to take the Vow that protects them from the worst of the spirits' wrath. Except it isn't my youth that's furrowing Willa DeLongpre's brow as I pass by DeLongpre Apothecary. And the hasty, last-minute planning of my ceremony that no one—least of all me—thought would come this soon isn't what's curling the lips of the locals gathered around the memorial fountain. They're watching me because, even after all these years, they're still afraid I'll follow in my mother's footsteps.

They're afraid I'll run.

The bell above the door to Curious Blooms jingles as I walk in, and Francesca looks up from arranging a bright yellow Euphoria bouquet behind the counter. Everything about her is a direct contradiction to the gloom outside, from the fuchsia scarf tying up her tight black curls to her colorful floral blouse and bright red lipstick.

Her large eyes search my face and her brow immediately creases, but unlike Willa DeLongpre, it's not in wariness or suspicion.

"Nev, sweetie. You look exhausted."

"Hey, Cesca." The door closes behind me and I'm engulfed in that dewy, floral-scented air no perfume could ever replicate. "I'm a little tired, but I'm fine."

She hums softly, like she wants to say more but is holding herself back. I suspect my mom's former best friend knows more than she should about where I go and what I do after a drowning, but we've never broached the subject directly, and we never will.

"Are these new?" I wander over to a display rack half full of pale blue bouquets. "I don't think I've seen them before."

"Bea's latest creation." The motherly pride in her voice is impossible to miss. "Forget-Your-Worries bouquets. Flew off the shelves yesterday."

I skim the pad of my finger over one of the velvety, bell-shaped flowers. From a distance, the arrangement looks like one solid color, but up close, it's several shades of blue. My fingers twitch with the urge to take out my sketchbook and pencils, but I don't have time today.

"Willa DeLongpre didn't think I'd notice," Francesca continues, her brown eyes sparkling like they only do when discussing her rival across the street. "But she sent her grandson over to buy *two* yesterday. I have no doubt she'll be rolling out a Forget-Your-Worries tea in a week tops."

She pins me with a look because, five years later, she still hasn't forgiven Gran for stocking some of DeLongpre's more popular tinctures and teas in the Blackwell House of Spirits gift shop. But I know better than to wade into that particular battle, and I'm saved from having to change the subject because at that moment Bea flies in from the back of the shop. In the week since I've seen her, she's added a fresh streak of pink to go with the fading purple in her thick, wavy bob, and her arms are brimming with more of her new blue bouquets.

It takes her an extra second to notice me, and when she does, she narrows her eyes at me like I'm the guilty perp in a police lineup. Hastily, I try to calculate just how many of her text invitations I failed to respond to this week. She doesn't normally hold my lack of response against me—Bea's always been better at keeping up her end of our friendship—but she's clearly pissed about something.

"Um. Hi, Bea. Is everything—" She cuts me off with a shake of her head.

"You're *early.*"

It's not the accusation I was expecting, but before I can ask what she's talking about, she rushes over to the counter, unceremoniously dumps her beautiful bouquets in front of Francesca, and points at me. "Don't *move!*"

Without another word of explanation, she darts back through the saloon-style double doors. They're still swinging when Francesca turns to me, eyebrows raised, but I shake my head. "I honestly have no idea."

4

Her mouth quirks, and she points at the blue bouquets Bea dropped on the counter. "Would you mind putting these with the display up front while I pop back for your arrangements?"

"Sure."

"Thanks, mijita." She smiles at me before following Bea into the back, and I gather up the flowers and start arranging them in the galvanized buckets. I've known Bea long enough to guess that she's up to something, and if I thought a bouquet to ease my worries would help me get out of whatever that something is, I'd buy a dozen. But Beatrice Diaz is a difficult person to say no to, magic-infused flowers or no. We may not spend as much time together as we did in the years after my mom left, but she's still the closest thing I have to a friend my age in this town, and when you're a Blackwell, that's not something you take lightly.

The double doors creak open again and Bea bounds back into the shop. This time, she's holding a spray of dark and light purple flowers that have been artfully fastened onto the back of a hair barrette. "These are for you." She holds them out to me. "For tonight."

I take the flowers gingerly. "They're beautiful. But what do you mean they're—"

I break off as realization dawns.

The party.

I forgot about her party.

"The star-shaped ones are astrantias," she continues, pointing at the varietal in question as if I hadn't spoken. "And the tiny light purple ones are thyme. Both are good for courage."

She looks up from the hair clip, her flashing eyes making it crystal clear that she has no intention of letting Mr. Harrison's death nullify my promise to attend the party she and her friends have been planning at the cove for tonight. Canceling it would of course be out of the question. Clinging to life amid death is a lesson the people of this town learn early, and if anything, the news of the latest drowning makes the party even more necessary.

But it's not the same for me.

And Bea knows it.

"Bea," I begin, but she cuts me off with a wave of her hand.

"I'm sorry, but no. You're not hiding away tonight. This is your last chance to let loose before the ceremony, and I refuse to let you miss it." She plucks the flower barrette from my hand and moves behind me. "But look, I know you're nervous."

"That's not—"

"And I know the last time you came out with us, it wasn't exactly . . . ideal." I flinch at the memory of my ill-advised appearance at a graduation party earlier this month. Bea's a year below me and didn't graduate this year, but she and her friends were far more welcome at the party than I was.

She separates a few curls from my perpetually messy mane of black hair and pretends not to notice my reaction. "But it will be different tonight because this is *my* party, Nev. And you have to trust that I've got your back." The barrette clicks softly into place, and she turns me around by the shoulders. "I absolutely promise that you'll have fun. *Way* more fun than you ever would have had at those sad-sack art college parties."

I shrug out of her grip. "Can we please not—"

"Not what?" She gives me a shrewd look. Bea and Francesca are the only people, apart from Gran, who I told about my acceptance into the Rhode Island School of Design. An acceptance I turned down the day after we got Gran's diagnosis. "Not admit that you're disappointed?"

"Here we are, hon."

We both turn as Francesca backs in through the double doors carrying a cardboard tray of the clean, white flower arrangements that Gran loves. We order them every Friday to place in the entrance hall where the tours begin, and the familiar sight now, in the midst of so much change, is surprisingly comforting. Here, at least, is one part of our lives that hasn't been turned on its head.

I take the tray from Francesca and as soon as my hands are full, Bea squeezes my arm. "I'll pick you up at eight. Don't forget to wear the flowers."

I open my mouth to protest, but she skips out of the shop before I can, and Francesca offers me a sympathetic look. It's been just the two of them since Bea's dad drowned when she was a baby, and Francesca is just as bad at saying no to her daughter as I am. She asks if I need help getting the arrangements to my car, but I tell her I'm okay and step back out into the grey June morning.

The sidewalk is clear since everyone has retreated into their shops and cafés to prepare for the horde of summer tourists who'll be descending on these picturesque streets in less than an hour. They flock to our small coastal town two hours north of San Francisco because of Alma Blackwell's legacy and the world-famous Blackwell House of Spirits that she built. But there will be repeat visitors in the crowds today, too. Vacationing families and couples who return to our hazy shores year after year to sample the offerings of a town that pretty much every tour book and travel guide has summed up in a single word.

Magical.

But they don't call Hollow Cliff magical because of our majestic coastal redwoods that rise up through sparkling layers of fog. Or because of our dramatic bluffs, sweeping ocean views, or even our Victorian-era charm. They say Hollow Cliff is magical because when someone reads your tea leaves at Mystery Grounds Coffee and Tea, the future they reveal often does come true. Because the thrill of inhaling one of the Euphoria bouquets at Curious Blooms can be more potent than the strongest of drugs. Because the Dreamless Tea at DeLongpre Apothecary will give you the best sleep of your life, and because the protective crystals you buy on Ocean Avenue really do warm in your palm when danger is near.

They call our town magical because as children, they rode through the redwoods in a handcart on the Railroad That Never Was and will swear for the rest of their lives they heard the echoing screams of the people who died that horrible day. They say it's magical because when they grow up, they bring their own kids here and give them a penny to throw into the memorial fountain in the center square, reminding them to think carefully about what their wish will be because, in Hollow Cliff, some wishes do come true.

My steps slow now as I pass by that fountain, the stone carving of Alma Blackwell kneeling in its center shrouded by silvery mist. But it's the thirty-four names carved along the base of the pool that draw my eye this morning. Names that were carved over a century ago to honor the victims of the 1903 massacre that only ended with Alma's Vow.

Tom Harrison's name won't be added to this stone even though he, too, had his mind seized by the spirits. Even though he, too, was a victim of their vengeance. Even though he, too, was driven by them to his death. But that's the way it is in Hollow Cliff when the spirits break free and take one of our lives. The ghost-hungry vacationers who crowd our streets browsing for mood-enhancing chocolates and protective talismans will hear no mention of the former water polo coach. Nothing will be written about his death in the *Hollow Cliff Gazette*. No investigation will be launched by the sheriff. In our town's public record, the coroner will record yet another drowning as an accident. It's not good for business otherwise. Not good for the town. It's better for everyone if the world believes that our ghost stories stayed in the past.

I turn away from the fountain and immediately crash into someone's side. The box holding the flowers slips from my grip and

I tighten my hold, grunting as the sharp cardboard corners dig into my palms.

A yelp and a thud draw my attention to the ground, and when I see the wispy white hair of Fern Fairchild—her multicolored skirts and scarves sprawled out on the ground around her—I crouch down and set the flowers aside.

"Fern?" I help her back up to sitting. "Are you all right?"

Her perpetually hazy, unfocused eyes settle on me and her thin, wrinkled lips break out in a delighted smile that's completely at odds with the situation. "Well, aren't you a sweet one, pet?"

I check her over, but Fern doesn't seem to have sustained any damage from the fall. The contents of her patchwork bag, however, have spilled out onto the ground, and I quickly gather them up. Several of the tarot card decks have mixed together, there's a crack in her crystal ball that may or may not have been there before, and a couple of her loose-leaf tea bags have emptied onto the pavement. But Fern just keeps smiling at me as I repack her possessions like I'm the hero here instead of the person who sent an almost-eighty-year-old woman tumbling to the ground.

When I'm done, she pats my cheek. "Home is where the heart lives, pet," she says like she always does.

"I know, Fern," I say like I always do in response.

She nods, pleased by this exchange, even though it's the same one she'll have with every Hollow Cliff resident she encounters today. Sometimes, she insists on repeating the ritual a couple dozen times with the same person, but everyone is always patient when it comes to Fern. Outsiders may look at her and see a rambling, eccentric old lady with a few screws loose, but we all know the truth.

Fern Fairchild stayed away too long.

I help Fern to her feet and hand her back her bag, but when I move to pick up the flower arrangements, she snatches my wrist, halting me. "Come along now, pet. I've got a new brew all ready for your reading."

Her grip is surprisingly strong as she tries to tug me toward the patio of Mystery Grounds, but I set my feet and gently pry her fingers loose. "I'm sorry, Fern. I can't today."

She clucks at me, shaking her head because this is also a thing I always say. Except for the one time. And one time was enough.

When I bend down to pick up the flowers again, she cocks her head and peers at me knowingly from behind her red-rimmed glasses. "Go on then, pet. But don't take too long. Not all futures are content to wait."

I stiffen, my gaze flying to hers, and when our eyes meet, I'm reminded of why I never told anyone—not even Gran—about the words Fern Fairchild muttered into a chipped blue teacup three years ago. The expectation in her gaze—the fervent, breathless hope—shook me to the core in a way the coldest, meanest look from Willa DeLongpre could never do.

It still does.

Overhead, seagulls shriek, and one of them swoops so low that the flap of its wings ruffles Fern's frizzy white hair. She turns to follow the bird's flight, and when it lands on the ground a couple of feet from her, she makes a *tsk*ing sound in the back of her throat. "Taking your time as well, I see."

Reaching into her coat pocket, she pulls out a small paper bag and tosses what looks like crumbs from a blueberry muffin in front of the bird. It immediately dips its curved yellow beak and gobbles up the offering. Fern tosses another handful of crumbs and—without so much as a backward glance in my direction— ambles away toward the coffee shop patio.

The prickle of unease I always feel in her presence follows me as I leave the square and head toward the bluffs where I parked the car. I'm almost there when an entirely different kind of prickle runs up the back of my neck. Less of a prickle, actually, and more of an unsettling, whole-body tremble. There must be eyes on me, but when I look over my shoulder at the front patio of Mystery Grounds, there's only Fern with her back to me as she sets up her table.

A cold wind pushes in from the sea, plastering strands of my hair against my cheek, and I turn my face directly into the breeze, shaking off my unease. Then I dart across the narrow road, look up, and freeze.

Not two dozen feet away from me is a guy I've never seen before leaning back against the wooden railing at the edge of the bluffs. His arms are folded, his head is tilted to the side, his dark hair is wild in the wind around his face . . .

And he's staring directly at me.

Our gazes lock, and the second they do, my stomach jumps into my throat as if I just missed a step going down a flight of stairs.

A jolt of recognition moves through me, and I know at once that it was *his* stare I felt so strongly on the back of my neck a moment ago. I expect him to look away now that I've caught him staring, but he doesn't. Instead, he raises his brows in what feels like a challenge. My body tenses with a strange urge to march right over to him and say . . . what, I have no idea. But the echo of Gran's voice in my head stops me.

You need to be careful now, sweetheart.

A lot of national news sites picked up the quirky human-interest story about the teenager in a tiny Northern California town who's taking over a haunted legacy from her dying grandmother. And most of the articles featured at least one photo of me. My lack of social media presence has shielded me a bit, but Gran has warned me repeatedly that the interest—in me, specifically—might get intense. Aggressive even, especially amongst the ghost-hunting set. And going off this guy's black hoodie, black jeans, and general un-tourist-like demeanor, that's likely what he is.

I turn away and balance the flowers on the roof of the car while I fish in my bag for the keys to the blue Volvo my mother had the unexpected decency to leave behind. But I know, without having to look, that his eyes stay on me as I settle the flowers in the trunk and slip into the driver's seat. I pull away without looking back and press down hard on the gas, but even though I roll both front windows down and let the damp, salty wind freeze my cheeks and fingers, the unsettling heat of his gaze lingers on my skin all the way up the winding hill to Blackwell House.

The witch-capped Victorian mansion teetering on the edge of a sea cliff is still shrouded in a thick layer of marine fog as I pass through the wrought-iron gates, making it difficult to separate the gables, turrets, and columned porches from the towering coastal redwoods that surround it on three of its four sides. Just before the wooden sign welcoming visitors to the Blackwell House of Spirits, I veer right and take my usual back road past the old caretaker cottage so I can loop around and park in the former carriage house.

Thanks to the excitement surrounding my once-in-a-generation Vow ceremony, both our morning and afternoon tours are fully booked, and there are already a few early birds wandering the misty sculpture garden and gazing out at the white-capped sea beyond the bluffs as they wait for us to open. A few of them catch my eye as I rush by with the cardboard tray of flowers, and I recognize the wary, hesitant look in them. It's always like this after a drowning when the simmering fury of the spirits is stronger and more perceptible. Tourists who would normally only feel the graze of their touch will shiver violently without cause as they tour our twisting hallways and snap at friends and family with an anger that isn't their own.

I slip through the side door into the kitchen, and Tabitha greets me with the chirping *meow* she saves only for me. She's a consistent favorite amongst the tour guests because she has one blue eye and one orange eye and is suspiciously good at striking ominous poses that make the house seem even more haunted than it already is. But Tab's not-so-secret secret is that she hates every single person

THE LIES OF ALMA BLACKWELL

in the world except for me, and even though it's selfish, I love her for it.

After setting down the flowers, I scratch her silky white head and open a can of her food. She mews her approval and digs in while I heat some soup and toast a few pieces of bread I hope I can coax Gran into eating. I force down another half cup of coffee from the pot I made before heading out to check the Anchors this morning, but even though I know I should, my stomach is too knotted to eat anything.

Once Gran's soup and toast is ready, I set it on a tray and start down the twisting hallways of the only wing in this house that wasn't opened to the public as an economy-generating tourist attraction by my great-great-grandmother after World War I. Shafts of morning light slant across the gloomy landscape paintings that line the walls, but the shadows in the corners are restless, and they slither out to meet me as I pass. Their unnatural chill surrounds me like a cloak, and I think about that fisherman I overheard at the harbor who said that every time he heads out to open sea, every time that first spray of salt water mists his face, it feels like coming home. But he also never forgets—even for an instant—that the moment he lets down his guard, those same dark waters will drag him to his grave with glee.

The spirits bound to Blackwell House are my sea. The icy touch of their dark fingers skating across my skin, pressing at the barriers of my mind, is as familiar to me as the steady rhythm of the waves crashing into the cliffs beneath my window. And on days like

15

today, that touch is a vicious, angry squall. A reminder, like the red whistle floating next to Mr. Harrison's body, that if they ever get the chance, they'll kill us all.

I pause in the hallway outside Gran's door and a voice—so much thinner than the melodious alto I grew up with—calls out from within.

"Don't hover, sweetheart. It's not an attractive trait."

I stifle a small smile and try to look appropriately chastened as I balance the tray of food against my hip and push open the door to Gran's room. She's sitting up in the middle of her old-fashioned canopy bed, the shadows cast by the hangings emphasizing the dark bruises underneath her eyes. Large chunks of her salt-and-pepper hair that were always so smooth and perfectly styled before have escaped their braid to hang limp and damp around her face. Her shoulders slump against the headboard, telling me this isn't going to be one of her good days, not that she has many of those anymore.

"I didn't want to wake you." I keep my tone light as I walk inside. Gran abhors sympathy, but more importantly, the only time she truly loses her composure is when she thinks I'm upset. "But I thought you might be hungry, so—"

"So you decided to bring me a tray of rations straight out of a Dickens novel?"

I set the tray over her lap without comment and rearrange the dark blue coverlet so it lies flat across her legs. Until a few months ago, Gran wouldn't have even considered eating a meal that didn't include a colorful array of in-season vegetables harvested directly from her garden. Apart from her passionate dedication to upholding our family's legacy—and her sometimes overzealous protection of me—her vegetable garden is her one pride and joy. But it's been a while since she's been able to keep anything but bland foods down.

She snorts in protest when I tuck a cloth napkin into the collar of her nightdress, but I ignore her and take a seat in the antique armchair that now lives permanently at the side of her bed. "If you're still hungry after the soup, I can bring you—"

"I'm not an invalid, darling girl. I can get my own food. You have more than enough on your plate as it is."

I say nothing to that because it's rare she has the energy to make it down the hallway, let alone to the kitchen. It might be different if she didn't keep stubbornly pushing back her stay at the hospital for pain management, but I know better than to bring that up again.

Gran picks up the spoon, fills it with broth, and brings it to her lips. When she grimaces after the first swallow, we both pretend that it's because of the bland taste and not because she's finding it difficult to keep even that small amount of liquid down. Just like we pretend, when she returns the spoon to the tray, that in a few minutes, she'll pick it up again.

"So?" Her amber eyes, still sharp even through the haze of pain, study mine with a mixture of apprehension and concern. "The Anchors. Are they—"

A violent cough swallows up her words, racking her too-frail body, and I hastily sweep the tray off her lap. There's a cup of water on the nightstand, and I hold it to her lips as she takes a small sip. Drops of liquid dribble down her chin and I use the corner of my sleeve to dab them away.

When her coughing fit subsides, I return the water to the nightstand and study her from under my lashes. She looks utterly exhausted. A thin sheen of sweat glistens on her brow, her shoulders tremble from the strain of sitting upright, and the alarmingly greyish tint to her skin makes me want to cry. I came up here to tell her what I found this morning at the Anchor sites because even though I'd love to spare her the knowledge, I can't. Until the sun sets on the solstice, she alone holds the Vow. It's because of the blood *she* added to the heart of Alma's charm that the spirits remain leashed. If the Anchors that extend that spell's protection are compromised, she needs to know.

But maybe the full details can wait a few hours more. Just until she's had a bit more rest.

"You look a little tired," I hedge. "Why don't you take a nap and I'll come—"

"Nev."

The upward tilt of her chin, the flash of steely determination in her eyes is so like the old Gran—so like the indomitable Marie Blackwell she shows to the rest of the world—that for one shining moment, I almost forget that she's sick. I almost forget that the one constant I've always depended on—the one source of unconditional love that's kept me from falling apart in a town riddled with death and grief and guilt—is leaving me. I almost forget how terrified I am that without her strong, sure arms around me, the seams that make me up will unravel.

Gran's eyes soften, and her too-thin, skeletal hand reaches across the bed toward me. She's always been able to sense the things I can't say, and when my hand meets hers halfway, her dry, papery skin envelops it.

"Tell me what happened with the Anchors, sweetheart."

She squeezes my hand, and I let out a breath. "Two pieces of the southern Anchor were drained."

She watches me closely. "And were you able to replace them?"

I nod. "Yes. But . . ."

"But what, hon?"

"It wasn't just the southern charm. Pieces in the east and west were drained as well."

She blinks once. Twice. "I see."

I watch for her reaction, but that carefully blank mask slips over her features. It's the one she wears whenever we talk about things she can't tell me until I take over the Vow. But I already know what will happen if all four Anchor charms fail, so it's not hard to guess that three blinking out at once isn't a good sign.

When the silence continues to stretch, I give up waiting. "Should I be worried? Have you sensed that they—"

"My strength is failing."

I blink in surprise. Gran isn't one to admit a weakness out loud, even to me.

"The Anchors will need to be reinforced again," she continues, her words slurring slightly, exhaustion heavy on her tongue. "Soon. I'm not . . ."

She trails off, shakes her head, and then grimaces at the pain that small motion causes. I squeeze her hand because she doesn't need to say the rest out loud. "It's okay, Gran. I'll check the Anchors again. I can handle it."

The tired smile she gives me is so full of trust, so full of love, that it's all I can do not to break down and sob right here in front of her.

"I know you can, sweetheart." She slumps back against the pillows, her eyes drifting shut. "She never could . . . but you will."

Her hand goes slack in mine and her breathing shallows, but but I'm too shocked to move. I can count on one hand the number of times Gran and I have spoken about the woman who abandoned me—abandoned this town—without so much as a goodbye seven years ago.

From deep inside the house, the grandfather clock chimes the hour telling me it's time to open the doors and let in the hordes. Without Gran's help, I'm running the tours, gift shop, and front of house solo, and although I placed a help-wanted ad a month ago—with Gran's grudging approval—there haven't been any replies, and I doubt there will be. Most locals do their best to avoid crossing the threshold of Blackwell House. Even Bea insists on picking me up at the top of the driveway, and the only cleaning and ground crew that will work with us travel in from over an hour away every other week. No one but family has ever worked inside the house itself, and unfortunately, it's likely to stay that way.

Carefully, I tuck Gran's hand back under the covers, stand up, and stare down at the slight form of her figure in the giant bed that used to belong to Alma herself. The first time the spirits distorted my nightmares, gleefully digging up my deepest fears to parade before my unconscious mind, Gran made a pillow fort in this bed, promising me that within its walls, I would always be safe. She seemed so big to me then, this woman who had the power to solve all of my problems. Who everyone else was a little bit in awe of, but who could make me laugh so hard that milk squirted out my nose. This woman who'd always been there, watching over me. Who leapt into the role of full-time parent with unbridled enthusiasm. Who met the pain of my mother's abandonment with a love so deep, so constant, not even my broken, betrayed heart could ever doubt it.

It's why, in every drawing I have of her, she takes up the entirety of the page. I had to stop putting her in group portraits and land-scapes years ago because she swallows everything up, even the sea. But it's been months since I've been able to finish so much as a sketch of her. Maybe it's because she seems so tiny to me now, so frail in the middle of this massive bed.

Maybe it's because I can't bear to make her small.

Chapter Two

Our feet kick up sand as Bea and I scramble down the steep
path to Smuggler's Cove. The crescent-shaped beach is a favorite spot amongst locals because the jagged rocks jutting out from
the black waters make it a dangerous area to swim, and thus
an excellent place to avoid tourists. Tonight, sparks from the
bonfire light up the silvery night sky, music is thumping from a
speaker balanced on a stump, and the narrow stretch of black-
and-white-speckled sand is crowded with my former Hollow
Cliff High classmates.

We pause near the bottom of the hill, and Bea reaches up
to adjust the flowers I dutifully pinned in my loose hair because
honestly, I could use the courage. Once she's satisfied, she hooks
her arm through mine and pulls me into the glow of the flames.
Two seconds later, the first head turns. By the time I count to five,
every eye on the beach has found us.

So much for slipping into the party unnoticed.

But Bea either doesn't notice the ripple of palpable unease, or she's decided to ignore it. Pulling me closer to her side, she steers me past a group of girls I've technically known all my life but who are currently looking at me the way you would an undertaker who brought a gift-wrapped coffin to a three-year-old's birthday party. My presence is an unwelcome reminder of what they came here tonight to forget. It's always like this after a drowning, but in a couple of days, the initial spike of fear and grief will ease, and they'll go back to treating me with the careful detachment we're all accustomed to.

"Bea! Over here!"

The sleek blonde head of Bea's best friend Darcy separates herself from a water polo player whose name I can't remember and makes her way toward us. Going off the slight sway in her hips, she's already a few drinks in.

"Look at *you*." Darcy holds Bea's arms out to the sides so she can better admire the vintage paisley miniskirt and matching halter top from her latest thrifting haul. After a long and enthusiastic inspection of the outfit, she turns to me, and when her eyes land on my faded black jeans and green knit sweater, her nose visibly wrinkles. "Nev. Hi."

Her voice is flatter than a pancake, but Bea must have threatened her with something drastic because this is the warmest welcome Darcy has ever given me. I send her a wide smile back, which annoys the hell out of her because with Bea watching her like a hawk, she has no choice but to return it. Except what Darcy doesn't get is that we have more in common than she realizes. She can't understand why Bea is so determined to integrate me into the social fabric of a town I was quite literally born to stay separate from, and frankly, neither can I.

A plastic cup is shoved into my hand, and before I can offer up a protest, Bea is clinking the rim of her cup against mine. Then, with a smile that's easy and loose, she raises her cup high in the air and cries, "To a night of wandering youth!"

A cheer goes up around me, as if more alcohol is all that's needed to forget the tension my arrival brought, and everyone takes a drink. Over the rim of her cup, Bea winks at me, the flames from the fire dancing in her eyes, and I send her a rueful smile back as I lift my drink in salute. It's rare for Gran to talk about the years she spent away from Hollow Cliff before selecting my mother's paternal DNA from a clinic and returning to take over the Vow from her own mom. But she made an offhand reference to her *years of wandering youth* once in front of Bea and me, and Bea's never forgotten it.

I finish the rest of my drink, and when Bea refills it, I swallow that one down, too.

Like pretty much everyone on this beach, Bea will have her own version of a *wandering youth* once she graduates. A handful of precious years away from Hollow Cliff before the pull to return becomes too strong to resist. My mother had one, too. Four years at a small college in New York before joining a band, hopping aboard a tour bus, and traveling this country from end to end. She didn't come back until she was four months pregnant with me and fresh off a breakup with a guy who was visiting from overseas and had no interest in relocating to America. Or in sticking around to meet me. At least, that's what she told everyone. For all I know, it was another one of her lies.

Gran's always wanted me to have my own taste of freedom before the Vow binds me to the borders of this town. It's why she was so insistent about me applying to art schools. But the cancer changed all that. Alma took the first Vow at sunset on the summer solstice, and that's the only time it can be passed down. Gran won't make it another year, which means my turn is up. It also means I won't have the *wandering youth* my mom and grandmother and the rest of the people around this bonfire will have. I'm going to stay here, in Hollow Cliff, for my entire life.

I know it.

I've accepted it.

But as Bea refills my cup again and the music and laughter swirl around me, I decide that maybe she's right. Maybe this is one night I can afford to wander through.

Smoke from the bonfire whirls around us, and each sip of vodka burns less and less as it goes down. I hadn't planned on drinking tonight. I definitely hadn't planned on getting drunk. But as the hours wear on, I find myself liking the warm, floaty feeling that's taken over my limbs. Liking the way Bea and I sway to the music blaring from the speakers, the sparks from the fire dancing with us as they twist up into the glow of the waxing moon.

At some point, I find myself swaying with my arms wrapped around two of the sneering girls Bea steered me past earlier, our faces flushed from the heat of the flames, our backs chilled by the wind from the sea. We laugh together, these people who have never been outright cruel to me, but who have always kept their distance. Who after tonight, will keep their distance still.

When my head begins to spin too much to stand, I sink down by the ring of stones that circle the fire. Every inch of my body is flushed and hot, so I peel off my sweater, pull off my boots, and sink my bare feet into the sand, burrowing them until my toes reach a layer that's cold and damp. Laughing faces flicker in the firelight and a few snatches of slurred conversations about college plans and post-graduation travel float my way. I try to ignore it, but the alcohol has made me selfish, and the bitter taste of jealousy claws up my throat even though I know it's unfair to begrudge them this small taste of liberty. Even though once this town is in your blood, nobody can truly get it out.

Fern Fairchild was a celebrated historical scholar before she left, and her now-addled mind is a daily reminder of what can happen if you resist the pull for too long. My mother hasn't stayed away as long as Fern did, but she's getting close. Does that mean she's feeling it now? In whatever exotic part of the world she's in? Is she consumed with that empty, heartsick feeling people describe? The one that hollows you out so deeply, you can't get out of bed? Does she feel like she's lost a part of herself? Does she yearn to come back here to find it? Does she think about coming back for me?

No. I shake my head because she's not someone I want to think about now.

Not now. Not ever.

I press my forehead to the tops of my knees and dig my fingers hard into my temples, but it's not enough. That night still flashes in my mind. The memory of us at the kitchen table that's been knocking at my carefully erected barriers since the day my Vow ceremony was confirmed. I try to push it away. I try to keep it from breaking through, but my brain is too slow, too sluggish from the alcohol to stop it.

I didn't understand then. I was ten, and I thought I was my mother's whole world. I thought she loved me more than anything, and I thought the game we played with the atlas was just that: a game.

That night was my first big hint, but I didn't see it then. We'd just finished clearing the dishes from dinner and Mom had taken out the atlas. We'd charted a route through Berlin the day before and now we were on to Prague. Gran knew the atlas game was our special thing, so she didn't normally intrude, but that night, she stayed in the kitchen after dinner. My mom smiled at her. I remember that because I'll never forget the grotesque way that smile froze on her face when Gran announced it was time for her to step up and take over the Vow. And I remember her eyes. I remember how wide and wild they grew. The frantic dart of them, like she was a rabbit with one leg caught in a trap.

She was gone a lot in the months and weeks after that. She'd leave the house for hours at a time, and when Gran asked where she'd gone, she would lie. I don't know if Gran knew she was lying at the time, but I did. I could tell by the way her voice went flat.

I didn't say anything though, because I knew she'd never lie to *me*. I knew that right up until that day in the Rose Room when I surprised her and she slammed her laptop shut. It's the only room in the house with semi-consistent Wi-Fi so I asked her what she was looking at, and she said she was shopping for clothes. I knew it was a lie then, but now I know it wasn't her first. Now I know she'd been lying to me my whole life.

This time when my head spins, it's not pleasant or warm. The fire is suddenly too hot. Too suffocating. I lurch unsteadily to my feet. My stomach lurches, too, and I swallow against the bitter bile that rises in my throat. Through the flames, I catch a brief glimpse of Bea deep in conversation with Darcy, Darcy's boyfriend, and a few other guys from Mr. Harrison's water polo team who I've managed to avoid so far tonight. I wait for Bea to turn away from me, and then I back away from the fire and pick my way across the sand toward the shore.

An evening wind slices across the black waters of the cove, blowing my loose curls against my face. I push the strands out of my eyes and realize that at some point, Bea's flowers fell out even though I swore I'd wear them all night. I could go back and look for them. I could go back and grab the sweater I left by the bonfire, too, because it's cold away from its warmth, but there's something in me that needs to keep moving. Some urgent impulse I can't control that won't let me go back.

So I don't. I keep going. Once I reach the water, I turn left and stumble my way toward the jagged rock caves that mark the sudden end of the beach, their outline just visible under the light of the half-moon. I don't stop, even when the world spins beneath my feet. I take deep breaths instead. Focus on the damp salty taste of the sea coating the back of my throat and the sulfuric tang of the seaweed washed up along the shore.

I'm so focused on breathing through the spins, on not tripping over the sharp bits of driftwood jutting up through the sand, that at first, I don't hear the steps behind me. And by the time I turn around, it's too late.

Robbie Harrison comes to a stop inches away, his tall, athlete's body towering over me. The grief etched on his face is stark in the silver moonlight, and his eyes are puffy and rimmed with red. If I'd known he was already back from college, I never would have let Bea drag me here. His loss is fresh and raw, and I'm the absolute last person he should see right now.

"Robbie. Hi. I'm so sorry about your da—"

"Did you see it?"

The hair on the back of my neck rises at the angry, desperate slap of his words. I throw a glance over his shoulder, but he came out here alone, and I've wandered too far from the bonfire for anyone to hear me call out.

I start to back away. "I'm sorry, Robbie, but I don't know what you're—"

"*No.*" His arm snakes out with the lightning-fast water polo reflexes his dad helped him hone, and his fingers clamp around my upper arm, holding me in place. "You have to tell me if that's why. You have to—"

His face crumples and his whole body shakes in a violent, racking sob. His grip on my arm doesn't ease, but my heart breaks at the sight of this grief-stricken boy who bears no resemblance to the cheerful, affable guy I used to pass in the hallways.

"Robbie, I really am so sorry. I know you're hurting, but I don't—"

"*Stop.*" His eyes slam shut, and he shakes his head violently like he's trying to dislodge a fly. "I have to unlearn what I've been taught." His eyes fly open and he blinks several times in rapid succession. "The true history has been hidden."

His words make no sense, and I try to pin his gaze with mine, but his eyes are moving back and forth too fast. "Robbie, I don't know what you're talking about, but you need to let go. You're *hurting* me."

He shakes his head again, like he doesn't want to hear me. His lips keep moving, but no sound comes out, and I'd think he forgot I was here if it wasn't for his bruising hold on my arm. But when I try to pull free, his lips stop moving and he pulls me close, so close that I can smell the sour taste of coffee lingering on his breath. Icy shards of panic race up my veins at the anger simmering in his eyes, but there's confusion there, too. Confusion and naked, heart-wrenching grief.

"You." He blinks several more times, like he's having difficulty keeping his focus on me. "It's because of you Blackwell *witches*. It's because of *you*."

Guilt and fear war within me as I dig my feet into the sand and try to wrestle my arm out of his grip, because Robbie's not wrong. The spell my family wove to protect this town may hold the spirits back, but it's not enough. It's never been enough.

"Robbie, I understand how angry you must—"

"Stop!" He shakes his head again and closes his eyes. "I can't—"

"But the spirits still seek their vengeance, and all we can do is hold—"

"I said *stop!*" His yell echoes off the caves at my back, repeating into the night. He makes another sound that's somewhere between a roar and a howl, and then his hands are circling my neck. I gasp and kick out, my legs and arms flailing in a frantic effort to get away, but Robbie's fingers are already digging into the tender skin of my throat. He's already cutting off my air. His eyes turn wild. They bounce between me and the sea and the caves and the sky like he's tracking a horde of invisible ghosts. Tears stream down his cheeks. His forehead glistens with sweat, and his lips begin forming silent words again.

I pummel my fists against his chest, but my strength is rapidly fleeing my body and my hits are sluggish and weak. I open my mouth wide, gasping, but nothing can get past the constriction in my throat.

Does he know he's killing me? Does he know my lungs can't suck in air?

Black spots fill my vision, and in one last surge of strength, I kick out blindly with my legs. This time, they connect with Robbie's shin. He grunts, traps my legs between his, and together we sink to our knees in the cold, rough sand.

Robbie's wracking sobs fill the air around us, but his grip on my throat isn't loosening. I'm starting to lose consciousness. I can feel my body use up the last of my breath. If Gran were here, she could stop this. She could weave a spell to soothe Robbie's mind.

But she's not here. I'm alone. And I'm going to fail.

There's a horrible irony to knowing that after all my efforts, I'm going to end up following in my mother's footsteps after all. It doesn't matter that she abandoned her responsibility to this town of her own free will while I'll be abandoning them because I'm dead. The end result will be the same. The cancer will take Gran, and when it does, there won't be a Blackwell left to take over Alma's Vow. The bind on the spirits may not be perfect, but it's the best we have, and it will fail. The full force of their wrath will be unleashed for the first time since the 1903 massacre, and it won't be one life at a time they take anymore, it will be the entire town. No one will be able to outrun them, not even the boy whose hands are currently stopping my last breath. His mind will be invaded and seized like all the rest. He might even be the first they drown.

It's the thing I was raised to prevent, the purpose that's been waiting for me since the day I was born, and that reminder jump-starts something in my fuzzy, panicked brain. I *can't* fail. But I can't fight, either. I can't even breathe. So I do the only thing I can do. I stop struggling and let my body go limp.

My full weight slumps against Robbie, and he jerks in surprise. His grip on my neck loosens enough for me to suck in a sliver of air, and I use that tiny thread of strength to lift my eyes to his. He blinks down at me, dumbfounded confusion shuttering his gaze like he doesn't understand how I got here.

And then several things happen at once.

A person materializes out of the darkness on my right.

Robbie's eyes go wide and wild again and then he's crying out. His fingers fall away from my neck, and I pitch forward onto the sand, catching myself on my hands and knees.

My lungs immediately start sucking in cold gulps of air as the thrum of my blood pounds like a drumbeat in my ears, but it's not loud enough to drown out the sound of flesh hitting flesh or the deep grunts punctuated by Robbie's enraged cries.

I try to push myself to standing but only manage to raise my head enough to see the profile of a long, lean body in a black sweat-shirt using his knee to pin Robbie's flailing body to the ground. I need to call out. Stop this before it goes too far. But when I try to wet my dry, aching throat with a swallow, the burn is so sharp, I whimper with pain.

At the sound, the head that's bowed over Robbie spins toward me. Overhead, a cloud shifts in the sky, clearing a path for the silver half-moon, and when it lights on the face staring back at me, my stomach lurches in immediate recognition.

It's the guy from this morning—the one I caught staring at me from the bluffs. There's a fierce set to his square jaw now and a bruise forming on the pale skin of his upper cheek where Robbie must have gotten in a hit. A swath of freckles is spread out over his nose and across his cheeks, and above his left eye, I can just make out the white lines of a crescent-shaped scar.

My eyes linger on that scar. It reminds me of something, but before I can wonder what, he tilts his head, drawing my gaze to his. His brows rise in a gesture that looks . . . expectant, and that same unsettled feeling from this morning washes through me. It's like he's waiting for something.

Does he want me to thank him?

I don't have a chance to find out, because at that moment, Robbie bucks beneath him, sending up a spray of sand that flies into his eyes. He turns back to Robbie, an annoyed growl in the back of his throat as he pulls back his elbow and curls his hand into a fist.

I throw out a hand and croak, "*Stop!*"

The guy's arm freezes midair, but he doesn't turn to look at me. His gaze stays pinned to where Robbie lies beneath him, tears streaming down his face as he mutters the same words over and over again in a voice that's barely above a whisper. *"The true history has been hidden . . . the true history has been hidden."*

"He's grieving." Each whispered word is a burning knife in my throat. "He doesn't mean . . . he's confused. That's all."

This time, when the mystery guy turns to me, a few pieces of his hair fall onto his forehead, shadowing his eyes from my view. But I can still feel them, flitting over my face. Robbie's twisting and muttering under his hold, but he doesn't seem to notice or care. The guy just keeps studying me until, finally, he says in a voice that's low and hoarse from disuse, "Is that what you really believe?"

There's a disappointment in his tone that I don't understand, even though I get the strangest feeling that I should. But before I can ask what he means, I'm interrupted by a new voice calling my name.

"Nev! *Oh my God.* Are you okay?"

Bea is sprinting down the beach, Darcy and her boyfriend fast on her heels. Trailing behind them are the other two water polo players who were sitting with them by the fire. They would have been Robbie's teammates last year before he graduated.

I manage to sit back on my heels for about two seconds before Bea crashes into the sand in front of me. She reaches to pull me into a hug but stops when I wince from her touch.

"What is it?" she asks. "Are you hurt? Where—"

"I'm okay," I croak, although I'm not sure that's true.

Bea's eyes narrow. "Oh my God. You are definitely *not* okay. You're shaking like a goddamn leaf. And what the hell happened to your voice? Josh said Robbie showed up. And then I couldn't find you, and—"

A scuffle behind us cuts her off and we both turn to see the water polo guys haul Robbie up from the sand so he's suspended between them. He sags in their hold, his blond head bowed, his broad shoulders shaking with silent sobs.

The mystery guy has taken several steps back and is now shrouded by the shadows of the cliff, so Robbie's former teammates don't even spare him a glance as they collectively steer their sagging charge back toward the bonfire. Darcy starts to follow them, but then she stops and looks over her shoulder at me. Our gazes lock, and I read accusation in hers, but confusion, too. As if she doesn't know how to feel about what just happened here.

I don't know, either.

Darcy blinks and turns away to jog after the guys as Bea helps me to my feet. "God, Nev." She scans me from head to toe, her face pinched in worry. "I'm so sorry I made you come tonight. I know you said it wasn't a good idea, but I never thought—"

I raise my hand to cut her off because I don't have a voice to protest with, but none of this is her fault. The grief immediately following a drowning can make people say and do extreme things. Gran says that people need someone to blame, and it's only natural when they choose us. Alma may have halted a massacre, but the spell she wove wasn't strong enough to protect everyone. One hundred and twenty years later, it's still not, and it's not as if the Blackwell name is innocent in any of this. Jonathan Blackwell drew the wrath of the spirits to begin with, and his blood runs through our veins as surely as Alma's does.

But the fury in Robbie's eyes, the frantic fear and confusion and grief radiating off of him as his hands wrapped around my neck . . .

Nothing like that has ever happened before.

I look over to where the guy from the bluffs was lingering in the shadows, but he's already walking away. Panic sends my pulse racing because he can't be leaving yet. I stumble after him, trying to call out for him to wait, but all I get from my vocal cords is a barely audible croak.

He must hear me though, because he slows his steps and turns around. The entrance to the sea caves is at his back and . . .

Is *that* where he's going? Is that where he came from a few minutes ago? Is that why he was close enough to hear me and Robbie struggling?

I study him in the silvery night. He's the longer, leaner answer to Robbie's bulkier frame, and I wonder how he was able to hold him down for so long. I'd assumed this morning that he was one of those ghost-hunting kids with an EMF reader, but now I'm not so sure. He could be a normal tourist. Most of the local inns are booked up ahead of my Vow ceremony at the end of the week, but if he's looking for a place to camp, I'd expect him to go to the campground inside the state park. I spent a couple of nights as a kid sleeping alone in one of the few caves that sit above the tide line here, but those entrances aren't easy to find. And although he could be a drifter, I don't think he is. His dark jeans and black hoodie are a bit rumpled but clean. So who is he? And what is he doing here?

He tilts his head, waiting for me to say or do something. His hands are shoved into the front pockets of his jeans and his shoulders are hunched forward, like he's protecting his chest against another attack. With the shadowy caves looming behind him and the churning black waters of the cove stretching out endlessly on his other side, he looks strangely . . . lost.

I have the sudden urge to run to him, but Bea catches up to me and puts her arm around my shoulders. She looks between me and the guy, her brow wrinkling.

"Thank you," I gasp out at him.

Bea winces at the pathetic crack of my voice, but the guy just gives me one last searching look before nodding and turning back to the caves. We watch him leave in silence. When he's no longer in sight, Bea looks at me with her eyebrows raised, but I shake my head and use the very last of my voice to ask her to take me home.

Chapter Three

We're running through the house. Our shadows are long in the hall as our feet slap against the hardwood floors in the same galloping rhythm. The phantoms hover at the edge of my vision, their vaporous forms shifting like smoke.

Always just out of reach.

Always just out of sight.

We race past the Séance Room, cut through the library, and climb two flights of stairs before stopping for a breath in front of a door with a stained-glass panel in the pattern of a spiderweb.

I turn, like I always do, trying to catch a glimpse of the faceless figures that haunt me night after night. But also like always, they disappear before I can, scattering in the air like fog run through by the sun.

Except—

my heart stutters.

—this time, one phantom stays.

It detaches itself from the corner, its hazy, featureless form flickering in the glow of an old-fashioned gas lamp as it drifts, smokelike, toward me.

A hand reaches out.

But these aren't the twisting wraithlike fingers I sometimes glimpse in the corner of my eye. This hand is made of solid pale flesh.

And it's reaching for my neck.

I open my mouth to scream, but first one fleshy hand and then another clamp down on my throat, cutting off my air. I beat my hands against a chest dense with hard muscle and look with frantic desperation into Robbie Harrison's face. His eyes are wide, his mouth is twisted, and silent tears are streaming down his cheeks.

And then his face changes. It melts like the wax of a fast-burning candle, and when it re-forms, I open my mouth again to scream, but the hands around my neck won't let me make a sound. They're slimmer now. Long, delicate fingers that end with neatly filed nails painted a deep, dark blue. But they're just as strong, just as capable of not letting go as I gasp and try to break free. And the face staring down at me now—oval with a slightly upturned nose, alabaster skin that glows between wavy curtains of chestnut hair—is equally etched with fury and pain.

Mom.

Her hazel eyes are round and unfocused. Her lips are moving in a soundless, frenzied litany I almost recognize. Her fingers dig

THE LIES OF ALMA BLACKWELL

into the soft skin of my throat, but when I try to beg her to stop, I can't suck in enough air to form the words.

Black spots fill my vision as she leans down and presses her lips against my ear. The heat of her breath skips across my skin, but when she speaks, it's with Robbie's deep, hoarse voice.

The true history has been hidden.

Pain shoots up my arm, sharp and sudden.

I jerk awake, throw off my covers, and tumble out of bed. My bare knees land with a thud on the hardwood floor as a white shape arcs over my head, a loud, hissing *meow* filling the air.

Tabitha lands on the floor next to me, back arched, orange and blue eyes narrowed. "Oh, God, Tab. I'm so sorry." I reach out to soothe her, but she prances out of my grasp, her white tail fluffed and high as she snakes her way through the narrow crack in my bedroom door.

I pull my legs into my chest and press my forehead to my knees, heart racing as Tab silently flees from me. I must have been having one of my dreams if she woke me like that, but when I close my eyes and try to remember images from it, it's like closing my fingers around wisps of smoke. Familiar frustration tightens my chest, but I'm shaking too much to take out my sketchbook to try to capture what I can of the faceless phantoms this time.

A minute or two later, the ringing chime of the grandfather clock penetrates my groggy mind, and even though my head and throat are both aching, I force myself to get up, shower, cover the bruises on my neck with concealer, and dress in the vaguely Victorian pin-striped blouse and long blue skirt costume Gran picked out to help our tours feel more immersive.

I down several strong cups of coffee throughout the morning, but the Saturday rush still almost kills me. We're busier than normal thanks to the publicity surrounding my upcoming Vow ceremony, and when a busload of camp kids shows up without tour reservations, I have no choice but to turn them away and hope Gran doesn't find out about it.

Without her help, I'm barely managing two tours a day, but after my mom left us high and dry, Gran ran four daily tours in addition to handling the ticket reservations and gift shop solo. I didn't understand how difficult that was for her when I was a kid, but now I'm not only in awe of it, I truly don't understand how she did it. But Gran has always been a superwoman, and her passion for upholding the Blackwell legacy knows no bounds. She's immensely proud of the role our family has played in keeping the lifeblood of this town flowing, since industry in most coastal towns like ours dried up years ago. Our cold, foggy beaches aren't exactly a compelling reason for tourists to keep driving past San Francisco, but she always says that Hollow Cliff has one thing those other towns don't.

Hollow Cliff has a ghost story.

I make it through the morning tour without losing my voice but the soreness from Robbie's bruising fingers hasn't gone away, so I'm downing a thermos of hot honey-laden tea as I ring up the last of the ten-thirty tour guests in the gift shop. But it's more than the pain in my throat that's lingered. All morning, I've been haunted by flashes of Robbie's grief-stricken face. The furious movement of his bloodless lips. The panicked fury in his wide, dark eyes as he tried to squeeze the life out of me.

I wish I could talk to Gran about it, but when I went to her room this morning, she was in so much pain that she actually asked me to move the start of her hospital stay up to tonight, and I knew it wasn't the right time. Gran keeping up her strength for the ceremony next week matters more than anything else right now.

For what feels like the hundredth time today, I wrap butcher paper around a glass jar of the Sweet Dreams Tea from DeLongre Apothecary, pop it into a Blackwell House of Spirits paper bag, and hand it to the—hallelujah—second-to-last customer in line. But when I try to discreetly wipe a sheen of sweat off my brow, my elbow knocks over a basket of anxiety-reducing moonstones, and they scatter on the floor at my feet.

"Sorry," I call out to the next customer as I duck to pick them up. "Just one second."

"Take your time."

I freeze, my heart kicking into a gallop at the sound of a voice I shouldn't recognize but instantly do. Slowly, I rise to my feet.

He's standing across the counter from me in the same zip-up hoodie he was wearing at the cove last night. His black hair is damp, and there's an aroma of salt water drifting off his skin as if he came directly from a swim in our freezing cold ocean. The pale freckles across his nose and cheeks are more visible in the light of day, but it's the piercing blue-grey of his eyes that I can't look away from.

They remind me of something. The sky, maybe? Yes. His eyes remind me of one of my first oil paintings. I used white and grey and a touch of blue to capture the sky as it looked over Blackwell House right after a storm. I couldn't get the color quite right though. I still can't. I have dozens more pencil drawings of the same landscape in my sketchbook right now.

"I was wondering," he says, "if you're the person I should talk to about the job."

I blink at him, realize how intensely I was just staring, and take an involuntary step back from the counter. His brows lift, the crescent-shaped scar above his left eye tightening.

"I'm sorry . . . what?"

Without dropping my gaze, he reaches into the back pocket of his jeans, pulls out a piece of paper, unfolds it, and slides it across the counter toward me. I look down.

It's a printout from the online edition of the *Hollow Cliff Gazette*.

The top of the page is a continuation of an article I've seen before that ran on the front page about a month ago. It includes a brief history of the first Vow made by Alma Blackwell, and it names me as its next successor. There's also a grainy black-and-white photo from when Gran took her Vow back in the eighties. She's kneeling on a stage overlooking the bluffs, her arms outstretched above her head as her mother places a small wooden box etched with carvings of the waxing and waning moon into her hands.

I skip over the information about ticket sales and skim down to the classifieds underneath the article. There's a used boat listed for sale, an offer for lawn mowing services . . . and at the very bottom, a help-wanted ad for a job with a generous salary and free room and board at the Blackwell House of Spirits.

I read the ad through, even though I'm the one who wrote it six weeks ago. When I look up, I notice for the first time that the mystery guy has a backpack slung over one shoulder. Is he not just here for the job, but for the promised room and board, too? In hindsight, that was a truly insane thing to offer, but I was feeling desperate when I wrote the ad, and we do have an abundance of rooms to spare. I thought it might help attract someone from out of town, but I never actually considered what I'd do if someone took me up on it.

I meet his eyes and ask the only question I can think of. "Why?"

He tilts his head. "Why what?"

"Why do you want to work *here*?"

"Is this part of the job interview?"

"Yes," I say, even though I've never conducted a job interview before and have no idea how they're supposed to go. His mouth quirks, as if my lack of HR experience is painfully obvious.

"All right." He crosses his arms. "I want to work here because I need a summer job and this one pays well."

I expect him to keep going. But he doesn't. "That's it?"

He shrugs. "I'm also good at memorization, which I assume will be useful for the tour guide part."

I arch a brow at him, waiting for him to say something else. Maybe something about how he came here with his family as a kid. Or how he's planning to be a history major. I'd even take a confession about an unhealthy obsession with ghosts. Anything at all that will help his appearance here make some degree of sense because I can't afford to turn him away. The desperation that led me to place that ad in the first place has only grown.

"What's your name?" I ask.

"Cal."

"Cal what?"

His eyes flick away before he answers. "The ad said you pay in cash."

Both of my brows lift. "What does that—"

He looks back at me, his face an unreadable mask. "If you pay in cash, you don't need my full name for a bank account deposit."

Well, *that's* not a good sign.

"Are you a criminal, Cal?"

Blue-grey eyes bore into mine. "Is that what you think I am, Nevinia?"

I jerk back. "Don't—"

I cut myself off, surprised by the force of my reaction to that name on his lips. His eyes narrow in interest, and I drop my gaze to the *Gazette* article he placed on the counter.

No one but my mom has ever called me Nevinia. She claimed the name came to her in a dream and that it was too musical to be shortened. But I'm fully aware that most of the articles written about my Vow ceremony—including this one—refer to me by my full legal name, which is obviously where this Cal guy got it from. Hearing it shouldn't send my heart pounding. It shouldn't be a shock.

I look back up and lift one shoulder in a shrug. "Most people call me Nev."

He holds my gaze, but instead of commenting on the weirdly extreme reaction I just had to hearing my own name, he leans forward and places both forearms on the counter so our faces are level. "Okay, *Nev*. Here's the way I see it. I need a job for the summer. And you . . ."

His eyes travel over the disorganized mess that is the space behind the counter. I discreetly shove a box of open but still unstocked magnets out of sight with my foot. "Well, it seems pretty obvious that you need the help." His lips twitch, but when he looks back at me, his face sobers. "And no, I'm not a criminal. And no, you will never be in any danger from me. But I think you already know that."

A prism of light from the stained-glass window dances across his face, illuminating the shadow of the bruise Robbie's fist left on his cheek. I think about the relief that washed through me when he materialized out of the darkness last night, and about his fist halting in midair the second I called out for him to stop. As I do, something my mom used to say floats through my head. Words I haven't thought about in years.

When your blood whispers, darling, listen.

Is that what's happening right now? Is that the source of this possibly irresponsible impulse to hire the stranger who saved my life last night and offer him a key to the front door? Is my gut telling me I can trust him?

"Oh," Cal adds like an afterthought, his lips curving in a crooked smile. "I should also mention, I'm available to start right away."

Chapter Four

Our newest—and first-ever—Blackwell House of Spirits employee is waiting in the front hall under the gas chandelier along with the rest of the afternoon tour guests. He has the blue cloth binder with this season's tour script tucked under one arm, and there's a pencil shoved behind his ear. When our eyes meet across the room, his lips kick into a grin and he raises two fingers to his forehead in a mock salute.

My face heats, and I look down at the clipboard with the reservation list. No one but family has ever worked at the house, so there's no practice in place for training new people. But since I learned everything I know from tagging along behind Gran, Cal shadowing me on the tour today seemed to make logical sense. Except now I'm questioning the wisdom of that idea. My gut may have told me to hire him, but there's something about his presence that unsettles me still.

Doing my best to ignore his gaze, I do a quick count to make sure all the registered guests are here and then climb to the fourth step of the grand staircase made of gleaming redwood. "Hello, everyone." The last of the conversations die down. "I'm happy to be the first one to welcome you to the world-famous Blackwell House of Spirits."

A couple of people in the crowd cheer—probably repeat guests—but more than a few cast nervous glances at each other, which is also a pretty common reaction. The spirits have never taken the life of anyone born outside of Hollow Cliff, and they aren't as restless as they were right after the drowning, but their presence is chilling even on the best of days.

"Very soon," I continue, "we'll learn all about the woman who transformed this house from a family home into a twisting mansion for spirits to roam, but first, we have a few ground rules to go over."

When I explain that everyone must stay with the group at *all* times, I make eye contact with each person. I don't have time to deal with any stragglers getting "lost" on purpose today. There are the usual number of groans when I explain that photos aren't allowed, and I can tell that two ladies in the back are immediately going to break that rule, which is fine with me. By the time their third or fourth photo comes out blurry beyond all recognition, they'll give up.

"Blackwell House," I continue once the rules are out of the way, "has been a public fixture in Hollow Cliff for over a century. It was a private home until 1921 when Lily Blackwell, the daughter of Jonathan and Alma Blackwell, opened the house to the public a year after her mother's death. One of the house's first visitors was the famous magician—and known paranormal skeptic—Harry Houdini, who came with the stated aim of debunking claims that spirits reside within these walls. Instead, he is the one who gave this house the name it goes by today: the Blackwell House of Spirits."

A ripple of interest moves through the crowd, and when I catch Cal's eye, he gives me an encouraging wink. I smile but shake my head because I've been giving this tour since I was fourteen and hardly need the encouragement. *He's* the one who should be trying to remember all of this and taking notes.

"Now, if you'll follow me," I call out. "We'll head to the Mariner Dining Room, named for its dramatic view of the Pacific, where I'll tell you more about the history of this house and the family who built it. On the way, pay attention to the abundant and often elaborate use of redwood design elements. As you'll soon discover, Hollow Cliff's towering coastal redwood forests are foundational to this house's story, in more ways than one."

I lead the group through an arched doorway made of said redwood filagree and down a series of twisting hallways lit by flickering gas wall sconces. A few shadows slither out as we pass, bringing their unnatural chill with them, but they seem less interested than usual in terrorizing the guests. I pause a few times to point out some of the more ornate architectural and historical details that my family has painstakingly preserved for over a century, including flamboyant onyx fireplaces, full-length stained-glass windows, gilt-framed mirrors, and ornate ceiling cornices.

When we reach the dining room, I launch into a recitation of the Blackwell family history, starting with Jonathan Blackwell's father who, after failing to strike it rich when he came out west for the Gold Rush, found his fortune instead in the Northern California redwood belt. A decade later, the small logging town of Hollow Cliff had sprouted up to support the Blackwell Redwood Company, which employed nearly everyone who lived in the area.

But as impressive as the profits from the logging company were, this was the era of industry in America. The era of the railroad tycoon. And a tycoon is exactly what the young, ambitious—and, as some would say, ruthless—Jonathan Blackwell wanted to become. So when his father died, leaving him the company, Jonathan decided he would go head-to-head with the famous Big Four railroad industrialists by transforming the short railroad line the logging company had built for hauling lumber into a passenger line. He wanted to own the railroad that would connect the Redwood Lumber Belt to the outside world, and he wanted Hollow Cliff to be its hub.

He had little trouble recruiting investors and business partners from amongst the prominent members of this town for his project, but unfortunately, the construction of the rail line met with multiple delays. This became a problem in the summer of 1903 because the agreement the Blackwell Redwood Company had with the federal government expired at the end of June of that year. If a rail line between Hollow Cliff and the town of Willits wasn't completed and fully operational by the time the representatives from the federal government arrived, the company's right of way would be revoked and given to a competing line.

Jonathan forged ahead, finished his railroad, and—in honor of the visiting federal delegation—planned an elaborate celebration to mark the engine's maiden voyage.

"But what only a handful of people knew at the time," I continue, my eyes scanning the crowd, "is that a week before the maiden rail voyage, an assistant engineer submitted a report about a trestle bridge that he believed the lead engineer had—in his haste to hurry construction—not anchored correctly at the bottom of the ravine. Jonathan, as well as many high-positioned men in his company, were given copies of this report, but they buried it, and the grand opening celebration went ahead as scheduled."

The expected murmurs break out amongst the group, and I pause briefly before continuing. "A week later, the first and only train to ever travel from Willits to Hollow Cliff derailed when that exact trestle bridge collapsed. In addition to the engine, three train cars flew off the bridge and crashed into the rushing river below. Those who didn't die instantly drowned in the icy water before help could arrive. All told, forty-three men, women, and children perished that day.

"The tragedy quickly became a national story, and when the same assistant engineer who had tried to warn the company about the engineering flaws in the bridge—although the public didn't know this yet—threw himself off the edge of the same ravine as the crash site, people began asking questions.

"Jonathan Blackwell, however, maintained that it was a tragic accident. And to squash rumors that he was at all concerned about what an investigation might turn up, less than a week after the crash, he threw a dinner party here, at this very table, with this very china, under these matching alabaster chandeliers with his closest business associates and their wives. He sat in this exact chair."

I point to the ornate Chippendale chair at the end of the table, and every head in the group swings toward it.

"His young wife, Alma, sat at the other end. But it was as Jonathan raised his glass to offer up a toast to his bride—they had only recently learned that she was expecting their first child—that tragedy struck. Instead of giving the toast he had planned, Jonathan Blackwell smashed his crystal wineglass against the table. And then, before anyone grasped what was happening, he jabbed the crystal stem into his own neck. Moments later, he was dead."

Every eye goes to the spot at the dining room table where Jonathan Blackwell collapsed a hundred and twenty years ago. Well, every eye except Cal's. He's studying me instead of the chair, which should not give me that itchy, unsettled feeling again because it's what he's supposed to do. He's supposed to watch me and learn.

I actively ignore his gaze and take a deep breath before launching into the next part of the script. What I'm about to say is the most sanitized version of events that we can get away with while remaining historically accurate, but speaking it aloud—even after years of practice—still makes me queasy every time.

"Unfortunately," I say, drawing back the group's attention, "what the rest of the dinner guests that evening didn't know is that the strange nature of Jonathan Blackwell's death was only a harbinger of things to come. Within three days of his death, the other six men who sat at this table that night would also be dead. And each of their deaths would be even more unexplainable, even more tragic than the last."

The room fills with its usual mix of horror and fascination as I tell them about the dozens of employees at the Blackwell Redwood Company who threw themselves out of windows and hurled themselves off cliffs. About the sheriff of Hollow Cliff's eight-year-old son and the rifle he took from the gun cabinet. About the shrill laugh his mother heard echo throughout the house before the boy shot his sobbing father in the head.

And the hush only deepens as I go on. As I tell the story of the factory manager, Jonathan Blackwell's cousin on his aunt's side, who was hanged without a trial in the center of the town square by a mob of townspeople who, the moment the man took his last breath, had no memory of what they had done or why they had done it. About the local judge who tried to flee town only to be found on the side of the road disemboweled by his own knife.

And it doesn't end there. I continue to recount horrible death after horrible death until at last, I get to the one that no one ever wants to hear. The one about the thirteen local kids who were found washed up on the shore by the harbor, their bodies bloated with seawater.

"And that," I say, looking out at faces that are both horrifically disturbed and helplessly transfixed, "is when Alma Blackwell stepped in."

I unlock the door to the Séance Room and usher the group inside.

"You might notice that the room we are entering now is perfectly square and perfectly symmetrical. There's a reason for that. Just like there's a reason that this door"—I gesture to the pale green door we just filed through—"is the only entrance to this room, but not the only exit. In fact, this room has three exits. Can anyone spot them?"

A girl with blonde hair and braces immediately raises her hand. I smile at her. "Found one already?"

She nods and points over my shoulder at the door we just came through. There's a soft laugh on my right, and even though I don't look, I know it belongs to Cal.

"You are absolutely correct," I say to the girl. "A lot of people don't get that right away, but yes, the door we came through is the first exit. But there are two others."

It only takes about a minute for the same girl to walk over to the single wooden chair in the center of the room and point at the floor below it. "Is that one?"

The other guests drift over, gazes following the point of her finger. I know they've noticed the outline of the trapdoor when heads start bobbing.

"You're good at this," I say to the girl.

She lifts one shoulder in a shrug. "I know."

I make the mistake of glancing at Cal over her shoulder, and when our eyes meet in shared amusement, I have to bite my lip to stop from laughing.

"Well, let me know if you want a job in a few years," I say, looking back at the girl. "But yes, you are again one hundred percent correct. The trapdoor you're currently standing on has been sealed shut for safety reasons, but in Alma's day, it opened onto a fifteen-foot drop to the cellar below, making it an exit—although not a very safe one—but not an entrance. So that's two out of three."

I wait about a minute, but when no one finds the last one, I cut through the group to the opposite end of the room, make my first two fingers into a hook, and slip them into a notch in the wall that's well camouflaged by the faded yellow wallpaper. One firm tug later, and a portion of the wall slides open to reveal a small antechamber on the other side.

"The sliding door only opens from *this* room." I step aside so people can peek their heads into the cozy sitting room beyond. "There's no notch, latch, or handle on the other side, so it's another exit you can't enter through. It's believed that Alma used this small chamber to compose herself privately after her communions with the spirits. But I'm getting ahead of myself."

At this point in the script, Gran has written that we're supposed to raise our eyebrows in a way that is both *suggestive* and *mysterious,* but I've never really been able to pull that off. So instead, I walk in a way that is neither suggestive nor mysterious to a framed black-and-white photograph hanging on the pale yellow wall.

"If you're wondering why Alma Blackwell would have a room like this built, the answer starts with this photograph. It ran along with an article in the *Hollow Cliff Gazette* in 1903, five days after the spirits first attacked. The woman on the left"—I point to a young woman dressed in black staring directly into the camera lens, her hair piled high in a fashionable tumble atop her head—"is Alma Blackwell. She's twenty-two in this photo, widowed only four days. The black mourning colors she's wearing here are the same colors that she'll continue to wear for the rest of her days.

"But it's the woman next to her"—I move my finger to indicate the middle-aged woman next to Alma, clad in flowing layers of white, her arms raised theatrically in the air above her head—"who is responsible not only for the curious layout of the room we're standing in now, but for helping Alma put a stop to the massacre of Hollow Cliff's residents."

An interested murmur spreads through the room. Even though most of the people on this tour already know this part of the story—it's the first thing that comes up when you search us—they like hearing it again. The only person who doesn't look interested is Cal. The amusement we shared earlier is gone from his eyes, and his lips are pressed together in a thin line.

Confused, I look away from him and back at the rest of the group. "The woman's name was Penny Margaret, but she was more commonly known as the *Portland Medium*. She came to prominence during a time of intense public interest in the Spiritualist movement, and she is the famed trance speaker and spirit medium who Alma turned to for help.

"It was Penny Margaret who revealed to Alma that the horrific deaths taking place in Hollow Cliff were being carried out by the spirits of those who had lost their lives in the train crash. This was the reason Jonathan Blackwell and his business partners were targeted first. But since it was the entire town of Hollow Cliff that stood to benefit from the rushed construction of the passenger rail, Penny Margaret decreed that the spirits would continue to seek vengeance on the entire town, unless they were given a concession."

I spread my fingers, gesturing to the walls of the house we're all standing in.

"That concession was *this* house. The Portland Medium charged Alma with making a home for the lost souls who were doomed to forever walk this earthly plane due to the violent, unjust nature of their deaths.

"She charged Alma with caring for those spirits by making a lifelong vow that would bind her to this house and this town. She charged her with building a room in the center of this house that had one way in and three ways out because it was only in such a room that Alma would be able to commune with the spirits and hear their will.

"She charged Alma with the monumental task of making amends for the lives that had been lost to the greed of Jonathan Blackwell. To the greed of this town."

I sweep my eyes across the group and pause to let them feel the hush that's taken hold. As if the spirits themselves are listening to this story. As if they too want to hear how it ends.

"That very same day, at sunset on the summer solstice, Alma Blackwell made a public Vow in front of the entire town. She stood on a hastily constructed stage on the western edge of these grounds with the sea churning at her back, and she swore to maintain a house for the spirits whose lives had been so cruelly taken. She swore that she and her descendants would uphold the charge of making amends. For four days, the spirits had wrought havoc on this town, but the day after Alma Blackwell's Vow, the killings in Hollow Cliff ceased."

For a long moment, no one speaks. Then the girl with the braces raises her hand. I nod at her and she asks, "Are the spirits happy now? Or do they still want to hurt people?"

I look her straight in the eye when I lie to her. "No. The spirits don't hurt people anymore."

Chapter Five

I place a carton of aura-cleansing chocolates from Miranda's Patisserie into a bag and hand it to our last customer of the day.

"Thanks for visiting the Blackwell House of Spirits." With my best customer service smile, I watch her leave while silently wondering exactly how many blurry photos she and her friend attempted to take on the tour before finally giving up. Once she's gone, I transfer the signed credit card receipts into the envelope for filing and shoot a surreptitious look at where Cal is unloading a shipment of crystal balls in a far corner of the shop. He's been noticeably quiet since the tour ended, and I can't make out his expression now thanks to the late afternoon shadows cloaking his face.

I could chalk it up to the amount of new information he's had to absorb while helping me with the post-tour gift shop rush, but he's also been throwing me intensely searching looks when he thinks I'm not looking. When I can't stand the tension-filled silence a moment longer, I close the cash register, walk over to the built-in shelf he's arranging the crystal balls on, and lean sideways against it. "You could just ask me and get it over with, you know."

He turns to me, glinting crystal clutched in each hand. "Ask you what?"

I raise an eyebrow because this isn't my first rodeo. "Ask me if I truly believe this house is haunted. If spirits are actually trapped in these walls. If all of this"—I make a sweeping gesture with my hand—"is real."

Cal tilts his head, an assessing look in those cloudlike eyes. Then he turns back to the shelf and sets down one of the crystal balls. "No. I don't think I will."

His mild, controlled tone is weirdly frustrating. I cross my arms and study his profile. I didn't peg him as a hard-line skeptic, but maybe that's what he is. "So . . . what? You're so sure ghosts don't exist that you won't even entertain the possibility?"

He places the other crystal ball on a shelf above his head and then turns to lean his shoulder against the built-in, mirroring my position. "I don't have to ask you if this house is haunted because only a supremely close-minded person could spend more than a half hour inside these walls and not acknowledge that *something* out of the ordinary exists here."

Oh.

I try to hide my surprise at his answer, but the slightly smug expression on his face tells me I don't do a great job. "So what you're saying is that you consider yourself an open-minded person?"

He lifts one shoulder in a shrug. "I prefer to think of myself as a person who questions."

"Questions what?"

He holds my gaze for a long moment. "Everything."

Something shifts in the air between us, and a strange shiver races down my spine. Then Cal's eyes dart to a spot over my shoulder and widen ever so slightly. A heartbeat later, the familiar *tap tap* of the walking stick Gran absolutely loathes using sounds from the doorway behind me. I whirl around, my eyes flying to the clock on the wall. We were supposed to leave for the hospital ten minutes ago.

I hurry over to her. "Gran! I'm so sorry. I lost track of time."

She's dressed in one of her signature all-black ensembles, and her salt-and-pepper hair has been pulled back into a sleek bun that gathers at the nape of her neck. The asymmetrical top and flowing silk pants hang slightly looser on her than they would have even a few weeks ago, but the proud tilt of her chin compensates for any frailty.

Before I have a chance to offer her my arm for support, she throws her shoulders back and tosses a quick, pointed glance to where I left Cal standing half-buried in shadows by the crystal balls. Then she looks back at me. "I assume this is the young man you mentioned?"

I raise my eyebrows at her lofty tone, but Gran pretends not to notice. She could barely keep her eyes open when I checked on her before my last tour, but apparently, she's decided to exhaust what little energy she has left to conjure up a show for our new employee, starring the invincible, iron-willed version of Marie Blackwell she presents to the public.

I glance back at Cal's carefully polite expression, realizing I probably should have warned him that she might do this. He may be living in our house, but Gran doesn't show her soft side to anyone but me.

"Gran, this is Cal. He took notes during my tour today, and he's already been a big help in the shop. Cal, this is my grandmother, Marie Blackwell."

She tosses him another textbook definition of a cursory glance. "May I also assume that by tomorrow he'll be wearing appropriate attire?"

"*Gran!*"

Her brows raise. "We've gone to great lengths to create an atmosphere, sweetheart. This isn't the time to get sloppy. Now." She straightens her back and juts out her chin, but the lines of exhaustion on her face make it clear she pushed herself too far with this little display. "Are you ready?"

I shoot an apologetic look in Cal's direction, but he's already turned around and resumed unloading the crystal balls. "I . . . uh, should only be gone an hour," I say to his back. "Are you okay to finish up in here?"

"No problem."

I wait for him to turn back around. When he doesn't, I add, "There are leftovers in the fridge in the kitchen. I'm sorry it's not—"

"I like leftovers."

His tone is polite, but his voice is lower. Flatter. I aim another annoyed glance at Gran, but she doesn't see it because she's already halfway to the doorway, her stride as impatient as her cane will allow. I shout out a hasty goodbye to Cal and hurry to catch up to her. This time, when I offer my arm, she takes it with a sigh of gratitude and immediately gives me the bulk of her weight.

I stay silent as we cross the echoing central foyer, but once we're in front of the Séance Room and out of earshot, I look over at her. "That wasn't exactly the warmest welcome, you know."

She gives me a wholly unapologetic look. "I said I wouldn't interfere with your decision, hon, but I'm still your grandmother. I understand you're almost an adult. I understand we need help. But that doesn't mean I have to like it. And it doesn't mean I'm obligated to warmly welcome the young man you've invited to take up residence in our home."

The stubborn set of her jaw and the mother-bear protective fire in her eyes reminds me of that time in seventh grade when she wanted to call the school and threaten to pull all of the Blackwell legacy donations to Hollow Cliff Junior High if they didn't formally reprimand the five kids who made me leave their lunch table. I begged her to let it go, and she did. But a swell of tenderness rises in me at the memory. Gran has always been my fiercest protector.

I throw my arms around her neck and whisper into her ear. "I love you, you know." The arm that isn't clutching her cane snakes up my back and squeezes tight. "I know you're worried about me, but I'm going to be fine. I promise."

When I pull back from the hug, Gran's eyes are suspiciously bright. And since I know how much she hates showing emotion in public, I offer her my arm again and don't say anything else as we continue down the hall. We're almost to the side door when she stops walking abruptly, her body stiffening against mine.

"Gran? What's—"

"Did you bring your charm bag?"

I frown at her. "No. It's in my room. Why—"

"You should get it." Her eyes glaze in the way they do when she senses something from the spirits. I'm not picking up on any unusual agitation or anger, but Gran's more sensitive than I am, thanks to the Vow. She blinks, focusing back on me. "I'll wait here, but go now, hon. Bring everything you need to tend the Anchors. You need to check them before you come back tonight."

After settling Gran at the hospital, I drive south until I reach the forest at the edge of town. The sun is a low ball hovering in the sky by the time I park the car where the unpaved road abruptly dead-ends. From there, it's only a short hike through an underbrush of green ferns to reach the hill where the more than two-thousand-year-old sequoia tree Alma herself selected still proudly stands.

The southern Anchor is dangling from a knot in the tree's bark like a wind chime. I rise on my toes, untie the pink fishing rope that binds the pieces, and lower myself to a seat on the damp forest floor. Leaning back against the sequoia's rough, cinnamon-colored bark, I settle the charm in my lap, close my eyes, and listen until I can pick out the individual vibrations of each object bound within the braided rope. Yesterday morning, these pieces combined to form a perfect working harmony. But today, a note is missing.

Frowning, I test each object one by one. The pad of my pointer finger hovers over a pink and white scallop shell, a smooth piece of light green sea glass, and half of a white seagull feather until I find the piece that's gone silent.

It's an acorn cap. The brown, textured dome drained like a dead bulb in a string of holiday lights.

An image pushes itself into my mind. Me as a child, pouring a few careful drops of milk into an upside down cap just like this one. Leaving it out on the forest floor along with a collection of fruit.

The fairies will come for it, darling. But only once we turn our backs.

I shake my head against the memory. Against the image of a mother I thought I knew. Reaching into my bag, I pull out my sketchbook and thumb past countless drawings of the faceless phantoms from my dreams until I get to the diagram I made the last time this particular Anchor failed six months ago. We're lucky that this time, Gran sensed the failure before the spirits had a chance to break through and seize another mind.

Last time, it was a butterfly wing that burned out. According to my notes, I replaced it with the seagull feather, hoping the slightly higher note of the feather would make the charm more potent. Had that thrown the acorn out of balance?

I stifle a sigh as the futility of what I'm doing threatens to overwhelm me and take out a pencil, forcing myself to draw a new diagram of the latest failed charm while trying not to think about the pitying look Gran gave me when I first told her about my study of the Anchors. For one hundred and twenty years, they've been the weak link in the spell Alma wove with her Vow to bind the vengeful spirits from the train crash. She extended her spell's protection to everyone in Hollow Cliff by placing these Anchor charms at the north, south, east, and west borders of the town, and, for the first six months after the massacre, she believed it had worked. But then one morning at dawn, a fisherman witnessed a woman throwing herself off the bluffs to her death. Alma went to check the Anchors immediately after she heard the news only to discover that the east charm had blinked out, allowing the spirits to slip their bind like they would through a hole in a fence.

There are a few surviving accounts from staff members who worked at the house back then, and they all note that something shifted in Alma after that first drowning. A deep melancholy took hold of her, and it only grew darker and more pronounced in the years that followed. But she never failed to repair and maintain the

Anchors, eventually training her daughter to do the same. Not once since they were first created have all four failed, and as a result, the full wrath of the spirits has never again been released.

But Alma never succeeded in strengthening her spell enough to protect everyone in this town. No one in my family has.

It ends with you, pet. It all ends with you.

I breathe through the memory of those words, forcing myself to focus on shading in the barbs of the seagull feather.

I was eight the first time the spirits drowned someone I cared about. Mrs. Price was the only teacher at Hollow Cliff Elementary who treated me like all the other kids instead of using the gloves-on approach most teachers adopted with the Blackwell heir. And then one morning she was just . . . gone.

I knew enough back then about the drownings—just enough about the role I would one day play—to naively think that when I took my Vow, I could stop the drownings for good. I truly believed that the promise I made to myself after Mrs. Price's death was one I could keep.

And then Mom left, and—with as much love and care as she could—Gran took the kid gloves off. My promise became an ignorant, childish hope deflated by reality. Until the day after my fifteenth birthday. Until I succumbed to Bea's blatant peer pressure, downed one of Fern Fairchild's bitter, noxious brews, and asked her if the spirits could ever truly be bound for good.

It ends with you, pet. It all ends with you.

I finish the diagram, make a note about the drained acorn cap, and slip the sketchbook back into my bag. Then I take out my bulky charm pouch and sort through the seemingly random collection of shells, feathers, fabric scraps, twigs, ribbons, and other odds and ends that have called out to me over the years. Hearing their call, sensing how to work them into existing charms, is the only sliver of magic I inherited from Alma so many generations later. For now, it's all I can contribute, but in less than a week, I'll be able to do more than repair the Anchors. In less than a week, I'll add my blood to the central charm Alma wove, and just like Gran and all the Vow-holders in my family before me, I'll become a living, breathing part of the spell she cast.

In less than a week, the power the Vow gives to Gran will become mine.

I chose a tarnished copper key I found buried in the sand a couple of weeks ago to replace the acorn. It has a lower, deeper note, but should still meld. Carefully, I unbraid the pink fishing rope, toss aside the dead acorn cap, and braid the key in along with the shell, sea glass, and feather. The charm is back in harmony even before I tie the last knot.

Flickering sunlight glints off the copper key as I hang the Anchor back on the sequoia. Taking a step back, I watch for a few moments as it sways gently in the early evening breeze. No one in my family has succeeded in strengthening Alma's spell. No one has found a way to truly live up to the vow of protection she made.

But that doesn't mean it's not possible.

Every time I visit the Anchors, I become more convinced that there's something about them that I'm not seeing. Some detail hovering at the edge of my understanding that I won't be able to fully grasp until I take the Vow.

Not all of Fern's predictions come true, especially because people often make the mistake of interpreting her meandering conversation style as words of prescience. But a lot of them do, and so for two years, I've lived with this fragile, secret hope.

What if she's right?

What if after I take the Vow, I can find a way to steady the Anchors? What if I can finally finish what Alma began? What if the death and grief that's gripped this town for over a century could truly be lifted?

What if it *could* all end?

What if it could all end with me?

Tabitha greets me with an accusing yowl as soon as I step through the side door into the kitchen. I snatch her up and scratch behind her ears in that way she loves but pretends to hate as I croon my apologies. Then I dish out her dinner and open the fridge to retrieve my own.

There's a sizable dent in the leftover lasagna, which means Cal must have found it. I cut a piece and slide it onto a plate, my heart thumping oddly at the simple realization that our meals tonight came from the same dish. I take out a fork and eat the noodles cold, but what started out as a peculiar, unbalanced tingle grows into a full-fledged anxiety spiral by the time I wash, dry, and put away both my and Tab's dishes.

The only way I'm going to get a wink of sleep tonight is if I look Cal right in those cloudy grey eyes and remind myself that he's a normal guy—a guy who all but pulled Robbie Harrison's fingers off my neck—and *not* a serial killer who's going to murder me in my bed.

I drop my backpack with my charm pouch in my room and take the twisting stairwell up to the third-floor room I gave Cal. Tab follows at my heels the entire way, her chirping meows of displeasure making it clear she still hasn't forgiven me for the unacceptable delay in her dinner. If his door is closed, I'll turn around, go back to my room, and get ready for bed. I tell myself this multiple times as I climb the stairwell. Except when I do finally get to his room, and when the door *is* closed, I immediately break my promise and knock with three quick raps.

There's no answer, but the door drifts open at the light pressure from my knuckles. Unless you lock these old doors from the inside, they rarely stay shut. I hesitate on the threshold, debating if I should call out, but Tab has no such reservations. Before I can stop her, she streaks past me and bounds into what turns out to be an empty room.

"*Tab!*" I whisper-yell as I inch inside. "Get out of there!"

But Tab ignores me. In the soft glow of a lamp from the bedside table, I can see her furry white body leap up onto the large oak bed, turn in three tight circles, and plop down on top of a pillow to lazily lick her paw.

I really hope Cal isn't allergic to cats.

After a quick look over my shoulder, I dart into the room to grab her. But when I catch sight of a black backpack lying on its side on the tufted bench at the foot of the bed, I stop in my tracks.

I shouldn't.

I know I shouldn't. But that itchy, unsettled feeling is even stronger now than it was in the kitchen, and I can't stop myself. Tab doesn't stir from her nest of pillows as I kneel in front of the bench, slide the backpack onto the rug, and start taking out its contents.

It's frustratingly sparse.

There are only a couple sets of spare clothes, a canvas toiletry bag, a flashlight, a couple of granola bars, and a slightly damp beach towel.

I want to believe my guilty conscience is responsible for the sinking in my gut, but I know what I am is disappointed. And I also know, as soon as I start returning Cal's things to the backpack, that I did *not* miss my calling as a spy. I paid zero attention to how this bag was packed before I started pulling things out, so it's very likely he'll know I rifled through it. Still, getting caught in the act would be worse, so I choose speed and start stuffing his things back into the main compartment. It's as I hastily pick up his spare black T-shirt that something heavy falls into my lap.

It's a locket, hanging on a tarnished silver chain.

The back of the oval pendant is silver and slightly scratched, but the front has a vintage glass clasp allowing the locket to display strands of human hair that have been braided into the shape of a heart. One of the strands is a dark raven's wing black like my own, and the other is a fiery sunset red.

I've spent enough of my life surrounded by early-twentieth-century antiques to know this is over a hundred years old. An heirloom, maybe. I turn it sideways so the hair catches the glow from the bedside lamp. Jewelry containing the locks of a deceased loved one was fairly common in the Victorian era, but there's something about this locket that makes me think it wasn't made with mourning in mind.

I have no right to unclasp the front glass casing, but I do. And without the glare, a small reddish-brown smudge is visible in the center of the heart. An icy, unnatural chill dances across my skin, and I reach out to touch the dark stain. The second the pad of my forefinger comes into contact with the center of the heart, a strange vertigo washes over me. Pain explodes in my temples, and my eyes snap closed.

Red dots swim behind my eyelids, a cool breeze slides over my cheeks, and the brine-like scent of the ocean invades my nose. I force my eyes open and have to immediately squint against the glare of bright light.

It's only when I feel sand beneath my feet, only when I see the aquamarine water of the Pacific Ocean spread out before me, its white-capped waves sparkling in the afternoon sun, that I understand.

I'm not in Blackwell House anymore.

Chapter Six

Two girls are running up the path from Smuggler's Cove. They look around my age, but they're wearing long skirts and blouses that are more elaborate versions of what Gran and I wear for our tours. One of them has a mane of black curly hair; the other a sleek braid of bright carrot orange.

The black-haired girl—

Millie.

Somehow, I know this.

—stumbles on her way up the path. Her arms are full and when she trips, two large work boots land in the sand at her feet with a soft thud. They're followed by a linen shirt, a pair of trousers, and a bundle of small clothes that Millie was very careful—I know this, too—not to touch too much when she gathered them up.

"Mil!"

Sand sprays her face as the other girl, the girl with red hair— her name is Jenny—catches up.

"Mil, are you all right?"

Jenny drops her own bundle of clothes, almost identical to Millie's except hers contains a pair of oxfords in place of work boots, and kneels next to where Millie landed on her hands and knees. As she does this, the bright afternoon sun catches on the glint of a silver chain around Millie's neck, the pendant hanging from it a newer, shinier version of the one I found in Cal's bag.

I move closer to the locket, but the girls don't react. It's as if they can't see me. As if—

All at once, I understand. That reddish-brown smudge I touched my finger to only moments ago in Blackwell House wasn't dirt or discoloration. It was a drop of dried blood. This Millie girl's blood, to be more precise. Because it's *her* memory I'm in.

Millie opens her mouth to answer Jenny, but before she can, a shout sounds from behind them.

"*Oy!*"

The two girls share a look. Then Millie straightens and looks over her shoulder at a blond-haired boy standing waist-deep in the blue water of the cove. And I know—because *Millie* knows—that this is a favorite swimming spot for all the young people in Hollow Cliff, but it's a particular favorite for the boys, who have the luxury of forgoing any pretense of a bathing costume and leaving their clothes strewn atop the rocks instead.

Millie pushes herself to her feet. Then she reaches out a hand, helps Jenny up, and together, they turn to face the water.

A wide smile stretches her lips as she lifts her hand in a cheery wave. "Hello, Eddie. Lovely day for a swim, don't you think?"

Next to her, Jenny stifles a laugh.

A second figure pops up next to Eddie, and Millie brings up a hand to shade her eyes. "Oh, is that you, Charlie? How *is* the water today?"

This time, Jenny's laugh rings out loud, and when it reaches the boys in the water, they both produce furious scowls. The first one—Charlie—calls out, "Give our clothes back now, Millie. You've had your fun."

But Millie makes no move to gather up the clothes piled at her feet. She just cocks a hand on her hip. "*Had my fun.* What an interesting choice of words, Charlie."

Next to him, the one named Eddie lets out a snarl. "Now listen here, you little bi—"

Millie slices through his words. "I'd be careful throwing around insults, Eddie Smothers." An icy chill of anger races up her spine, and I feel it as if I *am* her. "I know you aren't the sharpest tool in the shed, but surely even *you* must know when to keep your mouth shut and let the grown-ups talk."

The insult hits its mark, and I feel Millie's delight as she watches Eddie's face turn a pleasing shade of crimson. He jerks forward as if to run up the shore—clothes or no—but he's stayed by Charlie's hand on his shoulder.

At this, Millie's smile widens even further because she knows that Eddie is a handsome, mindless brute, but that Charlie

Anderson is calculating. She knows he will have already noticed her and Jenny's bicycles standing at the ready behind them. That he will have realized that one wrong word, one wrong *move*, and Millie and Jenny will be pedaling away with the boys' clothes stuffed in the wicker baskets attached to their handlebars. Even if he and Eddie do attempt to chase them—naked and shoeless— there's no possibility they'll catch the girls on foot.

And that will be a *long* walk back to town.

Charlie leans down to say something in Eddie's ear—something Eddie clearly does *not* enjoy hearing—and then straightens and lifts his chin. "Okay, Millie. What do you want?"

Millie crosses her arms, throws a searching look in Jenny's direction, then turns back to the boys and calls out, "I want an apology."

"For what?" Eddie explodes. "For stealing our—"

"I want an apology for what you two did to Jenny."

Both boys shift their gaze to Jenny. Her skin is pale and cov- ered in freckles which do little to cover the furious blush taking over her face. Millie knows how much Jenny hates to be the center of attention and so she reaches out, takes her hand, squeezes it.

Down in the water, Eddie snorts loudly. "We didn't do anything to her. It's not our fault if she—"

"If that's all you have to say," Millie calls, cutting him off again, "then I wish you both a very pleasant walk." She lets go of Jenny's hand, and both girls reach down, pick up the piles of clothes at their feet, and turn toward their bicycles.

"Wait!"

Millie stops first. She turns, takes a step back toward the water, and looks down at Charlie with her head tilted and her eyebrows raised. Beside her, Jenny lets out a small, terrified whimper. And it's hard to blame her. The look on Charlie Anderson's face promises murder.

But instead of meting out threats as Eddie did, Charlie draws himself up to his full height and shifts the direction of his gaze from Millie to Jenny.

"Jenny." He says this with as much dignity as he possibly can, given that he's standing naked, waist-deep in the middle of crashing waves. "I'm sorry about the diary. It was wrong of us to do it, and I deeply regret any pain or suffering our thoughtless actions may have caused."

Jenny's jaw drops, her thin lips parting in shock. Even Millie is a little taken aback by the sincerity of the apology. Charlie Anderson is the son of the local judge. A prince in this town.

He must—I hear her think the words clear as a bell—*really want his clothes back.*

There are several long seconds of silence. Then Charlie very obviously elbows Eddie under the water. Eddie, however, only shakes his head. "No way, Charlie. I'll be damned if I let that little bi—Ow!"

Eddie splashes sideways into the water as if someone just elbowed him in the ribs. He surfaces, spluttering, and throws a rueful look at Charlie. Then, with considerably less dignity, he addresses Jenny. "I'm sorry. For what we did and all." He turns and glares up at Millie. "There. That good enough for you?"

"I don't know, Eddie." Millie turns to Jenny. "Jenny, was that good enough?"

Eddie makes a loud sound of protest, but he's quickly silenced by Charlie.

Meanwhile, Millie has kept her gaze on Jenny, whose body is shaking ever so slightly. It's been torture for her, watching Jenny collapse in mortified sobs this past week. Seeing her normally cheerful face marred by shame. It stoked a rage inside Millie that she's only ever felt once before.

She was so angry it took her three full days to come up with, and then plan, a suitable form of payback. Not only a way to punish the perpetrators, but a way to restore to Jenny some of the dignity their cruel prank tried to take.

And, of course, to ensure that nothing like it *ever* happened again.

Now, she meets Jenny's eyes and whispers under her breath, "You can do this, Jen."

It's the boost Jenny needs. Sucking in a breath, she lifts her chin and turns to look down at the beach. "Yes," she calls in a loud, clear voice. "I accept your apology."

Eddie mutters, "Well, hallelujah."

But Charlie ignores his friend. "Thank you, Jenny. I appreci-ate your generosity. Now, if you ladies would be so kind as to leave our clothes on the rocks by the—"

But Millie and Jenny have already turned on their heels. They're already running toward their bicycles, shoving the boys' clothes and shoes into the baskets hanging off their handlebars.

"Hey!" Eddie cries. "What are you doing? Charlie, what are they—"

"Enjoy your walk back to town," Millie cries over her shoulder, swinging a leg over the center tube and hopping onto the leather seat. "And next time"—she brings her bicycle around so she can peer down at the cove—"remember that upsetting Jenny Murphy is upsetting *me.*"

She slants a look at Jenny, checking she's ready to go. When Jenny nods, Millie pushes off and pedals fast down the dirt road. The wind catches her hair, sending it streaming out like ribbons as she lets go of the handlebars, spreads her arms like wings, and lets out a loud, triumphant *whoop*! Jenny doesn't take her hands off her handlebars, but she answers Millie with a victorious cry of her own.

Behind them, down by the cove, an enraged roar echoes off the bluffs. It's soon followed by the sound of footsteps racing up the steep path, and then running behind them on the packed dirt road. But Millie and Jenny don't turn around. They just keep pedaling as fast as they can, their peals of laughter filling the warm summer air.

I fly with them up the hill, both with Millie and apart from her at the same time, and I feel the joy surging through her. I feel the triumphant thrill—the rightness—of avenging the person I love.

She and Jenny pedal all the way up the hill to Blackwell House, but they turn off before the drive and bump down a dirt path that leads to a clearing in the woods between the main house, where Millie lives, and the newly finished caretaker cottage where Jenny lives with her father's cousin and his family. They slow to a stop and dismount their bikes. The second Millie's feet touch the ground, Jenny throws herself into her arms and peppers her lips and cheeks with kisses.

"Oh, Mil." She leans back with her arms still around Millie's neck. "That was *wonderful*. I still can't believe it. The look on Charlie Anderson's face when he apologized. And Eddie!"

The look on your *face*, Millie thinks, loud and clear as she looks down at Jenny, her cheeks flushed pink from the climb. She's smiling in that way Millie missed so much this past week. Radiant and full of hope again. And Millie decides she can't help herself, and really, why would she want to? She wraps her arms around Jenny's waist, darts forward, and steals a kiss.

Jenny responds at once, pressing herself against Millie's chest, threading her fingers through the loose curls of Millie's hair in the way that Jenny knows she loves. And somehow, even now, even with Jenny wrapped up in her arms, Millie still can't quite believe this is something she's allowed to have. After two years of being the new girl in town—and not just the new girl, but the younger sister of the upstart who married the heir to the Blackwell Redwood Company—months of watching Jenny from afar after her adopted family moved from town into the caretaker cottage. Four months of being the best of friends, and now . . .

Everything.

I try to wonder at how I could never have known that Alma Blackwell had a sister, let alone one who lived at Blackwell House, but I can't tear my mind away from Millie's, and hers is full of the feel of Jenny's lips moving against hers as their kiss transforms from something fevered and needy to tender and slow.

Jenny lets her hand fall down the back of Millie's neck and lifts her head. "And you're sure, Mil? That it will work? That they won't—"

"I'm sure." Millie draws circles on the small of Jenny's back. "If you think that Charlie is going to tell *anyone* that two girls got the jump on him—"

"But his father—"

"Is firmly in Jonathan's pocket. And whatever my swollen-headed brother-in-law may think of me in private, to the public, I'm part of his family. Judge or not, Charlie Anderson and his father wouldn't dare cross him."

Jenny nods, but Millie can tell she's still unsure. Reaching up, she lifts one of Jenny's hands away from her neck and threads their fingers together. "Don't worry about it so much, Jen. In a few months, it won't matter what Charlie or anyone else in this town thinks of us, right?" She gives Jenny's hand a gentle, reassuring squeeze. "Did you mail your essay in?"

"This morning. But Mil, what if we don't both—"

"We will. I promise. Did you bring it?"

Jenny slides her hands away from Millie's, reaches into the pocket of her skirt, and pulls out a torn piece of stationery. "I took it from the corner. It doesn't have any of the writing on it, but—"

"That's perfect." Millie plucks the torn piece of Jenny's essay from her hand, closes her eyes briefly, and then, satisfied with the vibration the torn piece of paper gives, slips it into her pocket. She doesn't think she'll need the charm. She's confident they scored high enough on their university entrance exams to gain not only admittance but scholarships as well. But when it comes to her and Jenny's future? She's not taking any chances.

Millie pulls Jenny close again. Wraps her up in her arms and speaks softly in her ear. "Everything will work out just like we want it to. I promise."

A twig snaps behind them, and they both immediately jump apart. Jenny's eyes go wide, and Millie whispers, "Go."

Jenny hesitates, her eyes bouncing between Millie and the path behind her. Then she nods and scurries to where her bicycle is leaning against a tree trunk. She darts one more glance over her shoulder and then turns and hurries down the path toward the caretaker cottage.

I can feel Millie's heart racing in her chest, but she only allows herself a few calming breaths before tucking her and Jenny's pendant under her blouse, grabbing the handlebars of her bicycle, and turning up the path in the opposite direction. She's sure no one heard them. Sure no one saw. But if the wrong person—

"Where the devil have you *been*, Mil? I've been looking for you *everywhere.*"

A young woman is racing toward Millie, the skirts of her pink silk dress billowing out behind her. One hand is holding the side of an elaborately plumed hat as if she's afraid it might topple off her head, and the other is clutching a newspaper. Her cheeks are flushed pink, and as she draws closer, Millie silently laments her sister's recent insistence on lacing her corset so tight that she can hardly breathe. It's getting harder and harder each day to find any trace of the carefree farm girl Alma once was.

Alma.

This woman running down the path is *Alma Blackwell.* But not the stationary, black-and-white version of her I've seen in photos all my life. And not the dark-eyed woman draped in mourning clothes, either. This is a beautiful young woman full of life and color with shiny chestnut hair that's so like my mother's they would look like twins if viewed from the back.

"Alms," Millie begins, but she's cut off when Alma waves the front page of the *Hollow Cliff Gazette* in her face.

"It's horrible, Mil. Just . . . oh, just look already."

Millie stifles a sigh and leans her bike against a tree. She takes the paper from Alma and looks down at a political cartoon depicting a man sitting with his legs splayed across a broken rail line. His thumb is stuck in his mouth like a toddler, and behind him, the cartoonist has drawn a derailed train. The headline underneath reads: BLACKWELL REDWOOD CO. FLOUNDERS.

"Skip down to this part here." Alma jams her finger farther down the page, and Millie follows, reading the section aloud. "'. . . but delays have already plagued the small operation, and government officials have begun to question if Mr. Blackwell is the right man to connect the Redwood Belt to the Northwestern Line. A delegation from Washington has been dispatched to—'"

"You see?"

Millie does see. She sees proof that her brother-in-law's obsessive desire to go toe to toe with the Big Four railroad tycoons is as foolish now as it has always been. But she's also quite sure that's *not* the conclusion her older sister wants her to draw.

"John insists it's libel," Alma continues when Millie doesn't answer right away. "He said the writer, whatever his name is, is in Central Pacific's pocket, and—"

"But, Alms. There *have* been delays. It's not libel when it's the—"

"You're not *hearing* me, Mil. They're sending a delegation from *Washington* to oversee the inaugural train from Willits. It's scheduled for next week, and if anything goes wrong, if they encounter any further delays, they can revoke his right of way. John says it's a technicality. That they would never do this to someone like Leland Stanford. But he says that he can't do anything about it because he doesn't have the *influence*."

Millie lowers the paper, understanding her sister at last. She thinks back to two summers ago when Alma first met Jonathan

Blackwell in Newport. It was widely known then that the rich California bachelor had come east in search of a bride who had connections his money couldn't buy. So it had raised more than a few eyebrows when he'd eloped with a former farm girl working at the nearby general store instead.

"You do see now, don't you?" Alma turns on her heel and leans dramatically against one of the massive redwood trees that made her husband's family rich. "I overheard him in his study this morning talking with that horrible Rodney." She wraps her arms around her waist. "He said things would be different if he'd married Clara Prentice like he'd planned. That her uncle would have smoothed things over with Congress."

"Clara Prentice ended up married to a German *prince*. I highly doubt her uncle would have consented to a match between—"

"But that's just it! I *can* help him. More than that rat-faced Clara ever could. It's only that he doesn't know I can."

"Alma." Millie's voice is full of warning. "You said you were done. That after the love charm, you—"

"Oh, posh. I see you collecting pieces for that box of yours. Are you going to stand there and tell me that *you've* given it up?"

She thinks about the scrap of Jenny's essay tucked in her pocket, and her face reddens. Alma gives her a shrewd look and straightens, pushing herself away from the tree. "I didn't think so. Now, if you're done being a little hypocrite, I can tell you about the new charm I need your help—"

"No."

Millie grabs her bike and starts walking away, but Alma rushes in front of her, blocking her path. "That's it? You're going to sashay away without so much as an explanation?"

A muscle jumps in Millie's jaw. "I don't *sashay* anywhere. And I gave you my explanation after the last time. Whatever you're planning, Alms, I won't be a part of it."

Alma's light brown eyes flash, and she lifts her chin in a gesture so like Gran when she's annoyed that it's downright eerie. "What is it then, Mil? Do you want me to beg?"

"You know that's not–"

"Do you want me to admit that I can't do it without you? That I tried and I failed and I need your help. Is that what you want from me?"

Sparkling tears pool in Alma's eyes, and a stab of guilt sears through Millie. She knows how much it hurts her sister's pride to ask for her help. When they were kids, Alma refused to admit that her little sister was the more powerful of the two. And when she finally had no choice but to accept it, she made Millie's life hell in every way she possibly could. A behavior, Millie reminds herself, that she reciprocated.

But the desperate determination in Alma's eyes now reminds Millie so much of the girl she was at eighteen. After the fire, all of that petty jealousy between them fell away. It was Alma who took charge. Alma who found work and held them both together.

In so many ways, their grief broke them. But it brought them together, too.

Millie searches her sister's face. The distance between them started to grow again around the time Alma's obsession with Jonathan Blackwell began. She knows it will only get worse when she and Jenny leave. She wishes it were different. She wishes she could bridge this growing gap.

"Isn't it enough, Alms?" she asks softly. "Isn't it enough to have his love?"

Alma's face twists, and she wraps her arms around her middle again. "You don't understand. That's *why* I need your help. This railroad business, it has him twisted all around. He hasn't brought me flowers in weeks. He barely *looks* at me unless we have an audience. He stays locked in his office after dinner, pacing around all night. The only time he bothers to talk to me at all anymore is when he's peppering me with pointless questions."

A shiver of premonition runs up Millie's neck. "What do you mean? What sorts of questions?"

Alma waves her hand. "It's so boring, Mil. He keeps asking me to tell him about the farm."

Millie's body goes tight as a bowstring. "And what—exactly— do you tell him?"

Alma narrows her eyes. "What do you *think* I tell him? That a mob burned it to the ground because they thought Mama was a witch?"

"*Alma!*"

"Oh shush. No one can hear us. And you know very well what I tell him since you're the one who came up with the story. Why are you harping on this? The questions aren't the point."

"I'm *harping* on this because Jonathan is supposed to be a man madly in love. Not a bloodhound looking into our family history!"

"Don't yell at me, Mil. If he's not in love enough for you, it's as much your fault as mine. I did the best I could with the help you deigned to give me."

An angry retort rises to Millie's lips, but she checks it when she sees a tear slip down Alma's cheek. Closing her eyes, she takes a deep, calming breath. The truth she will never admit to Alma is that she does sometimes regret not making the love charm herself when her sister asked her two years ago. Altering the course of someone's life without their knowledge—even someone as unpleasant as Jonathan Blackwell—went against everything their mother taught them. But when she realized Alma was determined to weave one anyway, she offered to check over the construction of the charm to make sure nothing went wrong.

The thing she regrets the most is telling Alma that the spell would only be powerful enough to soften Jonathan's heart, at best. If she hadn't, maybe Alma wouldn't have offered the sacrifice she did to strengthen it. Maybe there wouldn't be a grave in the Blackwell cemetery with only a single date. Maybe Jonathan's howl of grief from the night he lost his newborn son wouldn't still echo in her mind. Because while she'd always understood that her brother-in-law was a dangerous man with a long arm, it wasn't until that night she understood with stunning clarity that if he ever discovered the price his wife paid for his love, neither she nor Alma would ever be safe from his wrath.

She heard Alma's wracking sobs that night, too, and she believes that she regrets it. That she was blinded by a need for love. That even though she knew what she was offering, she didn't truly *understand.* But Jonathan would never see that, and a strong, working love charm is their guarantee that he won't ever have to try.

"I'll check the charm tonight," she tells Alma. "If anything has fallen out of tune, I'll repair it. I should have checked it before now anyway."

Alma juts her chin again. "I suppose I should thank you. For cleaning up after me."

"That's not what I—"

"I know what you meant, Mil, and it's fine because I *am* grateful." She places her hand over Millie's on the handlebars and squeezes. "Truly, I am. And I'm sorry if I . . ." She trails off and shakes her head ruefully. "It's only I do hear them, you know. The whispers whenever John and I walk into one of those rooms. In San Francisco last month, I thought some of those women were going to set my skirts on fire with their eyes alone." She attempts a laugh, but it comes out more like a muffled sob. "I try to hold my head high, but they know. They know what I really am. They know that I'm a fraud. And it's only a matter of time before he sees it, too. Before he's as ashamed of me as they expect him to be."

Millie squeezes Alma's hand back. "Alms, you are a wickedly clever, fiercely determined person who will do *anything* for the people she loves. *That's* the truth of who you are beneath these absolutely ridiculous ruffles and silks."

Alma laughs weakly, and Millie smiles.

"And Alms?" Millie waits for her sister to raise her teary eyes. "That's a person no one could ever be ashamed to love."

Chapter Seven

I gasp, surfacing in my own body.

My own mind.

A cold, salty breeze blows hard against my face, and I open my eyes. But when I do, it's not a room inside of Blackwell House that I see.

"Damnit, Nev! *You need to let go.*"

Sharp pain shoots through my upper arm. It feels like fingers digging into my flesh, but I'm too transfixed by the crashing waves beneath my feet to wonder what it is. Too caught up in imagining how wonderful it would feel to step forward, soar through the air, and meet the jagged cliffs below.

Another burst of pain in my arm, this one sharper than before. It's a distraction that I don't want, so I uncurl my fingers from what I distantly realize is the edge of an open window frame and swat the thing away.

It doesn't work. My hand is crushed between something warm and strong instead. A tug pulls me backward, but I lean out to the sea, fighting it. Another tug. Harder this time. It's enough to break my other hand's grip on the window ledge, and then . . .

I'm falling.

Not in a graceful arc through the air, but in an awkward, fumbling backward tumble. And I don't land with a dramatic flourish on the jagged cliffs but crash into something warm and soft. Something that nevertheless smells like sand and sea.

"Nev?"

This time, the voice—hoarse and strained—breaks through the fog in my mind.

I blink and twist around.

I'm lying on top of Cal, my back pressed against his front. Our legs are tangled together, and his arms are wrapped around my shoulders and chest. There's a clicking sound from somewhere near my ear and when I try to open my mouth to speak, I realize it's the sound of my teeth chattering. Even with Cal's arms around me, I'm freezing. It's as if someone injected ice water straight into my veins.

I try to sit up, but Cal's hold tightens. "Wait. I need to know you won't jump."

Jump.

Yes. That's what I was just about to do. Moments—*seconds*—ago, I yearned for nothing more in the world than to throw myself out that window. And there's only one explanation for that. The same explanation that the people of Hollow Cliff first discovered one hundred and twenty years ago when their family, friends, and neighbors got that glazed look in their eyes before engineering their own deaths.

Somehow, some way, the spirits gained control over my mind.

That shouldn't be possible, not with Alma's blood running through my veins. Not while the Vow still holds. But that must be what happened. That must be why I can still feel the chill of their touch from the inside out in a way I never have before.

Was it the memory? Did it expose my mind in some way?

I try again to sit up, but Cal's arms are a vice around me. "I need you to tell me you won't—"

"You can let go." My voice is hoarse but reasonably steady. "I'm okay now." He hesitates for a moment, but then his arms slowly fall away.

I roll off him and push myself to my knees. Cal sits, too, and watches me with wary eyes that are more grey than blue in the low lamplight. When I don't immediately sprint for the open window again, some of the tension leaves his face.

"Are you sure you're okay?" He scans my face, neck, and arms in clinical perusal. "I almost didn't get there in time. You almost—"

Abruptly, he stops talking, his face paling. I follow his gaze to the palm of my hand where his locket is nestled, its glass case glinting in the lamplight.

But it's not his locket. Not really.

It's *Millie's*.

It's the locket of a girl I should know about, but don't. A girl who might have been even more powerful than her famous sister, but who has disappeared from our family's well-recorded history. It's the locket of a girl who, for a reason I don't understand, left a memory of herself behind.

I close my hand around the glass pendant and shift back onto my heels. Cal's eyes shoot to my face. "What are you doing with that necklace, Nev?"

His voice is low and careful, like he's having to work hard to control an emotion he doesn't want me to see. But although his jaw is tight, he doesn't seem overly angry that I went through his things.

"I could ask you the same thing. What are *you* doing with a locket that holds a memory of *my* family?"

His brow crashes down. "What are you talking about? What memory?"

I study the outline of his shoulders. The disheveled black hair that makes his skin look far too pale. The freckles scattered along his cheeks, and that crescent-shaped scar above his left brow. *Who is he? What really brought him here?*

From the first moment I laid eyes on him, I've felt unsettled and off-balance. Is this locket the reason? Did I sense it? Did I intuitively know what it held? Did my gut get it wrong? Is he not someone I can trust after all?

"Is this necklace why you really came here? Is it why you wanted a job?" I watch his face closely, alert for any reaction. He may have saved my life twice now, but he's hiding something. Could it be this? "Did you steal it?"

A muscle in his jaw jumps. "I didn't steal anything. That locket was given to me."

"Who—"

"What did you mean about it holding a memory of your family?"

I press my lips together and don't answer.

"Is that why you were on that ledge?" he presses. "Did the necklace have something to do with that?"

The naked concern in his expression, his insistence earlier on not letting me go until he was sure I wouldn't try to jump again, the very fact that he stopped me . . . it's all telling me that whatever else may be going on, he didn't intentionally put me in danger.

But that doesn't mean I can answer his question.

Gran and I don't talk about our magic with people. Although it's a widespread assumption in Hollow Cliff that Alma's Vow was more than just a simple promise, the specifics have never been revealed. No one knows there's an actual charm in the moon-marked box that's glimpsed once a generation. No one knows about the Anchors we maintain or the influencing spells Gran can weave thanks to the power granted to her by the Vow. And the memory this Millie girl preserved with her blood is—at its core—a more advanced version of what my family can do. Which means I've already said more than I should.

I rise unsteadily to my feet. The chill inside me is beginning to fade, but my heartbeat is still erratic and my limbs haven't stopped trembling from the spike of adrenaline. I don't have control of myself right now. I'm unbalanced and confused. That's why I'm having to fight the urge to tell this complete stranger exactly what he wants to know when the only person I should be talking to about *any* of this is Gran.

"Thank you," I say once I'm up, "for saving me. Again. But—"

"Christ, Nev. You don't have to *thank* me. Just tell me what—"

"But it's late." I step back and turn toward the door. "And I should—"

"*Wait.*" He jumps to his feet and moves to block my exit. "You're leaving because you don't trust me."

I shake my head. "Look, I don't know you. And I really am grateful for what you did, but right now—"

"Let me prove it to you." He steps forward, something almost desperate in his expression. "Let me prove that you can trust me."

I tilt my head back to meet those swirling storm-cloud eyes. The thing I don't understand, the thing I can't say aloud, is that I already do trust him, even though I have no reason to.

"You can't just *tell* me to trust you. That's not how—"

"I can show you something. Something that's been hidden from you."

I still. "What are you talking about?"

He holds my gaze. "There's something you . . . deserve to know. I can show it to you."

"Something *hidden* from me?"

I stare at him. He doesn't just look desperate now, he looks . . . conflicted. His eyes are bouncing back and forth in his head, and his teeth are digging into his bottom lip like he's considering taking back his offer. Suddenly, I don't want him to. Whatever it is he thinks he knows, I want to see it.

"Okay," I say before he can speak again. "Prove away."

I follow Cal down the hallway, a distant part of me impressed at how quickly he's learned to navigate the trick turns and mazelike stairways Alma built into the house after she bound the spirits, but I'm too distracted by the unusually strong presence of the shadows to dwell on it for long. More and more wisps of icy darkness slither out to trail me as Cal and I wind our way through the house, and the chill that only just began to fade from my bones comes back with a vengeance.

The spirits are furious, and I understand why.

It was Jonathan Blackwell who doomed them to their deaths. It was his wife who bound them to this house. And it's their descendants who have kept them leashed. And tonight, after over a century of hooking their claws into the minds of innocent townspeople, they finally seize control of a Blackwell mind, only to lose her at the final moment.

We step out into a violet dusk sky, and Cal strikes out east across the grounds, away from the crash of the waves pounding against the cliffs below. It's a steady, rhythmic sound that's always soothed me, but now . . .

I shudder and pick up my pace to match his as we weave through the Greek and Roman section of the sculpture garden, the old gods and goddesses casting long shadows in the gathering twilight, their outlines mixing with those of the mythical monsters they sometimes became and sometimes fought. Cal cuts a wide arc around Gran's withering vegetable garden and strides directly toward the edge of the redwood forest with the same confidence he showed navigating the house's twisting hallways. I have no idea where he's taking me, and I'm just about to call out to ask when he stops walking so abruptly that I run into his back.

"Shit." He turns and steadies me with a hand on my forearm. "I'm sorry. I should have "

"It's fine."

He nods and lets go of my arm. Then he shoves his hands in the pockets of his jeans, takes a step back, and fixes his gaze a few inches above my head. I look up, too, squinting at the canopy of tree cover overhead, trying to figure out what could be so important about this unremarkable stretch of woods.

"It's not here," he says.

I look back at him. "Then what—"

"There's something . . ." He exhales slowly and his throat works in a swallow. "Before I show you this, there's something I need from you. Something important that you aren't going to understand right now."

"What does that mean?"

"It means I need you to do something you won't understand now, but hopefully will. Later."

"You aren't making a lot of sense, Cal."

"I know. I'm sorry."

He looks at me with an expression that's so . . . torn. So deeply apologetic and concerned that all I can do is cross my arms and ask, "What is it? What's this thing you need from me?"

He holds my gaze. "I need your promise. A real one. I need you to swear that what I show you tonight stays between us. I need your word that you won't tell a soul. Not your grandmother. Not a friend. *No one.* Can you do that?"

An evening wind rustles the leaves overhead, and as I stare back into Cal's light grey eyes, I instinctively understand two things. The first is that if I give my word right now, he will trust me to keep it. The second is that if I lie, he'll know.

I'm also very aware that even though I'm not the one who asked to see whatever it is he wants to show me, my curiosity is past its boiling point now.

"Fine," I say. "Whatever this is, it stays between us."

He doesn't ask me to repeat it, and he doesn't ask me if I'm sure. He just nods, like my word is all he needs. Then he says quietly, almost reverently, "It's through here."

It's not until we reach the edge of the clearing that I recognize this place. The woods on the east side of the grounds aren't entirely empty; they have the dubious honor of housing the Blackwell family graves. It's a small cemetery. Only about a dozen or so headstones nestled amongst the green ferns. Jonathan Blackwell and Alma, of course. Their daughter. Their daughter's daughters. It's the place where I'll be buried, one day.

The grave closest to the edge of the clearing is the first one that was erected here. Smaller than the others, it bears only a single date. The day Alma and Jonathan's stillborn child both came and left the world. Is this the sacrifice that Millie girl was thinking about in the memory?

I shudder as Cal passes by the small, unnamed grave. He strides past Jonathan's and Alma's white marble markers, too. Past Lily Blackwell's grave, who was born six months after Jonathan's death, and past one of the few gravestones in the family cemetery that doesn't belong to a Blackwell: Lily's fiancé Patrick, who died of the Spanish flu the night before they were meant to wed.

He keeps going. Not stopping until he reaches a grave deeper into the clearing. I follow him slowly, a strange sense of foreboding tingling in my veins that I don't understand. I may not come out here often, but it's not my first time, either. Cal finally stops and kneels in front of a headstone that, like Lily's fiancé, doesn't bear the Blackwell name. The white marble stone is engraved for someone named Theresa Vale. A distant cousin, I vaguely recall. Someone my grandmother knew.

I open my mouth to ask why he brought me to what's probably the least historically significant grave in this cemetery, but before I can speak, Cal looks up at me in a way that makes me shiver. He motions for me to kneel next to him, and when I do, he holds out his hand, palm up. "I need you to take my hand. And I need you to not let go."

I place my hand in his, unable to speak through the strange blankness that's taken over my mind. Directly in front of me is the simple white headstone for a woman I've never met, and even though I sense Cal's eyes searching my face, even though I feel his hand giving me what I think is meant to be a reassuring squeeze, and even though I hear him whisper my name along with the words, *I'm here,* for some reason that I don't understand, I can't make myself look away from this simple white marker.

I'm still staring at it when Cal leans forward and places his other hand palm-flat against the stone. The moment he does, the engraving of Theresa Vale's name blurs before my eyes.

I blink through what must be tears, but when I open my eyes again there's an entirely different name etched into the white marble. A name that doesn't make any sense.

Because my mother isn't dead.

Chapter Eight

Celia Blackwell.

That's the name staring back at me from the white marble headstone now. The name that won't change back, no matter how many times I blink. No matter how hard I stare.

A name that doesn't make sense, floating above a pair of dates that makes even less. The first is my mom's birthday. The day and year she was born. And the second date, the one that's standing in for where her death would be, that's . . .

The day she left.

Left.

Not died.

Left.

I lurch to my feet. My hand slips out of Cal's, and the second it does, the name on the white stone blurs again. By the time I'm standing up, my mom's name is gone, and the grave is marked for Theresa Vale once more.

Distantly, I'm aware that someone somewhere is speaking to me, but the words are drowned out by the roaring echo of my heartbeat hammering in my ears.

My mother is dead.

My mind doesn't want to believe it. It wants to tell me that this is a mistake. A misunderstanding. I didn't see what I thought I saw. This grave isn't real. She could still come back.

But my bones know. They hum with a sickening truth I can't deny.

When your blood whispers, darling, listen.

My mother is dead. That's what my blood is whispering—*screaming*—at me now. My mother is dead, and my grandmother buried her. She buried her, and she wove a spell to hide this grave— my *mom's* grave—from my mind.

Cal calls out to me, but his voice is too far away to make out, and soon, the only sound I can hear is the drum of my feet pounding against the dirt-packed forest floor. A sharp sting from a low-hanging branch blooms across my cheek. Another rises on my bare forearm. But I don't stop. Don't slow down. I can't. Not when every instinct I possess is screaming at me to run as far and fast as I can.

I don't know how I get to the car. Or how many tries it takes for my shaking hands to insert the key into the ignition. It's not until I'm halfway down the hill, squinting against the last rays of the setting sun, that I consciously realize I've left the Blackwell House grounds. And it's not until I jerk the wheel, pull over beside the bluffs, and stumble up to a shop window filled with bright, colorful blooms that I understand where I instinctually came.

The side entrance leading into the back house is locked, so I ring the buzzer once.

Twice.

Three times.

I ring it again. Over and over and over until at last the door is yanked open by Francesca clad in a yellow fluffy robe with a matching towel wrapped around her head.

"What the hell is—*Nev*?"

Her eyes go wide and she darts a glance over my shoulder as if scanning the twilight for some sign of pursuit. "Is everything okay, mijita? Jesus, you're pale as a ghost."

She reaches out to me, but I shake my head and take a step back. There's something I need to ask her. A reason I came.

"Francesca, I need you to tell me about my mom."

I'm bustled down the hallway and into an armchair that faces the darkening sea. A soft, flamingo-patterned blanket is wrapped around my shoulders and a mug of steaming hot chocolate is placed between my hands. My body is shaking too much to drink it, so I hold the mug tight on my lap and stare down at the swirling liquid.

My mom didn't leave me.

My mom is never coming back.

Francesca sets a plate of warm buñuelos on the small table between us and sits in the armchair across from me. She's changed out of her robe and into sweats, her black hair damp and curling around her face. "Bea's out with Darcy," she says softly, her eyes searching my face. "So it's just the two of us."

I nod. Francesca picks up her mug of cocoa and takes a small sip, her brown eyes continuing to watch me over the rim. For seven years, my mom has been an off-limits topic of conversation between me and her once-best friend. The last time Francesca tried to broach the subject, I stormed out of her shop and refused to see her for three months.

She must be wondering what changed.

So far though, she hasn't asked. And when I meet her gaze, I beg her silently not to. I'm barely holding the pieces of myself together as it is. I'll crack open if I have to think about—let alone try to put into words—the shame and sorrow and *fury* boiling in my blood. Because for the past seven years, I've been living with a false version of my mother in my head. A version of her that I cursed, resented, blamed, even *hated* for leaving me. But it was all a lie. And now I can't trust myself. I can't trust my mind. I can't trust my own corrupted memories.

A full-body shiver racks through me, and hot chocolate splashes onto my hands. Francesca jumps up, grabs a cloth napkin from the table, and dabs at my hands with it.

"I'm sorry." My voice comes out as a hoarse whisper. "I didn't—"

"Don't worry, hon. This chair can handle a bit of chocolate."

The sympathy in her voice, the kindness—it's all too much. I'm going to break. The tethers that are barely holding back the dark waters are going to snap and I'm going to fall and I don't know if I'll ever come up again.

But I can't do that. Not yet. Not until I know who my mom really was. Not until I know who I lost.

"Please, Cesca." I grab the hand that's holding the napkin. "I need to know. I need you to tell me . . . tell me who she . . ."

I can't say *was*.

I can't say *was* because my lips won't form the word. And I can't say *was* because if Francesca knew the truth about what happened to her, she would have already told me. And because there's a distant part of my mind that remembers I made a promise.

"Please."

I sound desperate.

I am.

I sound lost and afraid, and I'm those things, too. Francesca must sense this because after a quiet moment, she nods, returns the now-stained napkin to the coffee table, and sits again in the chair across from me. She takes a sip of her cocoa and tilts her head. "Do you know how your mom and I became friends?"

Before I can answer she says, "No, of course you don't. It's probably not a story she would have told you before . . ." She trails off. Shakes her head and then starts again. "I always knew who your mom was, of course. Everyone did. But we didn't become real friends until our freshman year when your mom, well—I guess you could say she kidnapped me."

I blink. "She . . . *what*?"

"It was only a temporary kidnapping," she rushes to explain. "She told me later that she didn't want to take the chance that I'd say no, and honestly, I probably would have so . . ." Francesca shakes her head and laughs. "You look *horrified*, mijita. I'm sorry. I've gone about this backward."

She tears one of the buñuelos in half, pops it in her mouth, and dips the other half of the cheesy bread into her mug. "Your mom has always loved music. And as a kid she'd always dreamed about being in a band. But she didn't exactly have an easy time recruiting the other kids in town to . . . well, I probably don't need to explain that part to you."

No. She doesn't. I haven't thought much about what it was like for my mom as a teenager here because I rarely let myself think about her at all. But she must have been on the fringes like me. Not rejected, but not welcomed, either.

"Anyway," Francesca continues. "Somehow your mom convinced two counselors at that camp they used to run at the state park to start a band with her. One guy played guitar, the other played bass, and your mom was going to write the songs and sing them. But they didn't have a drummer. And so your mom staked out the concert band summer rehearsals, saw me in the percussion section, and decided that I'd do."

THE LIES OF ALMA BLACKWELL

Francesca shakes her head fondly, and for the briefest moment, a flicker of warmth flares amidst the grief and guilt knotting my chest. I can see it, the two of them. Francesca wailing on the drums. My mom singing into the mic, her chestnut hair wild and long.

"Were you good?" I ask.

Francesca laughs. "No! We were terrible. And we broke up after our first gig, which was at the summer camp, by the way. Twelve-year-olds are *not* a forgiving audience." The buñuelo is heavy with chocolate now, and she expertly transfers the fried dough from her mug to her mouth without spilling a drop. "But it bonded your mom and me, although not musically. I went back to concert band and she decided to try being a solo artist. All of sophomore year, she would carry this yellow leather notebook around with her every-where in case inspiration struck. And then she started dressing like Stevie Nicks—*full* hippie moon-child—which drove your grand-mother insane, of course."

I tense at the mention of Gran. "Why?"

Francesca reaches for another buñuelo. "Why what, mijita?"

"Why did it drive Gran insane that she started dressing like that?"

"Oh." She rests her mug on her lap. "Well, I think your grand-mother thought it was . . . inappropriate for your mom to go around dressed like . . . well, in a *witchy* way. And I'm pretty sure your mom's response to that was that she, quote, *might as well dress the part*, unquote. And *that* sent your grandmother into a . . . well . . ." She lowers the ball of dough into the cocoa slowly, like she's searching for the right words. "I guess you could say that Celia and your grandmother haven't always seen eye to eye."

"What does that mean?" I lean forward. "What exactly don't they see eye to eye about?"

The words must come out too sharp because Francesca blinks again. "It's nothing all that horrible, hon. A lot of mothers and daughters have similar bumps, especially in those teenage years. And Marie was . . . well, your grandmother has always had a strong . . . passion for tradition. There's a certain way she thinks things should be done, and your mom, well, I guess you could say she's always had a bit of a rebel heart."

A rebel heart.

I lean back against the chair cushion and study the dark brown depths of the chocolate cooling in my mug. Gran's never used those exact words, but in the rare moments that we have discussed my mom, that's pretty much how she talks about her. Not as a bad person, or even as a weak person, but as someone who liked to rebel for the sake of it. Someone she loved deeply, but who never truly understood what it meant to be a Blackwell.

I thought I understood why. I thought Gran was disappointed and hurt that she abandoned me. Abandoned *us.* Abandoned her responsibilities to this whole town.

But she didn't abandon anyone.

And although I have no idea how Cal was able to temporarily lift the spell on that headstone, I *do* know it was Gran who wove it.

She's the only one capable of altering a mind's perception like that, thanks to the Vow.

But why?

Why have a secret headstone made and then hide it? Why *lie* to me? Why let me believe—for *seven years*—that my mother had deserted me without a word?

It doesn't make sense. They may not have always seen eye to eye, but I *know* Gran loved my mom. And I know she loves me.

So *why*?

And if my mom didn't spend those last few months preparing to leave, what was she doing when she left the house on those secret trips? Why did she lock herself up in the Rose Room for hours on end?

What really happened to her?

And why doesn't Gran want me to know?

Francesca tells me more stories about my mom, and I cling to them like a life raft in a storm. As the night wears on, the numb shock that's acted like a shield around my heart wears off and the flood of tears begins.

Because I was wrong.

I *did* know her.

I knew this bright, funny, slightly mischievous person in Francesca's stories. I knew that she smelled like cinnamon and that she hardly ever cut her hair. I knew that she didn't just sing at the top of her lungs in the shower, but also in the kitchen, the hallway, the garden, and sometimes in the middle of the grocery store aisle.

I knew that she liked to take me on beach picnics and that she always swam in the sea no matter how cold the water was. I knew that every night before she put me to bed, she kissed me on the forehead and told me I was her world.

And I knew she would never intentionally leave me behind, but I made myself believe it anyway. I locked her out of my mind. I pushed away any memories that didn't corroborate the monster I'd made her out to be. I told myself that her love for me was a lie. That it was a hollow, weak, fickle thing.

But it was *my* love that failed, not hers.

It was me who let *her* down.

When Francesca finds out Gran will be at the hospital for the night, she insists I stay over, and I don't argue. When Bea comes in after midnight and puts her arms around me like we haven't done since our sleepovers as kids, I lean into her and cry some more. When I finally drift off into a restless sleep, it's with an image of my mom in my mind. I want so desperately to dream of her. I want so desperately to find some small comfort in seeing her again, only I don't get it. I get more of the shadowy, faceless figures that haunt me instead.

But when I blink open my eyes to the dawn light, I do find a memory. One that Francesca's words about Mom and Gran's relationship must have triggered. She said they didn't always see eye to eye, and even though I'm not sure I knew that, I did always have a vague awareness that their relationship wasn't like mine and my mom's, or even like mine and Gran's. I confided in my mom about absolutely everything, and she told me every day—sometimes multiple times a day—that I was her favorite person in the world. And Gran used to leave presents underneath my pillow. Toys that my eye had lingered on downtown, but that I hadn't mentioned out loud. My very first set of professional drawing pencils. Little things that told me she was watching. Paying attention. That she knew me. That she cared.

But Mom and Gran weren't like that. They were always very . . . polite to each other. And yet I only heard them truly argue with each other once, late at night, a couple of weeks before Gran announced that she wanted Mom to take over the Vow. It was back when I wasn't as good at guarding my mind against the spirits, and I'd just woken up from another harrowing nightmare featuring my own death. Sometimes, after a particularly bad dream, I'd crawl into bed with my mom or Gran, and I was padding down the hallway toward my mom's room that night when I heard the sound of both her and Gran's upset voices spilling out into the hall.

Gran's voice was the loudest, but she sounded more scared than angry. I pressed my ear against the closed door, but their voices were muffled, and I could only make out every third or fourth word. There were enough key ones though—like *victims*, *spirits*, and *death*—for me to understand that they were arguing about the thing they'd been—much more politely—discussing for months. Mom wanted to turn one of the rooms in the house into a memorial for the victims of the 1903 massacre and include it on our tour. She wanted to create a display that included photographs or portraits of the twenty-one adults and thirteen kids who were killed, along with stories about their lives. But Gran wasn't sure about the idea. She thought the memorial fountain her great-grandmother built in the town square was a more fitting way to honor the victims.

I'd heard them talk about the idea in matter-of-fact tones before, but they were arguing with real heat now. So much so that my normally poised and regal grandmother raised her voice in a shrill, agitated tone I'd never heard from her before.

"Enough!"

I was so shocked by the terror shaking her voice that I jumped back from the door and missed her next few words. But I got my ear back in place in time to hear the end.

". . . to survive. We always have. Our traditions are in place for a *reason.* Think of your daughter, Celia. You are a Blackwell. The *next* Blackwell. And you need to start acting like it because *that* is what she needs you to be."

The door flew open so fast, I didn't have time to run before my mom burst out into the darkened hallway. But she turned left instead of right, so she didn't see me huddled in the shadows against the wall as she stormed away.

It's been a long time since I thought about that night. And when I have, it was Gran's accusations that my mom didn't care

THE LIES OF ALMA BLACKWELL

about upholding our family's traditions that I remembered. It was another example of the many signs I'd missed. More proof that Mom never wanted the responsibility of becoming the next holder of the Blackwell Vow. More evidence to explain why she left.

Except she didn't leave. And now, Gran's accusations don't even make *sense*. We talk about the 1903 victims on our tour. We openly state that Jonathan's greed was the cause of the retaliation that resulted in their deaths. So why would adding another stop honoring those victims go against our family's traditions? Why would that suggestion from my mom cause Gran to accuse her of not acting like the next Blackwell?

Unless I jumped to the wrong conclusion all those years ago. Unless that wasn't what they were arguing about at all.

Bea's a heavy sleeper, so she doesn't stir as I slip out of bed and get dressed. Francesca greets me in the kitchen with a nod and a grunt because even though she's always up early, she's not a natural morning person. I accept a cup of coffee, pour in some milk, and sit on one of the kitchen stools waiting for the caffeine to take effect. She said a few things last night that made it clear she assumed my desire to talk about my mom—and my subsequent breakdown upon doing so—was brought on by the stress and pressure of my upcoming Vow. I said nothing to dissuade her of that, and I have no intention of doing so now. She deserves to know the truth, but I made a promise to Cal. And there's so much I don't understand. So much I need to make sense of before I can share this with anyone.

When Francesca finishes her first cup and gets up to pour her second, I brace my forearms on the counter and lean forward. "Cesca?"

She keeps pouring her coffee. "Hm?"

"I was wondering if my mom . . . if she said anything. Or if you noticed anything before she . . ."

I trail off because I can't say *left*. Even though I'm letting Francesca believe it for now, I can't bear the lie on my lips.

She turns around and leans back against the counter, studying me as steam rises from her mug. "If you're asking me why she left the way she did, mijita, I can't tell you. I wish more than anything that I could. I didn't understand it then, and I don't understand it now."

I drop my eyes, a fresh wave of bitter, hot shame washing through me. I'm her *daughter*. I should have had this kind of faith in her. I should have known she wouldn't leave me. I should have turned the world upside down trying to find her.

"But if you're asking if I noticed anything strange about your mom's behavior before she left, then I can tell you that yes, I did."

My head shoots back up. "You did?"

She nods. "I'd noticed that she seemed . . . distracted. But every time I asked her what was wrong, she brushed me off. Then one night a few days before she left, she was here—late—and she was more than distracted. She was . . . agitated." Francesca takes a large sip of her coffee. "I decided I was done taking no for an answer, and I demanded she tell me why she was pacing around my kitchen like a caged lion. She finally told me that something wasn't right and she was running out of time."

She gulps another large swallow of coffee and then sets the mug on the counter behind her. "I assumed she was talking about her Vow ceremony since it was going to be announced at the end of that month. But then she said something that didn't make sense to me. Something that still doesn't. I asked her what she meant, but she gave me this sort of—I don't know, almost terrified look, like she hadn't realized she'd spoken out loud—and then she left. A few days later, she was gone."

I lean forward, my chest tight. "What was it? The thing she said that didn't make sense?"

Francesca holds my gaze. "She said that the true history has been hidden."

Chapter Nine

Francesca's words play over and over in my mind as I wind up the misty hill to Blackwell House.

The true history has been hidden.

A hazy fragment of a dream I'm only just remembering. My mom's face. My mom's lips.

Robbie Harrison's voice.

I shiver and crank up the heat, but it does nothing to stop the goosebumps from springing up painfully on my arms as I pass through the gates and take my usual loop around the old care-taker cottage. But this time, I slow as I drive down the dirt lane, peering out at the modest two-story house cloaked in a veil of grey fog.

When I was a kid, I discovered that this empty cottage was the only outbuilding on the grounds where I could reliably escape the chill of the spirits' touch. I don't know if it was the same for my mom and Gran because I never asked. And after my mom *left*, the dusty, vacant house became my secret place. A sanctuary I still retreat to whenever I'm feeling particularly alone or afraid. The temptation to pull over now, to run in, and bury myself in the musty old couch in the living room is strong, but so is the sudden realization that this house—the cottage I've come to think of as mine—is where the other girl from the memory lived.

Jenny Murphy.

The name doesn't mean anything to me, and I don't know much about the Murphy family besides the fact that—until only a couple of decades ago—the role of caretaker here on the Blackwell grounds was passed down through their family, much as the Vow is passed down through ours.

I press down hard on the gas, and force myself to leave the cottage behind. I may want to run and hide, but I can't. I've already spent seven years failing my mom. Seven years thinking she was a selfish coward for leaving. Seven years agreeing with every horrible thing people said about her. As desperately as I want to, I can't take those years back. But I can use the time I have now. I can find out what really happened to her.

I can find out the truth.

There are already a half dozen or so tour guests wandering the misty grounds, and after I hang up the key on the rack and lock up the carriage house, I duck my head to avoid their eyes and make my way around the side of the house. I expect to hear Tab's angry yowl demanding her very late breakfast the second I step in through the kitchen side door, but instead, I'm greeted by the smell of butter frying in a pan and the sight of Cal in front of the stove, a spatula in his hand.

I freeze in the doorway, and he turns. His eyes are a clear blue this morning. So light that if I painted them, I'd use mostly white.

"Have you eaten?"

He asks the question so casually, like we're people who eat breakfast together instead of strangers who laid eyes on each other for the first time two days ago. Only there's nothing casual about the way his eyes search my face. Whatever he sees makes him frown and, without waiting for my response, he opens the oven, takes out a plate of perfectly round pancakes, and places them on the kitchen table. Then he leans back against the counter, crosses his arms, and watches me under his lashes like I'm a wild animal who'll run for the hills at the first sudden move.

I watch him back. He's in his black hoodie and jeans, and there's a fresh smudge of flour on the collar of the grey shirt he's wearing underneath. A small streak of the soft powder has drifted onto his skin, resting right at the base of his neck where his pulse beats.

A soft *mew* pulls my attention away to the corner of the kitchen where Tabitha is lounging in the one ray of sunlight that's managed to break through the morning fog. Her belly looks fat and full, and she's licking her fluffy white paw the way she does after a satisfying meal.

I glance at her water bowl and the empty ceramic food bowl next to it.

"*She* was very vocal about wanting breakfast."

I look back at Cal, surprised. "Tab let you feed her?"

Both of his brows lift. "If by *let*, you mean she jumped onto my chest and yowled at me until I got out of bed, then yes, she let me feed her."

His lips twitch in a half smile, but I shoot a confused look at Tab who's busy ignoring me in favor of her bath. The last time Gran put out her dinner, it sat untouched until I got home and dished out a new can.

"They're strawberry, by the way."

I whip my head around. "What?"

"The pancakes," Cal says. "They have strawberries inside."

It's like someone sliced me open with a meat hook and yanked out all my insides. My head spins, and I rear back, gripping the kitchen door handle to steady myself.

"Nev?" He drops the spatula and rushes forward. "What is it? Are you—"

"*How did she die?*"

He halts mid-step.

"My mom," I choke out when he doesn't answer fast enough. The tears are already falling hot and fast against my skin, but I don't even try to stop them.

They have strawberries inside.

She used to slice the strawberries paper-thin, and we ate them with melted butter and powdered sugar on top. And I told myself she didn't love me. I convinced myself she didn't care.

I grip the door handle tighter. "How. Did. She. *Die?*"

"She fell out of a window." Cal's voice is soft and full of apology. "Here, at Blackwell House."

My hand slips free. My knees are seconds away from slamming into the floor when strong hands grip my shoulders and pull me back up. I land in one of the kitchen chairs, the stack of strawberry pancakes swimming accusingly before my eyes. I curl myself into a ball. Knees bent into my chest, hands gripping the sides of my head, eyes squeezed tight.

I don't want to imagine it. Her body crumpled and broken on the ground. I don't want to see it.

"Nev."

I shake my head because this is what I wanted to know—what I *needed* to know—but I can't do it. I should have pulled over at my cottage. I should have buried myself in the musty old couch for a week. A month. For seven more years, and seven more after that.

Plates clatter. The lid of the trash can opens and closes. Water runs in the sink.

"I'm sorry. I didn't realize the strawberries . . . I'm sorry about the pancakes, Nev. I'm so sorry about her."

I choke on a sob, and then a chair scrapes and Cal is pulling one of my hands away from my head, wrapping it in his bigger one. Some distant voice in my head tells me to pull away, that this isn't a person I want comfort from, but my fingers have already curled around his, and the moment they do, a current of warmth washes through my blood.

His grip tightens until I can feel the rough calluses on his fingers and palms. The harder I shake, the harder he holds as if he somehow knows that *this* has become my tether. That this single point of connection is all that's keeping me from sinking into the dark cold depths below.

We stay like that for what might be minutes, seconds, hours, or days. I don't know because I fall out of time. I only know that eventually, tissues are pressed into my hands, and then those tissues are followed by a cold glass of water that I gulp greedily down. When I finally clear my eyes enough to look around, the strawberry pancakes are gone, and Cal is watching me carefully from across the kitchen table, our hands no longer linked.

More sunlight is streaming in through the window now, revealing dark purple shadows underneath his eyes that weren't there yesterday. I don't think he got any more sleep than I did.

"I'm sorry to do this now, Nev. But I need to ask you something important."

His hair is too dark today.

I don't know why I think this. I don't know why it's the thought that runs through my head the second I move my gaze from his arms to his face, but that's what I think: that his hair is too dark. Even though it must have been the same color yesterday.

"I need to ask you about what happened last night," he says. "I need you to tell me what you saw when you touched that locket."

I blink at him several times.

"I understand that this isn't—"

"No."

"I wouldn't ask if it wasn't—"

"I don't care about what happened in some memory from a century ago!" I push my chair back and stand up. "I want to know how you know about my mom. I want to know why the spell Gran cast on her headstone lifted when *you* touched it."

Cal's gaze sharpens. "You think your grandmother did that? To the headstone?"

I press my lips together because I shouldn't have said that.

Except . . .

Not talking about the Blackwell magic with outsiders is Gran's rule. And Gran is the one who lied to me. Gran is the one who wove a spell that affected *my* mind.

Cal stands and braces his arms on the table, leaning toward me. "Nev, you need to listen to me. Your mom died after she fell out of a window in *this house*."

His words conjure the scene I'm so desperate not to imagine. Her body, broken on the ground. Her eyes, glazed with—

"Less than twelve hours ago," Cal continues, "*you* almost died jumping out of a window in this house. You would have if I hadn't stopped you."

I shake my head, still trying to dislodge the sickening image. "I know. And I thanked—"

But I stop talking as his meaning sinks in. My pulse rises, and I turn to him with wide eyes. His aren't clear anymore. They're back to a stormy grey.

"Cal. Where did you get that locket?"

His jaw tenses and his eyes dart away.

But I know.

I already know.

The spirits were angry after Mom disappeared. I never understood why. I was too angry myself to question it, and I didn't understand them as well back then. But I remember that they weren't just restless. They were agitated, the same way they are after a drowning. Pushing against their binds like they do when the taste of a single kill makes them ravenous for more. Like they did last night when they had me on that window ledge and I slipped through their fingers.

Is that what happened to her? Was her mind seized like Tom Harrison's? Like Mrs. Price's? Like every victim in the 1903 massacre? Like everyone who's been drowned since?

Blackwells have always been able to resist the spirits' control because of our connection to Alma's spell, but my mind wasn't protected last night. Going into Millie's memory made me vulnerable. It's the only thing I can think of that would have made my mom vulnerable, too.

I reach into my pocket and pull out the locket I never gave back last night. "She had this with her, didn't she? When she died?"

Cal presses his lips into a thin line and doesn't answer, but I know I'm right. It's the only thing that makes sense.

I stare down at the pendant, turning it over in my hands so the silver back is facing up. Last night, I thought the thin scratches on the back were signs of wear, but it's actually a shaky, inexpert design of three nested circles shot through with wavy perpendicular lines. Did Alma's sister make these? Did my mom?

I shake my head and pace to the other end of the kitchen.

I don't know why accessing her memory—*Millie's* memory— opened my mind to the spirits like an all-you-can-eat buffet. My only guess is that it pulled me into the same plane as the spirits, allowing me to experience the events this Millie girl preserved in the locket as a kind of unseen, unfelt specter. But that could be one of a dozen explanations. The only person who could truly help me understand what happened is Gran, and the idea of confiding in her now makes me sick. But even if I don't understand *how* it happened, I'm positive that accessing the memory is what made my mind vulnerable.

Did my mom find this locket seven years ago? Did the spirits drive her to that window like they did me, except no one was there to pull her back?

I whirl back to Cal, brandishing the locket. "You said someone gave this to you. Who?"

He looks torn. Like he wants to tell me, but something is holding him back.

"It was my mom, wasn't it?" I press. "She had this locket with her when she fell. You were there. That's how you know what really happened to her. *She's* the one who gave it to you."

He drops his head. Shakes it. "No. It wasn't her."

"You're lying. This locket . . . *this* is why she jumped. It's the only thing that makes sense. You're the one who brought it back here. You *know* what happened to her and . . ." My voice breaks. "Please. I *need* to know. You have to tell me."

A heavy silence falls between us. Cal's all but frozen in his position braced over the table, his palms flat, his shoulders tense, his head bent, but I can *feel* the internal debate raging within him. Finally, after a long moment, he raises his head. When our eyes meet, the stark agony on his face makes my breath catch.

"Your mom didn't give me the locket. But I think . . . I think it's very possible she had it with her when she fell."

"How do you—"

He shakes his head. "But I don't know where she got it. And I don't why she fell. I swear to you, Nev, that's all I know about what happened to her. And that locket? I mean, Jesus, I thought that it was just . . . a necklace. I had no idea it would—"

He swears under his breath and pushes himself away from the table, his face clouded and miserable. I know there's more he's not telling me, but I also know—with a flash of understanding—that he's in pain. That the conflict I sensed in him earlier goes even deeper than I realized.

I'm still trying to understand what this means when the grandfather clock chimes. It shares a wall with the kitchen so the echo in here is so loud, it's all but impossible to speak over it. Cal's eyes find mine, and we stare wordlessly at each other as the bells toll out the hour with long, ringing gongs. There's an apology in his expression. A plea for understanding. And something else, too.

It might be a promise.

I think about last night. About the promise he asked from *me*. He said I wouldn't understand why what he showed me in the graveyard had to stay a secret, but that he hoped I would soon.

Is that enough? Can I trust this person even though I know he's holding things back? I don't know. And before I can figure it out, some distant part of my brain realizes that the chime for the tenth hour just rang out. Which means—

My eyes dart to the clock above the wall, and I curse under my breath. The front doors should have been opened fifteen minutes ago.

"We're late," I cry out, turning on my heel to go change into my costume. Then I stop and turn back to Cal. "Are you staying?" I ask. "For the job?"

He angles his head. "Do you want me to?"

I do. Desperately. That's what I don't understand. That's what doesn't make sense.

I nod, and his eyes flare in what might be relief. I look him up and down. From his scuffed sneakers to his faded black jeans and equally faded black hoodie. "But you're going to have to change."

Chapter Ten

The day passes in a blur.

So many people show up without reservations that I have to add two extra tours, leaving Cal to manage the gift shop solo. We aren't alone together for the rest of the day, but every time I lead new guests into the gift shop after the tour, I catch a glimpse of him in the makeshift costume I shoved at his chest this morning before running to open the doors. We've never had a male employee before, but one advantage to living in a house that's essentially been trapped in time for a century is that there's a treasure trove of old things lying about in chests.

He put on the vest and set the newsboy cap at an angle on his head so the thick waves of his black hair peek out from beneath the brim, but he left off the coat I gave him, rolling the white linen shirt sleeves up his elbows in a casual way Gran would have a minor fit over. And even though technically, he's wearing more clothes than he was this morning, there's something oddly . . . revealing about him in the ensemble. As if the loose, nondescript hoodie and jeans were some kind of disguise, and it's only now that I'm seeing the real him.

I have no idea what Cal does for lunch, but I only have time to shove an insufficient amount of deli turkey into my mouth. My stomach grumbles all afternoon, but by the time the last tour ends in the early evening, I'm too sweaty and exhausted to eat.

I run up to my room intending to wake up with a shower before finding Cal to finish our conversation from this morning, but one minute I'm lying down on my bed just for a second as my hair dries, and the next I'm staring into Robbie Harrison's face as he leans over me. His lips are moving again with frantic, soundless words as his hands wrap around my throat and squeeze. I try to scream, but I can't get enough air. And then—

His hands are gone and I'm climbing. Scrambling up the limbs of a gnarled oak tree as fast as my legs will carry me because I know as soon as I reach the top, I'll be safe.

Except I'm not.

I'm three-quarters of the way up the tree when a narrow limb snaps beneath my foot. It happens just as I'm taking one hand off a branch to grab another, so I'm only able to catch myself with one hand.

And that hand is already slipping.

My pulse ratchets up. I throw a frantic look at the ground.

It's so far below.

So incredibly far.

My hand slips another inch down the branch, and I know I'm going to fall. No. Not *going* to fall. I *am* falling. My grip has failed, and I'm reeling back. A scream rips my throat as my arms flail frantically, trying to find something—*anything*—to grab onto.

And then—

My phantoms come.

They swoop beneath me, gather me up, and carry me back to the tree. Their grey, featureless forms wrap around me like a blanket made of clouds. They press in from all sides, holding me as I sob. Their embrace tightens as I fight to catch my breath, and it's warmer than I imagined it would be.

Softer, too.

And I'm so grateful, I don't care that I can't see them. I don't care that they refuse to show me their faces. I only care that now, in this moment, I finally feel safe.

Sunlight streams through my window, and I blearily blink open my eyes. My head is pounding, and there's a chill to the morning air that the bathrobe I fell asleep in is in no way protecting me from. A glance at the clock on the side table tells me I slept past ten, and I tense for a moment, thinking I'm late opening up the house again. But then I remember it's Monday. The house is closed, and Gran is scheduled to stay at the hospital for another night.

For once, I have time.

I pull on sweats and slowly walk to the other side of my room, my heart rate climbing as I approach a place I've carefully avoided for seven years.

I think we should have a secret. Just for us.

I hook my first two fingers into the smooth notch in the floorboard, just like Mom did the first time she showed me the secret compartment underneath my bedroom floor. Her hazel eyes sparkled when she demonstrated how to wrap the dog-eared atlas in a dark cloth and nestle it into the shadowy cranny below so no one but us would ever know it was there.

The atlas itself wasn't a secret. We pored over it publicly enough at the kitchen table, brought it with us on beach picnics, and lugged it regularly to the library downtown. But its hiding place *was* a secret. It was all part of the game we played. A way to make us feel like daring explorers or covert spies as we plotted our imaginary routes through the cities and countries of the world.

I loved it.

I loved cuddling with Mom as we read about far-off places, debating which cities we wanted to travel through. I loved staying up late with her in bed, huddled under the covers as I used a highlighter to trace the route we decided on. And I was so enamored with the idea of an underground hiding spot that I began storing my other treasures in here, too, right along with our atlas.

But it's been seven years since I lifted this floorboard. Seven years pretending this secret cubby didn't exist because I couldn't bear to come face-to-face with the physical reminder that my mom was out in the world, living the real-life versions of the adventures we'd planned.

Except she wasn't.

I yank the floorboard loose, lean forward, and pull out several years of bent sketchbooks. The dusty, formerly white shoe-box I used to store my childhood treasures in comes out next. Then another stack of sketchbooks, followed by a one-eyed elephant stuffed animal that I used to love but completely forgot about. The atlas should be next. It should be at the very bottom, the grey cloth camouflaging it so it blends in with the dust. I pitch forward on my knees and reach deeper into the hole. I sweep my fingers into the corners. I press my palm flat against the crumbling brick.

There's nothing there.

Except that's not possible. *This* is where the atlas was kept. This is where it's been for the past seven years. This is the one piece of her I still have.

I run to my bedside table, yank my phone free from its charger, and shine its flashlight into the dark compartment.

It looks empty, but it can't be. It has to be here.

I shine the light into the corners again. I reach in with both hands but only find dirt, brick, and air. A sob crawls up my throat and I try to swallow it down, but it's too big. Too seismic. It cracks me open, and when the tears come hard and fast, I don't want to stop them. I want to break. I want to succumb to the cold despair storming in my chest.

But I can't.

Not yet.

My hands shake, but I force them to reach forward and slide the floorboard back into place. I make my trembling legs stand up so I can get my sketchbook out of my backpack and sit down at my desk. Then I turn to a fresh page, pick up a pen, and start writing down everything I remember or have learned about the weeks and months leading up to Mom's death. I start with her wild-eyed reaction to Gran announcing it was time for her to take the Vow. I add her secretive, unexplained outings, the hours she spent holed up alone in the Rose Room, and her strange conversation with Francesca.

I tape that page up on the wall above my desk. Then I write all the questions I have on yellow sticky notes.

Why did Gran lie to me?

Where did Mom go when she left the house?

Why did she tell Francesca she was running out of time? Time to do what?

Did she find Millie's locket? If so, where and when?

What were Mom and Gran fighting about that night?

What true history has been hidden?

What does Robbie Harrison know?

When I'm done, I add all the sticky notes to the wall and stare up at what I've written. This is what I can do for her now. *This* is why I can't fall apart.

Three short knocks sound on my door, and I spin around just as a white, furry body streaks through the crack I always leave open at night. Tab leaps onto my bed and burrows into the unmade comforter, but she's not my only visitor. Cal is standing on the other side of the doorway. He's wearing grey sweats and a white T-shirt, and—unlike Tab—he seems to be waiting for an invitation to enter.

"I thought I'd keep it simple today. This one is black with sugar." He lifts the steaming coffee mug in his left hand. "And this one"— he indicates the mug in his right—"has milk."

My eyes dart automatically to the coffee with milk, and the corner of his mouth quirks.

"Looks like I guessed right."

He takes a single step into the room and then pauses as if waiting for me to object to his presence. When I don't, he makes his way across the room and hands me the mug of coffee with milk. I take it, but before I can say thank you, his eyes dart to the wall behind me and I tense, realizing what he's reading.

But then he does something I wasn't expecting. He looks away from the taped-up notes, walks around to the side of my desk, and angles himself so his shoulder is perpendicular to the wall. It takes me an extra second to realize that he has deliberately positioned himself so that he can't see what I've written unless he turns his head.

It feels like a test.

Or maybe a question.

Like the two of us are standing on opposite cliffs with a yawning canyon between us, and it's my choice if I want to swing the rope.

I don't have to invite him into this. That's what he's telling me. And maybe I shouldn't. Nothing has changed since yesterday.

He's still holding information back, and we both know it. But at the same time, I've never felt more alone or confused in my entire life than I do right now.

I take a sip of my coffee and watch Cal over the rim. I know so little about him, but in some ways, it feels like he's always been here. And I like him. Or maybe it's that I like myself when I'm around him. There's something calming about his presence. Something . . . bracing.

I lower my mug. "You can look. If you want."

His grey-blue eyes sweep my face. "Yeah?"

I nod. Cal gives me one more searching look, and then he turns and begins reading the notes on the wall. I wrap my fingers around the mug, letting the hot coffee warm my palms as his eyes move slowly down the list I made of what I *do* know before turning to the questions on the sticky notes.

"What does that mean?" he asks, nodding at one of the yellow notes. "What history has been hidden?"

My fingers squeeze the coffee mug. "The other night at the cove. When Robbie . . ." Cal's face darkens, but he nods at me to go on. "He kept saying the same words over and over again—"

"The true history has been hidden," Cal finishes for me. "Yeah. I heard that, too."

I nod. "And then the other night, after . . ." I breathe through the fresh swell of grief. "I went to see a friend of my mom's. I didn't tell her about the . . . I didn't tell her anything. But I asked her if my mom did or said anything strange before she . . . left." I fill him in on the details of what Francesca told me about how distracted my mom seemed in those last couple of months, and about the night she was agitated, pacing around the Diaz's kitchen.

"She said those exact words?" Cal asks. "That she was running out of time, and that the true history had been hidden?"

"I think so. Francesca seemed to remember it all pretty clearly."

He takes a large sip of his coffee. "And you think there's some kind of connection with Robbie. Because he said the same thing?"

"I have no idea," I admit. "The other night I thought that he was just . . . confused. Grieving because his dad—"

I cut myself off, unsure of both what and how much I should tell Cal about the spirit drownings.

But he surprises me again.

"I know about the drownings, Nev."

My eyes go wide. "You do?"

He nods.

"How?"

He lets out a breath, sets down his mug, and walks over to perch on the edge of my bed. "They aren't exactly secret. The bodies are buried in the town cemetery. The death records are public, and accidental drowning isn't a particularly common cause of death. Even in seaside towns."

"But what made you think the spirits were involved?"

Drownings have been a leading cause of death in Hollow Cliff for one hundred and twenty years. But as far as I know, no one from outside has ever connected that to our haunted past. Maybe because, even though the spirits prefer drowning their victims now, in the stories we tell about their first attack, the deaths they caused were significantly more varied.

Cal raises a single eyebrow. "Maybe I heard someone mention it. Maybe people talk."

I shake my head because that can't be the reason. "No. We *never* talk about the drownings with outsiders."

"Why not?"

I blink at him. "Isn't it obvious?"

His only answer is a shrug.

"We don't talk about it," I say, "because even though the spirits have never attacked an outsider's mind, if the public found out that they still killed—that Alma's Vow only holds them at bay—the crowds, the families, the buses of camp kids . . . they would stop coming. This town would crumble. People would lose their homes. Their shops and businesses that they've been passing down for generations."

"And would that be so bad?"

"Would it be so bad if this town fell apart?"

He just stares back at me, his expression unreadable.

I shake my head. "You don't understand. Our connection to this place . . . it runs in our blood. It's not a place we can let go of. It's not a place that lets go of *us*."

He studies me, tilting his head. "Did you know that Robbie Harrison has a blog?"

I blink, confused at the sudden change of topic. "What?"

"He has a blog about conspiracy theories. He writes about them in detail, but he also posts shorter videos to his socials." Cal slips his phone out of his back pocket and holds it up. "Here, I'll show you."

He motions me over and, still lost, I set down my coffee and perch next to him on the edge of the bed. When I jostle the mattress slightly, Tab lets out a disgruntled *mew*, her single orange eye blinking open to glare at me. Cal shifts his arm so we can both see the screen of his phone and for a second, our shoulders brush.

"These are his most popular videos," he says, navigating to the top of Robbie's profile where several videos are pinned with titles like "*Fake Alien Invasion: Project Blue Beam Undercover*" and "*The Truth Behind the Lost Stargates.*" They all have a few thousand views.

"But he also has this one." Cal scrolls down the page and points at a video posted about a week ago that has a lot fewer views. The cover image shows Robbie, his blond hair styled in an artfully messy way, his eyes bright as he looks directly into the camera. "Not his most successful. But interesting because in it, he talks about the reason he got into the conspiracy game in the first place."

Cal hits play on the video. It takes a few seconds to load thanks to the terrible connection in this part of the house, but then the frozen version of Robbie springs to life.

"A lot of people," Robbie says into the camera, his white teeth flashing in a conspiratorial smile, "have been asking me how I first started to see beneath the darkness. So I've decided to let you all in on a little secret." The video jump-cuts to a shot of Robbie leaning closer to the camera. "I'm from a town—I can't tell you where, but some of you have probably been there for your summer vacations—and let's just say that there's a lot more to the story than the tourists get told. I'm talking about an entire brainwashed population, people. It's the real shit. I can't say a lot more on here, but if you want to know more, comment below, and I'll DM you. And then follow this account if you—"

Cal pauses the video, and I stare at Robbie's freeze-framed face. Could this be what he was talking about that night at the cove?

Did you see it?

You have to tell me if that's why.

I turn to Cal. "Robbie said something to me-at the cove that night. I think it might have been the reason he wanted to talk to me. He asked me if I'd seen *it*, but I didn't know what he was talking about. And then he said: you have to tell me if that's why. It almost seemed like . . ."

"Like what?"

"I don't know." I shake my head. "Like maybe he thought there was a reason the spirits targeted his dad. Like he thought that I'd be able to tell him if they did, and why."

Cal watches me intently. "What did you say back?"

"He didn't exactly give me a chance to respond." I hug my knees into my chest. "But the drownings are random. The spirits don't target specific people anymore."

Cal tilts his head. "How do you know?"

"What?"

"How do you know their victims are random?"

I start to answer, but then cut myself off because . . . I don't actually *know*. It's more that that's the logical assumption we've all made, since after killing Jonathan Blackwell and the rest of the railway board, there's been no discernable patterns to the people the spirits target.

"I think we should talk to him," Cal says.

"Talk to Robbie?"

"It's one of your questions, isn't it?" He nods toward the sticky notes. "What does Robbie know?"

I bite my lip, shifting on the bed. I've been desperate to talk to Robbie since my conversation with Francesca yesterday morning, but it's not that simple.

"I want to talk to him," I admit. "But you have to understand that my presence—*any* Blackwell presence—can be . . . upsetting to someone who's lost a loved one to the spirits. Especially at first. They blame us because the Vow is not—because it's never been enough. And I understand that. I do. But you saw Robbie at the cove . . ." A shiver runs up my spine. "Something that . . . extreme has never happened to me before. What if it's still too soon?"

Cal watches me for a long moment. I get the feeling that there's something he wants to say but isn't sure he should. Finally, he says, "It will be okay this time."

I look at Robbie's freeze-framed image on Cal's phone, but I don't see the bright-eyed version of him on the screen. I see him as he was at the cove. His eyes wild and desperate. His lips moving in a soundless, fevered litany as he tries to stop my words by wrapping his hands around my throat.

"You can't know that," I whisper.

"Nev?" He waits for me to meet his gaze. "It will be okay."

And for some reason, I believe him.

Chapter Eleven

Bea grudgingly confirms that Robbie is back at his old barista job for the summer. Guessing at why I asked, she then threatens to make Darcy stop her car and turn back from their shopping trip to San Francisco, but I manage to hold her off by swearing on all of Tab's seven lives that I won't go see him alone.

Gran checks in with me, too. One call that I let go to voice mail, and a text giving me an update on her first day of treatment and saying she misses me already. I force myself to respond to the text, but I don't say that I love her like I normally do. *Can* you love someone who lies to you about something like this? Even if she thinks she's protecting me from something I don't yet under-stand, it doesn't change what she did. It doesn't undo the damage of her lie.

The fog has already started to burn away as Cal and I walk across the grounds to the car, and I tell him about what I saw in Millie's memory.

"Did you know Alma Blackwell had a sister?" he asks after I tell him who Millie was.

I shake my head. "We don't know a lot about her family before she married Jonathan. A fire destroyed all the records in the town she grew up in. But . . ."

"But what?"

I pull off my sweater and fold it over my arm since it seems like it's going to be one of our rare warm summer days. "It's just if this memory is real—and I think it is—Millie lived here, at Blackwell House, for at least a couple of years. Considering how meticulously Jonathan's and Alma's lives were documented, I don't understand how I've never heard of her."

I open the combination lock on the carriage house and grab the car keys off the hook.

"This memory," Cal asks, "is it from before or after the train crash?"

I slide into the driver's seat and start the car. "I think it was a couple of weeks before." The white-capped waves of the Pacific sparkle in the morning sun as we head down the drive, but instead of going straight through the wrought iron gates, I turn left and loop around the house so we pass by the old caretaker cottage. "Millie was in love with a girl named Jenny," I say as we approach it. "In the memory, they were sixteen and planning to leave Hollow Cliff for college together."

"This Jenny was a girl from town?"

I shake my head and ease on the breaks. "No. She lived there." I point to the cottage through the window. Without its blanket of fog, the vines climbing up the walls are visible, making it look a bit like a storybook house. "I only know what Millie was thinking about directly during the memory, but I gathered that Jenny's parents died and she moved in with her cousin's family, the Murphys. They were the caretakers of Blackwell House in Alma and Jonathan's time, and the family stayed on for several generations after Alma's death."

Cal's quiet as he stares out at the cottage, his lips pressed into a firm line. I flex my hands on the steering wheel, once again resisting the urge to run into its familiar comfort and hide away from the world. "It's been empty for years," I explain. "But it's still furnished. I actually . . . I come here sometimes."

Cal turns to me, his eyes wide like I've surprised him. "You do? Why?"

"I don't know," I lie, the intense scrutiny in his gaze making me regret the confession. He already knows so much more about me than I do about him. "I've just always liked it here, I guess."

I switch my foot to the gas and accelerate past the cottage as I launch back into the story of what I saw in Millie's memory. We wind down the twisting hill, and I tell him about the boys she enacted her revenge scheme on at the cove, about her and Jenny's budding romance, and their plans to leave together that fall. He leans in when I tell him about Alma interrupting them with her request that Millie correct the love charm she wove on her husband. And he stiffens when I explain the sacrifice Alma offered to enact the charm in the first place.

"She sacrificed her *child*? So that Jonathan Blackwell would *marry* her?"

I think of the small headstone in the family cemetery. The one with only a single date. "Her future child, yes. Or, *their* future child, I guess."

"Jesus. Is that normal? To offer a life to—"

"No," I cut him off quickly.

Discovering the truth about my mom pushed this revelation about Alma to the back of my mind, but reflecting on it now is deeply unsettling. I'm used to thinking of her as a selfless hero, and I don't know how to reconcile the young woman of legend who saved this town from a massacre, with someone capable of not only sacrificing her unborn child, but of using her abilities to change the course of someone's life. Jonathan Blackwell may have been a callous, ambitious man I'm ashamed to be related to, but that doesn't make what Alma did okay.

"Spells," I continue, "don't usually require any kind of sacrifice. A life or otherwise. But . . . even though it's not something my grandmother or I would *ever* do, the truth is that, yeah, adding a sacrifice as an element of the charm you weave for a spell, would—technically—make it stronger."

"And that's not extreme? To offer a life for a *love* charm?"

"It's horrific and wrong," I agree. "But a love spell isn't . . . simple. It sounds quaint, maybe. But what you're really doing is planting a belief in someone's mind. A belief they won't question. One they will continue to build upon once it's there. It's not an easy thing to do."

"Could *you* do it?"

I glance sideways at him, the green-blue waters of the ocean flickering in and out through the trees behind his head. "Could I weave a love charm?"

He nods.

I look back at the road and shake my head. "No. The most I can do now is work with existing charms that power spells. I can sense what . . . notes are missing. And I can find objects that will strengthen or repair them."

"What do you mean it's the most you can do *now*?"

A flash of sun hits the windshield and I pull the visor down. "The magic we inherit from Alma is diluted by each generation. But when I take the Vow, I'll be able to do . . . more."

"*More?*"

I bite the inside of my bottom lip and keep my eyes straight ahead. This is something I shouldn't tell him. Something no one outside my family is supposed to know.

"We become a part of it," I say quickly before I can change my mind. "That's what the Vow ceremony truly is. It's the moment we become a living, breathing part of the spell Alma wove to bind the spirits. And once we're a part of it, we have access to the power Alma poured into that spell all those years ago."

"And that . . . power allows you to control someone's mind like Alma did to Jonathan?"

"She didn't control his mind. She influenced it."

"What's the difference?"

My tongue darts out to lick my dry lips. "I've never done it, obviously. But . . . the way it would work is that you weave a charm to introduce a thought into someone's mind. Something simple like: *I'm in love with Alma.* A lot of people don't understand just how powerful a single thought can be, but that's all a belief really is: a thought repeated over and over again."

"That's it?"

I nod. "It sounds simple, but it's not. And it can go wrong."

"Wrong how?"

I try to remember how Gran explained it to me years ago. Her lessons never included a lot of specifics because she said that once I took the Vow, weaving the magic it grants would come to me intuitively.

"Minds are complicated," I say after a moment. "And delicate. If a belief has taken root, then it can usually withstand . . . contradictions. But sometimes, if someone is faced with a different truth that refutes the belief that's been given to them, and if the charm that *gave* them that belief is still intact, it can—in extreme cases—cause a fracture."

"A fracture?"

"Of their mind."

Cal goes very still beside me. I glance sideways at him, but he turns to look out the passenger window before I can catch his expression. It's not until I brake at the stop sign at the bottom of the hill that he turns back to me and asks, "That's what your grandmother did, isn't it? You said she cast a spell on your mom's gravestone."

I stiffen, my foot still on the brake.

As furious as I am at Gran, I still want—*need*—to believe that what she did, she did to somehow protect me. But a glance at Cal tells me that he now understands something I've known for going on two days now but haven't wanted to examine too closely because if I do, I won't make it through this day. Let alone hold myself together long enough to question Robbie Harrison.

But he's right.

The spell Gran wove on that grave put minds at risk, including mine. She's the one who told me how volatile a spell like that could be, but she did it anyway. Why would she go to such an extreme? What about my mom's death could be so dangerous to know?

I don't realize I'm trembling until Cal's hand curls around mine on the steering wheel.

"Do you want me to drive?"

There's no pity in his voice when he asks the question, and something about that helps me snap out of my spiral. Or maybe it's the subtle brush of his fingers moving over mine that helps me find my voice again.

"I'm okay." I sit straighter and check the rearview mirror. Cal removes his hand from mine, and I immediately mourn the loss. For a moment there, I almost felt like I was on solid ground again.

We don't speak as I ease my foot off the brake and turn right toward downtown, but I can't stop thinking about his question. I want so desperately to believe that tomorrow, Gran will come home from the hospital and say something that will make sense of this. I want her to be that larger-than-life parent who solves all my problems. The woman who made me draw her portrait night after night for weeks after she found me sobbing in the kitchen, convinced I'd never be a real artist because I couldn't get noses right.

But she's also the one who taught me that a belief is made up of our own thoughts. And right now, when it comes to my grandmother, I have no idea what to think.

Robbie's working behind the register at Mystery Grounds when Cal and I first walk in, but he's too busy ringing up colorfully clad tourists and calling out their coffee orders to the barista at the espresso machine to notice us as we slip into the back of the line. I try to gauge his mood from a distance, but the bland customer service smile he's pasted onto his face makes it hard.

"Hey. You okay?"

I look over at Cal and start to nod, but that's when I realize I'm unconsciously rubbing circles at the base of my throat in the exact spot where Robbie's fingers pressed and squeezed two nights ago. The bruises have faded enough to not need makeup, but I can still feel them, pulsing beneath my skin.

I drop my hand and face forward, but the knot of anxiety in my stomach only tightens when I see that we're three customers away from the front now. What if it's too soon? What if Robbie has another violent reaction the moment he sees me? What if he refuses to talk to us? I need to know if there's anything he can tell me that will help me understand what happened to my mom, but what if my presence here is sabotaging that?

The line shifts forward again, and as it does, the back of Cal's hand brushes mine. It's a quick touch. Just a fleeting moment of the heat of his skin pressing against mine, but it's like a lit match. The fear and anxiety that was rising in me burns up, and this time, when the line moves, I'm able to take a deep breath in preparation for coming face-to-face with Robbie Harrison again.

Except his reaction is not at all what I was expecting.

"Hey, Nev. What are you having?"

Robbie tilts his blond head, that same mild, polite smile he's been using on every other customer stretching his face. I shoot a quick, confused glance at Cal, but he looks just as thrown as I am.

"Uh, hey, Robbie," I say after waiting a beat too long. "How are you . . . doing?"

His smile falters and he shrugs one shoulder. "You know. Not great. Keeping busy helps."

His eyes are slightly puffy like he might have cried during his last break. His skin looks pale beneath his tan and there are careless wrinkles in his shirt, like he got dressed this morning and didn't bother looking in the mirror.

It's obvious to anyone with eyes that he's grieving. That even now, at this very moment, he's struggling to keep his head above water. But where is the desperation in his gaze? Where is the blame and accusation? I'm used to people's censure slowly dying down after a handful of days—I only got about half the looks this morning as I did on Saturday—but this quietly sad boy asking me what kind of coffee I'd like is a night-and-day difference from the wild-eyed son who chased me down the beach two nights ago.

Someone clears their throat behind us in line. Cal shoots me a glance and then takes a small step forward. "We were wondering if you had a break coming up?"

That was supposed to be my line, but I'm so thrown by Robbie's complete one-eighty that I forgot to say it.

"Nev and I were hoping to talk to you about something important."

Robbie's gaze shifts from me to Cal, his forehead wrinkling. "Hey, man. We've met, right? What's your name?"

Surprise flits across Cal's features, but he hides it quickly. "Yeah, it's . . . I'm Cal."

Robbie nods a greeting as if he doesn't remember that the last time he and Cal were face-to-face, Cal was shoving him into the sand while Robbie did everything he could to punch his lights out.

Is his memory of Saturday night really that hazy? Was it too dark for him to see Cal's face clearly? Or is this some kind of act?

"And look," Cal continues. "We're sorry to bust in on you at work. If this isn't a good—"

"Nah, dude. Don't worry about it. I can take a quick break after this line clears out. What are you guys drinking? I'll bring them over."

Cal orders an Americano and I somehow manage to choke out a request for a latte. Robbie rings us up with one more disconcert-ingly pleasant nod, and after sharing another puzzled look, Cal and I find an empty table on the patio to wait. Neither of us expected the conversation to go that smoothly, and from the troubled look on Cal's face, he's as unsettled about it as I am.

Two kids run by our table, laughing and screaming, a copper penny held high in each of their hands like a prize. Their parents are a few paces behind, calling out for them to wait, but the kids don't stop until they reach the memorial fountain in the center of the town square. There are about two dozen people already crowded around it, some clutching coins of their own as they prepare to make a wish, others leaning forward to read the names of the victims from the 1903 massacre engraved along the base of the pool.

The two giggling kids worm their way to the front, and—after moving their lips in whispered wishes—they launch their coins deep into the sparkling water. Both pennies land with a splash, and a spray of water mists the stone skirts of the woman immortalized in the fountain's center.

I've always liked this statue of Alma. It was commissioned by her daughter when Alma was still alive, and it depicts her in a supplicant-like position, kneeling, with her hands raised in the air. It's the position Alma took when she made the first Vow with the aid of the Portland Medium, and I know from the photos I've seen of Gran's ceremony that it's the same pose I'll assume in the moments before I add my own blood to the moon-marked box that holds the charm at the heart of Alma's spell.

She looks young in the statue. Humble, but also powerful and determined, like the weight of the world just fell onto her shoulders but she's refusing to crumble beneath it. I always assumed those same qualities shone through in the flesh and blood version of her, but as my eyes trace the stone likeness, I struggle to reconcile this version of Alma with the slightly vain, almost callous young woman I saw in Millie's memory.

"That woman hasn't stopped staring at you since we sat down."

I tear my eyes from the fountain and look at Cal. "What woman?"

He nods to the corner of the patio where Fern is sitting, clad today in bright yellow linen along with her usual collection of scarves. The table she's sitting at is larger than ours, and it's covered in a shiny purple cloth, a single crystal ball, several stacks of tarot cards, a chipped teapot, and a handful of mismatching teacups. She's one of about a half dozen fortune tellers set up on the Mystery Grounds patio today, but she's the only one staring directly at us. And when she sees me looking over at her, she smiles so wide, the pinks of her gums flash.

"Home is where the heart lives, pet," she calls out, loud enough to startle several of the tourists chatting at nearby tables.

"I know, Fern."

She nods, satisfied. When I turn back to Cal, his eyebrows are raised. "That's just Fern," I say quietly, trying to ignore the slight tightening of my stomach that always occurs when I'm around her. *It all ends with you, pet.* "She's harmless."

Cal's eyes narrow, like he knows I'm not being completely honest. Then he shoots another wary glance in Fern's direction, his jaw shifting. "If she's harmless, why is she looking at you like she wants to eat you?"

In my periphery, I can see that Fern is still staring intently at us, but I just shake my head. "She wants to read my tea leaves. That's all."

"And you won't let her?"

He's too good at reading me, so I settle for a partial truth. "I did once. And once was more than enough."

He tilts his head. "You didn't like what she said?"

"That's not . . . it's more complicated than that."

I look away because I don't want him to guess that what I actually am is afraid. Afraid she'll take it back. Afraid she'll say it's no longer supposed to be me. Afraid that I've already failed in whatever destiny I was supposed to grasp. "But really," I add with a shrug, "I'm just generally not a fan of spending the night with my head over a toilet."

Cal blinks. "You . . . sorry, what?"

I snort at his baffled expression and lower my voice. "Fern likes to experiment with the teas she has you drink before she reads your leaves. Mostly, it's harmless. But Bea swears she put something psychedelic in hers once, and more than a few people have reported, um . . . stomach problems after a reading."

Cal glances sideways again. "Isn't that dangerous?"

"No one's ever been seriously hurt. And people like to humor her."

"Why?"

A high-pitched laugh from Fern's table draws our attention. She's no longer staring at us but has instead turned to face the seagull perched at the edge of her table, pecking at what's left of her croissant. As we watch, she throws her head back and laughs again, like the seagull just told a hilarious joke.

"Fern stayed away too long," I say quietly.

Cal looks confused for a second. "You mean away from Hollow Cliff?"

I nod. "Most of it happened before I was born, but the story goes that she married her high school sweetheart, and when they got divorced, she left and stayed away for . . . I think it was fifteen years, which is a lot longer than most people manage. She finally came back for her ex-husband's funeral. Some people say she tried to leave again but couldn't go through with it. Others say she never even tried. All anyone knows for sure is that she's been here ever since."

Cal's expression turns solemn as he watches Fern continue her one-sided conversation with the seagull. "How did he die?" He looks back at me. "Her husband?"

I hold his gaze. "He drowned in his bathtub."

"Um, hey again."

We both startle at Robbie's approach. "One Americano and one latte." He sets a cardboard tray of drinks on the table, plucks an iced coffee from the middle slot, and sits down in the empty chair between us. "So, uh, what did you want to talk to me about?"

I'm still thrown by how night and day his attitude is toward me, even though I guess it's a good thing he's not hurling wild accusations in my direction. "First, Robbie, I just wanted to say how incredibly sorry I am about your dad."

His face sobers. "Yeah. It's uh . . ." He runs a hand through his hair. When he speaks again, his voice is gruff, like he's holding back tears. "I miss him, you know? I didn't know you could miss someone this much."

His simple, straightforward words gut me because I know exactly what he means. Two days ago, I thought I knew what it was to miss someone so much it felt like a piece of you was gone forever. Even though I thought she'd left me, even though I thought I hated her, the lack of my mom's presence in my life followed me like a shadow wherever I went. I didn't think that emptiness could get any worse until it did. Because two days ago, I still had hope that one day, she would come back. I still believed deep in my bones that I would see her again.

Robbie takes another sip of his iced coffee, and I look sideways at Cal, biting my lip. Am I a monster for doing this? What if bringing up what happened at the cove on Saturday night forces Robbie back into that dark place? Grief is complicated and nonsensical, and maybe Robbie's shift in behavior toward me is simply a symptom of that. Am I prioritizing my own need for answers over Robbie's legitimate grief?

Maybe Cal understands the hesitation behind my glance because he takes his coffee from the tray and says, "You know, man, I've seen your videos. That project Blue Beam stuff is wild. You do some really deep dives."

Robbie's face lights up. "Dude, you've seen those?"

Cal nods. "I've only just started getting into that world, but yeah. Your stuff is great. And it was interesting, you know, watching the one about how *you* got into it. You were talking about this place, right? About Hollow Cliff?"

I'm watching Robbie's face closely, and—once again—his reaction to Cal's question is the opposite of what I was expecting because he blushes. Hard. The flush is so deep it bleeds through his tan. "Aw yeah, well. You know how it is, man." He rubs the back of his neck and gives Cal a sheepish smile. "People like it when you've got a personal connection to that shit."

Cal frowns. "You're saying you . . . made up what you said on that video?"

"Look, dude. It's cool that you like the page." Robbie picks up his almost empty iced coffee and pushes back his chair. "But I've got to get back to—"

"You said the true history had been hidden," I blurt out. "You said that to me at the cove on Saturday." Robbie freezes, his startled eyes widening. "What does it mean, Robbie? Have you heard someone else say that before?"

His face darkens, and for a second, I swear I recognize that wild, desperate look in his eyes. Cal must see it, too, because he visibly tenses and leans forward in his chair, but then Robbie shrugs and shakes his head. "That's just a thing we say in the community. It can mean a lot of things, but usually, it's about looking deeper, you know? To forget the story you've been told and make up your own mind about, like . . . life."

I stare back into Robbie's guileless expression. I don't think he's lying, and I don't think he's hiding anything, either. He seems completely genuine as he gives me another sheepish smile and stands up. "I have to head back in." He looks at Cal. "But uh, thanks for checking out the videos. It's cool to meet a fan."

He tosses his iced coffee cup in the recycling bin, and I watch his back as he winds through the customers to the register. Was it a coincidence after all? Did Robbie just happen to stumble into an internet conspiracy community that uses a similar phrase to something my mom said to Francesca—as far as I know—exactly one time? Am I so desperate to understand what happened to her—so desperate to understand why Gran hid it from me—that I'm making up wild connections that aren't there?

"I don't buy it," Cal says.

I lean back in my chair, feeling defeated. "It didn't seem like he was lying to us."

"No," Cal agrees. "It didn't, but . . ." He trails off and takes a sip of his coffee. I do the same. "At the cove the other night, did he say anything specifically about the spirits?"

I think for a moment and shake my head. "I don't think so. But when I tried to remind him that all we can do is hold them back, he . . ."

I gesture to my throat, and a muscle in Cal's jaw clicks. He glances through the window into the café, and for a second, it almost looks like he wants to throw Robbie into the sand all over again. But before he gets the chance, a familiar voice calls my name.

"Nev, honey. Bea said you might be here."

Francesca, dressed in a bright pink and blue sundress, walks up to our table, a purse on one shoulder, a white canvas tote bag on the other. When she notices Cal, she stops and tilts her head. "Who's this?"

I stand up from the table and Cal does the same. "Cesca, this is Cal. He answered our ad for the open position at Blackwell House and he started this weekend." I shift my gaze to Cal. "Francesca's a good friend of mine and she owns Curious Blooms down the street."

Cal's eyes flick to Francesca and he conjures a bland, polite smile. "It's nice to meet you."

The look on Francesca's face, however, is the opposite of polite. "Where are you staying while you're in town, Cal?" She crosses her arms, eyes glued to his face. "Because I know you aren't from Hollow Cliff."

Cal shoots me a glance before answering. "The job comes with room and board so . . ."

Her brows shoot up. "So you're living at Blackwell House. With Nev."

"Cesca . . ." I begin, but she cuts me off.

"And what brings you to our little town?"

I can't help it. My eyes fly to Cal, hoping to witness his reaction to a question he still hasn't given *me* a satisfactory answer to. But a carefully blank mask takes over his face, and I know instinctually that he's about to lie.

"I'm here because I need a job for the summer."

Francesca takes in a breath to continue her interrogation, but this has gone on long enough.

"We're *incredibly* lucky to have Cal working at the house," I say, forcing her attention back to me. "You know how overwhelmed I've been for the past couple of months. Gran's very happy to have him, too."

"Very happy" is a stretch, but the twitch of Francesca's mouth tells me that the subtle reminder was received. Until I turn eighteen in a month and a half, Gran is the only adult whose permission I need for anything. Still, when she looks mulishly between me and Cal, I play it safe by catching his gaze and widening my eyes. He gets the hint.

"I need to call someone back," he says to Francesca. "But it was nice to meet you. I'll meet you by the car, Nev?"

"Yeah," I say. "I'll be there in a minute."

He nods, tosses his coffee cup into the recycling bin, and leaves through the patio gate. Once he's out of earshot, I turn to Francesca with my eyebrows raised, but she doesn't say anything about Cal. Instead, she sighs and slips the canvas tote off her shoulder.

"Bea said you might be down here this morning, and I wanted to see you because of this." She holds the bag out to me. "Your mom left this at our house before she . . . well. I know you haven't wanted any reminders of her, but I thought that after the other night, you might have changed your mind?"

I stop breathing, every ounce of my attention zeroing in on the canvas bag. Three years ago, Gran cleaned out Mom's bedroom at the house because an article online said that would be healthy for us. She asked me then if I wanted to keep anything of hers, but I didn't. Not then.

My hand visibly shakes as I reach out to take the bag. It's heavy and somehow I know—even before my fingers brush the paperback edge inside—what this is. Slowly, carefully, like it's made of the most delicate blown glass, I take out the dog-eared atlas and hold it in both of my hands.

It's exactly as I remember it. Not bigger. Not smaller. It has the same heft, the same shape, the same faded drawing of a world map on its cover. And when I open the front flap, the same two names are written inside.

The first one is hers. Celia Blackwell, written in the clumsy cursive of someone still perfecting their penmanship because she got this atlas when she was in elementary school. The second name is mine, this one written in the more confident scrawl of my mom's adult hand.

There's a whole world inside these pages, darling. And now it belongs to us both.

I don't realize I'm crying until a tear splashes onto the page, blurring the black ink of my mom's name. I swear, dabbing frantically at the splash of water with my sleeve, desperate not to lose this piece of her, too.

"Nev? Honey, are you okay?"

Francesca reaches for me, but I step out of her grasp and lift the atlas spine side up so that the water from my tear doesn't seep through and damage the next page, too. It's as I'm holding the atlas sideways that two sheets of paper slip out and flutter to the ground.

Francesca and I see them at the same time. She bends to pick them up, but I cry out, "No!" and she halts mid-movement. Startled brown eyes snap to my face, and I belatedly realize how completely unhinged I must sound.

Sucking in a breath of air, I slowly set the atlas down on the patio table, careful to make sure the tear-marked page is facing up to prevent further smudging. "Sorry," I mumble to her as I bend down to pick up the loose papers. "It's just, I've got it."

One of the pages that fell out of the atlas looked like a print-out of a digitized article from the *Hollow Cliff Gazette*. The other is a lined piece of notebook paper folded in half. Francesca says nothing as I scoop both pages up, and by the time I straighten again, there's a forced smile pasted on my face.

"Thank you for giving me this, Cesca. And thanks for keeping it safe for so long."

She eyes me, likely not fooled by the smile, and it looks like she's going to say something, but then her gaze flicks to her right and she seems to notice—at the same time I do—that we've drawn a few stares, including Fern's. She has abandoned her conversation with the seagull and is now watching us with the wide-eyed intensity of a spectator at a competitive tennis match.

"Home is where the heart lives," she calls out to me and Francesca. Several tourists startle again at the booming volume of her voice.

Francesca turns to Fern and gives her a tired smile. "Yes, Fern. Thank you. I know."

Fern nods, satisfied by her response, and Francesca turns back to me, clearing her throat. "You don't have to thank me, hon. I . . ." She darts another look around and lowers her voice. "I hope you know that I'm always here if you ever want to talk about anything. Anything at all. All right?"

Guilt tugs at me because she knows there are things I'm not telling her, but she thinks it's about my anxieties around the Vow ceremony. She has no idea that her best friend since high school didn't really leave her without saying goodbye. She has no idea that Celia Blackwell is never coming back.

Francesca hugs me before leaving, but I'm too aware of Fern's eyes on the side of my face to unfold the slip of notebook paper here. It could be blank for all I know, but I still don't want an attentive audience when I open it. After testing the page in the atlas where my tear fell to make sure it's dry, I return it to the tote and step out onto Ocean Avenue.

The crowd around the memorial fountain has slimmed, so I slip around to the shade on the east side of the fountain where the most devastating names from the 1903 massacre are carved— the thirteen kids who were the first, but not the last, to drown at the hands of the spirits—and unfold the piece of notebook paper.

It's a list of names.

First names and last names, written in the half-cursive, half-print scrawl I recognize as my mom's. Some of the names are circled, others are crossed out, with no notation as to why. But I've seen these names before.

They're all people born in Hollow Cliff.

They're all dead.

And all of them—like the kids whose names are carved onto this fountain—drowned.

Chapter Twelve

Gran calls again after lunch, but I ignore it and send her a text instead updating her on my excruciatingly long meeting with Elaine Taylor of Taylored Events. Her family has been coordinating the Vow ceremonies ever since Alma directed Elaine's great-great-grandmother to plan her daughter Lily's Vow with as much public fanfare as possible to distract from rumors of Alma's mysterious illness. Unfortunately, Elaine takes her inherited responsibility very seriously, and with the ceremony only four days away, there was no chance of me getting out of that meeting early.

Now, I shift uneasily on my armchair perch as I watch Cal set up my laptop on the Rose Room's ornate writing desk, the pink light from the setting sun soft on his face through the window.

"I know you said you recognized all the names on the list as drowning victims." He keeps his eyes on the screen as he connects to our consistently unstable Wi-Fi. "But I think we should confirm that first, and then start looking for a connection between the names that your mom circled."

I bite my lip and hug the atlas to my chest. I recognized most of the names on the handwritten list still tucked inside these pages because I've made it a point to learn and remember as many of the spirits' victims as possible, but some of them I recognized because they're people I knew. Like my third-grade teacher Beverly Price, whose death prompted my childhood promise to end the drownings for good. Cal's right, though. There are a few names I'm not sure about that I need to look up. And I want to understand why my mom circled Beverly's name, but not others.

I do have a pretty good idea of why she printed out the *Hollow Cliff Gazette* article that was tucked in along with the list though. It was written in 1903, two weeks before the train crash that led to the spirit massacre, and it lists the top three students in years eight through twelve who finished with the highest marks in their respective grades. It goes on to say that all the students had been invited to join a brand-new student advisory board created and chaired by the school's biggest donor: Mrs. Alma Blackwell. There are fifteen students listed, but it's the two names under grade twelve—in the number one and number three slots—that made me gasp aloud when I first saw them.

Millicent Fayette and Jennifer Murphy.

There's no surviving copy of Alma's birth certificate, but Fayette is the maiden name she listed on her and Jonathan's marriage license, which means Millicent Fayette must be the same

Millie who left behind that memory. Does that mean my mom was researching Millie's history before she died? Did she already know that Alma had a sister before she found the locket? *Before* she accessed a memory that allowed the spirits to seize her mind, just like they seized the mind of every drowning victim on her list?

Cal looks at me over his shoulder. "Nev? Did you hear me?"

I tighten my hold on the atlas. "You lied to Francesca."

He blinks. "What?"

"At the coffee shop. When she asked you why you're here in Hollow Cliff, you said you came here for a summer job. But that's a lie. It's the same lie you told me."

His eyes widen slightly as he scans my face. "I told you there are things—"

"No." I stand up. This atlas and the pages inside it are all that I have left of my mom. Whatever this list meant to her, it's for *me* to figure out. And if Cal wants to be a part of that, he needs to come clean about who he is and why he's here. "You asked me not to tell anyone about my mom's grave, and I agreed. I lied to her *best friend* the same way Gran has lied to *me*. You said I'd understand why later. Well, this is later. I want to know the real reason you're here. I want to know how you really know about the drownings." I yank at the chain around my neck and pull Millie's silver pendant out from under my shirt. "And I want to know how you got this locket. I want to know who gave it to you."

Cal sits frozen in the chair, his lips parting and his eyes darkening as some inner conflict plays out on his face. The silence stretches until the only sound between us is the distant crash of waves outside the window and my shallow, uneven breath. I stare at his unmoving mouth and realize I have no idea what I'm going to do if he refuses to answer. In the last forty-eight hours, my entire world has tilted on its axis, and somehow in that short time, I've come to depend on the steady presence of this stranger. Every instinct I possess is screaming at me to keep him close, but how can I when I'm still reeling from the bitter blow of Gran's lies? How can I let myself trust him if he refuses to be honest with me?

"I knew someone," he says at last, his eyes on mine. "We spent some summers together, but she was from here. She lost someone that mattered to her. Someone she loved."

He doesn't look away, and he doesn't descend behind the carefully neutral mask he wore for Francesca earlier today. The face he presents to me now is open. Raw. Simmering with barely contained emotion. I don't need to ask myself if he's telling me the truth.

I know that he is.

"There was a lot she wouldn't talk about, but she's the reason that I know about what happened to your mom. It's because of her that I know she died, but that no one knew. She's the one who gave me the locket, but she made me promise to keep it—and everything she told me—a secret until she came back for it. And I so waited. But I . . ." He looks away. Swallows. "I waited too long."

My breath catches at the grief in his voice.

"The spirits," I whisper. "Did she—"

171

He looks back at me, and the anguish there is so horrifyingly familiar that for a second, I forget to breathe. This is how Robbie looked the other night at the cove. This is what I've seen on the faces of everyone in Hollow Cliff who's lost someone they loved.

"You want me to tell you the real reason I came here, but the truth is, Nev, I have no idea."

I've seen flashes of this pain before. Flickers of this raw wound. I wanted to know what he hides under that carefully neutral mask, and this is my answer.

"I don't know what I thought I could do by coming here. I don't know what I thought I would *find*." He runs a hand up the back of his neck. "I just knew she was gone, and that what happened to her didn't make sense, but that no one—not her family, not the authorities, *nobody*—gave a shit. So, I found out everything I could about this place. I looked up coroner reports. I read what I could find about the other drownings—which was almost nothing, by the way. And then I got on a bus, and . . . I don't know." He spreads his hands, and the look he gives me is almost pleading. "Maybe I just needed to understand. Maybe some part of me knew I wouldn't be able to let her go until I found out the truth about how she . . . died."

His voice breaks on the last word, and his gaze drops again. I stand up from the armchair and turn around to give him space.

The spirits' youngest victim was a twelve-year-old boy who was killed in 1903 along with the twelve other kids whose bodies washed ashore the morning before Alma took the first Vow. Since then, it's less common for kids my age to drown, but it does happen. I can think of a few from the past couple years who may be the girl Cal knew. I didn't know any of them well though, and I'm not going to make him tell me any more about her. Especially because if he came here for answers about why she died, he doesn't have to look much further than my family. The spirits are only a threat to this town because of what Jonathan did. And because Alma's spell isn't—has never been—enough.

It ends with you, pet. It all ends with you.

The memory of Fern's expectant, hopeful gaze pushes its way into my mind, and I shiver.

"I meant what I said about your mom, Nev." I turn back around. Cal's standing up now, his arms folded protectively over his chest. "I told you everything I know about what happened to her. If you believe nothing else, please believe that."

I don't know what to say. I'm not sorry that I asked him to tell me the truth, but I'm sorry that I made him dredge up this pain. I'm sorry that even if Fern is right, even if I *do* find a way to end the drownings once I take the Vow, there are already so many who are gone. So many I'll be too late to save.

"And I know you don't know me," he continues. "But . . ." His gaze dips to the atlas still clutched to my chest. "Now that I'm here, I'm even more convinced that there's something . . . *more* to what happened to her. I don't know what it is or even what I'm looking for, but . . ."

His stormy eyes flash to mine, and I'm caught in a gaze that makes me feel both safe and strangely exposed all at the same time.

Like he can see through all the layers of skin and bone that make me up. Like there's a secret place he's discovered within me that even I don't know about yet.

"We both lost people, Nev. We both have questions. I'd like to help you find the answers to yours because you deserve them, and also because I think it will help me find the answers to *mine*." He swallows. "If you'll let me, that is."

His gaze holds mine and the only thing I can think is that I don't want him to leave. I don't want to face whatever this is alone.

"Okay."

His eyes widen. "Okay?"

I nod. "Yeah. But I have . . . conditions."

"Conditions." He nods. "All right."

"There has to be complete transparency between us from here on out."

He doesn't hesitate. "I can do that."

"And . . . you have to answer three questions about yourself with total, unfiltered honesty."

"Only three?"

"To start. Ultimately, I get to ask as many as I want."

His mouth twitches. "That sounds fair. Do you know what your first one is?"

I nod and perch again on the arm of the cushioned chair so I can watch him closely. "Where do you live?"

"Eugene, Oregon." He braces himself on the desk and leans back. "It's a very outdoorsy city. We like to bike and hike a lot. For the past two summers, I worked as a white water river rafting guide."

I blink, somewhat overwhelmed by this deluge of everyday life details from someone who's been about as forthcoming as a black hole until now. "You know that only counts as one answer, right?"

"I know, but I'm a bit of an overachiever. That's another fact about me, but I'll give you that one for free." He winks, and I have to press my lips together to stop from smiling.

"Fine, as long as we're clear. Second question. What's your favorite color?"

"Black."

"Black?" I shake my head. "No. Black isn't a color. Black is the *absence* of color."

"Your hair's black."

"So?"

"So, if someone asked you what color your hair is, you'd say black. Which means it's a color." He flashes me that crooked smile. "Next question. And it better be a good one because I'm not answering any more for at least thirty seconds after this."

His eyes dance, and this time, I can't stop my lips from twitching. I like him like this. I like *me* like this. I feel . . . lighter. Easier than I have in a long time. So much so that for a minute there, I actually let myself forget about everything that's happened in the last two days. I let myself forget that the tattered reference book I'm clutching to my chest isn't just the only thing I have left of my mom, it's also the only clue I have that might explain what she spent the last few months of her life doing. The only thing that might help me figure out the truth about what happened to her.

"Last question," I say softly. My fingers dig into the spine of the atlas. "Do you promise that I can trust you?"

His face sobers. "Yes." He pins me with his gaze like he wants to make sure I hear his words. Like he wants to make sure I feel the truth in them. "I can promise you that."

Chapter Thirteen

Cal groans and falls back against the couch cushions, his hand running down his face in a gesture of frustration that mirrors my own.

We've been holed up in the Rose Room milking its Wi-Fi signal for hours, and so far, the only thing we've been able to actually confirm is what I already knew: everyone on my mom's list tragically drowned in a manner consistent with a spirit attack. But if there's a connection between the names that she circled versus the names she crossed out, we haven't found it yet.

I stuff my mouth with the last of the surprisingly delicious grilled cheese sandwiches Cal made us and take the laptop from him. The names on my mom's list aren't the only dead end we've struck. Still unsettled by Robbie's strange reaction to the question about his video, Cal went back to watch it again, only to find that sometime between this morning and now, Robbie deleted his entire account.

I scan the document up on the screen. In the left column are the names my mom circled. On the right are the ones she crossed out. Under each name are notes and URL links with whatever potentially relevant information we've found about each person, which—apart from the date and manner of their death—largely consists of their birthdate, known family members, and occupations, which range from former police officers and shop owners to fishermen, lawyers, homemakers, and everything in between.

My third-grade teacher Beverly Price isn't the only teacher on this list, but she's the only one whose name is circled. We also found out that she served on the city council, but so did some of the people whose names are crossed off. My most recent project has been trying to figure out how long each of these people stayed away from Hollow Cliff for college or whatever else, but so far, there's been nothing to distinguish the circled names there, either. Mrs. Price, for example, went to an out-of-state college and then came back to live here permanently, like pretty much everyone else on this list.

One of the circled names is Arthur Fairchild, who was the longtime local coroner, and—perhaps more interestingly—Fern's ex-husband. The one whose funeral she finally came back to town for. But since Fern is the only person I know of who left Hollow Cliff for over a decade and then came back . . . *changed*, his connection to her isn't much help when it comes to finding similarities with people like Maria Rodriguez, who worked as a barista at Mystery Grounds, and the Brown brothers, who both worked construction and drowned within three months of each other in a rare instance of the spirits' striking twice in less than six months.

My mom circled their names, too.

There must be a connection. There must be some reason she was looking into this. And the fact that I have no idea what it is, the fact that I can't see it, makes me feel like I'm failing her all over again.

"Can I ask you a question?"

I look over at Cal. I've been peppering *him* with questions all night, which is why I now know that he's had two near-death experiences—the first one while ice fishing, and the second one involving a very stupid freshman-year dare and a very pissed-off horse. I've also learned that his parents got divorced when he was really young and that he rarely talks to his dad. I know he's close to his mom, has a younger sister who he used to find adorable but who now drives him crazy, and that he's starting UCLA in the fall on a partial scholarship, but that he hasn't decided on a major yet. I guess it's only fair for him to ask a few questions in return.

I turn to face him fully, pulling my legs into a cross-legged position on the couch. "Sure."

"Okay, first question. Does the deal go both ways? Full honesty from both of us?"

I nod, the irony of what I've demanded of him hitting me at full force. I insisted on complete and total honesty from him even though my whole life, I've dedicated myself to keeping my family's secrets.

His lips kick into a smile. "Then my next question is: Can I see what's in there?" He points to where my sketchbook is lying open on the couch cushion behind me. It's what I've been using to record my notes about how long each person on my mom's list stayed away from Hollow Cliff.

"That's more of a request than a question," I hedge.

He shrugs and watches me expectantly, like he's waiting to see if I'll renege on our bargain this quickly.

"Fine." I pick up the notebook and hand it to him. "But they're just sketches. Most of them aren't even finished."

He doesn't say anything to that, just pulls his legs onto the couch so he's matching my cross-legged position, settles the sketchbook on his lap, and flips to a random page with a colored pencil drawing of Francesca standing behind the counter at Curious Blooms. It's an explosion of color because that's how everything around Francesca is. Her apron is a floral pattern of bright reds, purples, and blues, the scarf tying up her black curls is a sunshine yellow, and the hyacinths she's arranging into a bouquet are the playful pink of spring.

Cal flips the page to a black-and-white charcoal portrait of Gran, her face taking up the entire page. Her eyes are crinkling because we'd just found out I'd been accepted into RISD, and we didn't know she was sick yet, so we both still thought I'd get to go. She's not much of a baker, but she made me a yellow cake that night, and even though the bottom was burned, I ate every crumb.

THE LIES OF ALMA BLACKWELL

The next page is an unfinished sketch of one of my phantoms skulking in a shadowy corner of the house. I used charcoal here, too, and I smudged the lines with my finger so everything appears hazy and out of focus, just like it is in my dreams. He flips again to one of my many colored pencil studies of the sky over Blackwell House after the rain. Clear—almost white—blue shot through with sheer streaks of grey.

"These are . . ." Cal looks up at me. "These are incredible, Nev."

My face heats and I look down at my hands. Gran has seen a lot of my drawings. She frames her favorites and puts them up in her sitting room. Francesca and Bea have seen some, too, and of course, I submitted a bunch in my application for school. But I'm still not used to showing them to people.

"Thanks."

"You graduated this year, too, right?"

"Yeah."

"Is this . . . is art something you've thought of pursuing?"

I shift on the couch. I could lie, but I'm insisting on the truth from him, so . . .

"I was actually going to start at a design school on the East Coast in the fall. But then Gran got sick, and once I take the Vow, I can't leave Hollow Cliff, so . . ." I shrug. "It'll always be a part of my life, though. Just as a hobby."

Cal's expression turns thoughtful, but instead of saying anything, he looks back down at the sketchbook and flips a few more pages. As he studies my drawings, I study him. The waves of his hair, tousled from running his hands through them so many times tonight. The subtle constellation of freckles across his nose. The crescent-shaped scar above his eye.

"What's this one of?"

He looks up, catching me staring, and I immediately drop my eyes to the page. He's reached the back part of the sketchbook where I record my studies of the Anchor charms. The one staring up at me now is the sketch I made of the southern Anchor less than two days ago. This is another thing Gran warned me never to talk about. Another rule I've followed blindly.

"It's a part of Alma's spell," I say. "We call those Anchors because they're charms that extend its protection to the whole town."

He looks back down, angling his head. "Why did you draw it this way? With all the parts separated? It almost looks like—"

"A diagram. Yeah. They . . . fail sometimes. That's how the spirits break through the binds Alma placed on them. When I take the Vow, it will be my job to maintain them. Replace the pieces that fail. But I've always . . ."

I trail off.

"Always what?" he prompts.

I shake my head and stare at my hands because there are some things—some hopes—that are too fragile to say out loud.

"Does this have anything to do with why you won't let Fern Fairchild read your tea leaves?"

My head snaps up. "How do you know that?"

The words come out accusatory and both of his brows lift. "I don't *know* anything. It was just a guess."

"A guess."

"Yes, Nev. A *guess*." He leans forward, bringing our faces closer. "You may not know this, but you can be . . . kind of easy to read."

I stare at him because that's not something people usually say to me. Bea has in fact accused me on multiple occasions of having a face like a steel trap.

But isn't that because I've never allowed her to see beneath it? It's not like I've ever opened up to her. Not truly. I never even told Gran the real reason I decided to start studying the Anchors. Maybe if I don't want any more secrets or lies in my life, it has to start with me.

I take in a breath and let it out. "Two years ago, after I started to really understand how the Anchors worked, I drank some of Fern's tea and I asked her if there was a way to truly bind the spirits for good. She looked at my leaves and told me that it would end with me. Her exact words were: *it all ends with you.* And I've always thought—hoped, I guess—that she meant that when it became my turn to take the Vow, I'd be the one to figure out how to strengthen the Anchors so that they would hold. So that the drownings—the spirit attacks—would stop. Forever."

Cal's brow creases and his lips press into a firm line.

"I know it probably sounds naive to think that after so many generations, I'd be the one—"

"I don't think it's naive."

I blink. "You don't?"

He shakes his head and leans in closer. "People are *dying*, Nev. What's naive about you doing absolutely everything you can to stop it? And what does it matter if no one else has figured it out? Why *can't* it be you?"

I inhale softly. The conviction shining in his eyes isn't at all like the hopeful expectation I always try to avoid in Fern's. My stomach isn't twisting with fear that I'll fail, it's tingling with something . . . strong. Something confident. Because Cal isn't looking at me like I'm the last in a chain of Blackwells destined to fail. He's looking at me like whatever I am—*who*ever I am—is enough. Like maybe it always has been.

Suddenly, I'm intensely, acutely aware of all the ways we're almost touching. His face is so close to mine that I can see the thin rims of gold around his pupils. I can feel the heat of his knee centimeters from mine on the couch, and if I flex my hand, our fingers will brush. My tongue darts out to lick my dry lips, and his eyes follow the movement. The air between us tightens, and a shiver races down my spine as his eyes continue to linger on my mouth.

He swallows, his muscles tensing beneath his shirt. I lean forward slightly, and his eyes snap to mine. They aren't just stormy now. They're dark as a thundercloud. My breath turns ragged. Cal's lips part, and—

"Can I ask another question?"

I freeze. Cal straightens on the couch, pulling his legs closer to his body. It creates a minuscule amount of distance between us, but it might as well be the Grand Canyon considering how quickly my face flames.

I scoot back until I collide with the plush arm of the couch. What was I thinking? What did I almost just do? Cal came here for someone he loved. Someone his heart is clearly still breaking for. And I was about to—

I grab one of the small couch cushions and hug it to my chest. "Of course. Ask away."

I make a thorough and unnecessary study of the embroidered roses on the cushion so that I don't have to look at him, but his voice is almost apologetic as he asks, "Have you ever thought about not taking the Vow?"

My head jerks up. I'm too surprised to remember I'm supposed to be embarrassed. "Of course not. That would be . . . that's not an option."

He tilts his head. "Are you sure?"

"I . . . yes, I'm sure. Alma's spell may be far from perfect, but it's still the only thing holding the spirits back. They killed thirty-four people in *three days* the last time they were unbound. And unlike her, I'd have no hope of binding them again if they were allowed to break free."

"But you told me yourself that you aren't just making a promise. You're becoming a *living part* of a spell that still allows people to die every year. Doesn't that seem . . . I don't know. Wrong somehow?"

His words cut like barbs, and I rear back from them. "What happened to me being the one who could change things? Was that just something you said?"

"No. Of course not."

"Because, believe me, I won't have a *chance* of strengthening the Anchors without the power the Vow will give me." I stand up from the couch and hold out my hand. "Can I have my sketchbook back, please? I'd like to get back to work."

Cal's eyes search my face in that deeply unsettling way of his that makes me feel like a dissected frog with my guts on display. When he silently hands me the sketchbook, I take it and sink into the armchair across the room, but the unsettled feeling doesn't go away. It stays with me, like the last stubborn ray of sunlight fighting against the dusk. I've always known what my life would look like. I've always understood and accepted the role I would play. But I was wrong about my mom. Wrong to trust Gran blindly, no matter her intentions. What if there's more I was wrong about? More I don't know?

And what if it changes everything?

I'm falling from the twisting oak again.

My arms are flailing at my sides. My fingers are reaching for purchase, but all they find is air. A scream rips through my throat because I know I'm going to die. I'm too high up. The ground is too far away.

But it won't be soon. Soon, I will meet it. Soon, I—

I scream again, but this time it's not in fear. This time, it's in relief because my phantoms have caught me. They swoop beneath me and snatch me up, but they don't return me to the limb of the tree. They wrap me up in their warm, mist-like embrace, and the next thing I know we're running together through the halls of Blackwell House. We tear through the library and tiptoe past the Séance Room. We barrel up the stairs and pause to collect our breath in front of the door with the web-patterned glass panel.

I turn, like I always do, trying to catch a glimpse of the shifting forms that hover in the far corner of my eye. All the phantoms but one scatter, and I remember with a jolt that this has happened before. My heart pounds, and somehow I know it's the same faceless figure that detached itself from the corner last time, flickering in the glow of the gas lamps as it cuts through the air toward me.

For years, I've drawn my phantoms like shifting grey smoke hovering above a fire. But now that I'm facing one head-on, I realize how wrong I was.

My phantoms aren't made of smoke.

They are the clouds of a storm.

I blink my eyes open slowly, disoriented for several long seconds as I try to figure out where I am.

My neck is stiff, my legs are tucked underneath me, and soft moonlight is pouring in through floor-to-ceiling windows that don't belong in my room. It's only when I see Cal sprawled out on the couch across the room, his long, jean-clad legs hanging off the end, that I realize we're still in the Rose Room. We both must have fallen asleep, no closer to understanding the purpose of my mom's list than we were hours ago.

There's a throw blanket covering me that I don't remember getting for myself, but even though it's cozy in my armchair bed, there's no chance of me going back to sleep. Images from the dream that woke me up flicker through my mind, and the usual frustration surges through me as I try to piece them together.

I remember falling out of the tree. I remember thinking I was going to die. And I remember a fleeting feeling of safety when my phantoms swooped me up. But something was unsettling about the dream, too. Something I can't identify, but that makes my skin feel tight when I try.

I'm too rattled to face Cal right now, so I slip as quietly as I can from under the throw blanket and plant my bare feet on the floor. Tab, the traitor, is curled up in the crook of his arm on the couch, but neither of them stirs as I slip my feet into my sandals and scoop up my empty glass of water.

As soon as I step out into the hallway, a familiar icy touch glides up the back of my neck. Even with the glow from the almost full moon, it's impossible to separate the shadows from the inky black of night. They kept their distance earlier today, but I feel them now, falling in around me, twisting and turning as they snake their way beneath the collar of my shirt, raising goosebumps on my arms.

I pass by a large bay window, and a swath of moonlight snags on something in the corner of my vision. I turn toward it and immediately recognize the cobweb design in the glass panel of the door I ran past in my dream only minutes ago.

I've studied this door a handful of times, along with the collection of partially broken, cast-off pieces of furniture covered in white dustcloths stored in the room behind it. I used to hope it would trigger something that would help me remember more about the dreams, but it never has. Except now, as my eyes linger on the design in the glass panel, there's something about it that seems familiar in a way I don't think has anything to do with my dreams. I bite my lip, trying to make the connection as I absently fiddle with the silver chain around my neck, but it's only as I'm about to give up and turn away that my pulse skips and I realize what it is.

Reaching under my shirt, I pull out the locket and study the silver backing. The scratches I noticed before are thin and inexpertly done, the circles nestled within each other aren't perfectly round or particularly proportional, and the lines that extend out from the center are more wavy than straight. But as I look between the glass panel and the back of the locket, it's impossible not to see a resemblance.

Are these scratches supposed to be a web? Or am I seeing things that aren't there again? Grasping for connections since the rest of this night has been a series of dead ends and disappointments?

I leave the door open behind me so as much light as possible can trickle into the narrow, cramped space. It's been at least a year, maybe more, since I've been in here, and like all of those times, no images from my dreams come rushing back. But that's okay, because this time, I'm here for a different reason. This time, I'm looking for some explanation for why Millie might have singled this room out. If that's even what she did.

I can barely make out of the shadowy lumps of furniture covered in white sheets, their jagged shapes more ominous now than they've ever been during my daylight visits. I'm leaning forward to lift the sheet off what looks to be a chair with a missing slat when I catch a movement out of the corner of my eye.

I spin toward it, my heart jumping into my throat.

There's another flutter. And then another as I take a few tentative steps forward, each of my subsequent movements causing a corresponding blur of motion, almost as if—

A mirror.

The glass is tarnished and cloudy, and the white sheet that was covering it is slipping off the corner as it flutters slightly, as if it's caught in a gentle breeze. Except there are no windows in this room.

So where is the breeze coming from?

Something tugs at the far recesses of my mind, and I walk forward, scoot the free-standing mirror aside, and lower into a crouch. In front of me is another spiderweb design, this one made of a waist-high metal grate set into the wall. And as soon as I see it, I feel like an idiot because I already knew this was here.

I spent countless hours as a kid exploring every inch of Blackwell House, and the secret passageway behind this grate was no exception. There are enough hidden entrances and passageways in this house that it *is* hard to keep track of them all—especially the ones that aren't useful shortcuts—but I'm surprised that this one slipped my mind.

I grip the grate, muscle memory knowing exactly how to lift it to dislodge it from the wall. A quick duck of my head confirms it's pitch-black inside the passageway, and although I should go back and get a light of some kind before going farther, before I'm fully conscious of the decision, I'm crawling into the dark, musty room and feeling my way down the passageway, my hand skimming the cold stone walls. I stumble up a narrow flight of stairs and eventually come to a vaguely familiar tapestry that I push aside. There's a door behind it, and I unlatch it, push it open, and step into a large room awash in blue moonlight.

It takes a moment for my eyes to adjust after the complete darkness of the passageway, but once they do, I take in the dusty attic, my gaze lingering on the domed, cone-like ceiling that meets in a triangular apex in the center of the round room. I have vague memories of exploring this attic as a kid, but nothing specific or unique comes to mind. Unlike the storage room downstairs, the furniture here hasn't been given the benefits of protective cloths. The scattered chairs and side tables have been left exposed to the dust, giving what might otherwise be a cozy space a derelict, abandoned air.

And it's not only the dusty furniture. There's a large, oval window taking up almost all of the southern wall, and the soft glow filtering through it highlights a section of wallpaper to the window's right that has been messily ripped away. I must not have appreciated this as a kid, but it's rare to find a room in Blackwell House that hasn't been meticulously maintained.

Curious, I walk over to the ripped wallpaper. I'm only steps away when a loud creak sounds from behind me.

I whip around, my heart skipping, and I'm immediately blinded by a flare of bright light. My eyes squeeze shut, and I throw up a hand to shield them just as a familiar voice says, "I thought you might be tired of wandering around in the dark."

"Cal?"

His name comes out as a squeak. Footsteps sound and seconds later, a warm hand is lightly cupping my elbow. "Yeah, it's me. Sorry. I didn't mean to scare you."

I blink several times, and my eyes finally adjust to the added light in the room, even though it's not really that bright. Cal's carrying one of the small camp lanterns that Gran and I stash around the house for emergencies since about a quarter of the rooms were never updated with electric lighting.

"How did you know I was up here?" My heart is still beating fast. "And how did you *get* up here?"

His eyes sweep my face, and I'm suddenly very aware of the heat of his fingers curled around my bare elbow. He must become aware of it at the same time because he lets go and steps back.

"I woke up and you weren't there." His voice is still a little gruff from sleep, and he shrugs. "I went to find you, saw that the door to that storage room was open, noticed the open grate, and guessed that's where you'd gone."

I press my lips together because even though he gives the explanation matter-of-factly enough, there was more than one open door in the hallway that he could have investigated.

His brows pinch and he makes a beeline for the large oval window before I can press him on it. I start to follow but stop when the light from his lantern swings onto the section of wall-paper I was looking at earlier. It looks like someone ripped it on purpose rather than normal wear and tear, and there's something on the wooden slats that I can see now, too. Something that would have been hidden by the paper before it was torn.

I step forward and reach out my hand.

"Nev? What are you doing?"

I hear Cal, but I don't answer him. I'm too transfixed by an odd, oval smudge on the exposed wall.

My finger extends. Behind me, Cal shouts, "Nev, wait!"

But it's too late.

The pad of my finger has already connected with the wall, drawn like a magnet to the reddish-brown smudge. A cold, familiar touch races under my skin, and I feel her, drawing me in.

Taking me into her mind.

Chapter Fourteen

Millie is tiptoeing in the dark, a thick dressing gown belted over her white nightdress, her wild mane of black curls braided in a rope that hangs down her back. In one hand, she holds a flickering oil lamp, its buttery-yellow light revealing brief flashes of an enclosed corridor that feels instantly familiar.

I'm ready this time when her thoughts tangle with mine. I understand what's happening as my unbodied form hovers in the air around her, both with her and apart from her as she mounts a narrow flight of stairs.

Her feet don't slow as she climbs because this is a path she's taken many times. And I know—because this is something Millie learned from the staff—that in the original, more modest structure of Blackwell House, these stairs were out in the open. It's only when Jonathan decided to add yet another wing to his ever-expanding mansion on the cliff that they were enclosed.

Presumably, this passageway was preserved so the staff would still have access to the attic, but Millie is the only one who uses it now. She knows for a fact that her lady's maid, Lucy—a snoop and unapologetic spy for her brother-in-law—is deathly afraid of both enclosed spaces *and* heights, which is only one of the reasons the attic is Millie's favorite place to escape to.

Her lip twitches as she thinks about sour-faced Lucy and the valerian root she slipped into her nightly tea this evening. She mixed in enough to knock out someone twice her size, but this is a night for caution. She's still rattled from her conversation with Alma in the woods this afternoon, and she also couldn't ignore the tense energy in the house this evening. Jonathan was even more upset about that ridiculous cartoon of him in the paper than Millie had anticipated he would be. And after dinner, she heard him yelling at his cousin Rodney in his study, railing on and on about an assistant to the head railroad engineer who did something—she didn't overhear what—that Jonathan is deeply displeased about.

She reaches the top of the stairs, pulls aside the heavy tapestry, flips the lock, and slides open the panel door. Silver moonlight streams in from the oval window on the south wall, illuminating the poorly maintained armchairs and cast-off tables that Millie assumes were placed up here for storage before she and Alma arrived.

Half of the walls are covered in cheery wallpaper with a pattern of yellow daisies that Millie put up herself. It was only six months ago that she finally convinced the man in charge of papering the newest wing of the house to give her some extra sheets along with a couple of brushes, a bucket, and paste. Her application isn't perfect, but she's pleased with how the color brightens the space during the day. As much as she dislikes Blackwell House and everything it represents to her brother-in-law, she'll miss this little room when she and Jenny leave in the fall.

Some nights, when she can't sleep, Millie comes up here to work on the papering, imagining the home she and Jenny will one day make for themselves, but tonight she passes the buckets, kneels in front of the oval window, and works her first two fingers into a groove in the floor until, with a pop and a groan, a single floorboard comes loose. In the hidden space below, there's a rectangular-shaped bundle wrapped tightly in a dusty black cloth. Millie lifts it out and unwraps it, revealing a delicate rosewood box engraved with the waxing and waning phases of the moon.

The design reminds me of something, but Millie's thoughts sweep mine away before I can remember what. She's thinking about another charm box, similar to this one, that belonged to her mother. It was passed down to her from Millie's grandmother, and her mother's mother before that. It was larger than this one, and each phase of the moon was reverently depicted with shimmering inlays of mother of pearl. The last time Millie saw it was the night her parents died.

The neighbors set the fire. Millie can't help but see it now in her mind's eye. The bright orange flames that burned her parents' house to the ground. The bar they placed over the door to keep her mother and father locked inside. They'd screamed that she was a witch. Millie heard them chant it from where she and Alma hid huddled in the woods behind their house. She'd tried to break free, tried to run to the fire, pull them out, but Alma had wrapped her arms around her like a vice, chanting over and over again that they had to stay hidden. That the mob would kill them, too.

But Alma didn't understand. She didn't know that it wasn't their mother who brought the Thompson babe back from death. She didn't see the look of horror on their mother's face when she came upon Millie, still crackling with power from the charm clutched in her hand, the babe everyone had seen take its last breath only minutes ago alive and screaming in her arms. Their mother knew better than to plunge that deep. She knew better than to touch that place where life and death are held.

She'd snatched the babe from Millie's arms and made her swear she'd tell no one—not even her sister—about what she'd done. Then she'd rounded Alma up and ordered the two of them to run.

Millie didn't understand why.

Not until she saw the flames.

And her greatest shame, the thing she forces herself to admit now, is that she still didn't learn her lesson. When she saw her parents' burned bodies, she wanted nothing more than to plunge into that dark, forbidden place again.

Only this time, it wouldn't be life that she sought.

Millie closes her eyes, a shiver running up her spine. Alma will never know the degree to which she saved her that night. Not only her life but her soul as well. Because if Alma hadn't dragged her away, if she hadn't ignored Millie's pleas and cries to let her go, she doesn't know what she might have done.

She doesn't know what she might have become.

A tear slides down her cheek, and she wipes it roughly away. These memories, this bitter descent into her ever-present ocean of anger and guilt, isn't why she came to the attic tonight. She sucks in a breath and holds it, not letting out the air until her head begins to spin. She does this several more times, holding her breath in and then letting it out, forcing her mind to clear. When she finally reaches a place of deep calm and focus, she opens the lid of the rosewood box and takes out the charm her sister wove with her grudging guidance two years ago.

It's a simple construction, bound in the shape of a braid. But the second she touches it, she knows something is wrong. *More* than wrong.

The charm is . . . broken.

She sucks in a breath because this is so much worse than she'd allowed herself to imagine. She was horrified when she discovered what her sister had sacrificed in order to strengthen this spell, but the ugly truth is that it should have worked. This charm should have endured for a couple dozen more years before needing any attention.

Except it didn't.

The fact that Jonathan hasn't kicked them both to the curb already is a minor miracle. Or perhaps the seed of love Alma planted in her husband's mind was strong enough to take root and grow on its own?

But she can't risk that. She had planned on weaving her own charm around Alma's original one, commandeering what her sister already made and strengthening it with a complementary spell of her own. But now, she'll have to make a new one from scratch. There's no clock in the attic, but it was nearing three in the morning when she slipped out of her room. That should give her plenty of time to dismantle Alma's broken charm and reweave it with new additions. Still, she works fast, bending over and undoing the braid made of the tennis strings that Alma plucked from her now-husband's racket. Fully drained objects—the corner of a bird's nest, a perfectly round pebble, the scrap of a letter Jonathan penned—are placed to her left. Objects that will be rebound in the new charm—locks of both Jonathan's and Alma's hair, a single piece of red string—are placed to the right.

Once that's done, Millie pulls her charm box onto her lap and begins sorting through the collection of objects she keeps inside. I feel my own jolt of recognition at the realization that these materials, like the assortment of odds and ends I keep in my own pouch, are items that have called out to her over the years. Pieces she's carefully collected so she might one day use them in a charm. Her fingers comb through pebbles and feathers, moth wings, stray eyelashes, and torn newspaper corners. She discards bits of dried seaweed, broken-off pieces of redwood bark, scraps of lace, and a spindly piece of silver wire. She keeps searching, passing over rusted pieces of metal and several brightly colored ribbon snippets until she finds a tattered scrap of blood-soaked linen that she wishes she didn't have. But it called to her that night, after Alma's screams had faded, and she took it not out of want, but *need*.

Now she understands why.

The scrap of linen goes to the right, an echo of the sacrifice that was made, even though, unlike her sister, Millie doesn't need to offer up life for her spells to take.

She sets the charm box aside, knots the tennis strings at the top, and begins to weave. She's so intent on the task, so focused on the individual vibrations rising from her nascent charm that she doesn't notice the step behind her. By the time her brain finally does catch up to the sound, there's already a large hand clamped over her mouth.

Millie screams, but the sound is muffled by the hand. She surges back, trying to rise to her feet and fight herself free, but a second arm wraps around her waist, pinning her back against a hard, muscled chest.

"None of that, you little witch."

She freezes, sudden, horrible recognition washing through her as a laugh sounds in her ear, cold and cruel.

Jonathan Blackwell pushes her forward, forcing her to her knees on the hardwood floor. But he doesn't release her. Doesn't face her. He keeps her back pressed to his front, and when he speaks, his hot breath skips down the back of her neck.

"I believe, little sister, that this is what they refer to as being caught in the act."

Millie's entire body shivers violently, and Jonathan laughs his cruel laugh again.

"Did you know, Millicent, that for a time, I believed I had changed? Truly *believed* I had been transformed . . . by love."

Millie goes very, very still.

He couldn't know, she thinks furiously. It's not possible that he could—

"I was so in *love*, Millicent, so enamored that at first, I didn't believe what my own man told me he discovered about my dear wife's family. The humble circumstances I had guessed, to some extent. That I could forgive. But the stories from your former neighbors about your baby-killing witch of a mother? Their vivid, detailed descriptions of the devil-worshipping daughters she had trained?"

He makes a *tut-tut* sound in the back of his throat, and it's more than Millie can take. She surges up again, jabbing back with her elbow, aiming for his ribs. But her brother-in-law is a large man. Fit and athletic. He subdues her so easily that he laughs. A real laugh, this time, full of mirth.

He lets her struggle for a bit longer. Lets her wriggle like a fish on a line before pressing his palm so hard over her nose and mouth that he cuts off her air. She tries to breathe through it, but it's not long before Millie's head is spinning. Before her limbs give up, and she goes limp in his arms.

"May we continue with our conversation now, Millicent?"

She doesn't attempt to answer, but as much as it sickens her to do it, she doesn't renew her struggle, either. After a moment, Jonathan makes a sound of approval in the back of his throat and eases the press of his hand. At once, Millie sucks in air, filling her lungs to the brim.

"Now, I think it's best if we skip over my initial reaction to the discovery that I had not only been robbed of the wife—of the *life*—I deserved, but that I had brought into my home at least one viperous harpy capable of controlling my very *mind*."

The air Millie only just pulled in leaves in a rush.

It's not possible that he knows this. It's not possible, but somehow he does.

I underestimated him.

The thought rings clear in her mind.

"But as I said, we'll skip over that. My marriage to your grasping sister may have temporarily weakened me, but I'm not a man who lies down at the first sign of defeat. And if I have one talent, Millicent, it is the ability to recognize the tools—*all* the tools—at my disposal."

It's as if the entire room is collapsing in on her, squeezing her from every side. She's desperate not to let him see her break, but her entire body is shaking and the tears are pushing painfully at her eyes.

"Now, I had a conversation with my dear wife earlier this evening. I explained to her that I'm having a small . . . issue at the office. An overly ambitious assistant has submitted a report about a bridge on my route. It's a blatant attempt at sabotage, of course, but I sadly do not have time to expose it as such before the delegation from Washington arrives. My wife was very distraught to learn this. Particularly because, although she is quite *motivated* to help me make this little problem go away, she is, apparently, not the right sister for the job."

He pauses and leans in closer so his lips brush Millie's ear. "But you, Millicent. You are exactly what I need."

Millie twists around. Looks up into Jonathan Blackwell's cruel, handsome face and then—

Black.

Darkness closing in on me from all sides.

It feels wrong. Like I'm folding in on myself. Like I've lost myself in a place I'll never come back from. Like I no longer—

Light. Soft and pink, streaming in through an oval window. I'm with Millie again. We're still in the attic. She's still dressed in her robe and nightgown, but they're soiled now. Stuck to her skin with sweat. Her knees are pulled up to her chest and both of her hands are cupped around something silver and sharp.

It's a nail.

It took her two full days to pry it out of the floorboard with her fingernails, but it was worth it. In the four days since she's been locked in this attic, this nail is the only thing she's found that she might be able to use.

Not for a charm, though, or for any kind of spell. She searched every inch of her attic prison, but she didn't find a single item with a resonance strong enough to weave even the weakest forgetting spell. It was a blow, but not a surprise. Some places suck the life out of the things they hold, and in the two years Millie has lived at Blackwell House, she hasn't heard even the faintest note from an item within these walls.

When she acceded to Jonathan's demand and wove the spell to alter the mind of that young engineer, she tried to squirrel away a few objects from her charm box, but Jonathan's rat-faced cousin Rodney caught her in the act. She shivers now, not wanting to remember the menacing glint in that hateful man's eye as his meaty hand clamped around her arm. Not wanting to think about his sour breath as he taunted her with warnings of what he'd do if she disobeyed again.

Millie doesn't want Rodney's face in her mind, so she banishes him and stares at her hard-won nail instead. She twists it in her fingers so it glints in the faint morning sun, and she thinks about how Jonathan Blackwell made her a killer.

The belief she planted in the young engineer's mind was simple: the trestle bridge is sound.

It was enough for him to withdraw his report. Enough to stop him from going to the press ahead of the Washington delegation's visit, as he'd threatened to do. But when the bridge did collapse, it became *too* much.

The mind is a delicate thing. She tried to warn Jonathan of this, but he didn't care. And now that confused, broken man's death is on her hands, along with every soul she prevented him from saving. And Jonathan wants her to do it *again*. This time, to dozens and dozens of minds.

Her belly rumbles. Proof that her brother-in-law is making good on his threat to starve her as long as Millie continues to, in his words, *render herself useless* by refusing his request.

There's a footstep in the hall outside followed by the sound of a key sliding into a lock. Millie quickly slips the nail up the sleeve of her blouse before turning her head. She's expecting Rodney. She's had no food for two days, but Jonathan doesn't want her dead yet, so water is sporadically brought. But when the door opens, it's not Rodney's weasel-like face she sees. It's—

"Alma?"

Millie pushes herself to her feet, eyes roving over her sister, looking for any sign of harm. She's carrying a tray laden with food, but not the mush Millie was given before her starvation diet began. This is *real* food. Chicken in cream sauce with asparagus and whipped potatoes on the side. But while the smell alone makes her stomach growl, it's the sight of her sister that Millie truly devours. Only Alma doesn't look hurt or traumatized. She's even dressed in one of her fashion-plate silks of soft lilac with bows on the sleeves.

"Mil!" She places the tray of food on the floor, rushes forward, and throws her arms around Millie, pulling her into a lavender-scented hug. "Oh, Mil. I'm so sorry. I've been begging John to let me come see you, but he's only just agreed."

Millie squeezes her and pulls back, searching her face. "You're okay, Alms? He hasn't—"

"No." Alma takes both of Millie's hands in hers and squeezes them. "I'm fine. Really. Now come." She pulls Millie forward and gestures for her to sit before the tray. "It was wrong of John to leave Rodney in charge of your food and comforts. He understands that now. Things are going to be better now. I promise." There's no table to eat at, so Alma sits on the floor in her beautiful dress and slides a piece of chicken onto a small flower-patterned plate. "It's only that he's been so distraught the past few days. There was a horrible crash. A bridge collapsed and—"

"I know, Alms. He wants me to—"

"It was a horrible accident, of course." Alma adds whipped potatoes to the plate of chicken. "John can't forgive himself, even though it's not his fault. He fired the engineer who built the bridge, but—"

"Alma, he knew the bridge wasn't anchored properly. There was a report, but he—"

"*No.*" She adds a fork to the plate, pushes it in front of Millie, and lifts her chin. "He put his trust in the wrong men, Mil. *That's* what happened."

A horrible, strained silence falls between them. Moments ago, Millie was starving, but now, when she looks at the plate of chicken, she thinks she's going to be sick.

"Why are you here, Alma? Why did he let you come see me?"

Alma sits back and takes a moment to rearrange the fall of her skirts on the wood floor. "I came to ask you to do what he wants, Mil. I came to ask you to make it go away. For me. For our family."

Alma lowers a hand to her belly. Millie follows the movement. "Alma. Are you—"

She nods, her face glowing. "Dr. Jacobs said the babe should come near to Christmas this year. Isn't it wonderful news? John is thrilled, of course."

Millie's heart sinks. Not because her sister is pregnant with the child of a murderer, the poor babe is innocent of that sin, but because she'd hoped that Alma would help her.

But will she go against Jonathan now?

"I've already given him what he wanted, Alma." She speaks slowly, needing her sister to hear her. Needing her to understand. "I gave him what he wanted, and forty-three people died, along with that young engineer who tried to *stop* the bridge from collapsing. I did it so no harm would come to *you*." She can't keep the accusation out of her voice. Alma hears it and flinches. "I carry those deaths with me now. Because I gave your husband what he asked."

Alma doesn't meet her eyes. "I know, Mil. And I'm sorry."

"If you were sorry, you wouldn't ask me to do this. That poor engineer killed himself when he was confronted with the truth *I* stole from him. What if that happens again? Are you truly willing to risk two dozen *lives* just so your precious Jonathan doesn't face public scrutiny?"

Alma reaches out to take her hands, but Millie pulls back. Hurt flares in Alma's eyes, and she straightens her spine, jutting out her chin. "We do what we must to survive, Mil. We always have. And besides, it will be different this time. You can alter the charm. Reduce the strength of the spell. That engineer, he . . . he knew more than these men do. It's only the report about the bridge, Mil. That's all you have to make them forget. As long as everyone believes it was an accident, everything will be well and all of this will be over."

But Alma's wrong. It will never be over.

If I have one talent, Millicent, it is the ability to recognize the tools at my disposal.

Millie saw the greed that flared in Jonathan's eyes when she agreed to weave a spell on that poor engineer. It was a mistake to let him see just how powerful of a tool she could be, but at the time, Millie had feared for Alma.

And now it's too late. Now he'll never let her go.

"I would do it myself," Alma says, a note of bitterness in her tone, "but you and I both know it's beyond me. So I'm asking you, Mil. I'm asking you to help my family."

Millie opens her mouth to respond, but Alma talks over her. "And if you won't do it for me, do it for yourself. I know how much you've always wanted to go to university, and if you help us, John has agreed to pay your tuition. All of it. If you'll just do this one last thing for us."

For us.

The words are a death knell. They are the sound of Millie's last hope that her sister might willingly help her fading away. One day, Alma will discover the truth about her husband, and Millie can only hope, for her sake, that it won't be too late.

But she won't see it now. That much is clear. Jonathan is a cruel man, but he can be charming. Convincing. And he already had an advantage with his ambitious, lovesick wife.

Millie fingers the silver chain at her neck, debating her next move. She'd hoped that Alma would find a way to see her. She'd hoped that together, they might find a way out of this mess. But at the very least, she'd hoped that Alma could get a message to Jenny because she can only imagine how wild with fear she must be after four days without a word. And Jenny is impulsive. Braver than she should be. Millie can't risk her doing anything foolish. She can't risk her drawing Jonathan Blackwell's attention.

Tears press against her eyes, but she blinks them away and makes an effort to school her expression into a neutral mask. "I'll think about it, Alms. That's all I can promise for now. I'll think about it. For you."

Alma's smile is quick and sudden. She yelps and pulls Millie into a hug, her relieved *thank you* whispered against her cheek. It's maybe the first heartfelt hug that the sisters have shared since moving into Blackwell House, and Millie hates that it's because of a lie.

When Alma pulls back, her eyes are bright and her color is high. Then her gaze slips down to Millie's soiled nightclothes, and her nose wrinkles. "I'll see about getting you fresh clothes, Mil. And a bath. John never should have left you in Rodney's care. But you know how men are. They never pay attention to these sorts of things."

Millie bites her tongue because she very much doubts her current state of cleanliness—or lack thereof—was in any way an oversight. But there's no point in saying that to Alma now.

"Thanks, Alms. That would be nice." It's an effort, but she manages to conjure up a weak smile. "Like I said, I promise to think about it, but I have a favor, a very small one, to ask in return."

Alma tilts her head, her curiosity evident. "I'll do anything I can to help you, Mil. You know that."

The obvious lie behind that answer is gutting, but once again, Millie doesn't let it show. She pulls a silver chain over her head and holds the glass pendant locket out to Alma. "Could you see this returned to Jenny Murphy at the caretaker cottage? She lent it to me, and I wouldn't want her to think I forgot to give it back."

Alma takes the locket, and Millie watches her closely, alert for any sign that she's able to sense the memory the pendant locket now holds. But her sister has always been attracted to more overt magic. The kind that—Millie suspects—speaks to a deep desire within Alma to match her little sister in power. And that means she's taken very little interest in the subtle, benign variety Millie used to implant this memory, which, while not the full story—it would ruin everything if Jenny came charging up to the attic in an attempt to rescue her—is hopefully enough to communicate to Jenny that Millie is well and that she herself should be on her guard.

When Alma slips the chain around her neck without hesitation or question, Millie's shoulders loosen.

"Leave it with me, Mil." She gives the pendant a reassuring pat against her chest. "I'll make sure your little friend gets her bauble back."

Chapter Fifteen

I suck in a breath, but the air won't come.

There's something heavy pressing on my chest. Something strong pinning down my arms. I fight against it, surge up and kick out with my legs, but the heavy thing on top of me doesn't move. Doesn't let up.

Jonathan Blackwell's face flashes in my mind. It's his fingers curled around my wrists, holding me down, his warm breath skittering across my face. If I somehow manage to open my leaden eyes, it will be his cold smile that I see. Because there's something he wants from me. Something he's prepared to take by any means.

A burst of fear erupts within me, and it gives me strength. This time, when I heave my body up, a hoarse scream rips through my throat.

"Nev."

The single word reaches me, but it's distorted, as if it had to travel through a heavy layer of fog to reach me. But somehow, I know what it is. My name.

Not Millie. *Nev.*

"Let it go, Nev. You're okay. Let it *go.*"

My eyes fly open. I'm staring up at a boy that I know. He has freckles scattered across his nose and a crescent-shaped scar above his left eye. His eyes like to shift between grey and blue and his hair . . .

I blink my eyes closed. Shake my head because what I'm seeing doesn't make sense. Gradually, I become aware of the hardwood floor of the attic beneath my back and a hand pulling at my fingers, trying to pry them loose from something that's clenched in my right fist. When I open my eyes again, Cal is staring down at me. His black hair is almost blue in the moonlight and there's rigid tension in every line of his face. "Let it go, Nev." His voice is shaking with what could be fury or fear. "Let it go *now.*"

I turn my head and blink several times at the sight of my fingers clenched around what looks like the broken piece of a chair leg. It's jagged and uneven, and it ends in a sharp, serrated spike.

A spike that could easily puncture my skin.

It takes me significantly more effort than it should to release the barbed piece of wood. But, one by one, I loosen my fingers enough for Cal to wrench the stick out of my hand and throw it skittering across the floor.

He heaves out a gasping, shuttering sigh, but I barely have time to take a breath of my own before I'm being lifted into the air. One of his arms is braced under my knees, the other cradles my upper back, and the rapid pounding of his heart beats against my side. Seconds after he lifts me, Cal sets me down on a stuffed armchair that's covered in decades of dust.

"Does anything hurt?"

He kneels in front of me, inspecting my face and neck with a clinical perusal that nevertheless sends my heart racing.

I shake my head. "I'm okay, I think."

He doesn't look convinced. His lips are tight, the light from the lantern on the floor casting harsh shadows across his pale face. He takes my hand—the one that was holding the wooden stake to my neck—and gently examines my wrist.

"You'll have bruises." His voice is hard and gruff, but the light touch of his fingers on the inside of my wrist is anything but. "I got to you in seconds, but you moved so damned fast. I didn't even see you get it . . . just the edge, pressing into your . . ."

His throat works in a swallow, his gaze remaining fixed on my wrist. "You were too strong. I couldn't make you let it go." He keeps his head bent, like a petitioner looking for absolution.

Except none of this is his fault.

"Cal." I flip my hand over and squeeze his fingers. "You *did* make me let go. If it weren't for you, I'd be d—"

"*Don't.*" Ravaged eyes snap to mine. "Don't say it."

My breath catches because there's so much more than concern in his eyes. So much more than worry or fear. "Cal," I begin, but he cuts me off with a shake of his head and stands up, putting distance between us. For a second, it looks like he's going to say something, but then he shakes his head again and looks over his shoulder at the ripped wallpaper, one hand reaching up to rub the back of his neck.

"It happened again, didn't it? Millie left another memory?"

I sink back into the musty chair and pull my knees into my chest. I don't know how to begin describing the enormity of what I just witnessed. I don't know if I even understand all of it myself. It's like that mile-long mural under the old flood control bridge that Mom and I used to walk along. It's too big, too sprawling, to take in all at once.

So I start with what matters most. I start with the truth that's gutted me to my core.

"Alma knew."

Cal looks back at me, but I drop my gaze, unable to meet his eyes. For almost as long as I can remember, I idolized Alma Blackwell. She was the measuring stick I judged myself by. She was everything brave and humble, resourceful, selfless, and kind that I wanted to be.

Except that woman never existed.

That woman was a lie.

"Alma knew about the report on the trestle bridge."

I force myself to look up into Cal's arrested gaze. I'm desperate to get this all out now. Desperate to not be alone with this knowledge.

"I think that's what she wanted Millie's help with in the first memory. I think Alma wanted to weave a charm to affect the mind of the assistant who submitted the report about the bridge engineering flaws. The police found proof after his death that he was planning to go to the press with his information before the congressional delegation from Washington arrived."

"The assistant engineer," Cal says slowly. "He's the one who—"

"Threw himself off the ravine after the crash, yeah." I hug my knees tighter. "Some people wondered later if it was him—not Jonathan Blackwell—who was the spirits' first victim."

"But he wasn't?"

I shake my head and tell him about Jonathan ambushing Millie in this very attic. About the family history he was able to unearth, and about the belief Millie agreed to plant in the young assistant's mind because Alma wasn't powerful enough to do it.

"So Millie made him believe the bridge was sound?" Cal asks, his voice tight. "And when it collapsed—"

"He might have jumped off that ravine out of guilt, but Millie seemed sure that his mind was affected when he was confronted with a competing truth."

"But you said that only happens in extreme cases."

I let out a breath. "Millie is, I mean, *was* extremely powerful. I can *feel* it when I'm there with her in the memory. Whatever charm she wove, I have no doubt it was strong. Unless she or Alma wove a countercharm to free his mind, I don't think that poor guy stood a chance."

Cal swears under his breath and paces over to the oval window. The anger that radiates off of him as he stares out into the night mirrors my own. All of this happened over a century ago, and even if that young engineer had lived, he'd be long gone now. But it doesn't feel that way. The injustice of it all feels fresh.

"Was there more?" he asks, eyes still fixed out the window. "In the memory?"

I wish I could say no. I wish I could forget everything I saw happen between Millie and Alma in this attic. But I can't. So I tell Cal about Alma's visit, and the longer I talk, the sicker I feel.

Alma knew what her husband was doing to her sister, but instead of helping her, instead of using the considerable resources at her disposal to help her escape *imprisonment*, the woman lauded as the *savior of Hollow Cliff* wanted Millie to cover up her jailor's tracks once again. She knew it meant risking even more innocent lives, and she didn't care.

Cal looks as disgusted as I am by the time I'm done, and for several long moments, neither of us speaks. I stay curled in a ball on the armchair, and he sits down hard on the end of a dust-covered coffee table, dropping his head into his hands. I squint out at the shadows lurking in the corners of the room. Nothing has slithered out to surround me since Cal arrived, but I feel them there.

Watching.

Waiting.

And maybe it's because I know now what once happened in this room, or maybe it's because the spirits almost succeeded again in seizing my mind and forcing me to engineer my own death like they did to my mom and all the drowning victims on her list, but there seems to be a new edge to their presence that wasn't there before. A deeper, more primal kind of anger that's stronger than anything I've felt after a drowning. As if they too sense the lingering imprint of injustice in this room.

I don't know how long we sit there in silence, but eventually, I push myself up from the chair. When I'm satisfied that my legs are no longer shaking like twigs in a storm, I walk over to the ripped wallpaper again, but a hand on my elbow stops me halfway.

"Nev. What are you—"

"It's okay." I raise both my hands. "I'm just going to look. No touching. I promise."

Cal reluctantly lets me go, but when I inch closer to the wall, he comes with me, his chest almost flush against my back, his hand hovering inches from my waist like he's preparing to snatch me back at a moment's notice. I stop about a foot away from the wall, but it's not Millie's blood mark that I study. It's the rip in the yellow-patterned paper.

In Millie's memory, the wall was only half papered. And I can see now that she placed the mark right at the seam where two panels meet. Two panels that noticeably don't align.

"Do you see the flowers?" I ask Cal. "The way the petals don't line up?"

He steps forward so his shoulder is in line with mine. "I see it."

"I think Millie put it up that way on purpose when Jonathan had her trapped in here."

"To mark the spot?"

I nod. "The memory she put in the locket for Jenny didn't reveal very much about what had happened to her. It was only supposed to be a warning, but . . ." I lift the locket in question out from under my shirt and turn it over so the silver back with the cobweb-like design is facing up. "I thought these were just scratches. But when I passed by the door to the storage room tonight, I recognized the pattern and wondered if Millie might have tried to scratch out an image of a spiderweb. I think she did. I think this was supposed to lead Jenny to this attic. To this new memory she left. I don't know if Jenny ever found it, but I think someone else did."

When I turn to Cal, he's watching me intently. "When you came in here tonight, you went straight over there." I nod toward the south-facing oval window. "There was a reason for that, wasn't there?"

His eyes don't leave mine as his chin dips in a nod. It's the answer I was expecting, the answer I already knew, but my stomach flips anyway because I'm finally beginning to understand.

"This where she fell from, isn't it? This is the room my mom came to before she died."

"I don't know." Cal's voice is low, barely above a whisper. "I truly don't. When I saw the window, I thought maybe . . . but I honestly don't know."

But I do. I know it with a certainty that defies all logic, and that I refuse to question.

"My mom was here," I say. "I don't know how she found the locket, but when she was pulled into that first memory, she must have survived it. That's how she knew about Millie. That's how she found her and Jenny's names in that newspaper article. And she must have recognized the spiderweb design in the door, too. She must have come up here and—"

I turn to the torn yellow daisies on the wall. "She's the one who ripped the wallpaper. She found the next memory Millie left, but this time . . ." A tear slips down my cheek, but I wipe it roughly away because it's not grief my mom needs from me now.

"Alma lied about her involvement in the train derailment." I look at Cal, his pale eyes glowing like two silver moons in the lantern light. "She told the world she wanted to make amends for her husband's actions, but she was a *part* of the attempted cover-up. Which means she lied. So what if that's not all she lied about?"

Cal's gaze sharpens. "What do you mean?"

I bite my lip and begin to pace. "It doesn't make sense that Millie's name doesn't appear anywhere in our family's *very* well-documented history. The most obvious explanation is that Alma scrubbed her sister from the family tree herself. I think my mom figured that out. I think she'd already found Millie's locket by the time Gran asked her to take over the Vow. I think she was starting to suspect that there was more to the story than we've been told. And if that's true . . ."

My feet still, because there's no way I'm right about this. I must be grasping at straws. This must be my grief-stricken, guilt-laden mind trying to find some deeper meaning—some larger purpose— in the injustice of my mom's death.

"Hey."

My gaze swings to Cal. He holds out his hand, and I instinctively slip mine inside it. His fingers intertwine with mine, and it's like someone has reached into my mind and turned down the volume on all of my screaming doubts.

Our eyes lock, and I take in a deep breath. "My mom told Francesca that the true history had been hidden. What if she meant *our* true history? My family's history. And this town's. Everything we know about the spirits—everything we know about the drownings—came from Alma. What if *that's* why my mom made that list of names? What if *that's* why she was researching Millie? We know now that Millie was more powerful than Alma, and that whatever happened here a hundred and twenty years ago, she was involved. What if that's why my mom came up here?"

I pause, collecting my breath. "What if she believed that the memories Millie left for Jenny would reveal a way to finally stop the drownings, once and for all?"

Chapter Sixteen

I trace the dotted line my mom drew through Northern France, the tears coming hard and fast.

When we used to play the atlas game together, either she or I would open the atlas to a random page and whatever map we landed on would be the section of the world we'd plan our travels through. So that's what I've been doing since I gave up on sleep an hour ago. Except I'm not making new routes, I'm retracing the ones we already made.

The sun is barely up, and while normally Tab would be yowling for her breakfast the second she realized I was awake, today her warm body is curled next to mine in bed, purring furiously. When I reach the end of the dotted line in the center of Paris, I move to tracing the doodles I drew in the margins. This must have been one of the early routes we plotted because the quality of the art here is below even my ten-year-old standard. There's an oblong shape that I assume is meant to be a baguette, a dog with curly fur that bears a vague resemblance to a poodle, and a little man with a small body and a very large mustache.

My mom was the one who always requested my doodles. She didn't consider a route complete until I'd added my *artistic flourish.* But it wasn't only the doodles in the atlas. She was always asking me to draw things for her.

I turn to a new page and once again I trace the dotted line she made, this time through the Swiss Alps. Even though the atlas was a game, there was a part of me that believed one day, she and I would really go to these places. That we would live out the real-life versions of the adventures we'd planned. And all this time, I thought that was what she'd done. I thought she'd taken our game and made it real, only without me. I imagined her sipping coffee by the river Seine. Hiking the base of Mount Kilimanjaro. Swimming in the Mediterranean Sea.

And I'd hated her for it. Hated her for choosing the world over me. It's why—in seven years—I never once looked for this atlas. It's why I never even realized it was gone. But now, as I look down at the dotted line she made through eastern Germany, all I can see is the life she didn't lead.

The routes she'll never take.

I close my eyes and try to remember the last time I saw her, but all I can think about is that night Gran told her that it was time for her to take over the Vow. I remember thinking she looked trapped. I thought it was more evidence to explain why she left. More proof that she wasn't—maybe never would be—ready to bind herself to this town.

Except she didn't run, and I understand now that wasn't frustration in her eyes.

It was fear.

Cal's words from last night come back to me. *Have you ever thought of not taking the Vow?*

I turn to a new page and trace my finger along the route we plotted through the islands of Greece. I was raised to follow in Alma Blackwell's footsteps. More than that, I *wanted* to. I admired her determination and ingenuity. I wanted that for myself. That's why when Fern made that prediction two years ago, I was so sure it meant that I could be the one to find a way to strengthen the spell *she* began. But Alma isn't who I thought she was. She wasn't even as *powerful* as I thought she was. So what does that mean about the spell she wove? What does that mean about the Vow I'm supposed to take in three days? The spell I'm supposed to bind myself to and become a living part of?

My mom didn't want to take it, but it wasn't because she was a coward, and it wasn't because she was selfish.

So why? Why would she even consider risking the lives of everyone in this town? Was it because she knew the truth about who Alma was? Was it because she'd lost confidence in the spell we're supposed to uphold? Was it because she knew—or hoped— there was another way? Maybe even a way to stop *all* the deaths?

What if Fern's prediction was never about me strengthening Alma's spell? What if it was never *her* work I was meant to finish?

⤸

I don't know what I was expecting to feel when I came into Mom's room, but it wasn't this.

It wasn't nothing.

I knew Gran had it cleaned out three years ago. I knew her clothes were gone, along with the racks that used to hold her beaded jewelry. I knew the bedding and furniture had been swapped out, the walls repainted, and that her framed vintage concert posters had been replaced with the same personality-less landscapes that decorate the rest of the house. But I still thought I'd feel *something*. I still hoped that coming in here for the first time in seven years would trigger some sort of . . . what?

A memory?

A realization?

I don't know. I only know that even though I think I'm beginning to understand what my mom was trying to figure out, I've also hit a dead end.

I'd hoped there'd be something in the attic similar to the spiderweb scratchings on the back of the locket that would lead us to another memory Millie left for Jenny, but Cal and I searched every inch of that attic until our eyes blurred with exhaustion

225

last night, and if Millie did leave some kind of marker, we didn't find it.

The grandfather clock chimes the nine o'clock hour, reminding me that I should be heading downstairs soon to help Cal open up. It also means that I only have three hours until I have to pick Gran up from the hospital, and I'm still too angry and confused to face her. I want to hate her for what she hid from me—what she *took* from me—but at the same time, I can't make myself believe she would ever do anything to intentionally hurt me. Not unless she truly believed it was the only way to keep me safe.

I sink to the floor because this, at least, wasn't replaced. These aged slats are the same ones that touched my mom's skin. The same dark wood that shared her air. And I don't know how it happens, but somehow, my cheek ends up pressed to the cold, varnished wood, my long blue costume skirt spread out in a circle around me. Tears slide down my cheeks, mingling with the light layer of dust, and I think about how unfair it is that when she died, I could feel the fury of spirits I never knew in life, but that my mom—who was equally innocent, and equally wronged—didn't leave so much as a shimmer in the air.

It was a mistake to come in here. A mistake to think this cold, empty room could help me get inside her head. If the atlas couldn't help me, if the visceral memory of her arms wrapped around me, her voice in my ear, her hand skimming across the yellowed pages, couldn't make me see all of this through her eyes, then what could

I have possibly hoped to accomplish by coming into this sterile, abandoned place?

I push myself up to sitting, and as I do, the floor creaks beneath me. Maybe it's only because the atlas is on my mind, but it makes me think of the attic compartment where Millie hid her charm box. I found the loose plank last night before Cal and I left the attic. It had a smooth finger groove just like mine, although there was nothing left inside. I wasn't surprised to discover that she, like me and my mom, hid her treasures beneath the Blackwell House floor since it almost seems like a requirement when you live in a house like this. Something nags at me though. Something about her charm box and our atlas that feels significant. But I can't put my finger on what it is.

I bite my lip and sweep my eyes across the dusty floor.

When I was a kid, it didn't seem at all odd to me that my mom suggested we keep the atlas in a secret place. It was another fun and exciting part of the game we played even though the only person we were actually hiding anything from was Gran, and considering how many times she saw us poring over the pages of the atlas together, it's safe to say she knew about our game.

Except Gran never knew about our hiding place under the floor. She still doesn't. In seven years, I haven't mentioned it once.

An idea forms, and I pitch forward on my hands and knees, scanning the one thing in this room Gran couldn't replace. The one thing that hasn't changed in seven years. Because this wasn't just my mom's room as an adult. This was her childhood bedroom, too. I think about the secret smile she gave me when she first showed me the loose floorboard in my bedroom, like she knew exactly how thrilling it was for a six-year-old to discover a secret hiding place in their very own room. And what if she *did* know? What if, like me, like Millie, my mom had a loose floorboard of her own?

I spot the notch in a board in the far corner of the room beneath the window. The groove is smooth when I hook my first two fingers into it, just like Millie's was.

Just like mine.

I hold my breath, and when I pull, the board lifts up and out of the floor without so much as a creak. Still not daring to breathe, I slide the loose plank aside and plunge my hand into the dark chamber below, feeling around until the back of my finger brushes against something silky and smooth. Carefully, I pinch the edge of what turns out to be a large ziplock bag and pull it into the light. Inside, there's a document covered in what looks like typewriter print, but before I can read what it says, a distant voice calls my name.

"Nev, sweetheart. Are you up here?"

I freeze with my hand clamped around the plastic bag. That's Gran's voice, but I'm not supposed to pick her up from the hospital until noon.

A distinctive metallic creak sounds, and I recognize it instantly as the in-need-of-oiling hinges that bracket the door separating the short stairwell from the second-floor hall. That means she's headed this way, and this is the last place I want her to find me. My body springs into action. I shove the plastic bag with the document under my costume blouse, slide the wooden plank back into place, and sprint for the open door. I'm only just closing it behind me when Gran rounds the corner.

She has her cane with her, but she's not leaning on it as heavily as she was before she left. Her skin is still too pale, but the alarming greyish tint is gone and there's some actual color in her cheeks. The relief that washes through me at the sight of her in relatively little pain is so automatic that it takes me a full second to remember why the sound of her voice sent panic racing through my veins.

"Nev?" She stops in front of me and reaches out her free hand to cup my cheek. "Honey, you look pale. Are you all right?"

I knew I wasn't ready to see her, but I underestimated just how unready I was. The concern, the love, radiating from her is so strong I feel it in my bones. But it's always been like that with her. This is the woman who held my hair back and didn't say a single judgmental word the first time I went out with Bea's friends and got sick after drinking too much. This is the woman who reread my art school essay *fifteen* times and squealed like a teenager when I got in. But this is also the woman who lied to me. Who I used to trust more than anyone in the world, but now . . .

"I'm fine, Gran." I force a smile and hope it doesn't look as false as it feels. "I'm just surprised to see you. I was going to pick you up after the first tour."

"I know you were, sweetie, but Deena was getting off her shift and she's just at the bottom of the hill. We wanted to save you a trip. Did you not see my text?"

I shake my head. "I left my phone in my room. I was just coming up to get it actually."

The lie falls too easily from my lips, and Gran nods, like this makes sense, but her brow is creased and she's studying my face. "Are you sure nothing's wrong, sweetie? You look like you've been crying."

Of course she knows that I've been crying. She's the person I've come to with almost every one of my problems for the past seven years. She knows when I'm upset. She knows when I'm holding something back. So why did I think I could do this? Why did I let myself believe I could keep her from noticing that in a matter of three days, my entire world has been blown apart and now the pieces of me no longer fit?

"I didn't sleep great, that's all. You're worrying too much again."

I'm impressed with how steady my voice sounds, but Gran doesn't look convinced. Her frown deepens as she continues to search my face. "It's my *job* to worry about you, sweetie." She presses her lips together and nods like she's come to a decision. "Come sit with me for a minute, hon."

It's the absolute last thing I want to do, but since bolting down the hallway isn't exactly an option, I let her lead me down the hallway past my mom's room and into the sitting room connected to her bedroom. Before her diagnosis, she spent most of her evenings reading in the armchair by the fire, but that's not the seat she chooses today. Today, she lowers herself onto the loveseat and pats the place next to her.

The urge to confront her, the need to grip her by the shoulders and demand she explain everything to me is all-consuming, but I can't risk it. Gran still has the power of the Vow, and she's proven she's willing to weave charms on my mind. What if she decides that the only way to protect me from whatever she's hiding is to make me forget what I've spent the past three days figuring out?

I sit down and her cold hand reaches out to take mine. "Let me start, sweetheart, by saying that we should have had this conversation some time ago. The fact that we haven't is entirely my fault, and I hope you can forgive me for that."

A breath sticks in my throat. She can't be about to admit to it, can she? She can't know that I know.

Gran notices my reaction and gives me a sad smile. "I suppose my only excuse is that you've always seemed so . . . ready. So much more competent than I ever was at your age. You've taken everything that's been put onto your shoulders with such grace. Such fortitude. And I'm so proud of you for that, sweetheart. I hope you know that. But it does make it easy sometimes for me to forget how . . . difficult all of this is. It's not an excuse. I just want you to understand."

I nod slowly even though I don't understand at all.

"I know we've talked about my own Vow ceremony before, but I don't think I ever mentioned to you that I was . . . well, a bit of a wreck leading up to it, have I?"

I shake my head. Gran was a wreck before her Vow ceremony? *Gran?*

"Yes, well. It's not exactly the story I want my only grand-daughter to remember me by, but suffice it to say, I was more than a little bit nervous. In fact, I believe *terrified* would be a more apt description." She lets out a small, rueful laugh. "And I was much older than you by then, of course. Thirty-five with a child of my own. And yet two days before the ceremony, I was sobbing to my own mother like a little child, convinced that I wasn't up to the task. Convinced that I would let my family—and everyone in this town—down."

I'm stunned to hear my doubts—my fears—coming out of her mouth. She's always been so confident in her role as the holder of the Blackwell family legacy. So committed, so passionate, so sure.

"I tell you this, sweetheart, because you need to understand that anything you are feeling right now—any fear, any nerves, any *doubt* . . . all of it is completely normal. It doesn't mean you aren't ready for this. It means the opposite. It means you understand the significance of the responsibility you are about to take on. It means you understand that this road won't be . . . easy."

Her eyes pierce mine, gauging the effect of her words.

"Do you understand what I'm saying, hon? Because there is nothing you can say to me right now—absolutely *nothing*—that would make me think any less of you."

The silence stretches. She's waiting for me to respond, and I know I should say what she expects me to. I should tell her what I would have told her four days ago. That I'm nervous but ready to step up and uphold this family's legacy. Ready to become a living, breathing part of Alma's spell. Only, for the first time in my life, I'm no longer sure I am.

Gran squeezes my hand and there's so much understanding in her eyes, so much love etched into every line of her face that I don't want to lie to her about this. I'm so angry at her, so hurt, so betrayed, but she's still Gran. She lied to me about Mom, but she also had a real headstone made. Doesn't that mean she intended for me to know the truth one day? And wouldn't she be as horrified as I am to discover the truth about Alma? To say she would be an asset when it comes to figuring all of this out would be the understatement of the century. There's no one alive who knows more about this family's legacy, or about the power and magic that's wrapped up in it. Isn't finding out the truth—potentially stopping the drownings forever—more important than my personal feelings of betrayal?

I wet my lips. "There is something that I've been thinking about recently." She squeezes my hand and nods at me to continue. "I guess, the thing I've been wondering is if we might be . . . wrong."

She blinks a couple of times. "Wrong about what exactly, sweetheart?"

I try to swallow, but my mouth is too dry. "It's just . . . have you ever wondered if Alma wasn't the person we think she was? If the spell she wove isn't the only way to stop the drownings? Have you ever wondered if she . . . lied?"

Gran's eyes flare in surprise. Outside the window, a cloud shifts, and the extra sunlight on her face makes her papery skin appear almost translucent. For a strange moment, I almost think I can see the grey shadow of her skull moving beneath her flesh.

"Sweetheart." She leans forward out of the light, and her skin becomes opaque once more. "I'm going to tell you something my mother told me when I came to her with my own doubts, all right?"

She doesn't wait for me to respond before continuing.

"She took my hand in hers, just like this, and she looked me in the eye and said: the moment you take that Vow, the moment you become a true part of the legacy Alma left us, all of your doubts, all of your fears will fade away. She said, your path will become clear again. Your *purpose* will become clear again. And she was right, Nev hon. She was right about all of it."

I try to hide the disappointment that surges at her response, but she must read some of it on my face because she squeezes my hand again. "I know you think I'm offering you platitudes, but I'm not. It's one of the greatest regrets of my life that I won't be here to guide you through those first few years of the Vow like my mother did for me. But as much as I want that, sweetheart, the truth is, I'm not worried, because I know you'll never truly be alone. When you add your blood—your *essence*—to Alma's spell, you'll join the generations of women in our family who have done the same. It's not only the Vow's power you gain, Nev, you also gain *our* strength. And it's that strength that will see you through every doubt. Every fear. We will be with you through all of it. And I promise you, sweet-heart, we will not let you fail."

The reverent gleam in her eye is one I've seen many times before. It's there on her face whenever she talks about the vital nature of our family's legacy. I used to envy it. I used to hope that someday, I'd feel the same faith and confidence in my life's purpose, but now it fills me with bone-deep unease. She's not only dodging my questions, she's telling me not to ask them at all.

My mom's face flashes into my mind. Her wide, terrified eyes the night Gran announced it was time for her to take the Vow. And even though I know I shouldn't ask it, even though it's too much of a risk, I can't stop myself from opening my mouth. I can't stop the words from tumbling out.

"Did Mom have questions? Did you tell her the same thing?"

Gran blinks, and I don't think I'm imagining the flash of guilt that crosses her face. But guilt for what? For lying to me? Or is there more?

She presses her lips together like she's considering my question. Then she places a second hand on top of mine so my fingers are sandwiched between the thin, papery skin of her two palms. "Your mother . . ."

She trails off, presses her lips back together, then begins again. "I love your mother dearly. Nothing will ever change that. But Celia . . . she's never understood what it means to be a part of this family. So yes, we had many conversations about the Vow, and I told her much of what I've told you today. But eventually, I had to accept that, although I'll always love my daughter, there's nothing I could ever say that would make her take her responsibility to this family seriously."

"Is that why you told her that she needed to start acting like a Blackwell?"

"Excuse me?"

Gran looks . . . *shocked* is the only word I can think of. I'm shocked, too. I didn't make a conscious decision to ask that question out loud, but when she was speaking, all I could think about was the fight I overheard between Gran and Mom in the hallway that night. I thought they'd been arguing about the room on the tour Mom wanted to dedicate to the victims of the 1903 massacre, but what if they weren't? What if they were having a version of *this* conversation?

Gran narrows her eyes in confusion, but I don't take the question back. Now that it's out, I want an answer. "I heard you. The night you said that. The night you and Mom fought. I was in the hallway. Neither of you saw me."

Gran's eyes flash and her chin juts out in a gesture so reminiscent of Alma that for a second, my heart stops. "And did you . . . hear what we were discussing?"

I don't want her to know that I'm not exactly sure what I heard, so I dip my head in a nod.

"Well." She gathers her composure and offers me a tight, pained smile. "If that's the case, then I'm sorry, sweetheart. It's not often that I lose my temper, but as you must know, I did that night."

I nod again, hoping she'll go on without asking me to elaborate on what I heard her lose her temper *about*.

She does.

"You have to understand, hon, even as a little girl, your mother was a dreamer. An idealist. And there's nothing wrong with that. Nothing at all. But this family has responsibilities. Duties that we are sworn to uphold. And as uncomfortable as it is, as much as we may not like it, the spirit drownings are kept quiet for a reason. You understand that, don't you, sweetheart? You understand why it's necessary?"

It takes every ounce of control I have not to let the surprise show on my face.

My mom didn't want to keep the spirit drownings quiet? That's what she and Gran were arguing about? That's why Gran accused her of not acting like a Blackwell?

The realization is staggering. The implications . . .

No. I can't let myself think about the implications right now. I can't start cataloging all the ways this might change the way Cal and I look at my mom's list of names.

Gran is watching me.

Closely.

And far from restoring my trust in Gran, this conversation has only confirmed that even though there's still so much I don't understand, I made the right decision not confiding in her. And that

237

means that I need her to leave this conversation thinking nothing has changed. Thinking I still believe the lie.

"Of course," I say. Solemn. Serious. "Of course I understand."

Relief softens her features, and a small smile lifts the corners of her lips as she pats my hand. "I know you do, sweetheart. I know you do."

Silence falls between us, and I glance at the clock on the mantel above the unlit fireplace. I need to head downstairs to meet the morning tour group soon, but before I can say as much to Gran, she speaks again.

"I want you to promise me something, Nev dear. Can you do that?"

I don't know how much longer I can fake the shining trust I'm forcing into my eyes, but I grit my teeth and nod again.

"If you have . . . doubts like this again, after I'm gone, I want you to remember that Alma should have died all those years ago, right along with the child in her womb." Her amber eyes bore into mine, determined and resolute. "She knew the spirits wouldn't spare her, but she refused to roll over and accept that fate. The only reason you and I are alive today is because Alma found a way to survive. For *us*. For this family. So when you have questions, sweetheart, when you have doubts, I want you to remember that *that* is the legacy you carry. *That* is what it means to be a Blackwell. We do what we must to survive. We always have."

Chapter Seventeen

A gust of wind rattles the windows of the old caretaker cottage, and the soft yellow lights in the wall sconces flicker. The couch cushions Cal and I pulled onto the living room floor so we could spread out aren't as good at combating the chill as the plush carpets of the Rose Room, but even though Gran's night meds usually knock her out, I don't want to be under the same roof as her right now.

I pull the musty, patchwork quilt tighter around my shoulders, and—for what must be the hundredth time in the past hour—trace my finger along the document spread out in my lap and read the line my mom underlined in Alma Blackwell's will.

To my neighbor Jennifer Murphy, I leave my heart-hair silver locket in the hopes that she will receive it with the love and friendship with which it is offered.

My mom wasn't hiding Alma's original will under her floorboards. As far as I know, that's safely tucked away in some lawyer's office. This is a photocopy. One I assume she obtained from said lawyer's office, and its presence in her room suggests a pretty obvious answer to how she knew about Millie's locket because there's no doubt in my mind that the *heart-hair silver locket* referred to here is the one currently hanging around my neck.

I look around the cozy living room that I've come to so often when needing comfort. Is this where my mom found the necklace? In the place where Jenny Murphy lived? And why did Alma leave Jenny the locket in her *will*? Clearly, she broke her promise to deliver it to Jenny when Millie asked her to, but why finally follow through with it in such an oddly dramatic way?

The line my mom underlined wasn't even in the original will. It was added as an addendum, witnessed and dated by the Blackwell lawyer two days before Alma's death. Apart from a few monetary pensions left to longtime staff members and a handful of sizable charitable donations, it's the only specific bequest that Alma made. Everything else—the house, the furniture, her jewelry, all her assets—were left to the Blackwell estate, which was inherited by her and Jonathan's daughter, Lily.

Not a lot is known about the illness that took Alma's life when she was a mere forty-seven years old. The doctor who attended her kept a diary that I read once because Lily Blackwell promptly obtained it upon the good doctor's death for our private family archives. In it, he vents his frustration that his patient's body was wasting away even though she was able to take in fluids and keep solid food down. He theorized that she might have been afflicted with an unknown disease of the mind since she often took to rambling over and over again that *her love would save them all* and frequently spoke about Jonathan as if he were still among the living.

I finger the edge of the will, wondering if Alma's reasons matter now. My mom seemed to believe there are answers buried in our family's past, but will any of them help me figure out what I'm supposed to do—what she would *want* me to do—at the Vow ceremony in just under three days?

I rub my eyes and look over to where Cal's sitting on the blue couch cushions next to me, his back against the sofa's frame, his head bent over the laptop screen. While I've been studying the will, he's taken the lead on going back through my mom's list of names in case the true cause of her and Gran's fight that night reveals any new connections between the people she circled.

Cal looks up from the screen when he senses my gaze. His eyes are especially blue tonight. They've been like that since we first got here, and I think it might be because he instantly liked my cottage, which makes me happy. I've always felt at ease here, and despite everything that's happening right now, it's nice to share it with someone.

"Figure anything else out?"

I shake my head and push the copy of the will off my lap onto the pillow-covered floor. "I'm pretty sure this is how my mom knew about the locket, but I don't know if it tells us anything else. What about you?"

"Not yet, but I'm only a quarter of the way through the list, and . . ."

"And what?"

"Maybe it's just wishful thinking, but I feel like we're close to something."

I turn sideways and lean my shoulder against the couch to face him fully. His jet-black hair is mussed again, and I have the most insatiable urge to run my fingers through it. An urge I need to tamp down. Quickly. Because my exhaustion is inches away from overpowering my self-control. "Can I ask you something?"

His lips quirk. "I think we've established that you can, yes."

I pause a moment, not sure if I want to ask this. Not sure if I should. "Are they on the list?"

He gives me a confused look. "Who?"

"The person she lost. The girl who you . . ."

But the words die on my tongue because even though it's only a flash, I see it. That careful neutral mask slipping into place. The one he wears when he's about to lie.

I rear back. "Oh my God."

"Nev, wait." He pushes the laptop aside and reaches out to me, but I scramble back on the cushions.

"No. Don't pretend, Cal. Don't pretend like you weren't just about to lie to me."

His face pales, but he doesn't deny it.

"Is she even real? Just tell me that. That girl? Or did you lie about her, too?"

He looks at me like his heart is breaking. "I've told you the truth about everything I can."

"Everything you can isn't the same as everything."

"I know."

"Oh, you know? Well, okay then."

He runs a hand down his face and swears under his breath. "I can imagine what you're thinking right now, but Nev, the *only* thing I've done since I got here is try to help you. If you think about it, you'll know it's true. And that's all I *want* to do."

I shake my head wordlessly at him.

"And before you ask," he continues, "I swear that I haven't held anything back about your mom. I've told you everything that I know."

"So it's just yourself you lied about?" Another rush of wind blows past the cottage and the windows clank and rattle in their frames. "Are you actually from Oregon? Do you have a sister? Do you even know how to *fish*?"

"Yes, I live in Eugene. Yes, I have an annoying little sister. Yes, I almost drowned going ice fishing. I'm still me, Nev. I'm—"

"I have no idea who *you* are. That's the problem!" I push myself to my feet and back away.

"Please, Nev." He stands, too, but doesn't move to approach me. "Please don't shut me out over this. That ceremony is in *three* days, and we have to figure out what all of this means before then. Whatever is going on here, it's too big for you to face alone. You need help."

I turn around because I can't bear to see the ravaged torment on his face. Not after coming face-to-face with Gran this morning. I can't take any more of this. I can't care about anyone else who's lying to me.

I wrap my arms around myself and try to calm my breathing by staring up at what's always been my favorite wall in the cottage. It's a gallery wall, but it's nothing like the formal displays in Blackwell House. Instead of gloomy professional oil paintings in gilt frames, this wall is covered in simply framed pictures that range from childhood crayon drawings to detailed sketches and even a few quite lovely watercolors. I've always assumed they were drawn by members of the Murphy family when they lived here, and I've always been jealous of it. Gran has dozens of my best drawings framed in her sitting room, but she would never display such personal, amateur work in a public-facing room like this.

Cal says my name again, but I don't turn around and the silence between us becomes a physical thing. A barrier separating him from me. After a few long, torturous minutes, I hear the sound of the laptop keys clicking again. I don't tell him to stop. I don't yell at him to get out. Because he's right. I do need his help.

My gut is telling me that my mom wouldn't want me to go through with the Vow, but I can't refuse to take it and risk the lives of everyone in this town. So if my mom knew of some other way, I need to figure out what it was, and I have less than three days to do it. Cal may be lying to me about who he is, but I also can't deny that his every action since arriving here tells me that he wants to find out the truth as much as I do.

I take out my frustration on my lip, biting it so hard I'm surprised I don't taste blood. My restless gaze flits over the frames on the wall until it lands, as it has before, on a charcoal drawing that doesn't fit with the rest of the joyful, family-friendly pieces that surround it.

It's a portrait of the mythical figure Medusa, her features split in two. The right side of her body looks almost exactly like the statue in the Greek goddess section of the Blackwell sculpture garden. Her hair is a writhing nest of snakes, her bare breast is exposed, the corner of her mouth is opened wide in a terrifying scream, and her larger-than-life right eye looks more than capable of turning every man it falls upon into stone.

Her left side, however, is not monstrous at all. Her hair is still a bit wild, but it falls in luscious waves down to her waist. Her eye is not only human-sized, but the artist added little creases next to it to match the soft smile on her lips. And while the hand on the right side is drawn with clawlike nails curled into a fist, her left hand's long, graceful fingers rest peacefully over her heart.

A rush of rain falls heavy on the roof, and I rub my hands up and down my arms. I'm used to our cold Northern California summers, but this storm feels like it came directly from the Arctic. The *tap-tapping* of keys quickens behind me, but I'm not ready to face Cal again so I let my gaze wander farther up the gallery wall.

There's a much smaller charcoal sketch higher up that looks like it was done by the same person who drew the split-down-the-middle Medusa. It's not one of the pictures I've paid much attention to before because it's a pretty typical landscape featuring Hollow Cliff's oft-depicted bluffs overlooking a turbulent sea. But now that I *am* paying attention to it, I wonder how I haven't noticed it before. For a simple landscape, there's a surprisingly evocative energy to it. It's so high up on the wall that it's hard to make out much of the detail, but even from a distance, it makes me think about something I read in an art book once about the kind of paintings that study *you* as much as you study *them*. Like they're waiting to see if you can still your mind long enough to hear what they have to say.

I step closer to the wall, curious to see it up close, but Cal's voice halts me.

"Nev. You need to see this."

I turn, tensing at the urgent clip of his voice. "What is it? What did you find?"

He shakes his head like he's too stunned to speak, and I'm across the room in a second. He hands me the laptop, which is open to a full-sized browser window with a transcript from an old Hollow Cliff city council meeting. The typed line at the very top of the screen is the chair recognizing a city council member named—

Beverly Price.

My eyes fly to Cal, but he just shakes his head. "Read it."

So that's what I do.

I read a speech that Beverly Price delivered while she served on the city council. A speech that not only publicly acknowledges the drownings, but that refers to them as an endemic that needs to be—

"She wanted the drownings categorized as *homicides*?"

Cal's leaning back against the sofa, his hands braced on either side of his head like he's trying to keep his skull from exploding. At my question, he looks up and gives a grim nod. "She says there that it would mean a documented investigation into each death. And look at the last two paragraphs."

I scroll down, my eyes scanning the text.

"Wait." I read the first line again. "She was running for mayor?"

"She was planning to. This speech was her announcement. And she also announces here that her position on the drownings will be a centerpiece of her campaign, so that win or lose, the issue will be a part of the public debate."

It feels like I've been punched in the stomach. I slump back against the couch, my mind racing as I try to figure out exactly what this means.

"You think that's the connection," I whisper. "My mom circled Beverly Price's name. My mom wanted to change the way we responded to the drownings, and Beverly Price did, too."

When I lift my eyes to Cal, he holds my gaze and despite everything, in this moment, I'm glad he's here. I'm grateful I'm not in this alone.

"Look at the date of that meeting," he says. "And then look at this."

He leans across me and navigates the cursor so it pulls up the typed list we made with information about each of the people on my mom's list, including the date of their death.

The date next to Beverly Price's name makes my stomach twist.

"Beverly Price called for the Hollow Cliff drownings to be investigated," Cal says. "She said the victims deserved true justice. Three days later, she became one of them."

Chapter Eighteen

The second Cal and I step out on the patio of Mystery Grounds, Fern Fairchild's head snaps up.

The storm continued all through the night, so most of the metal tables and chairs are still wet from the rain. Add that to the thick layer of marine fog currently hanging in the air, and it explains why the rest of the fortune tellers and morning caffeine addicts are all huddled inside the café. Not Fern, though. She's set up at her usual table, the crystal ball, tarot card decks, and chipped tea service all spread out on her shiny purple cloth. Her multi-layered scarves are varying shades of red and orange today, her curly, white hair is loose and frizzy around her face, and from behind her red-rimmed glasses, her owl-like eyes are fixed on us.

Beside me, Cal is quiet, waiting for me to take the lead. He's been like that since last night. Careful. Watchful. Like I'm a bomb primed to go off and he doesn't want to trip the wrong wire. It's driving me crazy, but I refuse to think about it right now because as desperately as I need the triple shot latte currently warming my hands, coffee isn't the reason we came here today.

After he found the transcript of Beverly Price's city council speech, Cal and I spent the rest of the night researching the names my mom circled, but this time, we looked for anything they might have ever said or written about the Hollow Cliff drownings.

Unfortunately, the local neighborhood boards don't make their meeting minutes available online, and if anyone else circled on that list made a bombshell city council speech, we haven't found it yet. But we did stumble across something potentially interesting about Daniel Wiley, who drowned two years before Beverly Price when he stole a sailboat and took it out to the open sea during a violent storm. Daniel Wiley served as a deputy in the Hollow Cliff sheriff's department for thirty years, but a week before he died, he was laid off. We knew that from our previous research into him, just like we knew that a week before that, there was a short bulletin in the *Hollow Cliff Gazette* announcing his intention to run against the town's long-standing sheriff in the upcoming election. But it wasn't until last night that we looked closely at the article itself. In particular, a quote from Deputy Wiley stating that he intended to run for sheriff on a platform of reform. And his first order of business? Changing the culture of the Hollow Cliff sheriff's department by addressing some *pervasive and harmful beliefs that have long been held within the department.*

There's no proof that he was referring to the lack of investigations into the deaths caused by the drownings, but the fact that he—like Beverly Price—announced his campaign two weeks before his death? It's too much of a coincidence to ignore.

But the reason I lied to Gran and said we ran out of coffee beans this morning is because last night, we also stumbled across an archived post hosted on one of those old-school web 2.0 blogs about local paranormal activity that—while it didn't mention any of the people on my mom's list by name—did include a reference to Blackwell House in a Halloween roundup post about the ten most haunted places to visit in California.

The fact that Blackwell House is listed in the number one most haunted slot isn't unusual. But what *is* unusual is that while most posts like this simply recount the basic story we tell about the train crash, the 1903 massacre, and Alma's Vow, this post continued on to say that a *friend of the blog* had alerted the writer to an interesting development about the local Hollow Cliff coroner who'd gained the attention of some amateur paranormal enthusiasts who work for the state government. Apparently, the coroner in question sent a letter to an official claiming that the spirit attacks on the people of Hollow Cliff never stopped.

And it just so happens that the coroner who was employed in Hollow Cliff during the time this post was first published? One of the names circled on my mom's list. And although he was older than both Beverly Price and Daniel Wiley when he died, he's the only one with a close family member still living in Hollow Cliff.

Well, ex-family member.

"Good morning, Fern."

I know she hears me because she watched our approach to her table with the same intensity Tabitha employs when she's stalking a spider through the house. But, in a rare occurrence, the intensity of her gaze does *not* immediately fix on me. Instead, she's staring at Cal. And she keeps staring at him as she tilts her head and says, "Home is where the heart lives, deary."

He doesn't say anything for a beat too long, and I nudge him in the ribs because we went over what he was supposed to say in the car.

"Oh, right. Um, hi, Fern. And yes, home is where the heart lives. I know."

It's not the perfect response, but as long as you agree with her, Fern's not very picky about the exact wording. That's why I'm surprised when her customary nod of approval doesn't come, and instead, she keeps staring at Cal.

No, not staring. She's *glaring* at him. Her dark brown eyes grow narrower and narrower behind those red frame glasses, and when she finally does speak, it's in a low hiss. "Little boys shouldn't *lie*."

Cal's eyebrows shoot up, and my jaw falls open.

I've never seen Fern snap at someone before. I've seen her get agitated when they don't respond the way she wants them to, but she usually just keeps repeating herself until she gets an answer she likes. And while she can be very insistent, she's always . . . well, sweet about it.

But there's nothing sweet about the animosity she's directing at Cal. I'm so thrown that it takes me a couple of seconds to gather my wits and draw her attention back to me.

"Um, Fern. We're actually here because I was wondering if you'd have time for a read—"

Fern jumps out of her seat before I can finish the word *reading*. She shoves her chipped teapot into Cal's chest and demands that he return *quick as a tick* with hot water from one of the baristas inside. The next thing I know, Cal and I are sitting across from Fern at her table and I'm throwing back a bitingly bitter cup of herbal tea that has an eerily similar taste to the cup I drank two years ago.

"Now don't drink it all, pet. They're young to drown, but sacrifices must be made."

Cal stiffens beside me, and I choke so hard on my last sip of tea that tears spring to my eyes. Oblivious to this, Fern plucks the small ceramic cup from my hand, and slams it enthusiastically on the table in front of her. She bows her head to examine the loose tea leaves stuck to the bottom, and over the rim of the cup, I can see that they're still covered in less than a fingernail's width of hot water. Not enough for them to float, but enough for them to look as if they . . .

Drowned.

Is that what she meant? Was she talking about the tea leaves?

"Mmmm-hmm." Fern hums softly in the back of her throat. "I think I see, pet. I do think I see."

She sounds pleased, like she's just figured out something of extreme importance, and when her eyes lift to mine, they're beaming with triumph. "What do you think about water in your future, pet? It could be rain, but it's hard to tell these days."

"I . . . um." I glance up at the overcast sky, which is all but covered in dark grey rain clouds ready to burst. I share a glance with Cal because this is what I was telling him about Fern's fortunes. What she tells you isn't always particularly mind-blowing. One time she told Bea that she should clip her nails, and when she didn't right away, Bea got a hangnail. Technically good advice, just not what you normally go to a fortune teller for.

"I could see some rain in my immediate future, yes."

Fern's teeth flash in a smile. "Yes. It's soggy, pet. Very *soggy.*"

She lowers her head to examine the soggy bottom of the cup again. If a weather prediction is all Fern's going to offer today, I'm fine with that. I wait another moment to make sure she's definitely finished, and then I lean forward and ask the question we truly sought her out for this morning.

"Fern, I was wondering if I could ask you about your ex-husband, Arthur. Would that be all right?"

Her head snaps up. "Art?"

I nod. "Yes, Art. He was the coroner here for a long time, right?"

Fern wrinkles her nose, like this is something she needs to think about. Then she nods. "They don't always see it right away. Men. But my Art did in the end. Said he was sorry it took so long. You'll see for yourself one day, pet. Or maybe . . ." She shoots a sly glance in Cal's direction, then winks at me. "Maybe you already have, hm?"

I have . . . no idea how to respond to that, so I ignore it and continue with the line of questioning Cal and I fine-tuned on the car ride here. "We were wondering if Arthur—Art, I mean—ever spoke to you about his . . . work?"

She tilts her head in a very birdlike movement. "Of course he did, dear. We were married for twenty years."

I blink, taken aback by how . . . lucid she just sounded.

Beside me, Cal leans forward, like he too has sensed this and wants to capitalize on it. "Did Art ever talk to you about the Hollow Cliff drownings, Fern? Did he ever say anything to you about the autopsy reports he submitted? Or about any reports he sent to the state?"

Apart from her not-so-subtle glance at him a moment ago— and a brief interaction when he delivered the hot water for the tea—Fern's done a pretty thorough job of ignoring Cal since we sat down. But now, she turns to him, and as she does, her eyes narrow again into slits. "Are you asking why he died, little boy?"

Cal's eyes fly to mine.

"Yes, Fern," I say quickly, my pulse racing. "Cal and I are here because that's exactly what we want to know. We want to know *why* Art died."

A seagull squawks overhead, the flap of its wings disrupting the air as it lands on the table next to us. Fern's eyes follow the bird's movement, and I follow hers, holding my breath as she watches the gull's curved yellow beak pick at the scraps of someone's abandoned, half-eaten croissant.

"He told me not to come back for it."

She's still watching the bird tear apart its pastry, so her face is in profile to me, but I can hear the bleak sorrow in her voice and see the sudden slump of her shoulders. I hesitate, not wanting to upset or push her too far. Under the table, Cal's hand presses against mine, and when I raise my eyes to his, he gives me a subtle nod of encouragement.

Taking a breath, I look back across the table. "What does that mean, Fern? What didn't Art want you to come back for?"

She blinks but doesn't look away from the seagull who, instead of gulping down the last scrap of croissant, picks it up in its beak and, with a flurry of wings, takes off from the table. It doesn't fly far though. Just about a dozen yards until it lands on the edge of the memorial fountain in the center square, its scaly yellow talons curved over the edge of the base where the names of the victims from the 1903 massacre are inscribed.

Fern twists her neck to follow the bird's flight, and my eyes bounce between her solemn expression and the stone fountain still dark with rain. Is she thinking the same thing I am? Is she thinking that her ex-husband's name should be inscribed there, too? Because it should be. So should Beverly Price's. And Coach Harrison's and Daniel Wiley's. So should every single person the spirits have killed, including my mom. No matter what Gran says, they all deserve to be mourned. Honored.

Known.

A second seagull lands next to the first, and when the new bird makes a dive for the croissant scrap, a lot of squawking and wing flapping ensues. It's not until both birds have taken flight and dis-appeared into the clouds that Fern turns back to me, her dark brown eyes sparkling with unshed tears.

"For his funeral, pet. He told me so that night." She closes her eyes and a single tear slides down her wrinkled cheek. "So young, you know. So young to drown."

Chapter Nineteen

Cal and I don't make it back to the cottage until after ten that night. With the Vow ceremony only two days away now, the number of daily visitors to Blackwell House is four times even our highest summer attendance numbers. I added three additional tours and we still had to turn people away.

When the last visitor finally left, the out-of-town cleaning and gardening crew arrived for a pre-ceremony spruce-up of the house and grounds. Right on their heels was Elaine Taylor of Taylored Events, armed with a preliminary day-of-ceremony itinerary and about a million mind-numbing questions and updates. But the worst part of the day was lunch with Gran and the smile I had to paste on my face to combat her constant probing looks.

Now, I'm curled up in an armchair in the cottage's living room, my fingers clutching my mom's atlas like it's a life preserver as Cal works a groove in the floor by pacing restlessly back and forth while he listens to me say the same thing I've already said several dozen times since we left the coffee shop this morning.

"It doesn't make sense. Arthur Fairchild was in his *early sixties* when he died. Of course his life was cut short, and of course it's horrific, but why would Fern say he was *young* when he drowned?"

I attempted to ask Fern this exact question this morning, but after her solemn and relatively clear-minded pronouncement that her ex-husband had instructed her not to come to his future funeral, she clammed up and refused to talk about anything except the weather and how she might have been wrong about the rain. A roundabout and increasingly frustrating conversation that also turned out to be somewhat prescient because twenty minutes after we left the coffee shop, the thick army of rain clouds cleared away to reveal a bright blue sky.

Cal shakes his head and runs a hand through his hair. "I have no idea." While I was stuck at the house, he got a roaring fire started in the hearth, and now the flickering light dances across his face. "Maybe to her, that *is* young. But I don't think his age is what matters here." He stops pacing and turns to face me. His stormy eyes are bloodshot from lack of sleep and his hair is sticking up at the back. "He wasn't sick. He was still going to work. So he must have known—or strongly suspected—that he was going to be attacked. Why else would he call his ex-wife and warn her against coming to his *funeral*?"

I look down at the atlas in my lap, but what I actually see is Robbie Harrison, his face hollow and pale in the moonlight as his dark eyes searched my face that night at the cove.

Did you see it?

Is that why?

No matter what he said later, I'm now positive that in that moment, Robbie believed his father had been targeted by the spirits because of something his son had done. Did Art Fairchild believe the same thing? Is that why my mom circled his name? Is it why she circled Beverly Price's and Daniel Wiley's names, too? Robbie may not have been running for local office or writing to state officials about the true cause of the drownings, but he *did* shine a public light on them. He did call the story we tell the world into question.

And there are seven more names circled on my mom's list. Did they speak out about the drownings, too? Right now, that seems like the most logical connection to make. Except . . .

"I don't understand why they would do it." I look up from my lap. "Why would the spirits target Art Fairchild? Or Beverly Price? Or even Robbie's dad? They didn't care if people knew about the deaths they caused after the train crash. If anything, don't you think they'd *want* the world to know that their retaliation—their vengeance—never truly stopped?"

Cal drops into the chair across from me. "I don't know." He props his elbows on his knees and stares down at his hands like maybe there's an answer lurking in the shadows between his fingers. "I honestly don't know."

My own fingers curl tighter around the edges of the atlas. The closer I get to understanding what my mom knew—or at least what she was trying to figure out—the closer I want to be to the physical objects I know she once touched. I left the copy of Alma's will here last night, tucked away in the drawer of the writing desk in the corner of the living room. And tonight, I decided to bring our atlas, her original handwritten list of names, and the copy of the *Gazette* article to store out here, too.

But it's not my mom's handwriting or even the maps inside the atlas that I'm thinking about now. It's the little landscape drawing high up on the wall across from me that I noticed last night. My eyes have been seeking it out since I got here, and this time, when I squint up at it, I think I might understand why.

Setting the atlas aside, I stand and cross the room so I'm directly underneath the drawing, my head tilted up, my hands on my hips. It's difficult to make out the details from this far away, but—

Yes. Right there. At the very edge of the cliff are two human figures standing side by side. I missed them before because they're tiny. Ants in comparison to the massive sweeping cliffs and stretch of stormy sea that takes up 90 percent of the composition. It reminds me of the way the Romantics chose to emphasize the sheer awesomeness of the natural world in comparison to our minuscule human lives.

Dragging a chair over from the writing desk, I position it underneath the drawing.

"Nev? What are you doing?"

I step up onto the chair, bring my face level with the frame, and then—

I see them.

Two girls dressed in long skirts and blouses strikingly similar to the costume I wear for the house tours. They're facing the sea with their backs to the viewer and their long hair is wild as if it's being pushed back by the wind. Each girl has one arm wrapped around the other's waist and their free arm flung out wide in the air. When taken together, their figures almost seem to merge into the outline of a bird eager to take flight, wings angled and ready to lift into the wind.

Like the Medusa drawing below it, the piece is unsigned, but I know in my bones who the artist is. Just like I know who the two girls in this drawing are meant to represent.

I lift the frame off the wall, and when I turn to step down, Cal is standing on my left with his foot braced on the bottom rung of the chair and his hand gripping the wooden back to keep it from tipping over. When he sees the drawing up close, his eyes widen.

"Is that—"

"Millie and Jenny," I say. "I think so."

He helps me down from the chair, and I place the frame gently on the ground, glass side down. Cal crouches beside me, but when he sees I'm having trouble getting the backing off the frame, he mutters that he'll be right back and quickly returns with a small kitchen knife. After a couple minutes of poking and prying, I lift the thin wood back. There's something there, flattened between the drawing and the frame. A letter, the words *Dear Jenny* written in looping script on the very top. And I know, even before I see the reddish-brown smudge at the bottom of the page beneath Millie's signature, what this is, because a shivering chill races through my blood.

I drop the thin wood backing and it lands on the floor with a thud. The urge to reach out and touch Millie's blood mark is all-consuming, but I force myself to scramble back a full foot. Except I'm not sure how long I can hold out. Already, the effort is causing my entire body to shake.

Cal looks from me to the letter and then back at me. "Do you trust me?"

It's a loaded question, and we both know it. The answer should be no, but this isn't a moment for lies.

"Yes," I whisper.

Relief softens his face and he holds out his hand to me, palm up. "Take my hand."

I don't ask why, and I don't hesitate. I slip my hand in his, and when his callused fingers close around mine, an entirely different kind of shiver races across my skin. And something else, too. A warm, gentle purr deep within my bones. It takes me a moment to realize what it is.

Safety.

Cal slides the picture frame across the floor until it—and the letter with the dried drop of blood—is within my reach. Flames from the fire flicker in his stormy eyes as he tightens his grip on my hand. "Don't let go of me, okay?"

He doesn't explain, and I don't ask him to. I also don't think about what happened the last two times I came into contact with one of the marks Millie left. Right or wrong, my mom told me that when my blood whispers, I should listen. And right now, those whispers are drowning out every other thought in my head.

Trust Cal.

Find out what Millie left.

I lower my gaze to the letter, and the second I focus on it, my hand shoots out. The pad of my pointer finger connects with the blood mark, and that unnatural cold shoves itself under my skin. I close my eyes, and when I open them again, Cal is gone. I'm in a small, cramped room bathed in shadow. The only hint of light comes from a narrow window high up on the wall through which the faintest trace of moonlight limps through.

Millie is huddled on a cold stone floor, her back pressed against the wall, her wrists tied together with rope in front of her body. Her face is lifted to gaze at the tiny slip of window as if she just might be able to steal a glimpse of the stars lighting up the night sky if she only tries hard enough.

She's not in her filthy nightgown and wrap anymore because Alma did come through on the promise of water to wash and a clean change of clothes. Both were delivered to the attic only a couple of hours after Alma left yesterday, although the fallout from that delivery didn't play out how either side had hoped.

The memory flashes through her mind, vivid and painful. Rodney's cruel, weasel-like face smirking as he tossed not her own clothes into the attic but a faded black dress so worn and thin that it wouldn't be fit for even the lowest member of the kitchen staff. He left an enamel bowl of ice-cold water, too, but no cloth, which meant Millie had to use the soiled corner of her nightgown to clean what she could of the grime off her skin.

She did it though. And she put on the thin black dress, too. And as she did, she promised herself that if she got out of this, she would never again fail to appreciate how good it felt to be clean. Once she was done, she picked up the very full chamber pot that Rodney had failed to take away and empty for the past two days, stationed herself by the entrance to the attic, and waited.

Even now, the memory of Rodney's shocked face—his horrified, spluttering wail as she dumped the chamber pot over his head and bolted into the passageway—brings a small smile to her lips. Her stunt gave her so much of a head start that she made it all the way to the storage closet before he caught up with her, his meaty hands gripping the flesh of her arms so hard, she can still feel their mark.

It had been a reckless and desperate thing to do, but once she realized that no one—not even her sister—would help her escape, reckless and desperate is exactly what she became. And now, as punishment, she's been locked away in a cellar room that she didn't even know existed.

It's not a room I recognize either, although there's something vaguely familiar about it. It's less than a quarter the size of the attic, and in addition to being dank and cold and miserable, it's completely and utterly bare. She hasn't been given so much as a single blanket to wrap around her shivering body.

The door flies open, and Millie turns her head, blinking at the sudden flare of lantern light. When her eyes adjust, it's to the unwelcome sight of none other than rat-faced Rodney. The room is so small, it only takes three strides for him to reach her. And once he's standing in front of her, looking down, she sees the glint of silver in his other hand.

It's a knife. Rodney sees her notice it, and his teeth flash. "Not so brave now, are you, little witch?"

In one swift movement, he lowers to a crouch, sets the lantern on the floor, and seizes the rope binding Millie's wrists.

Her heart pounds. She knows she's no match for Rodney's physical strength. She knows she's at his mercy now, and the truth of that terrifies her as much as it infuriates her. Slowly, menacingly, he runs the tip of the knife up the underside of her arm. The pressure is light enough not to break the skin, but heavy enough to leave a thin scratch of red. Rodney must see something that pleases him in Millie's face because he laughs—a wheezy, high-pitched giggle that makes her stomach turn—and then in another swift movement, he uses the knife to cut the rope of her bindings in two.

Cold, hard fury chases away every trace of fear in Millie's blood. She's done with Rodney's games. She's done with allowing him to think he can terrorize her without consequences. Hauling back her head, Millie purses her lips and spits directly in his face.

Rodney rears back and splutters, but his outrage isn't quite satisfying enough, so she hauls back her head and prepares to do it again.

"I would reconsider if I were you, Millicent. Unless you want our dear Miss Murphy to suffer for even more of your sins?"

She whips her head around, mouth instantly dry at her brother-in-law's words. She can't see his face at first because he's cloaked in the shadows that lurk in the dark cellar room, but at her movement, he steps forward into the sphere of lantern light. He's dressed as immaculately as always. His perfectly tailored suit emphasizes his broad, muscular build, but it's his smile that chills Millie to the bone. All teeth, like a predator moving in for the kill.

She wants desperately to demand he explain what he meant about *Miss Murphy*, but she's also afraid of revealing too much. Of saying anything that might put Jenny in harm's way. And maybe he guesses at her thoughts because the next thing he says is, "Not to worry, Millicent. Your secret is safe with me. Young love. Always such a *joy*."

Millie's breath stops. Black spots cloud her vision, and the entire basement room blurs before her eyes.

How?

They were careful. So careful. How could Jonathan have—

"Alma."

She says it aloud, and even though it's not a question, Jonathan answers her. "Indeed." He tilts his head, examining Millie the way you would an animal at the zoo. *"Alma.* Not the wife I wanted. Not the wife I *deserve.* But she has proven to be not entirely useless."

Millie lowers her head, only vaguely aware of Rodney wiping his face and leaving the room as she swallows back the bile rising in her throat.

"I was quite sure her plea to you wouldn't work," Jonathan continues in that frustratingly mild voice. "But she insisted I let her try. My dear wife seemed to think that your sisterly bond would prevail where my methods had not. So you must imagine her disappointment, Millicent, when she discovered that despite your *promise,* you never had any intention of helping your family after all."

Millie lifts her head. "You are *not* my family."

Jonathan smiles like he's pleased with her reaction. He likes it, Millie realizes. He likes seeing evidence of the pain he's caused.

"Believe me, dear sister, I'm no more pleased about it than you are. Surely you don't think I set out to bring a pair of *witches* into my home?"

He means it as an insult, but Millie doesn't see it that way. She's grateful for his words. They remind her that she's not nearly as powerless as Jonathan thinks. "And that doesn't worry you, *brother*? You aren't concerned about the tales of what can happen to men who cross women like me?"

"Oh, Millicent." He huffs out a humorless laugh. "You insult me if you think I have so little care for my own well-being. No, no. You aren't seeing your situation clearly yet."

He aims a look over his shoulder, and a moment later, Rodney scampers back in. This time he's carrying a simple wooden chair that he places in front of Millie—just out of spitting range—before retreating again and closing the door behind him. Jonathan sits on the chair, crosses his legs, and aims an infuriatingly pleasant smile at Millie. "Now, shall we discuss your dear Jennifer Murphy? Pretty girl. Charming, in fact. It's a shame, isn't it? To discover she's no more than a common thief."

Millie's mind goes blank with confusion. "Jenny's not a—"

"Oh, there's no need for protestations. Dear young Jennifer confessed to the crime earlier this evening, straight to Judge Anderson's face. Not that she had much of a case to make seeing as it was her word against mine. One does like to help out the odd orphan, but when they are caught red-handed stealing your wife's jewels—"

"You dirty, lying—"

"Do try to pay attention, Millicent. I'm attempting to tell you that your sweet little Jenny is the dirty, lying thief and that she has already been tried, convicted, and sentenced. She's in the town jail now, as a matter of fact, bound for the workhouse in the morning. And while a twenty-five-year sentence does *seem* like a long time, it is truly unlikely she will survive that long. The guards are not known for their . . . gentle hands. Or their *restraint* when it comes to pretty young girls. And I'm sad to say that the conditions are such that very few keep their health for more than a year or—"

"*Stop.*"

The word is a sob. It's a display of weakness that she shouldn't allow, but Millie can't bear to hear anymore. She already knows that incarceration in a workhouse for someone like Jenny is tantamount to a death sentence delayed. A guarantee of a short, miserable life full of rancid meat, sunken cheeks, and long brutal hours of back-breaking work. There are women who have killed themselves to avoid such a fate.

There's a brief, brutal shattering inside of Millie as the life that she and Jenny had planned breaks apart into a million jagged pieces. They cut at her heart, the remnants of this life that hadn't been so grand. Hadn't even been particularly ambitious. A little life, really. A modest desire to find a small corner of the world where they could be together.

"I sense that this news is not pleasing to you?"

His voice is smug. Satisfied. He's so sure he's won. So confident in the absolute power men like him hold over silly little girls like her.

But it's power he didn't earn.

Power he doesn't deserve to keep.

Instead of answering, Millie just keeps glaring at him, and he leans back in his chair and smiles. "There is another option, of course. If you were to agree to complete the task I've set before you, I might be prevailed upon to speak to the esteemed Judge Anderson on Miss Murphy's behalf. He indicated he would be . . . open to releasing young Jennifer into my care. There would be conditions, of course."

Millie clenches her jaw. She doesn't want to ask, but he's going to make her. "What conditions?"

He smiles again, like she's just proven to be a good, obedient dog. "I would insist on her immediate marriage. It can be such a steadying influence, and I believe her cousin Paul, who will soon take over his father's caretaking role, would be an excellent choice. Judge Anderson would also require weekly reports from me. Should I fail to deliver them, or should I mention even a fleeting concern over young Jennifer's moral character, she would be immediately delivered to the workhouse to serve out her sentence without the trouble of an additional trial."

He cocks his head, gauging the effect of his words. When Millie says nothing, he continues. "Were you to agree to these terms, I would also acquire your assistance in writing a letter to ensure that Miss Murphy carries out her end of the bargain. Any deviation on her part would, of course, nullify any agreement you and I make here tonight, so I suggest you word the letter quite clearly."

With that, he stands, and this time when the door opens and Millie looks around, it's not Rodney's rat face that she sees, but an oval face with porcelain skin surrounded by a halo of chestnut curls.

"*Alma.*"

She spits her sister's name like it's poison on her tongue, but Alma doesn't even flinch. She walks straight to the chair Jonathan just vacated, the purple silk of her skirt swishing softly around her legs. She sets a fountain pen and a small stack of blank parchment on the wooden seat and then steps back so she's standing shoulder to shoulder with Jonathan. Only then does she meet Millie's eyes. "Write the letter, Mil. It's the only way you can help her now."

Millie looks up into Alma's cool eyes. "Who *are* you?" She whispers the words because she's asking herself the question as much as she's asking the sister she thought she knew. The sister she thought she loved.

Alma stiffens. "Don't look at me like that. Don't look at me like I'm some kind of monster for wanting to protect my *family*. We both know who the real monster is, Millie. We both know what you did to the Thompson babe."

Millie rears back so fast her head hits the wall.

Alma's lip curls. Beside her, Jonathan crosses his arms, looking bored.

"Did you truly think I didn't know?" Alma hisses. "Did you think I'd ever believe that our mother would defy her own rules? I knew the very night it happened because I've always known what your precious power could do. Even when you and Mama refused to see it."

Millie barely registers the naked jealousy in Alma's voice. Her shocked mind is too busy racing to understand what this means.

All these years, she carried this guilt alone. All these years, she thought Alma didn't know.

"You never said anything." Millie's throat is so dry, her words come out like a croak. "Why?"

Both of Alma's brows lift. "Why didn't *I* say anything? Why didn't *you*? I'm your older sister. But you never came to me for help. Not like you went to Mama. Because you thought I was weak. Because you thought I wouldn't be able to *comprehend* that kind of power."

"You're wrong. That's not—"

"But now?" Alma steps forward, her chin jutting up in a gesture so like Gran, a brief image of her flashes in my mind before Millie's thoughts take over again. "Now, I want you to admit that you're a hypocrite, Mil. You as good as *killed* our parents. You destroyed our lives, all to save some stranger's whelp. But when I come to you, begging you to help your *own* family, you treat me like I'm dirt under your shoe."

Alma's breathing hard now, her chest rising and falling rapidly beneath the tightly laced bodice of her dress. Her eyes lock with Millie, but there's no love in her gaze. No guilt or shame as she stares down at the little sister she was supposed to care for, but nursed resentment for instead.

Next to Alma, Jonathan makes an impatient noise in the back of his throat. "As heartwarming as this trip down memory lane has been, I do think we've strayed a bit from the point, dear."

Alma jolts like she's coming out of a trance, and Millie's gaze shifts to Jonathan. Only it's not him she's seeing. It's the bright orange flames that burned her parents' house to the ground that night. Afterward, she wanted to hurt the people responsible. She wanted to return to that dark, forbidden place where life and death are made and held, and she wanted to bring vengeance back with her. It was Alma who held her back. Alma who dragged her away like the grieving child she was.

But Millie isn't a scared little girl anymore. And Alma is no longer by her side. So when she looks at Jonathan, she doesn't just see flames, she *feels* them. White and hot, burning through her insides. They cleanse her. Transmute her. They give her clarity. A single-minded strength of purpose that chases away every lingering trace of fear or doubt.

Jonathan doesn't see this. His amused, condescending gaze makes it obvious that he sees only an angry young girl backed into a corner with no recourse but to obey.

"I believe I forgot to mention, Millicent, that I've also taken the liberty of appraising our esteemed sheriff of the situation with Miss Murphy, along with the members of my board. I mention this because I want to assure you that should I become . . . incapacitated in any way, there are just under two dozen men prepared to step in and oversee the proper *rehabilitation* of this young, misguided member of our community." He angles his head. "I trust we understand each other in this regard."

Millie understands, but she says nothing. She understands that Jonathan Blackwell is too much of a coward to act alone. She understands that he believes he has found safety in numbers.

"So tell me, Millicent." His voice is lazy. Arrogant. "Do we have a deal?"

Millie closes her eyes. She pictures Jenny's face in her mind, cloud-blue eyes blazing with trust and love. She sucks in a breath of air, stoking the fire within her, embracing the pain of the flames as they burn what's left of her hope away. Fire gives way to cold fury, and she wraps it around her heart like a bandage on a wound.

When at last Millie lifts her chin and meets Jonathan Blackwell's gaze, it's with an icy, emotionless calm. "A deal is exactly what we have."

The scream tears through me.

It burns a path up my chest and shreds the inside of my throat. It's the scream I tried to make Millie hear, but couldn't. The warning I tried to give over a century too late.

I can still see Jenny's eyes, blazing into mine. Blue-grey irises wide with worry. Frantic with concern. Was it like this for Millie, too? Could she feel Jenny's arms around her, holding her tight? I hope she did. I hope it burned through the icy rage that took over her heart.

But was it enough?

I don't know. I only know what she became. A part of me has known for a while, only I didn't want it to be true. I recognized her, in that first memory. The icy touch of the shadows that have haunted me my whole life, nudging at my dreams, pressing against the threads of the spell that bind her to this house.

Not spirits. There are no train crash victims haunting the Blackwell House halls.

It was Millie.

It was Millie all along.

The eyes—Jenny's eyes—blur through a veil of tears. And then . . . my name.

Mine, not Millie's.

"*Nev.*"

Not Jenny's voice. Not Jenny's eyes. *His.* Storm-cloud eyes that I know. Have *always* known. Eyes that I've chased for years. Drawing them over and over again. I thought it was the sky I was trying to capture. The exact right color after a storm. But it was him.

It was always him.

"You," I whisper. Those eyes move from side to side, and I follow them, twin lights to guide me in the midst of this storm. "*I know you.*"

The eyes disappear behind a pair of dark lashes, and I panic. My hand shoots out and cups the face they belong to. If I lose them now, I know deep in my bones I'll never find them again.

"Nev." The voice that speaks is rough. Hoarse and clipped. Deeper than it should be. Am I wrong? Is this—

No. There are his eyes again. Blazing. Warm. *Known.* "You saved me in the tree." Something tenses beneath my head. An arm, propped under my neck. There's another arm, too, draped over my legs. And a chest pressed against my shoulder. A heart pounding in my ear.

Cal.

It's Cal's eyes. Cal's heart. He's holding me, and we're on the floor of the cottage where Jenny lived. I'm clutching a letter in my hand. Millie's letter. The one Alma and Jonathan forced her to write Jenny. Cal is helping me. He held my hand. He kept me safe from . . . not the spirits.

From *Millie.*

From the thing she became.

He's Cal. The boy who appeared out of the darkness that night at the cove. But he's also . . .

"We were racing." I don't dare break eye contact. I don't dare to look away. "You told me to slow down, but I didn't. I stepped on a branch that snapped. I fell back. I was going to fall. I was going to—"

"No." He breathes the word like it's being ripped from his chest. His eyes are wide with confusion. With hope and fear. "I didn't let you go, Nev. I never let you go."

But I did. Somehow, I let him go. Somehow, I lost him.

I move my hand up from his cheek and trace the crescent-shaped scar next to his eye. "The branch snapped back." I can see the way it happened, but not clearly. It's like watching a reel of film that hasn't been developed all the way. "It cut you here." My thumb traces the curve of the scar. He closes his eyes and presses his head into my hand like he can't help it. Like he needs my touch. "You bled all over your shirt."

I try to see past this single reel. Try to play out the rest of the tape because there's more. I can *feel* that there's so much more. This is *Cal*. The person who fits me. Has always fit me. That first morning on the bluffs, I recognized him. My body, my blood remembered.

I press hard at the memory, but it's not enough. I can't see past the moment I'm safe in the tree. Once I'm wrapped in his arms, the images abruptly stop like a song in the middle of the chorus. But it's enough to know.

Cal is the phantom in my dreams.

Except he's real. He was always real. This person I told all of my secrets to. This person who told me all of his. This person who shaped the very core of me. Somehow, I lost him. But he came back. He came back for *me*.

"Nev." His voice is hoarse, strained. There's wonder in his eyes, and a deep, desperate longing that I understand. Because he's the color I've been living without. He's the reason I've been a ghost in my own life, haunted by pale imitations of the love, the *knowing*, we used to have. And these past few days, I found some part of it again. I tried to resist it because I didn't understand, but I couldn't.

"I lost you." Tears spill down my cheeks because it's only now that I understand what I've been living without. It's only now that I can see, *feel*, the full shape of the gaping wound at the very center of me.

Cal cups my cheek. His touch is warm and gentle, and his hand trembles slightly against my skin. I'm trembling, too. Because he's here. The friend who was always with me. The friend I never thought I would live without. He was gone for so long, and now he's *here*. "You never lost me, Nev." His stormy eyes blaze into mine. "You never will."

We move at the same time, our lips crashing together in something desperate and inevitable. His fingers slide into my hair, and his chest rumbles against the palm of my hand. He kisses me like he wants me more than anything, and I kiss him back the same way. He tastes like salt. Like sand. Like wind blowing through the trees. And when he pulls back to look at me, his breath mingling with mine, our chests rising and falling like the tide, it's not a plunging sense of confusion I feel, but a deep sense of knowing.

Knowing and being known.

I press my lips to his again and wrap myself up in a warmth that's both achingly familiar and thrillingly new. I let it fill the cold nothingness inside of me. Let it melt the remnants of Millie's fury that wrapped itself around my heart. And I make a promise against his skin. I promise that I'll never lose him again. I promise that this time, I won't let him go.

Chapter Twenty

My lips are deliciously swollen, my mind is racing, and *Cal Murphy* is sitting cross-legged on the cottage floor across from me.

His cottage floor. Because this is where he lived.

Faint flashes of memory flicker and fade like lightning. Laughter bouncing off these walls. The giddy feeling of discovery. Safety. Joy. It's not an accident this place became my refuge. It was Cal who drew me here. My best friend since birth. My mind may have lost him, but some part of me must have held on. Some part of me must have never stopped looking for him.

Clear blue eyes search my face. They were always like this when he was happy. Lighter. The clouds in them shrinking to tiny flecks of grey. His thumb sweeps back and forth across the inside of my palm. His breathing is shallow like mine. The waves of his black hair are mussed from my fingers running—

"Your hair was red."

His lips curve in a smile that's cautious, like he's still afraid to let go all the way. "I dyed it two days before I came back." His fingers flex around my hand. "Does this mean you remember?" His smile falters. "Your grandmother's spell . . . ?"

I pause, collecting what I can of the flashes lighting in my mind. But they aren't full memories. They aren't even images, really. They're more like impressions. Waves of emotions. Currents of deep, fundamental truths that don't connect with a specific event.

"I remember when you saved me from falling out of the oak tree," I tell him. "But I can't remember any details beyond that. It's more like, I remember how I felt about you. How we felt about each other."

He tries to hide his disappointment behind a soft smile, but I see it. He thought I remembered everything. He thought I was whole again.

I'm not.

I haven't been whole for a long time, and now I know it. Now I know that my grandmother did more than hide my mom's grave. She stole my best friend from me. And I don't think that's all. I think she took more.

"Tell me everything," I say. "Why did you leave? Why are you back now?"

His eyes bounce back and forth in his head. "I don't . . . I don't know if I should say."

"What? Why wouldn't—"

"Because you told me it could *shatter* your mind!" His mouth twists, and I see another glimpse of that torment he's been hiding beneath his careful masks. But it wasn't some stranger that he lost. I'm the one he came back for. That fear in his eyes is for *me*.

"That assistant engineer," he continues. "You told me his mind fractured when he was confronted with the truth. You said that was why he jumped off a damned *ravine*."

"I know, but—"

"Do you think I don't *want* to tell you everything? Do you think it hasn't killed me every time you've looked at me—at *me*—like I'm some stranger? I made myself wait at first, to make sure you and your grandmother . . . but then, when I knew you were still *you* . . ." He trails off, shakes his head. "What if that happens to you? What if I tell you everything and . . ."

He swears under his breath and rubs a hand down his face. His left hand is still holding mine, and I squeeze it tightly.

"I'm not going to break, Cal."

His eyes fly back to mine. The battle raging behind them is fierce, and it triggers another half-recovered wave of memory. These eyes, but younger. This face, but rounder. Softer. We used to beg for five more minutes with each other at the end of the day like it was a matter of life and death. He was the person I ran to with every new thought, every new idea, every new discovery. I try to remember what those discoveries were. What we whispered into each other's ears high up in our oak tree. What we talked about late into the night when we snuck out to meet each other because whatever we had to say was too urgent to wait until morning. But it's like my memories are stuck inside one of Fern's crystal balls. Foggy, frustrating wisps too fleeting to hold.

I force out a breath and focus on the Cal who's with me now. In some ways, he still looks like a stranger. The firm set of his jaw. The intensity of his stare. He's harder than the laughing boy he was, and I wonder if he thinks the same thing about me. That some of me is the girl he knew, and some of me is not.

"I'm not like Millie, or even Alma," I tell him. "I don't have anything close to the power they had, but I do have *some*. I can't create a charm to weave a powerful spell, but I can work with charms that already exist. I know how to hold them in my mind, how to sense what they're missing. What they need. It's how I've been able to tend the Anchors for months, even though I don't have power through the Vow. That's why I'm not going to break, Cal. I understand what the charm is doing. I know how to hold both truths in my mind."

He still looks wary. "But what does it mean that you only remember some things and not everything?"

I press my lips together. "I'm not sure, but I think . . . it might be because of my dreams."

"Your dreams?"

I nod. "I dreamt about you. Only I didn't know it was you. I called you my phantom because I couldn't see your face." His lips curve in a tender smile and my heart flips in my chest. "And then the night after I saw you again, I had a dream about falling out of an oak tree." I bite the inside of my lip, considering. "I think that maybe Gran's spell didn't—or *couldn't*—take all of you from me. That somehow, some small part of you stayed with me, and that's what's breaking through now."

He watches me intently as his thumb continues its sweeping path across my palm. Left, right, left. I never want him to stop. "Can you get them back?" he asks softly. "The ones she did take?"

I drop my gaze to our hands and try to breathe through this stab of longing. "Maybe. If I can find her charm. If I can figure out a way to counter it." I look up at him. "But she could have hidden it anywhere, and I can't wait that long. Please, Cal. You have to tell me what happened. You have to tell me why you left."

He draws in his lips and looks at the slowly dying fire. "We were there that night." His voice is soft, gentle. "You, me, my mom, and my little sister. We didn't see her . . . fall. But we saw her after."

Every single cell in my body stills. My lungs stop breathing. My heart stops beating. The blood racing through my veins halts in its tracks. The only thing that exists right now is Cal and the truth I'm finally going to hear.

"We were walking back through the woods from the cottage. You'd been here with me playing, and my mom and sister were walking you back with me. We all heard the scream, but you got to her first. She wasn't . . . she was still there when you knelt next to her. I think she said something to you, but I don't know what it was. And then you—"

His eyes drift close and he swallows. "And then you started sobbing. The sounds you were making . . . I still hear it sometimes in my nightmares." He shivers slightly and looks back at me. "Your grandmother came running out then. I tried to go to you, but my mom held me back and Marie took you inside while my mom called the paramedics. I used to leave my window open because you'd climb through it sometimes when you couldn't sleep, and you did that night. You gave me that locket and made me swear to keep it safe. I tried to talk to you, ask if you were okay, but you just told me I couldn't tell anyone about the necklace, and then you left. It was the last time I saw you. Until five days ago."

The realization that I was there when she died—that I saw her, *spoke* to her—sends shock waves crashing through me. A distant part of my mind is also realizing that this is something else Gran stole from me. But I also need to understand—

"I still don't understand why you left."

He swallows and holds my gaze. "Because we're immune. My family."

"Immune to . . . what?"

He leans forward. "My mom went to the grocery store the next morning to get food for you and Marie. She ran into one of the paramedics she'd called the night before. She knew him well from school, I think, but when she said hello he acted like he hadn't seen her in weeks. And when she said your mom's name, he cut her off and asked how Celia was doing these days. That's when she realized what had happened. You weren't the only one your grandmother made forget, Nev. But it didn't work on us."

My eyes widen, a glimmer of understanding lighting in my brain.

"It's like when we were kids," he continues. "We were always running around, plotting out all the secret passageways that we were convinced no one but us had ever discovered, and you were always complaining about the shadows following you. About the chill that snuck under your skin. I'd overhear tour guests talking about it, too, especially after someone drowned. But I never felt it. And it wasn't until my mom packed us up that night and marched us to the car that I understood why. She's never felt them, either. No one in my family has."

Because he's immune.

The whole *Murphy* family is immune.

"My mom told me what Marie had done to the paramedics, and she said that it wouldn't work on us. She didn't know if your grandmother knew that we wouldn't be affected, but she didn't want to risk us staying to find out. She said Marie Blackwell had other ways of silencing us. I remember screaming at her, refusing to leave. I said we could lie and pretend to do whatever your grandmother wanted, but she just pointed at my little sister—she was only six then—and asked me if I thought she was capable of lying, and did I want to risk that. So we left. And she made me swear never to contact you again, but I . . ."

A guilty look crosses his face. "I did anyway. I called your house line for a week straight until you were the one who picked up. But you had no idea who I was. You accused me of being a prank caller, and you hung up."

So much is starting to make sense. The realizations are pouring in so quickly that my mind is struggling to keep track of them all. I shoot to my feet and pace back and forth in front of the dwindling fire. But of everything I'm coming to realize, one glaring problem takes precedence.

"What the hell were you thinking coming back here?" I whirl to face Cal. "Your mom tells you that she's worried my grandmother is going to . . . to *silence* you and you just waltz on back? Christ, Cal. I told her your *name*. You're living in the same house. I don't know how she hasn't already—"

"Marie barely paid any attention to me as a kid, Nev. And she didn't know me by this name. No one here did. Except for you."

"What?"

"My first name is Oliver, but when we were about six I think, you decided we should have secret names to go along with some secret club we were starting. My middle name is Calvin, so . . ."

"Cal," I finish for him.

He nods. "You came up with it, and we were ridiculously strict about only ever using the names in secret. But when we left, I insisted that Cal was the name I wanted to go by. My mom didn't like it at first, but eventually, she gave in."

Our eyes lock, and a thread of understanding pulses between us. *You never lost me, Nev. You never will.*

"And the reason I *waltzed* back here is because I saw the article about your Vow ceremony, and I don't know. I panicked, I guess. I'd always planned to come back once I figured out a way to make sure my mom and sister would be safe, but that article made me realize I was out of time. So I lied to my mom about a trip with a friend and got a bus ticket. I was pretty sure you wouldn't remember me, and I knew that if I just showed up raving about what your grand-mother did, you probably wouldn't believe me and would tell her everything. But . . ."

"But you came anyway."

He dips his chin. "I'll always come for you, Nev."

My sudden tears blur his features, and I have to brace a hand against the mantelpiece to stay upright. It's too much. The risks Cal took. The potential danger he put himself and his family in for me. The fact that it's *my* family who *is* the potential danger to begin with. My head spins and I'm not sure how I make it to the nearest armchair, but somehow I sink into it and pull my knees into my chest because if I don't, I'm afraid I won't stay in one piece.

"Do you know why you're immune?" I ask once I get my breath-ing back under control. "Does your mom know?"

Cal shakes his head.

"I think I might."

He blinks. "What? How?"

I take in a breath and let it out slowly. "You may want to sit down for this."

Wordlessly, Cal sits in the chair across from me, and I proceed to tell him every single thing that happened in Millie's last memory. I tell him about Alma and Jonathan realizing they could use Jenny as leverage against Millie. About the false charges of theft that the judge in Jonathan's pocket upheld. I tell him about Alma's jealousy and resentment, and about the cold fury that wrapped around Millie's heart as she told Jonathan Blackwell that they had a deal.

"But she wasn't going to do it," I say. "It's hard to explain, but I felt her intention at that last moment. She wanted access to her charm box, but not so she could make a bunch of Blackwell Railroad Company board members forget about a memo. They'd crossed a line going after Jenny, but Millie also knew that Jonathan wouldn't stop there. She knew he'd continue to find uses for her, and that as long as he and his associates were alive, Jenny would be under constant threat. And that wasn't something she could allow to happen."

"What are you saying, Nev?"

"Think about it. Think about the first people who died in the 1903 massacre. Jonathan. Then his cousin Rodney, who acted as Millie's de facto jailor. Then the local judge who'd sentenced Jenny to the workhouse. The sheriff who Jonathan specifically told Millie had been *appraised* of the situation so that should anything happen to him, Jenny's sentence to the workhouse would be enforced. He told the members of his board the same thing and they—"

"Were killed next."

I nod. "And those kids who drowned . . . I don't know. Maybe that's when she started to lose control. But I think her initial intention must have been—"

"To kill anyone with the power to hurt Jenny."

Cal's words shiver around us, so heavy, they suck up all the air. I hug my knees tighter and twist my head to look at the gallery wall, my eyes once again seeking out the drawing of the Medusa split in two.

A girl on one side.

A monster on the other.

"Jenny knew," I say at the exact moment I realize it's true. "She knew—or figured out—what Millie became. She had the letter. She eventually got the locket. Maybe she found the memories Millie left for her after all." I keep my eyes on the drawing, but it's not the monstrous side I study. "Do you know the story of Medusa?"

Cal chews his lip. "I think so. She's the one who could turn people into stone with her eyes?"

"Men. Not all people. Just men. I read a few versions of the myth a couple of years ago because of this drawing." I nod to the wall and Cal follows my gaze. "Medusa was a young priestess for the goddess Athena, and one day when she was tending the temple, she was raped by the sea god Poseidon. Athena appeared then, and she turned Medusa into a Gorgon with snakes for hair and a stare capable of turning men to stone. Some interpretations claim that Athena was punishing Medusa for demeaning her temple. Others say that she was giving her young priestess the tools for her revenge against mankind. Either way, the result was the same. The girl became a monster. And then some young hero chopped off her head."

For several long minutes, Cal and I stare in silence at the drawing Jenny made. The human side of Medusa is wearing long priestess robes, and although it doesn't look exactly like Millie, now that I'm looking for it, I see a resemblance. The wild wave of her hair. The shape of her eyes.

But it's the pain and heartbreak Jenny poured onto the page that scream out to me now. I haven't read the letter from Millie that was tucked behind the smaller sketch, but the fact that Jenny received it at all tells me its contents. She married her second cousin. She lived here in this cottage for the rest of her life. And she watched the girl she loved—the girl who loved her—become a murderer.

"So the spirits," Cal says after a long moment. "They never—"

"There were never any spirits. Those people who died in that train crash did just that. They died. They never came back. They never haunted this town. Alma must have convinced that spirit medium to say what she did. She would have known it was Millie behind the unnatural deaths, but if she was going to tell the world a ghost story, she didn't want it to be one that might expose what she did to her sister."

"So it was Millie that Alma bound with her Vow?"

I frown and look from the Medusa painting to him. "It's the only explanation for why the killings slowed, but I'm not sure how she did it. Alma wasn't close to matching her sister's power in life. I don't know how she could have overpowered her once she became—"

"A monster."

I don't argue with his choice of word, even though the part of me that's come to know and care for the girl Millie once was wants to. But who she once was doesn't change what she is now. It doesn't change the fact that she seized control of my mom's mind and sent her flying out a window. It doesn't change the fact that she sent Mr. Harrison, Beverly Price, Art Fairchild, and countless others to their watery graves. It doesn't change the fact that each time I fell into one of the memories she left behind, each time I exposed my mind to her, she tried to kill me, too.

Except for one time.

I look at Cal. He's staring off into space, his brow furrowed, his teeth digging into his bottom lip. "Why did you hold my hand before I touched the letter?" I ask.

He looks at me. "Because the spirits—I mean Millie—has never affected me. And you said it was them—*her*—attacking your mind when you were in the memories."

I nod. "I think it's more than Millie not being able to affect you. I think she won't—or maybe *can't*—hurt you. I don't understand how Millie became what she became, but I'm positive she did it to protect Jenny. She must have known there was a possibility she might lose control."

I meet Cal's blue-grey eyes. The exact same color and shape as the eyes of the girl Millie loved. The girl she turned herself into a monster for.

"I think she wove something into her spell that protected Jenny from *her*. From the worst of what she might become. And I think that protection is still alive in you."

Chapter Twenty-One

Gran is leaning on her cane with her back to me, the sparkling sea stretching out before her as she watches the construction of the ceremony stage along the bluffs. I trace the outline of her slight, stooped form silhouetted against the blazing sun as a vee of geese flies overhead, a stiff breeze blowing my loose curls away from my face.

I want to scream at her. I want to shake her and demand she explain why she stole Cal from me. Why she poisoned my memories of my mother. I want her to tell me how Alma did it. I want her to explain how a woman who couldn't even maintain a love charm—a love charm she offered a terrible sacrifice for—was somehow able to bind Millie *after* she became a being powerful enough to seize thirty-four minds and send them to their deaths in a matter of days.

But I can't get my lips to open. The harder I try, the harder my teeth sink into my tongue. The coppery taste of blood fills my mouth and Gran's words from the other day in her sitting room echo in my head.

The moment you take that Vow, the moment you become a true part of the legacy Alma left us, all of your doubts, all of your fears will fade away. Your path will become clear again. Your purpose will become clear again.

That is what it means to be a Blackwell.

We do what we must to survive.

I try to walk toward her, but my feet sink into the sand. I fall deeper and deeper until I'm buried up to my knees, trapped on every side so the only thing I can do is stare wordlessly at her back. Does she know? Does she know it wasn't a trainload of angry spirits Alma bound that day, but her own sister?

What spell am I truly meant to bind my life to on that stage tomorrow? What promise did Gran really make when she made her Vow?

As if she can hear my thoughts, she turns around to face me, the sun bright at her back. But there's something wrong with her eyes. Something . . . shifting within them. And her skin is changing, too. It grows more and more translucent like one of those glowing deep-sea jellyfish bodies whose skeletons are always on display. Something moves underneath her skull, undulating like a wave. Her rippling eyes meet mine, and as she juts out her chin, her lips pull back in a sneer.

"You thought I was weak."

A sharp pressure on my chest jolts me awake.

My eyes fly open but I'm disoriented, my brain hazy and reeling. The dream I had of Gran flickers before my eyes, and I try to grab hold of it before it disappears. There was something wrong with her skin. With her eyes . . .

A silky tail brushes my cheek and a soft *meow* in my ear reveals the source of my sudden return to consciousness. Except Tab isn't the only one here with me. There's also something warm and solid radiating heat at my back. A hand draped over my waist. Steady breathing soft as a whisper against my neck.

Cal.

I blink, letting my eyes adjust until the soft moonlight is enough for me to make out the dark shapes of the cottage's living room. Cal and I escaped here as soon as we could last night after a tortuous day of leading tours, overseeing the ceremony setup for tomorrow, and trying my best to avoid more of Gran's probing stares. We spent hours talking in circles, trying to figure out what I should do about the next day's Vow ceremony, but we must have fallen asleep in this nest of couch cushions and blankets on the floor before coming up with a solution.

Tab's orange and blue eyes blink at me and her tail brushes my face again. I resist the urge to hiss at her in a language she'll understand because I'm not ready to leave the temporary oblivion that sleep brings, but it's too late now. I'm wide awake, and the tight chest, shallow breathing, and racing thoughts that plagued me all day are back with a vengeance.

Carefully, so as not to wake Cal, I slide out of his arms and pad over to where I left my jacket and shoes. Tab follows at my heels like a pale furry ghost as I let myself out into the night, tipping my chin up to gaze at the moon. When it rises tomorrow night, it will be full, and before that happens, I have a choice to make.

There's a blur in the air followed by a rustle of bushes as Tab pounces on some scurrying nighttime foe. She leaps back into the path a few seconds later, and I follow her, wrapping my arms around my middle. The fog is rising, and this jacket is no match against its grim, damp chill.

I no longer trust Alma, or Gran, or the legacy I'm meant to carry. But what does that change? If I don't take the Vow tomorrow at sunset, if Alma's bind breaks, the thing Millie became will be freed. I have to assume that Gran and I will be her first victims since we're the last in the family line that destroyed her life, threatened the girl she loved, and imprisoned her for a hundred and twenty years. But what about after? What about the rest of the people in this town? The last time she was unbound, she murdered everyone with the potential to harm Jenny, but then she lost control and drowned thirteen completely innocent and blameless kids. I read their names aloud to myself this morning, along with the names of every single person she's drowned since. I can't allow myself to forget even for a second that the Millie I've come to care about in those memories is gone.

It ends with you, pet. It all ends with you.

But how? *How* is it supposed to end?

A long, low hiss splits the night air, and I jerk my head up, expecting to see Tabitha locked in a standoff with some terrifying possum or raccoon. But it's not an animal she's hissing at. It's a white marble stone, its smooth surface glowing in the moonlight.

Did I wander here by chance, or is this clearing what I set out tonight to find?

I don't know. But as I stare at my mom's hidden grave, I can just make out the name *Theresa Vale* engraved in the stone. I hate seeing it, but it also confirms that despite the incomplete memories of Cal that I've managed to recover, the charm at the heart of Gran's spell is still strong.

I take a step forward, but Tab doesn't move out of the way. Her back is arched and her tail is fluffed up to three times its usual size. Is it possible that she knows what Gran did to this headstone? Is it possible she senses the wrongness here?

As I wonder that, something else occurs to me.

"You knew, didn't you?" I whisper. "You knew who he was when he first came. That's why you didn't scratch his eyes out."

Her mismatched eyes blink up at me, neither confirming nor denying this. She does, however, hiss again in the direction of my mom's headstone and back up a couple of paces.

"Hey," I soothe. "It's okay, Tab."

I reach down to pet her, but she bounds away before I can, disappearing into the night with an angry high-pitched yowl. I call after her a handful of times and make the clicking sound with my tongue that usually brings her running, but Tab doesn't come back. Something about this place definitely spooked her, and as I turn back to my mom's disguised headstone, I have a sudden guess about what it could be.

But would she really do it that way? Would she really hide it here? In the same place where, once she's gone and unable to refresh it, the truth she has hidden with her spell will be revealed?

My heart races as I approach the headstone and kneel down before it. I don't have anything to dig with, so I use my hands. I curl them into claws and try not to think about what—*who*—is underneath me as I gather up clumps of cold dirt and toss them aside.

I'm about a foot or so deep when I see it. The base is a salt-encrusted iron dock ring, and she's used a faded red fishing line similar to what binds the north Anchor charm to tie four objects at equidistant points around the circle. At the very top is a gold and red coral ring my mom rarely took off. The bottom holds a weathered piece of driftwood. The left, a small rusted key. And on the right side of the circle, a black raven's feather, the dozens of curved barbs crusted through with grave dirt.

This is Gran's charm. *This* is what's powering the spell that's currently hiding so much from my mind. The true inscription on this gravestone. My memories of Cal.

What really happened the night my mom died.

My hands shake as I lift it, the urge to tear the thing apart, to hurl the broken pieces into the dark wood, is almost irresistible, but I can't. Attempting to dismantle magically connected pieces will only damage—possibly kill—the person who attempts it. It was Gran who taught me that.

I close my eyes and force my breathing to slow, just like Millie did in the memory when she was preparing to reweave Alma's love charm. When I told Cal that I might be able to counter Gran's charm by undoing what she wove piece by piece, it was more theoretical than anything else because I doubted I'd ever actually find the source of her spell. But I did.

Gradually, my body and mind come back under my control and once they do, I bow my head and listen. Thanks to my training with the Anchors, I know how to pick out specific notes and identify the piece of a charm that has flickered out. I also know how to find replacement objects that fit, which means I should be able to find the pieces that *don't* fit.

It takes me a little while, but eventually, I tease out the first note. If I had my charm ingredients with me, it would be easier to find a piece that counters it, but I don't want to waste time retrieving it from my room, so I get up and start combing the woods instead. I'm lucky. In only a handful of minutes, I find a smooth oval stone that perfectly counters the piece of driftwood. I find counters for the rusted key and raven's feather soon after that. An ivy vine serves as my bind to attach each object to the corresponding piece it offsets on the iron ring, and when the notes of Gran's charm begin devolving from harmony to discord, I smile in grim victory.

But I can't find the right thing to offset my mom's coral ring. I search the woods for a full twenty minutes before I'm ready to admit defeat. And still, I'm reluctant to retrieve my charm pouch. Now that I've found Gran's charm, I don't want it out of my sight.

I thrust my hands into the pocket of my jacket and immediately still when my fingers collide with something that makes a soft crinkling sound. Carefully, I pull the folded piece of paper out of my pocket, and even though it's too dark to read the words printed there, I already know what they say. This is the copy of the article my mom printed out from the *Gazette*. The one that mentions Millie and Jenny amongst the top students in their 1903 class.

And it's also exactly what I need. The subtle vibrations rising from the page are the perfect fit to cancel out the last piece of Gran's charm.

I run back to where I left the charm by my mom's grave and tear off a single strip of paper from the bottom of the article. I layer it carefully over the coral ring, attach it with the ivy vine, and then sit back on my heels. A blast of warmth rises from the charm, and I close my eyes.

When I open them again, I remember.

I remember it all.

Chapter Twenty-Two

I'm laughing too hard to keep running, so I bend over and brace my hands on my knees as Cal streaks past.

"What's the matter, Nia? Can't keep up?"

He turns, grinning as he jogs backward down the path. The light from the setting sun filters through the tree canopy overhead making his dark red hair blaze. From far behind us, his mom calls out for us to wait, but neither of us listens.

"You *cheated!*"

Cal waggles his eyebrows. "It's not cheating if—"

A scream cuts off his words. It rips through the air, and before I understand what I'm doing, I'm sprinting past Cal's confused, petrified face. Branches cut into my arms and face but I don't slow until I reach the patch of glass on the south lawn.

She's lying on her side, her chestnut hair spread like a halo around her head. There's no blood, but her body looks ... wrong. I scream and fall to my knees in front of her. She croaks my name in a thin, strained voice, and everything inside me goes frighteningly still.

"*Nev.*"

She's in pain, like the time Cal sprained his ankle when we were camping in the caves at the cove. It was hard for him to talk then and I had to lean in close to hear his words, so that's what I do now.

"Nev. Honey." Her hand moves toward me on the grass, and I reach down to slip mine inside. "You need—"

She gasps and her face twists.

"Mom?" Hot tears stream down my cheeks. "Mommy, what—"

"The atlas." She's so quiet that I have to lean in until our noses are almost touching to hear her. "It's not . . . protection. It's control."

Running feet sound behind me. Gran is here. I can smell her flowery lotion, and it means everything is going to be okay. But why is she wrapping her arms around me and pulling me back? I lurch forward because I'm still holding Mom's hand, and I don't want to let go.

"It's us." Mom's eyes flutter close, and the hand around mine goes soft. "The Vow. Don't let her take you, too. I love . . ."

Her throat makes a scary gurgling sound and her body goes still. Too still. My hands shake. My chest shakes. I don't understand what's happening, only that everything inside of me hurts. There's a horrible sound. A wail like a dying animal.

I think it's coming from me.

Gran grips my shoulders and turns me around. Her eyes are red and streaming with tears. She's only wearing a thin robe, and her hair isn't smoothed out like normal. It's messy and twisted in a clip. "It's okay, Nev, sweetheart. It's going to be okay."

Her voice doesn't shake because this is Gran. Cal's scared of her sometimes, but I'm not. She's going to make everything okay.

"I'm not going to let it happen again. Okay? I'm going to keep you safe, sweetheart. Whatever it takes. I swear to you, *I will keep you safe.*"

The memory of Gran's tortured, determined face keeps swimming in my mind as I burst into the cottage, tears streaming down my face just like they did that night seven years ago. The present-day version of Cal is sitting up on the couch-cushion bed, but as soon as he sees me, he's on his feet striding toward me.

"Nev?"

Both of his hands cup my face and his eyes frantically search mine. I try to speak. Try to explain what I found. What I did. What I *saw.* But the sobs are coming too fast for words.

"Oh my God." Understanding dawns on his face, and he pulls me into his chest. I melt into the warm salt and sand scent of him, tears staining his shirt. I've cried into this same shoulder so many times before. The memories swirl wildly in my mind, each image stacking on top of the other. The afternoon he stayed home sick from school and no one would sit with me at lunch. The day I cut my foot open on a piece of glass at the beach and there was so much blood, I was afraid I would die. He let me cry then, just like he's letting me cry now.

"You called me Nia."

Somehow, Cal has maneuvered us to the armchair, my cheek resting on his chest, his steady arms around me as I sit sideways on his lap. "That was your secret name for me. Everyone else called me by the first three letters of my name, so you called me by the last."

His arms tighten around me.

"I'm sorry I forgot. I'm sorry I didn't keep more of you with me."

His lips press into my hair. "It's okay," he whispers. "I found you, and you found me. That's the only thing that matters now."

Tears blur my eyes, but I wipe them away so I can see the page in the atlas clearly.

It's a cross-section of Northern California, the town of Hollow Cliff near the bottom. It's one of the only pages in this atlas I've never looked at before because why would I study a map of the one place in the world I know like the back of my hand?

But my mom studied it. Closely. And she did something else, too. She marked the locations of the north, south, east, and west Anchor charms with small circles, then she connected the four dots, creating a rectangular border around the town. And inside the rectangle, she drew a series of horizontal lines.

It could be some kind of unfinished grid, but that's not what it looks like.

It looks like a cage.

It's not protection. It's control.

I think about Robbie Harrison's wild, grief-stricken eyes when he chased me down the beach the night he got back to town. He thought his father had been targeted because of his video, and if Cal and I are right about what happened to the other people circled on my mom's list, he may have been right. But then, two days later, he did a complete one-eighty, changing his mind about everything he said.

But what if Robbie didn't change his own mind? What if—after reentering the perimeter created by the Anchor charms—it was changed *for* him?

It's not protection. It's control.

Alma wove a spell that bound Millie, and the Anchors at the four corners of town are supposed to extend that sphere of protection to everyone in Hollow Cliff. But what if it's not *protection* the Anchors extend?

It's not protection. It's control.

I don't think Gran heard my mom whisper those words, but I know she heard the next ones.

It's us. The Vow. Don't let her take you, too.

Gran took my memory of those words away.

Why?

And who was the *her* my mom was referring to? Gran? Alma?

And now it's not my mom's voice I hear, it's Gran's after she came back from the hospital. After I asked her if we might be wrong. *The moment you take that Vow, the moment you become a true part of the legacy Alma left us, all of your doubts, all of your fears will fade away.*

I've always known the Vow would bind me in certain ways. Physically, to the borders of this town, and to the spirits—*no*, to Millie—in a unique way. But is that all? Because if it is, I don't understand how taking the Vow could ever truly erase my doubts about Alma as a person. Not now that I know what she and Jonathan did to Millie. Not now that I know the real reason this town is cursed with death.

Unless . . .

It's not protection. It's control.

Unless it can. Unless the spell Alma wove was never meant to protect. Unless it was meant to—

"You should drink some of this."

Cal slides a mug of coffee across the small table and sits in the chair next to me, but I'm only vaguely aware of the steam rising from the cup into the pre-dawn light of the cottage kitchen. My mind is too busy trying to snatch at the glimmer of understanding that's hovering just out of my reach.

But it's close.

Very close.

"What if that's how she did it?" I ask out loud. "What if Alma didn't need to *overpower* Millie? What if she only needed to harness the spell Millie *had already cast*?"

Cal looks down at the atlas and loose papers spread out on the round table. "I'm not sure I'm following you."

I stand up from the table and start pacing because I can taste how close I am. "Millie intended to—and she must have succeeded—in convincing Jonathan and Alma that she would weave the mind manipulation spell they wanted. But she only agreed so she could get access to her charm box. The manipulation spell she *actually* wove was even more powerful than they could have ever imagined. She turned *herself* into the spell's instrument, and once she did, she had the power to manipulate the minds of anyone who might have harmed Jenny, and she sent them to their deaths. She got to everyone on that list, except for one."

Cal leans forward. "Alma."

"Right. And Alma must have known she was next. In that last memory, Millie *hated* her. I don't know why she didn't attack her when she attacked Jonathan. Maybe she wanted to save her for last. Or maybe there was still some part of her that was hesitant to kill her own pregnant sister. But I'm sure she *intended* to kill her, one way or another."

Alma found a way to survive. For us. For this family.

"I don't know how Millie became what she became, but there's a charm at the heart of whatever spell she cast. What if Alma got her hands on it? She couldn't just take it apart. She'd have known that the blowback from the magic she'd release would be too unpredictable. It could kill her. Or worse."

I walk over to the kitchen counter, pick up Gran's charm with my own hand-selected pieces layered over it, and set it on the table next to the atlas. "She couldn't have broken Millie's charm, but she could have woven her own around it. Like I did."

Cal and I both stare at the thing that irrevocably changed both of our lives. The thing that powered the spell that forced us apart.

"But what if," I continue, "instead of countering Millie's charm like I did to Gran's, Alma hijacked it? What if she saw an opportunity to finally best her sister? To finally get her hands on that power she'd always coveted. Millie became a thing capable of seizing and controlling minds. What if Alma found a way to harness that same ability?"

Cal's eyes bounce from the charm to me and back to the charm again. Hesitantly, he reaches out to pull the iron ring toward him but the movement knocks some of the loose papers off the table. They flutter to land at my feet, and when I bend to pick them up, I see the page on top and freeze.

It's the torn article from the *Gazette* I used in my countercharm. It was too dark outside to make out the text earlier, but I didn't even try because I already know what it says. Just like I already know why my mom printed it out.

Unless I don't. Unless I got it wrong.

When I first saw this, I immediately focused on Millie's and Jenny's names, but they aren't the only students mentioned in this article. Thirteen other kids also finished at the top of their respective classes. Thirteen other kids were invited to join Alma Blackwell's student advisory board, and that's not the only thing those thirteen students had in common.

On the morning of Alma's Vow, every single one of their bodies washed up on the shore of the harbor. The names listed here are the same names I reread to myself this morning when I was looking for proof that Millie lost control and began attacking innocent kids.

So young, you know.

Fern said those words. But what if she wasn't talking about her ex-husband?

So young to drown.

I stagger back, catching myself on the edge of the kitchen counter. "This is how she did it." The words don't want to come. They want to stay lodged in my throat. They want to hide, run, bury this horrible, heinous, unthinkable truth.

The true history has been hidden.

"Nev?"

Cal stands and reaches out to steady me, but I hold the *Gazette* article out to him instead, the paper shaking in my trembling hands. "There are fifteen students listed in this article. Two of them are Millie and Jenny. The other thirteen are the kids who drowned the same morning Alma took her Vow. I thought Millie killed them. I thought she lost control. But she didn't. It wasn't her." I try to suck in a breath, but there's a band around my chest, squeezing my lungs, restricting my air. "It was Alma."

Cal jerks. "What?"

I meet his confused, horrified eyes. "She didn't counter Millie's charm. She made it her own. But she needed power to do that, and do you remember what Alma did the last time she wanted to weave a spell but didn't have the strength to carry it out?"

His face pales. "You're not . . . are you talking about the love charm? About her . . ."

I wrap my arms tight around my waist. I need the comfort now. I need the strength to face this. "She offered up the life of her unborn child to strengthen that spell. That much innocence, that much life that will never be lived. It's . . . horrible and evil, but it's powerful, too. And she knew these kids, Cal. The town was in chaos by this point. It would have been easy for her to make some excuse about needing to meet with the students she'd appointed as her personal representatives and advisors. Because all of the kids, they must have been so scared. So confused."

My stomach churns. I'm going to be sick all over this floor. My knees are going to give out, and I'm going to collapse into a heap of anger and shame.

But not yet. I have to hold myself together a little bit longer. I need to see it all.

"Those thirteen kids were the only ones to die who didn't pose a threat to Jenny. And they were also the only ones to drown. But ever since then, every time there's an attack—"

"Oh God." The horrified revelation on his face reflects my own.

"The drownings are a pattern," I say. "But it's not Millie's pattern. It's Alma's."

The first, faint strains of a morning bird's song floats through the window, but inside the little kitchen, it's horrifyingly silent.

"But Alma is dead," Cal says. "How can she be the one attacking people *now*?"

The moment you take that Vow, the moment you become a true part of the legacy Alma left us, all of your doubts, all of your fears will fade away.

I close my eyes. Is this the answer? Is this our true history? Is this what we've hidden all these years?

We will be with you through all of it. And I promise you, sweetheart, we will not let you fail.

"Nev?"

I open my eyes, and when I do, it's to Cal's worried gaze. I must look as unstable as I feel because he's gripping my elbows like he's worried I'm about to faint, but this isn't something I can escape from. This is something I have to face.

"When we take our Vow," I whisper, too horrified to speak the words any louder, "we become a *part* of Alma's spell. We become bound to it. We act in its . . . interest. It's extremely unlikely that the bind Alma wove on Millie was strong enough to last indefinitely.

That's why we have the Vow, to renew it. But I don't . . ." I swallow. "What if it has to be renewed the same way it was cast?"

My body convulses like it's trying to expel a poison deep within me. Cal's hold on my elbows tightens and I suck every ounce of strength I can from the warmth of his fingers against my skin. Skin that always knew him. Skin that never forgot.

"Millie isn't breaking free. She's not the one infiltrating minds, driving people to their deaths. It's us, Cal. It's my family." A shudder tears through me, but I force myself to keep my gaze on him. I force myself to meet those horrified blue-grey eyes. "The drownings are sacrifices to power Alma's spell. My family has been killing the people of Hollow Cliff to keep Millie bound."

Chapter Twenty-Three

Dawn is breaking, the first eager fingers of sunlight reaching through the fog to fill the cottage kitchen with a soft, tentative glow. Through the window above the sink, I can see the edge of the twisting oak tree that I almost fell from that day, but it's not only the climb or the fall that I remember now. I remember what I told Cal afterward. I remember promising that one day, I'd save him, too. I remember telling him that one day, I'd be the one protecting *him*. And I believed that. I was proud that the Blackwells of Hollow Cliff were protectors. Proud that my ancestor had saved so many. Proud that one day, I'd do the same.

But my family never protected anyone but themselves. Murderers and liars. That's the true Blackwell legacy. That's what I was raised to carry on.

Except I can't.

I won't.

It all ends with you.

"I have to end it."

Cal lifts his head from where it's been cradled in his hands for I don't know how long. He's sitting across from me on the kitchen floor, knees bent, feet flat like he's braced for impact. In the weak morning light, his skin looks especially pale against his black hair and I have a sudden, desperate urge to see it without the dye.

"I have to counter Alma's charm." I clarify before he can ask. Before the sudden thump of my heart renders me incapable of speaking. Because it knows what this means. It knows exactly what I'm saying. "I have to break the spell she wove to harness Millie. It's how Gran—how my family—has been controlling minds. They renew Alma's charm by forcing innocent people to drown in an echo of the sacrifice she used to create it."

Outside the cottage, birds chirp and sing as they fly from branch to branch. The woods are waking up, which means the vendors will be arriving soon to set up. There'll be a few merchants and musicians from out of town, but it will mostly be Hollow Cliff shopkeepers. And fortune tellers, like Fern. Fern, who studied history. Fern, who stayed away until Art's funeral. Fern, who everyone says wasn't the same when she came back.

Home is where the heart lives, pet.

What a simple but powerful thought. What a simple but powerful *belief.*

But what if Fern isn't the only one who believes it? What if she's just the only one who's *conscious* of believing it? People say that once this town is in your blood, you can never truly get it out. What if Alma's spell is the reason?

I focus back on Cal. "I think the spell also controls what people think about this town. I think it's why people like Robbie can't hold onto the truth, even if they figure some of it out. I think it's why anyone who's lived under its influence can't stay away from Hollow Cliff for long."

Trapped, like lambs in a pen for slaughter.

Cal looks over at the kitchen table where Gran's countered charm still lies. "Do you know where Alma's charm is? Where it's kept?"

I shake my head. "Only the Vow-holder does. I spent an entire summer searching for it a few years ago because I wanted to see what it looked like. I couldn't find it." I pause. "But I know where it will be tonight."

Just like me, Alma's charm—the thing that powers all this— will be on that stage atop the bluffs at sunset. And as soon as I repeat the words of my Vow, it won't matter how well Gran hid the charm because she will lower it into my hands herself. Because she'll be expecting me to slice open my flesh and spill my blood. She'll be expecting me to become one of them.

We will not let you fail.

"If you counter Alma's spell," Cal asks slowly, "what happens to the bind on Millie?"

My heart thuds faster. "It breaks."

"So Millie—the thing she is now—will just be . . . free?"

I nod, avoiding his gaze.

He jerks forward. "Then that's not going to work. Millie killed your mom, Nev. She's tried to kill you *twice*. What the hell do you think will happen if you free her?"

She'll kill Gran. And then me. Possibly in that order, possibly not.

I don't know exactly how I'm able to be so matter-of-fact about my own death, but somehow I am. Maybe it's because I've been living with lies for so long, and in some strange way, it feels good to know and embrace an unalterable truth.

I'm going to free Millie.

I'm going to lift the curse my family has inflicted on this town, and I'm going to die doing it. It's all going to end, and just like Fern predicted, it's going to end with *me*.

There's no point in denying it. At least, not to myself.

I look over at Cal from my balled-up position on the floor. "We were wrong about Millie, Cal. The only threat to the people of this town is my *family*. Millie won't hurt them when she's free. The only thing she wants—the only thing she *ever* wanted—is to protect Jenny."

That, at least, I believe. That I know in my bones is true.

But Cal's not having it. "If that's all she wanted, then why did she send your mom flying out of a window? Why did she try to do the same thing to you? Jenny is dead. Your mom wasn't a threat to her. Neither are you. So if protecting Jenny is all Millie wants—all she still wants—then why did she try to kill you?"

Because I'm a Blackwell. Because my mom was a Blackwell. Because Alma betrayed her sister and then my family imprisoned her for over a century, using her own spell—her own power—against her. Because I've felt her all my life. Because I know the freezing, haunting chill of her touch. Because she's waited to complete her revenge for over a century, and in that time, her desire for it—her determination and fury to have it—has only grown.

Because I'm the last of the Blackwell line.

Because Millie's vengeance will only end with me.

Cal knows this. And he must see the confirmation—the acceptance—in my eyes because he swears, stands, and slaps his hand against the wall.

"So you take the Vow." He paces to the edge of the kitchen. "You gain more power that way, right? You can use that power to weave your own . . . thing, right? You can do what Alma should have done. You can counter what Millie did. You don't have to free her. You can—"

"Cal." I push myself up to standing. "I can't—"

"You can, Nev. This is the obvious solution. If you'll just think—"

"Cal, my mom's last words to me were *don't let her take you, too.* I think she was talking about Alma. About what happens when we take the Vow. Alma may have died, but . . . I don't think she's entirely *gone.*"

He stops pacing and looks at me. "What are you talking about?"

I twist my hands in front of me. "Ever since I saw Alma in Millie's memories, there've been . . . things I've noticed about Gran. Certain similarities between them. The same gestures. The same way of . . . talking about things."

We do what we must to survive. We always have.

"They're related. It makes sense there would be similarities, Nev."

"It's not just that." I stare at my hands, but I'm thinking about the grief and guilt on Gran's face every time there's a new drowning.

Drownings—deaths—that she caused.

I'm going to keep you safe, sweetheart. Whatever it takes.

Was Gran born with evil in her heart? Was her mother? What about her mother before that? Because in the end, they all killed. In the end, they all murdered innocent people to save themselves. To save their families. I want to believe that I would be different. That I wouldn't make the same choice. I want to believe that I would be the first Blackwell in five generations to resist whatever corruption lives in the heart of Alma's spell.

But that's not a risk I can allow myself to take.

"I can't take the Vow," I whisper. "I don't know what I might become if I do. I don't know if I'll be strong enough to resist—"

He's across the room in seconds. Both of his hands cup my face, gently but determinedly lifting my chin so our gazes clash. "You won't *become* anything, Nev. You'll be you. And *you* will end it."

A tear slides down my cheek. "You don't know that. What if I can't stop myself? What if—"

"Then *I'll* stop you. I'm immune, remember? You won't be able to—"

"I may not be able to influence your mind, but your mom was right when she said there are other ways my grandmother could silence your family. She was right to run. And as much as I wish you could stop me . . . I know how strong Millie was. How strong she *is*. If Alma harnessed even a fraction of that power . . ." I step back and shake my head. "You won't stand a chance."

"I don't care." His arms drop to his sides and a muscle in his jaw jumps. "I came back to get you *out* of this. Not to stand aside and watch you offer yourself like some kind of . . . atonement for something your *family* did. You can't ask me to watch you do that, because I can't. I *won't*."

He's right. I can't ask that of him. If I were in his shoes, I'd do everything I could to stop him.

And I also can't fight with him anymore. The peculiar numbness that's insulating me from the horror of my extremely likely death in a handful of hours is thin and brittle. If anyone can crack it and shake my resolve, it's Cal. But that's not something I can let happen. At sunset tonight, the Blackwell legacy has to end with me.

I was raised to believe that I didn't have a choice in who I would become, or in what my life would stand for. But it turns out I always had a choice, I just had to find it. I wish I could explain that to Cal. I wish I could tell him that if he hadn't come back, I would never have found the courage to dig this deep. But I know he's not ready to hear that, just like I know there's nothing I can say now that will convince him this is the right—the *only*—choice I can make. And so I meet his gaze, and I do what my family does best.

I lie.

"I can protect myself from Millie."

He narrows his eyes like he knows exactly what I'm doing. "I know you think you know her, but she's not that girl in the memories anymore. You can't expect—"

"I know exactly who Millie is now. And that's why I'll be able to figure out a way to protect myself from her."

"*Figure out* a way?"

"Yes. I'll figure out a way because I *have* to. Because I don't have another choice. I may not have Millie's power, but I'm not helpless. I've been working with the Anchor charms for months. I countered Gran's spell and it *worked*. I can do this, and I need you to believe that, Cal. I need you to believe in *me*. I need you on my side."

He rears back as if I've slapped him. It's not fair to use his loyalty against him, but I don't have another choice. He swallows, his hands clenching into fists at his sides. "I'm always on your side, Nev. You know that."

"Yeah," I whisper, my smile sad. "I know."

The sun is rising properly now, and I can't risk Gran getting suspicious if she figures out I spent last night anywhere but in my own bed. I take a step back from Cal because if I don't leave now, I may never be able to. "I should go."

He shakes his head. "No."

"Cal, I have—"

He closes the distance between us and crashes his lips down onto mine. His hand digs into the curls of my hair, and I throw my arms around his neck, pulling him closer.

He kisses me like he's never going to let me go, even though he will. Even though he has to. And I kiss him back in the same desperate way. I dig my fingers into his back, holding onto this moment with everything I have. My skin, my heart, my lungs—all the pieces of my body that never forgot him, that thrilled in recognition the instant I saw him on that bluff—strain toward him. I taste the salt air lingering on his lips. I feel the steady beat of his heart thumping against my chest and my own heart turns wild and greedy. This is everything I want. Everything I need. But it's not enough.

I want more.

I want more of him whispering my name like it's his favorite sound in the world. I want more of his hands tracing the moon of my hips, the dip in my waist, the soft skin beneath the hem of my shirt. I want to know every story, every joke, every moment of his life that I missed. I want to curl myself into his body until I don't know where I end and he begins, and I want to take back the past that was stolen from us. I want to live every moment of the future we should have had.

But the sun is winning its battle with the morning fog. Bright light sifts through the kitchen windows, and even though I don't want to think it, I know this is the last sunrise I'm likely to see.

I want so many more.

A tear slides down my cheek. Cal lifts his lips just an inch from mine and wipes it away with his thumb. Our breaths rise and fall together, quick like the rush of the sea, and as our gazes lock and hold, I see it. Just a flash. A teasing, yearning glimpse of what would have been. My blood whispers with the knowledge, but I don't need to listen.

I already know.

I already know it would have been love.

Chapter Twenty-Four

"What do you mean I can't ask any *questions*?"

Francesca's eyes narrow in suspicion, and she crosses her arms over her bright floral blouse. I dart a look to the front of the Curious Blooms booth where Bea is wrapping up a Forgive-Me bouquet for a nervous-looking man who keeps glancing over his shoulder. The ten-piece brass band, all of whom are dressed in striped suits and straw hats to match the theme of a turn-of-the-century summer fair, finishes their last song with a flourish and launches into another upbeat, festive number. The aroma of freshly popped popcorn and spun sugar fills the ocean air as tourists and locals alike wander the western grounds of Blackwell House, popping into vendor booths styled with old-fashioned striped awnings to browse magical trinkets and sip lemonade as they wait for the sun to set.

As they wait for me.

Gran's been resting in her room to prepare for her big moment, but I look around anyway to make sure she's nowhere in sight

324

before pulling my bulky charm pouch out of my backpack and pressing it into Francesca's hands. I tried to find a way to conceal it in my ceremony costume, but it's too big, and I can't risk paring the contents down because I don't know exactly what I'll need, and time will be of the essence.

"Please, Cesca. I wouldn't ask if it wasn't important."

Instead of taking the pouch from me, she covers my hands with hers and frowns, her eyes searching my face. "What's going on, mijita? Whatever it is, you can tell me."

Tears well in my eyes, but I blink them back. I wrote a letter to Francesca explaining the truth about Mom. I'll leave it on my dresser for her to find, but I wish I could tell her now. I wish I could tell her that the Celia Blackwell she befriended all those years ago never changed. I wish I could be here to see that faith and love restored. I wish we could have mourned her together.

I squeeze her hands. "This is something I need to do for my mom."

Her eyes widen and she looks over my shoulder through the gap in the tent flap as if she's expecting her former best friend to materialize out of the crowd. "Celia? Is she—"

I shake my head. "I can't say any more. I'm sorry, Cesca, but please. I—*we*—need your help."

Her eyes fly to mine, and there's a glimmer of understanding in them that I don't know how to interpret. She swallows, nods once, and takes the pouch. Relief rushes through me, and I throw my arms around her neck. *"Thank you."*

I allow myself one full inhale of her unique, floral scent before pulling away. The impulse to tell her everything, to unburden myself like a child would to a parent, is strong, and I need to remove myself from the temptation. I dart another glance at Bea, but she has a line of customers and as much as I'd like to say some kind of disguised goodbye, I can't risk making a scene.

Stepping back from Francesca, I force a smile and pop the hood of my sweatshirt like I did on the way here to avoid too much attention. "Thanks again, Cesca. I'll see you after the ceremony, okay?"

Her lips press together, and she looks like she wants to say something more, but I duck out of the tent and join the milling crowd before I'm forced to tell any more lies.

Two hundred eyes follow me as I make my way up the center aisle to the stage where Gran is waiting, the setting sun silhouetting her features as it hovers on the edge of the horizon. She's clad in all white, her layered, flowing outfit deliberately chosen to invoke the ensemble worn by the spirit medium who presided over Alma's first Vow. I'm in black from head to toe, the skirt swishing at my ankles a theatrical nod to the mourning clothes Alma never took off after her husband's death.

The front of the stage has been decorated with elaborate ivory flowers, courtesy of Curious Blooms, but as I mount the stairs, I keep my gaze trained on the delicate pink and orange clouds stretched across the sky like cotton candy because every second spent looking at Gran is nothing short of torture. When she pulled me into her arms this morning, when her familiar gardenia scent wrapped around me as she whispered in my ear how proud she was of me for making it to this day, I had to blurt out an excuse about nerves so I could sprint to a bathroom and throw up the tiny amount of toast I'd managed to choke down.

Somehow, I make it up the stairs and down to my knees in front of Gran. Somehow, I hold my shaking body together as she turns and welcomes the crowd, her amplified voice crackling through the speakers as she tells the story I've heard—and recited—so many times before. I listen to her repeat the lies my family tells. I listen to her speak about Jonathan Blackwell's greed and his young wife's amends, and through it all, I study her profile from under my lashes wondering, as I have all day, if my mom saw the thing I never could. She was eight when Gran took over the Vow. Did she see the change in her? Did she sense the moment her mother became a cold-blooded killer? Is that what first caused her to ask the questions I never thought to ask?

Don't let her take you, too.

Tears blur my eyes, and I push all thoughts of Mom out of my mind as Gran finishes her story and turns to face me. The smile she gives me is one of reassurance, and I hope that means she's interpreting my shaking limbs as nerves instead of the bone-deep disgust and ice-cold terror it really is.

"Nevinia Blackwell."

I lift my chin and force my watery gaze to hers.

I'll never know if any of her grief—her guilt—was real. I'll never know if she tried to fight the evil at the core of Alma's spell or if she succumbed willingly. I'll never know if she meant to tell me the truth about my mom someday.

"You kneel before us today to honor the Vow of protection your ancestor Alma Blackwell swore to uphold."

She pauses, waiting for my scripted response.

"I do."

She nods. "Do you repent the blood on the hands of your kin?"

I look straight into her eyes when I answer. "I do."

She blinks, but if she's taken aback by the hard edge in my voice, she doesn't outwardly show it. "Do you vow to bind yourself in service to the souls of those who were lost?"

"I do."

"And do you vow to do all within your power to ensure this promise is upheld by the generations to come?"

"I do."

She nods, and with a dramatic flourish, she lifts her arms above her head, hands facing each other as if she's holding an invisible crown. A gust of wind blows in from the ocean and an audible gasp races through the crowd as between one blink and the next, Gran's hands go from empty to full. From holding nothing but air to holding the moon-marked box I've only seen in photos from past Vow ceremonies.

Except—

She lowers the box to my eye level, and I have to stifle a gasp when I get my first clear view of the waxing and waning moons carved on top.

This is *Millie's* charm box. The first time I saw it in her memory, there was something about it that seemed familiar. I couldn't place it then, but I do now. I reach up, and the second I touch the smooth, dark wood, my hands begin to shake. Quickly, before anyone can notice, I place it on the stage floor in front of my bent knees and open the lid.

An unsheathed knife is nestled inside the box, its tarnished silver handle cast in the shape of a serpent. At first glance, it seems like the blade is tarnished, too, but it's not rust staining the sharp edge.

It's blood.

Generations of Blackwell blood.

I lift the knife out of the box, and an excited hush spreads through the crowd. Anyone who's witnessed a previous Vow ceremony or read up on the traditional order of events knows that we're almost to it now. They know that next, I'll run the blade edge of this knife across my palm to seal the words of my Vow with blood.

But I don't do that. I study Alma's charm instead.

Except it's not truly Alma's charm. It's Millie's, with Alma's corruption layered on top. And while it's easy to see the original diamond shape Millie made with thick, silver wire, I can't make out the objects she secured to each of the diamond's four corners because they're covered with the pieces Alma laid over them.

At the top of the diamond, Alma secured a jagged piece of dark wood stained through with dried blood. The left corner holds a perfectly intact scallop shell, and the right a finely wrought piece of lace, still milky-white a century later.

But it's the bottom of the diamond that makes my stomach curl in on itself. It holds thirteen chunks of glistening hair secured with a ribbon of black velvet. Thirteen shades from the thirteen kids who were the first to drown. And even though these locks were gathered over a century ago, every single strand is still soaking wet.

Bitter, hot bile rises in my throat while in my periphery, Gran shifts the lower half of her body impatiently from left to right. The crowd murmurs, too. I've waited too long. I may not be able to stall much—

"FIRE!"

Cal's cry cuts through the crowd, and every head jerks around. A breath later, the first puff of dark grey smoke rises from behind the vendor tents and absolute pandemonium ensues. The stage erupts in chaos. Elaine Taylor herself bolts up the stairs and screams at the staff member assigned to help Gran up and down the stairs to get her out of here. Gran whips around to argue with Elaine, and I take advantage of her distraction to secure the box under my arm and dive for the flower arrangement on the left side of the stage. The pouch with my charm ingredients is exactly where I asked

Francesca to hide it, and the moment it's in my hands, I unzip it and dump the contents onto my lap. It will be several minutes before anyone realizes that the controlled burn of wet leaves and damp wood is more smoke than fire, and by then, the crowd should be cleared out. Gran is the more immediate problem, so I waste no time closing my eyes and listening to the notes of Alma's charm.

It has a remarkably similar feel and sound to the Anchor charms that disperse it, which makes me simultaneously angry that I never sensed their true purpose and fiercely glad because my familiarity makes it almost easy to select objects from my collection to counter the left and right sides of the diamond. It takes a beat longer to find the dried daisy petal that nullifies the sickening vibration emerging from the thirteen locks of hair, and I have to dig to the bottom of my pile before I find the pure white seagull feather that's able to balance out the blood-soaked scrap of wood, but even then, it's only a minute later that I'm lifting the diamond charm out of the box, settling it on my lap, and adding my own layer on top of Alma's.

I tie each new piece with a length of unbleached string, and it's not until I'm tying the final knot that Gran stops arguing with Elaine and turns back to me.

"Nev. We need—"

Her gaze drops to my lap. She sees the countered charm, and her eyes go wide with horror. *"What have you done?"*

She backs away from me, tripping over her own feet. Elaine Taylor jumps forward to stop her from slamming into the hard stage floor, but I don't know if she catches her. Every ounce of my focus has been pulled back to Millie's charm box. To the fingerprint-sized smudge of dried blood planted in the bottom right corner of the wood. It had been concealed by the diamond charm, but it's not anymore.

A blast of warm, dusty air wraps around me at the same time that a familiar chill shivers through my blood. My hand darts out. My pointer finger extends. A hoarse, frantic voice calls my name, the edge of my skin connects with Millie's mark, and my eyes slam shut.

Chapter Twenty-Five

Millie's face is pressed against a cold glass window, a single thought ringing through her mind over and over again like a prayer.

Please let me see her face. Please let me see her face.

There's a thick layer of dust and grime on the glass of the second-story window she's peering desperately through, and she has to squint to make out the white-clad figure stepping from the carriage parked in the Blackwell House drive. She curses silently at the wide brim of a straw hat that hides her face from view.

Please. Just one last glimpse.

She doesn't let herself think about the fact that the carriage has just returned from the town church, or that the young man in the ill-fitting morning suit handing Jenny down from the carriage, his strawberry hair a pale imitation of her brilliant orange, is no longer just her quiet second cousin who prefers horses to people, but her husband. She pushes aside the surge of possessive jealousy that tears through her when their hands touch, and instead, she focuses every fiber of her being on silently willing Jenny to *look up.*

But just as Jenny's slim shoulders begin to turn toward the house, Jonathan Blackwell—dressed in a perfectly tailored day suit that makes young Paul Murphy's best look like rags—follows Jenny out of the carriage and offers her his arm.

Jenny hesitates, and though it's hard to tell from this angle, it looks like she tilts her head toward her new husband. But Jonathan is not a man who likes to wait, and when she doesn't immediately take his arm, he grabs Jenny by the elbow and yanks her in the direction of the path that leads to the caretaker cottage that has, as of her wedding this afternoon, become her permanent home.

Millie still can't see Jenny's face, but even from this distance, she can taste her fear. Frustrated, impotent rage courses through her. And then—

Millie blinks in surprise.

Paul Murphy is stepping forward. He's shorter than Jonathan, but stockier. His thick neck and broad shoulders evidence of the years he's spent working with his hands on the estate. He blocks Jonathan's path, and although Millie can't hear what he's saying, she can see his face, and it looks like he might be protesting Jonathan's handling of his young bride.

A brief flare of hope ignites in Millie's chest, but it's short-lived. Whatever Jonathan says next brings a frown to Paul Murphy's face, and although he doesn't look happy about it, he sends an apologetic look in Jenny's direction and steps aside.

At the same moment, Jonathan twists his neck and looks up at the window Millie is peering out of. The glass is so dirty that she doubts he can see her, but that's not the point. What he wants is for Millie to see *him*. What he wants is for her to see the cruel smile that curves his lips. He wants to remind her that no one will—no one *can*—protect Jenny against him.

And then, as if he knows exactly how desperate Millie is to see Jenny's face, as if he knows *exactly* what he's robbing her of, he jerks Jenny's arm again and hauls her toward the path that leads through the woods.

Vicious fury rises in her as she watches Jenny walk away. The possibility of her disappearing into those trees without Millie seeing so much as a flash of her stormy grey eyes is too much for her to bear. Before she even realizes what she's doing, she lifts her bound wrists over her head and, with a cry of rage, slams a two-handed fist against the window glass.

But the glass is thick, and the rope tying her hands has severely limited the power of her thrust, so her efforts produce nothing more than a single hairline crack.

Behind her, Rodney barks out a sharp reprimand, but she ignores both this and the approaching thud of his boots. As fast as she can, she lifts her arms to strike the window again, only to freeze with her hands in front of her like a prayer as the distant white figure that belongs to Jenny stops walking.

Jonathan tries to tug her forward, but Jenny resists. She turns back toward the house, the brim of her hat dipping to the side as she lifts her chin. One pale freckled cheek comes into view, and Millie tenses in breathless anticipation. She's going to see her face. She's going to stare into those loving eyes one last time.

Is it too much to hope that Jenny will somehow see her, too? That she will sense her? Feel the force of Millie's gaze—Millie's *love*—when she lifts her—

"That's enough of that."

Strong hands grip Millie's shoulders, hauling her roughly back from the window.

"*Wait!*" The old Millie would have hated the pleading in her voice, but she's beyond pride now. "A moment. Please. Only a—"

"John kept his end of the bargain. You've seen your proof. Now it's your turn, little witch."

Millie thought she was beyond this kind of fruitless fighting, but when Rodney makes to drag her farther away from the window, she lifts her knee and jams it into his stomach. His grunt sounds more surprised than pained, but Millie lifts her knee again anyway, preparing to deliver another blow.

She's slammed against the wall before she can even try.

Rodney's face, red and full of fury, swims into her vision, his sour breath washing over her as he opens his lips in a sneer. "Do it again, witch. Do it again and I promise you won't be so eager to see your precious Jenny's face when I'm through with her."

And just like that, all the fight goes out of her. *This* is not her battleground. This is not the fight she can win.

Millie sags against the wall. When Rodney yanks her forward and sends her stumbling in front of him down the stairs, she doesn't let out so much as a grunt of pain. By the time they reach the cellar room, she's once again wrapped in the cold resolve she spent a wakeless night and day nurturing.

Rodney throws her to the ground, and she lands hard on her bound hands and knees. Behind her, the door slams and a bolt thuds into place. For a long moment, Millie doesn't move. Then, once it's clear he's not coming back immediately, she lets out the groan she's been holding in and pushes herself up to sitting. Pulling her legs into her chest, she loops her bound hands over her knees, stares up at the thin sliver of sunlight limping through the high-up window, and thinks about Jenny.

She so desperately wanted to see her face. She so desperately wanted to drink in those star-clustered freckles on her cheeks one last time. But that's not what she got. She got the taste of Jenny's fear instead. She got the echo of Rodney's threats ringing in her ears.

It's not what she wanted, but maybe it's what she needed. Because underneath the cold resolve, Millie is scared. Terrified. But she needs to push that aside and find determination and focus instead. She brought Jenny into this, and she's going to get her out of it. When Millie is through, scum like Rodney will never threaten her again.

That is what she can do for Jenny.

That is what she can control.

Her mind goes dark and quiet, a singular, shining purpose taking shape, eating up every ounce of focus. She closes her eyes, and when she opens them again, the sliver of sky visible through the window is dark with night. The basement door opens, but this time, when Rodney strides back into the room, he's not alone. This time, Jonathan and Alma Blackwell sweep into the room behind him.

Jonathan has changed from his church finery into an elegant evening suit. Alma is dressed in a similarly lavish bright red gown trimmed with hundreds of shimmering jet-black beads. She doesn't look at Millie when she strides in, but Jonathan does. He has her rosewood charm box tucked under one arm, and when their eyes meet, he gives her a lazy, condescending smile.

"Good evening, Millicent."

His eyes sweep over her dirty dress and smudged face, lingering on the thick rope tied around her wrists. Turning to Rodney, he raises a brow. "You may not be able to handle the chit, Rod, but I do require the use of her hands this evening."

Rodney's face flushes and he hurries forward to hastily untie the rope around Millie's hands. Once that's done, Jonathan nods at him and he leaves the room, closing the door behind him. Millie rubs her aching wrists and slides a glance in Alma's direction, but her sister isn't looking at her. She's inspecting the hem of her red silk dress, the wrinkle in her nose indicating she's displeased at how the dirt from the cellar floor clings to it.

"Now, Millicent. I do believe this is everything you require?"

Jonathan places her charm box on the floor a few inches in front of her and steps back. The goading, condescending smile he aims down at her would make Millie's insides boil if she weren't already filled with ice. But she's moved past the place where Jonathan Blackwell's words and taunts can hurt her. There's only one thing that matters now, and it doesn't require words.

Reaching forward, she pulls the rosewood box onto her lap.

"And Millicent, I do hope you can make this quick. Your sister and I are expecting dinner guests within the hour."

Giving no outward sign that she heard him, Millie lifts the lid of the box. Jonathan chuckles another condescending laugh anyway and turns to his wife. "Come closer, Alma dear."

He takes Alma's elbow and pulls her forward so she has an unobstructed view of her sister's hands. He does this, Millie knows, because he thinks his wife's knowledge of spell work will prevent Millie from going rogue with her charm. But the adjustments Millie intends to make are subtle. Far too subtle for Alma, whose obsession with her little sister's raw power blinds her in so many ways. The only thing Alma will see and sense is a potent charm with mind manipulation at its center. She won't understand the full scope of what Millie is building until it's too late.

And so Millie tunes out Alma's avid gaze and Jonathan's smirk. She chooses a binding from her box—a silver wire from a fence that bordered her parents' farm before the fire—and twists it into a diamond shape. Once that's done, she takes her time sifting through her collection, ultimately selecting a broken raven's feather, a dried tanbark leaf, a charcoal lump, and a jagged oyster shell fragment. Using twine, she attaches each object to the north, south, east, and west points of the diamond. Then she closes her eyes and listens, grim satisfaction coursing through her at the confirmation that it's almost ready.

There's only one more piece to add.

Heart racing, she sets the wire charm on the floor in front of her, pulls the open charm box higher onto her lap, and straightens in her cross-legged seat. "It's almost ready."

Jonathan casts a skeptical glance at the crude diamond while Alma steps back, her gaze avoiding Millie's once more.

"By all means"—Jonathan waves a hand in the air—"proceed."

Millie's heart is pounding inside her chest, but she forces her voice to remain calm when she speaks. "What you're asking me to do requires a great deal of power. I need blood."

He raises a brow. "You expect me to let you spill my *blood*?"

"No. I expect you to let me spill mine." She reaches out her hand, palm up. "I require a knife."

Jonathan angles his head, studying her for a moment. Then he shrugs, pulls a leather sheaf from his pocket, and tosses it to her with a carelessness that makes it clear he doesn't see her as a threat. Just as she had once underestimated this man, he is now underestimating her.

Leaning forward, Millie picks up the knife from the floor, curls her finger around the snake-shaped silver hilt, and tests the edge.

A bead of blood blooms on the pad of her thumb. At the same time, a hum of agreement rises from the charm below her.

Closing her eyes, Millie allows herself a selfish moment. A few, too brief seconds of remembering Jenny laughing the day they raced their bicycles away from the cove. She remembers how the wind pulled strands of her blazing red hair across her freckled cheeks. She remembers how fast their feet flew on the pedals. How it felt as if they were flying. She remembers eyes like the sky meeting hers across the road, shining with love and trust.

When Millie opens her eyes again, her vision blurs with tears. She looks to Alma, and at last, her sister meets her gaze. Something flickers there. Maybe it's shame. Maybe it's not. Either way, it's gone in an instant. "Are you waiting for an invitation, Mil? We don't have all night."

Her tone is haughty. So arrogant it's almost lazy. But Millie has known her sister all her life, and she sees right through the act. She knows why Alma's eyes so quickly flit away from hers.

Alma is scared.

She's trying to hide how desperately she wants this to work, but desperate is *exactly* what she is. This is her chance to prove to Jonathan that she—that their *marriage*—is an asset, and she's so afraid something is going to go wrong. She's terrified that her little sister is going to find a way to best her again.

Millie tilts her head. "You must know I'll never forgive you for this."

Alma's eyes snap back to hers.

"So I suggest you beg, Alms. I suggest you get down on those proud knees because Jenny's heart is all that can save you now."

Alma's eyes flare, first with confusion, and then with horrified understanding. Her gaze drops to the charm at Millie's feet. A cry escapes her lips. She lurches forward, her arms outstretched, but Millie moves faster. In one fluid motion, she lifts Jonathan Blackwell's blade to her neck and slashes a single line deep across her throat.

Distantly, she's aware of her brother-in-law's shout of alarm joining Alma's, but she doesn't make out the words because she's focused on pressing the bloody thumb she tested the knife with to the bottom corner of her charm box. She holds it steady, letting the blood seep into the wood because even though Jenny may never find it, she's determined to leave this one last memory behind.

I'm sorry, Jen.

I love you.

Pain like she's never known rips through her, but she forces her eyes to stay open. A flare of heat rises from the charm at her feet, and she lets its warmth sink into her skin as she holds the intent of her spell like a solid thing in her mind. As she sinks lower and lower into that forbidden place where life and death are held.

Her life's blood soaks the diamond, turning it and the wood floor below it a bright, vicious red. Rough hands grip her shoulders, but Millie only smiles, knowing it's too late now.

Beneath her, the sturdy redwood boards that were cut, cleaned, sorted, and stacked at the Blackwell Redwood Company melt away. They welcome her with open arms. They expand and shrink to accommodate the thing she is becoming. And she smiles. One last time. Because Jonathan and Alma's plan has failed.

She will never be their monster.

She has become her own instead.

Chapter Twenty-Six

I gasp, surfacing in my own body. Only something is wrong. Something is deeply, deeply wrong.

I'm lying on my side, curled into a ball with another body—a warm, familiar one that carries the scent of sand and sea—wrapped around me from behind.

Cal.

Only, his arms are wrong. Not strong and steady around me, but heavy and limp. And we're not curled on top of the ceremony stage, we're lying amongst its broken pieces, the sand and dirt from the bluffs mixing with the splintered wood that used to make up the platform.

It must have collapsed. And we must have fallen with it. Is that why Cal's arms are slack and unmoving around me? Is he hurt?

I try to turn my head to look at him, but there's a disconnect between my body and my mind. My muscles simply don't move, and when I try to speak, my lips don't part. And then, all at once,

I *am* moving. I'm roughly and coldly pushing Cal's unconscious body away from me. I'm pressing the underside of my palms painfully into the rubble of the broken stage. I'm standing up on shaking legs, and I'm lifting my chin high.

It's my body doing all of these things, but I'm not the one controlling it. And when my mouth opens, the word that emerges is in my voice, but it doesn't belong to me.

"Alma."

The name is directed at Gran's small, frail body. She's alone, curled into a ball amongst the splintered remains of the stage, the sky a riot of violet and crimson behind her. The shouts and yells from the retreating crowd are distant now, and I can hear her feeble moan as she rolls herself onto her knees. But when she lifts her chin and meets my eyes, it's not only Gran staring back at me.

It's not a trick of light. I know that this time. I can see her clearly, undulating beneath my grandmother's transparent skin. A watery, inhuman face twisting and shifting, never settling long enough to fully form.

And then, with the agility of someone half her age, Gran lunges forward. Her frail body flies over the sharp rubble, the now-dirt-stained gauze of her white ceremony attire billowing out around her. When she lands, the exposed skin of her right arm grazes a jagged piece of broken metal from the collapsed stage, but she doesn't cry out. She doesn't make a single exclamation of pain or alarm.

At the same time, something moves through me. It's so potent, so powerful, I'm afraid it's going to rip me in two. My limbs tingle.

My head spins. And then I feel it. The seizure of not one, but two minds.

Gran's body freezes. She's on her knees, torso leaning forward. Her arm is outstretched, and there's fresh red blood dripping from the deep gash along her forearm. I walk forward, and when I'm less than a foot away from Gran's stock-still form, I bend down and pick up the silver knife she was reaching for. Its handle is in the shape of a twisting snake, and I'm not the only one who recognizes it.

I can feel Millie's icy, cold darkness wrapped around me, but I can't hear her thoughts like when I was in her memories. There's a barrier between our minds. One she must have erected. But certain flashes come through, and when she looks down at this knife I was meant to use for my Vow, I know she remembers. She remembers Jonathan tossing it carelessly at her in the cellar that night. She remembers the bite of its blade when it sliced her skin.

Millie opens my mouth and laughs. It's a terrible, harrowing sound I didn't know I was capable of making. "You need new tricks, Alms. This knife has already killed me once."

The rippling grey outline of Alma Blackwell's face flickers behind Gran's skull. Her lip curls, and although it's Gran's voice that emerges, the hissing words are all Alma's. "It did more than kill you, Mil. I made sure of *that*."

She spits the words, but her fury is marred by the way Gran's slim, weak body is violently shaking, still suspended in the awkward position on her knees with her torso bent forward and one arm outstretched.

Millie laughs again, and the hate in it, the fury pouring out my mouth, makes me tremble. "Yes, you did, didn't you?" I wave a hand and seconds later, Gran's sitting on her heels, her arms glued to her sides. My head tilts, and I sense a flare of genuine curiosity from Millie. "Did you ever regret it, Alms? Adding your own soul to my cage? Because if you were so eager to shorten your life, it would have been much easier to let me take it."

Gran's chin tilts at a haughty angle only Alma could truly achieve. "Everything I did, I did to protect my family from *you*."

I smile and shake my head. "It's only the two of us now. Let's dispense with the pretty lies."

My hand twitches again, and Gran's body jerks to standing. Her eyes flare, and even though they retain Gran's shape and color, I can no longer see any trace of her in them. It's only Alma staring back at me now.

"Is it a lie to claim you sought the death of your own sister, Mil?"

I lift my shoulders in a careless shrug. "You should have known better. You should have known I would never let you touch her. You should have known you had no hope of outmatching me."

This time, it's Alma's laugh that's cruel, and there's a wild, desperate look in her eyes like a tiger backed into a cage. "But I did outmatch you, didn't I? All that power, all that strength, and it was me who won in the end, Millie. It was me who trapped *you*."

"*Yes.*" Satisfaction purrs through me. I jerk my head and Gran's body stumbles back, tripping over the rubble. I take a step forward and follow. "Because you craved it, didn't you, Alms? You still crave it. The deep descent. The rush of holding life and death in your hands. The thrill in that broken soul of yours every time you choose *death.*"

"*You're* the broken one!" Gran's body stumbles back another step. And then another. "And not because of me and John. *This* is what you always were. Mama cried after what you did to the Thompson babe because she didn't want to see it in you, but I always knew. The day you were born, I saw the monster in your eyes."

"At least I don't hide the monster I am, Alms." Sharp bits of rubble pierce through the thin soles of my ceremony shoes as I stalk forward. "*Home is where the heart lives.* So much simpler than your usual methods. I won't pretend I didn't expect you to get greedy. You had control of my spell. You could have used it to make them believe anything. For a time, at least."

The point of a loose nail pierces the underside of my heel, but Millie doesn't let me stop. She doesn't care that my left foot is limping now or that I'm trailing blood. She only has eyes for the remnants of Alma swimming in Gran's shaking, trembling body as she backs her up to the edge of the cliff.

"But you never overreached," Millie continues. "You simply tied their hearts so securely to this place that it caused physical pain to stay away. You made a nice little pasture for yourself. So much death, so much pain, all to keep your baby sister locked away."

"A baby sister desperate to murder my *family*!"

"No, Alma. I'll kill them now because you spread your poison deep, and they deserve to die. But I want whatever shattered, corrupt pieces of you that remain to understand that it didn't have to be this way. You could have ended it all when it began. I only ever wanted *you*."

Gran's arms lift and extend like a bird about to take flight. The white, dirt-stained fabric wrapped around her thin body flaps in the rising wind. Her amber eyes are wide, and for the briefest of moments, it's not Alma I see in them, but her.

Gran.

I see her fear.

I see her regret.

I see her tormented, silent apology.

It's not enough. Nothing ever could be, but I still try to reach out. I still try to open my mouth to say goodbye. But Millie won't let me. She keeps me pinned, relegated to a far corner of my mind. Helpless to do anything but watch.

"Millie," Alma pleads, her voice desperate and thin. "Please."

"Goodbye, Alms."

It happens quickly. Gran's eyes go wide and her lips part, but before she can speak, before she can even scream, she tips backward over the cliff. Another gust of wind kicks in from the ocean, the cold dancing across my skin. And then . . . I hear it. A soft, distant thud. And from somewhere both close and very far away, an echoing howl of inhuman pain.

On the inside, I scream for Gran. On the inside, I collapse into a ball as I try to hold the shattering pieces of myself together because even though I have no choice but to hate her now, even though she's a killer and a liar, she was also someone I loved. And now she's gone.

But there's no sign of my anguish on the outside. My unblinking eyes are free of tears, and my mouth is pressed into a thin, unsmiling line. And even though Millie is shutting me out, I know what's coming next.

My knees bend and I crash hard onto the harsh, debris-covered ground. The twisting serpent knife Alma failed to reach is still clutched in my grasp, and I lift it to my neck. The metal is warm from its time in the sun, and the tip is sharp, drawing blood at once, a hot trickle skating down my neck.

My heart pummels my rib cage with frantic, desperate thrusts, but no matter how hard I try, I can't make myself lower my hand. I can't force my lips to form my own words. But I also can't give up. Not yet. I promised Cal I would try, so I hurl desperate plea after desperate plea at the barrier Millie erected between our minds. I appeal to the girl she once was. The girl whose laugh was filled with careless, youthful joy as she flew down that hill on her bicycle. The girl who knew a fierce, deep love. The girl whose life was taken away before she could truly live it.

But either Millie doesn't hear me, or it's not simply enough to sway her. Not enough to counter the Blackwell poison running through my blood. The tip of the knife digs deeper into the delicate skin at my throat where Cal's lips hovered only hours ago. A century after it took her life, the same blade will finish Jonathan and Alma's line as well. Maybe there's a kind of justice to that.

It ends with you, pet. It all ends with you.

There's only a slip of sun left on the horizon. A shining slash of gold in a bloodred sky. It's a beautiful sight to die to, but it's not what I want to see. It's not *who* I want to see.

My muscles tense in preparation for the final slash.

"*Nev!*"

I can't blink. I can't turn. But it's as if I've conjured him. He sprints into my line of sight, leaping over shattered shards of wood and metal. His face is streaked with dirt, bleeding scratches crisscross his arms and face, and his determined, storm-cloud eyes are blazing.

And when those eyes meet mine, the shock that riots through Millie is so intense, so seismic, it blasts through the barrier between us and rattles me down to my bones. She doesn't lower the knife, but she lets my hand pause in its slicing motion. It's only a brief hesitation, but it's enough for Cal to reach me. Enough for him to tear the knife from my hand, toss it away, and throw his arms around me.

His salty, sandy scent wraps around me. Warmth floods my core and my body shudders. My jaw opens. My lips stretch. A deep, guttural howl tears out of my throat. And then—

She's gone. My body is mine again. The ice-cold fury she encased me in melts, and as it does, every suppressed emotion I couldn't express rises to the surface in a massive, terrifying wave. Hot tears blur my eyes, and all I want is to press my face into Cal's chest and sob until the safety of his arms drives all the fear away.

But I can't.

"Nev . . ."

I squeeze his arm because I see it, too. A disturbance in the air in front of us. A whirlpool of wind rising like a tornado, pulling in loose bits of dirt, sand, rock, and wood as it grows rapidly in size. There's a shattering crash from the house behind us, and Cal and I throw ourselves to the ground to avoid being cut to pieces by the gemlike shards of stained glass flying through the air over our heads. Stone cracks and wood groans as more and more fragments of the Blackwell house and grounds are torn apart and absorbed into the growing cyclone. A cyclone that's beginning to take on a distinctive and eerily familiar shape. A *human*like shape.

And then, she's there. Hovering in the rapidly darkening sky, her larger-than-life form a rippling eddy of sharp glass, twisted metal, jagged wood, and swirling grey dust. Her hair is a mane of black sand and stones writhing like snakes, and her eyes are shards of colored glass, eerily lifelike apart from the angry glow of red in their center.

"Hello, little Blackwell."

It's her voice. Millie's voice. Except it claps like thunder and rolls out past the cliffs to the churning sea. Except it's devoid of the youthful warmth it once held. Empty of that undercurrent of love and hope it had in life, and filled instead with fury and unsated rage.

The storm of her monstrous, ever-shifting body advances on us, its sharp edges glinting dangerously in the last rays of the setting sun. She brings her own punishing wind with her, and it lashes against our bodies like a whip. But it's not me that's the focus of this violent wrath.

It's Cal.

The indigo sky behind Millie darkens, blotted out by her growing cloud of dust and debris. Cal's arms tighten around me, and I frantically dig my fingers into his arm, but it's not enough.

With an explosive burst of speed and strength, he rips himself away from me and shoots to his feet like a marionette controlled by strings. I roll to my knees and scream his name, but he's already running away from me. He's already reaching for the glinting hilt of the silver serpent knife that he ripped from my hands and threw away. It landed blade tip down in the sand and dirt a foot away from the cliff edge Gran was standing on only minutes ago.

I gain my feet, but I don't even make it a step before Millie's deadly, glittering tempest blocks my path.

"How like my sister you are, little Blackwell. Cowering behind a human shield."

Through the swirling debris of Millie's monstrously fluid form, I see Cal pick up the knife. He stands and turns to face me with agonizingly controlled slowness.

"But unfortunately for you"—Millie's glass eyes glint, and her colorless, dust-made lips curve in a goading smile—"you chose a shield that only exists at *my* mercy. And you should have learned by now, little Blackwell, my mercy can only be stretched so far."

Cal lifts the knife to shoulder height, the tip of the blade pointing directly at me. He takes one step forward. And then another. All the color drains from his face, and his eyes flare wide in horror as understanding hits us at the exact same time.

Millie won't hurt a Murphy, but she has no qualms about letting one kill *me*.

Cal takes another halting step forward, the muscles in his neck bulging in futile resistance. A tear slides down his cheek, and I cry out with a wordless sob.

I was ready to die. I was ready to let Millie end everything with me. But it can't be Cal. I can't leave him to live with this.

He takes another step toward me, and I wrench my gaze from his and look up at Millie. She's staring down at me, her head tilted, her glass-made eyes glinting with grim triumph. I saw the same expression on her human face only minutes ago in her last memory, when she spoke her final words to Alma. Final words that—

I gasp and fall to my knees.

I suggest you beg, Alms. I suggest you get down on those proud knees because Jenny's heart is all that can save you now.

Is this why Alma left Jenny the locket in her will? She was dying. Millie asked her if she regretted adding her soul to the bind, and what if she did? What if, when it drained her body in that incurable way, she finally acted in some small way on Millie's parting words? It didn't work. Or it wasn't enough. But maybe—

"I'm sorry."

The words come out hoarse and thin, and I don't need Millie's dusty sneer to tell me they're not near enough. Cal takes another step forward. He's a foot away from me now. I have seconds.

"There's nothing I can do or say to atone for the harm my family caused you, Millie. For the harm we caused Jenny. You deserved to have the life you dreamed of with her. She deserved to have the life she dreamed of with you."

The violent maelstrom that makes up Millie's face swirls faster, but her expression is unreadable. Cal sinks to his knees in front of me. Sweat beads his brow, and his arm shakes furiously as he angles the knife to pierce the edge of my throat.

This is Millie's answer to my plea.

I could try to run, but she won't let me get far. And maybe it's selfish, but I don't want to die with a knife in my back. I want Cal's face to be the last thing I see.

Our eyes meet, and the anguish in his abruptly takes me back to that night at the cove when he came roaring out of the dark to pry Robbie Harrison's fingers off my neck. I felt the connection between us that night, but I held myself back. I wish I hadn't. Maybe then, we would have had more time.

Another memory. His face again, this time tense and desperate with worry as he shouts my name and pulls me off a window ledge.

Another. His hand wrapped around mine as he led me to my mom's grave. His forehead creased with guilt as I collapse in grief over a plate of strawberry pancakes. Cal sitting next to me on my bed, heat flaring through me at the brush of his arm. The fierce joy on his face when he held me in his arms and I told him I remembered.

They're my memories, all of them, but I'm not the one conjuring them. I'm not the one flipping through them like they're pages in a book.

They stretch further back. Flashes of memory I've only just recovered. A young Cal and I dragging our sleeping bags through the network of caves at Smuggler's Cove. The two of us giggling as we build a fort of blankets and pillows in the cottage living room. Screeching as we chase each other up trees and down the Blackwell House halls.

And then a much more recent memory. Cal's hands cupping my face as he pulls me toward him. His warm lips finding mine. The taste of our combined tears stinging my tongue. Both of us trying to pretend for one too-brief moment that there might be another way for our story to end.

Cloud-blue eyes blaze up at me. The exact same color and shape as Cal's, only they're set in a pale, heart-shaped face. Framed by a curtain of flaming hair.

Jenny's lips are pink and glistening because I've just kissed her for the very first time. And now those pink lips smile at me as she says in whispered awe, "Oh, Mil. I didn't know. I didn't know love would be as wonderful as this."

Jenny's face disappears, and my mind goes abruptly blank. I blink once. Twice. And it's not until the third blink that I see the silver serpent knife lying harmlessly on the sandy ground.

The air shifts and Cal pulls me to him as Millie's twisting form descends. Only she's smaller now. Almost human-sized. And maybe it's a trick of the gathering twilight, but when my gaze meets hers, it almost feels for a moment like I'm staring into the eyes of the girl she once was.

Her glass gaze shifts from me to Cal. Her grey lips lift, only this time, the smile is tender. Brimming with love and loss and regret. It lasts the space of a breath. And then, without word or warning, the bits and pieces of Millie's form burst apart. Only they aren't jagged, cutting weapons anymore. The glass and metal and stone break into thousands and thousands of tiny pieces that fly into the air as glittering grains of sand.

For a moment, the pieces hover, like a floating layer of fog. Then a gust of wind blows in from the sea, sweeping it away. All of it except for a shimmer in the air. A figure, made not of sand and stone, but etched with thin, silver light.

A girl.

She has a wild mane of curly hair and wide intelligent eyes. When our gazes meet, she tilts her head and gives me a sad, knowing smile.

The last of the sun dips.

I blink.

When I open my eyes again, the girl is gone.

One Year Later

The last shirt doesn't want to fit, but I shove it deeper into the main compartment, hold the two zippered sides together, and—with one final tug—

I'm done.

It's official. My entire life now fits into a forest green backpack half the size of my body. I step away from my former bed and admire the slightly overstuffed pack. I'd have a lot more room for clothes if my mom's atlas wasn't taking up about half the space, but I would never leave it behind.

My phone buzzes with a text from Bea saying she and Francesca have finished with the last of the floral decorations for the reception tonight. We're lucky that Curious Blooms is one of the handful of shops that survived the mass exodus this past year after Alma's spell broke. Once the natives of Hollow Cliff stopped believing that their hearts could only live within our town's borders,

.

several dozen families packed their bags and closed their shops and businesses. And something else happened, too.

The hum of magic thrumming through our town began to noticeably fade.

The summer that began as our biggest tourist season on record became a quiet one of shock and mourning as the entire town of Hollow Cliff struggled to come to terms with the true story of our past. But not everyone left, and not everything closed. Millie's harnessed magic may no longer encase the town, but there are still visitors who claim a Forget-Your-Worries bouquet at Curious Blooms is the only thing that can truly quiet their minds. The Dreamless tea at DeLongpre Apothecary is still a bestseller, and on sunny days, there's almost always a handful of people in the town square making a wish as they throw a coin into the memorial fountain. Although the fountain looks different these days, without the statue of Alma at its center.

No one knows how accurate Fern's fortunes are now because, after my aborted Vow ceremony, she gave up her usual table on the patio of Mystery Grounds and announced with a lucidity no one had seen from her in years that she'd signed up as a volunteer on an archeological dig in Turkey. But bright-eyed visitors continue to come and sip their tea on her old patio, eager to have their fortunes read because they still say that the predictions made in Hollow Cliff are known to come true.

And maybe they do. Maybe it's not only Millie and Alma who gave this town its touch of magic. Maybe there's always been something shimmering in the fog that feeds our towering red-woods. And maybe, just maybe, the longer we were surrounded by evil, the stronger it grew.

But in the end, it doesn't matter if our protective stones truly warm in your hand when danger is near or if people only want them to. The only thing that matters is that when it comes to what people believe about this town, they get to choose.

A light tap on the bedroom door turns me around just as a familiar voice says, "I've been sent to retrieve the lady of the hour."

"Cal?"

His storm-cloud eyes crinkle in a smile, and I'm across the room in seconds. I throw my arms around his neck and he laughs, pulling me closer, his hands locking behind my back. I tilt my head up at him. An errant lock of his dark auburn hair has fallen onto his brow, and I can't resist brushing it with my fingers. He looked good with the black hair, but with the auburn, he looks like *my* Cal. "I thought you couldn't come. Your final—"

He shakes his head and drops a quick kiss on my nose. "I wasn't going to miss this."

"You didn't skip it, did you?" My smile fades. "Cal, that class is important to—"

"No, Nia. I didn't skip anything. But I might have called in some reinforcements."

"Reinforcements?"

He smiles, and his thumb brushes the corner of my mouth in an incredibly distracting way. "It's possible that my mom didn't want me to miss this, either, and it's also possible that she and Francesca blew up my professor's phone until she agreed to let me take an alternate test early."

I laugh because even though Cal's mom, Lynn, still isn't ready to return to Hollow Cliff, I spent a month with them before Cal left for college, and the second she saw me, she swept me into a hug, sobbed an apology for leaving, and then declared that since we had a lot of time to make up for, we'd better start right away. And for Lynn Murphy, making up for lost time apparently means calling and texting me every day and insisting I drive up to Eugene for visits even on weekends when Cal's not back from college.

Cal pulls me closer, his hands sliding from my waist to the small of my back. "I've missed you, you know."

I wrinkle my nose. "Really? I wish I could say the same, but—"

He laughs and cuts me off with a kiss. It hasn't been easy with me here in Hollow Cliff overseeing the museum plans and Cal in LA navigating his freshman year. It will only get harder once I scan that one-way plane ticket to Europe that I bought with what was left of the Blackwell funds post-renovation. But we're not worried. We lost each other once. We won't let it happen again.

Cal ends the kiss, and when I hook my arm around his neck to pull him back down for another, he groans. "I swore to Francesca that I'd bring you down right away. She threatened to hide a cursed boutonniere somewhere I'd never find if I didn't, and I don't think she was joking."

I laugh at the look of genuine worry in his expression, and together, we make our way down the twisting hallways. It's a rare warm summer evening, and not a single shadow slithers out to greet us as we wind through the family wing that isn't private anymore. Its furnishings have been updated to match the historical accuracy of the rest of the house because it's now part of the Hollow Cliff Memorial Museum tour. Only starting this evening, the tours won't be led by members of the Blackwell family, but by guides who will tell the real history of Hollow Cliff.

And this time, my family won't be the heroes.

Whether people will believe that a girl turned herself into a monster for love, or that her sister began a bloody legacy that persisted for over a century, is up to them. Either way, the truth will be out there for all to know.

Our steps slow as we cross into the newly redesigned central foyer, which has been my primary focus for the past year. What used to be an empty room with high ceilings is now a mazelike gallery of display walls. Each panel features a photograph, portrait, or description of one of the three hundred and eighty-six people who lost their lives because of the Blackwell family, along with a brief story about their lives. Cal squeezes my hand as we wind our way through the pictures and stories I painstakingly collected and organized over the past year, but he stops abruptly when we reach a small black-and-white drawing in the far corner.

"You didn't tell me about this."

I smile as he steps closer to examine the sketch I found on accident when I was scanning through the microfiche of old *Hollow Cliff Gazette*s at the library, looking for information about my family's victims.

"It's from before the train crash," I say, stepping up next to him. "There was a Hollow Cliff community picnic, and it included a sailboat race. According to the article, it was a *surprise to all* when a pair of young ladies, both of whom were newly arrived in town, scooped victory from the hands of the local boys. The article doesn't mention the winners by name, but when I saw the sketch . . ."

Cal grins. "Oh, it's them all right."

I smile back at him. The staff artist at the *Gazette* was evidently more impressed by the lady winners than the writer of the article, because when choosing a subject to immortalize in commemoration of the day, he chose their moment of victory. In the sketch, two girls are standing side by side on the bow of the sailboat, their smiling faces tipped to the horizon beyond. The girl on the left is depicted with a riot of curly hair, and the girl on the right has a smattering of freckles across her cheeks. The caption underneath the illustration dubs them *The Ladies Triumphant*.

A crackle sounds from the newly installed speakers in the foyer, and a moment later, music fills the room. This museum and the land it stands on now belong to the people of Hollow Cliff, and a good number of them will be arriving soon for the opening night reception.

"We should go," Cal says quietly.

I nod. "Can you tell them I'll be there in a minute?"

His eyes soften. "Take your time. We'll be there when you're ready." He squeezes my hand one more time before heading down the hallway.

Festive, upbeat music continues to fill the air as I turn to take in the whole of the memorial this room has become. It's not enough to make up for the harm my family caused. Nothing ever will be. But I'm still proud of the part this house will play in honoring the true history that was hidden for so long.

I pause in front of the portrait I drew of my mom, the words that tell the true story of her life and death displayed to the left. As I trace the lines of her face and search the laughing crinkles in her eyes, I imagine telling her about my plan to travel as many of our routes as I can for the next year while drawing absolutely everything I see. But I don't have to imagine the beaming smile she would give me, because that's how I drew her. Smiling as bright as the sun.

After a few moments, I turn to follow Cal, but before I go, I let my eyes linger for an extra second on the sketch from the *Gazette* of Millie and Jenny on the bow of their winning sailboat. Their faces radiant, their arms flung out wide.

And that's when I hear it.

Laughter, echoing in the air.

It's clear and bright. As full of giddy joy now as it was that day Millie and Jenny rode their bicycles away from the cove, the wind whipping their hair, their feet soaring on the pedals so fast it felt as if they were flying.

It's a laughter full of hope.

Full of love.

It's the laughter of two girls who, for one brilliant moment, glimpsed a path before them that was shining and bright. A future that belonged only to them.

Slowly, the laughter fades. But it doesn't go away. It blends into the music crooning through the speakers. It joins the hum of electricity surging inside the walls. It becomes a part of the rattling windows as a summer breeze passes through.

And I know, as I turn to join the party, that it will always be here. Thrumming beneath the surface. Raising the hair on the backs of our necks.

A reminder. A promise. A warning.

Some loves never die.

ACKNOWLEDGMENTS

The initial spark for this story emerged from my childhood curiosity in the Winchester Mystery House in San Jose, California, and Sarah Winchester, the enigmatic and secretive woman who built it. I'm deeply grateful to the amazing tour guides, historians, and restoration experts who have worked so diligently to preserve this mysterious slice of history. You have lit a fire in countless imaginations, including mine. Thank you especially to the tour guides who took the time to answer my many questions, and for going into such wonderful detail about the unique personalities of the ghosts who haunt those twisting halls.

My eternal thanks to my wonderful and wise agent Sara Crowe, who not only shares my fascination with the Winchester Mystery House but who encouraged me early on to explore my own take on what might really have happened all those years ago. None of this would be possible without you. Thank you, too, to everyone at Sara Crowe Literary.

Endless thank-yous as well to editor extraordinaire Laura Schreiber, whose kindness and care is only matched by her intelligence and insight. Thank you for drilling deep into the core of this story with me and for helping me find the beating heart at its center. You are the editor an author dreams of, and my gratitude is endless. I am also extremely grateful to Ardyce Alspach for diving into the misty waters of this book with me and guiding our journey with such gothic-loving enthusiasm.

This book would not exist without the support of my friends and fellow writers, and I am especially grateful to Elana K. Arnold for swooping in like a guardian angel when I—and this story—needed it most. My whole heart to Olivia Swomley for reading a draft of this story very quickly and providing invaluable insight. Thank you, too, to Lindsey Olsen, Nina LaCour, Ari Tison, Gretchen McNeil, Veronica Derrick, and Susan Azim Boyer. Sometimes we find ourselves in holes (both of the plot variety and otherwise), and I'm so lucky to have generous friends like you willing to throw down a rope and haul me out. A shout-out, too, to the amazing Hamline MCAC community that I count myself so lucky to be a part of.

I'm indebted to Alexander at the Lomita Railroad Museum and the kind and generous folks at the Southern California Railroad Museum for patiently answering my many questions about trains, railroad tracks, and railroad politics during the turn of the century. I burn a never-ending light of gratitude for librarians everywhere for their unparalleled genius when it comes to tracking down historical documents, and for their dedication to maintaining such wonderful and thorough databases. As always, all mistakes are my own.

It's a special thing to work with a publishing team as talented and enthusiastic as Union Square & Co. Thank you to Emily Meehan, Tracey Keevan, Jenny Lu, Daniel Denning, Chris Vaccari, Stefanie Chin, Grace House, and the entire Union Square team. My mouth dropped when I first saw this gorgeous, creepy cover, and I'm very grateful to artist Elena Masci and designer Marcie Lawrence for creating it. Thank you also to Hayley Jozwiak for lending her eagle-eyed expertise to this manuscript.

To all my friends, but especially Meredith Wieck, Avalon Hernandez, and Preeti Hehmeyer, for being so patient and understanding when I disappear into my writing cave for months at a time and for still hanging out with me when I emerge, desperate for human contact. Thank you, too, to Francesca Pardo for always making me feel like a part of the family and for inspiring a character in this book.

I am forever grateful to my family for their never-ending support and encouragement. My parents, Nancy and Rick, my sister Georgia—who is thankfully nothing like Alma—Nato, Violet, Susie, Steve, Betty, Tom, Lynne, Kevin, Embry, Ty, and Toren. Cat MVP awards to Jenova and Dash for keeping me in the writing chair by meowing in annoyance every time I attempt to get up.

I would also like to sincerely and enthusiastically thank every reader, bookseller, reviewer, librarian, blogger, and

Bookstagrammer who has taken the time to read my books. Thank you for your gorgeous photos, reels, and posts. I'm so in awe of the creativity, insight, and enthusiasm you bring to this vibrant, bookish community.

And lastly, to Blake. Thank you for feeding me when I'm on deadline, brainstorming with me when I'm stuck, and for helping me find the end.

ABOUT THE AUTHOR

Amanda Glaze is the bestselling author of *The Second Death of Edie and Violet Bond*, a Barnes & Noble YA Book Club pick and a Rise booklist honoree. She grew up in Northern California where she spent most of her time with her nose in a book or putting on plays with friends. Since then, she's lived many lives: as a bookseller, a theater director, and an Emmy Award–winning film and television producer. When she's not running off to the mountains, she lives in Los Angeles with her husband and their two cat familiars. Find her online at amandaglaze.com.